SILVER-TONGUED DEVIL

JENNIFER BLAKE

 sourcebooks
casablanca

Published by Sourcebooks Casablanca, an imprint of Sourcebooks, Inc.
P.O. Box 4410, Naperville, Illinois 60567-4410
(630) 961-3900
FAX: (630) 961-2168
www.sourcebooks.com

Originally published in 1995 by Random House.

Library of Congress Cataloging-in-Publication Data

Blake, Jennifer.
  Silver-tongued devil / by Jennifer Blake.
      p. cm.
  "Originally published in 1995 by Random House"—T.p. verso.
  1. Louisiana—Fiction. I. Title.
  PS3563.A923S55 2011
  813'.54--dc23
                              2011039401

Printed and bound in the United States of America
VP 10 9 8 7 6 5 4 3 2 1

One

THE MAID WHO TENDED THE LADIES' STATEROOMS OF THE *Queen Kathleen*, the Natchez to New Orleans steamboat, was neat enough in appearance, with a clean apron and her hair tucked under a mobcap. Still, she carried about her the odor of corn whiskey like some raw perfume. Angelica Carew was no stranger to the smell; her fiancé had been known to take a drink too many, as had most of the men of Natchez society. She disliked it, however, and held her breath while the maid did up the row of tiny buttons that fastened the back of her evening gown.

The spirits had apparently loosened the young woman's tongue, for she crooned over the softness and delicate apricot color of the silk of the gown as she worked. She also asked a thousand questions about where Angelica was going and what she would be doing when she got there. Angelica's answers were not particularly informative. She preferred not to think about the journey, its purpose, or its end.

"You will be here to help me undress later?" Angelica said as the maid, finished with the buttons, began to lift and spread the gown's wide skirt evenly over the hooped petticoat underneath.

"Oh, yes, indeed. You only have to ring the bell just over there. I'll hear it at my station."

"I don't expect to be late. My father will be retiring early, I'm sure, and I have no reason to linger."

"Not even for a stroll along the deck with your young man? The moon is nearing full tonight." There was a hint of roguish humor in the other woman's voice.

"I'm sure he will find other entertainment."

"Will he? Then he's a poor sort in my book." The maid's laugh released an alcoholic breath strong enough to make a sailor reel.

Angelica managed a brief smile as she moved away toward the petticoat mirror in the side table. The lamplight shifted with a rich gold sheen in her high-piled hair as she turned slowly to check her hemline. Swinging gently to face the other woman again, she said, "Are you the only ladies' attendant?"

"Indeed I am. One ladies' attendant and one for the gentlemen on this boat."

"I expect you're kept busy?"

"Sometimes yes, sometimes no. Many ladies bring their own maids, of course, and some dress themselves. Will there be something special I could do for you?"

"No, no." Angelica glanced at the other woman, then away again. "It's just that—oh, some women are terrified of spiders or mice or snakes, but my horror is being trapped in my underclothes. I was punished as a child by being forced to sleep laced up tight in a corset with applewood slats up the back and—I can't quite forget that when it's time for bed."

"Now who would do such a thing to a child as sweet as you must have been?"

Wry humor rose in Angelica's dark blue eyes. "I'm afraid I was a handful growing up, especially for a maiden aunt with a great many fine things to protect. She felt her methods kinder than striking me. Truth to tell, I would have preferred the slap."

"Yes, well, never you fear, dearie," the woman said with ready sympathy. "Just you give your bell a good yank when you need me, and I'll be here before you can take your hair down."

Satisfied, Angelica thanked her. A short time later, the attendant held open the door while Angelica maneuvered her wide skirts through the narrow opening. She stepped out into the salon known as the ladies' cabin, then moved through into the main cabin.

This lounging and eating area was a cavernous space running more than half the length of the boat. Brass and glass chandeliers, glowing with the mellow light of whale oil, were spaced at regular intervals. They illuminated ornate woodwork, the stained glass in the great overhead dome, and the miniature landscapes that were set above the stateroom doors. The mahogany tables down the center had been laid for dinner with white napery, heavy silver, and centerpieces of roses and ivy.

It was possible, Angelica thought as she paused in the doorway, that she should have remained in her stateroom until her father or her fiancé came for her. The few ladies who had emerged to wait for the dinner bell appeared to be escorted by their menfolk. The remaining passengers standing around the room were all male.

An uncomfortable flush rose to Angelica's cheekbones as she hesitated, uncertain whether to advance or retreat. That was even before a man, who stood with a group which included the captain and a trio of older gentlemen, turned to direct a piercing stare in her direction.

Tall and broad-shouldered, he commanded attention with the sheer force of his presence. He was smooth-shaven, his features singularly handsome in their chiseled planes and angles. Crisp, black hair clung in sculptured waves to his head and curled just at his coat collar. The coat was of impeccable cut, the lapels bound with dark gray silk lying neatly against the black broadcloth. His gray trousers fit without a wrinkle over muscular thighs and were fastened under half boots that were polished to a dazzling sheen. The pattern of his waistcoat was a subtle gray shadow-stripe, and the heavy watch chain that emphasized his taut midriff was weighted only by a single gold signet fob.

He appeared a gentleman of refined taste and ample means, yet there was taut and watchful power in his casual stance. More, something in his stillness, some hint of violent impulses ruthlessly restrained, gave Angelica an odd feeling of vulnerability. He was not, she knew instinctively, a safe man to know.

The man's gaze narrowed. For a single instant, he was as alert as a wolf scenting prey on a warm wind. Then the severely molded lines of his mouth relaxed. His gaze, as cool and opaquely green as a lime pool, drifted downward from her face to her shoulders exposed by her gown, and from there to her slender waist. The lamplight shone with blue fire in his dark hair as he inclined his head in a bow that was both an acknowledgment of her presence and a devastating compliment.

Angelica stood statue-still while her heart beat high in her throat. Heat flooded through her and a strange confusion of impulses—to go, stay, run, hide, walk toward the man who watched—held her immobile.

It was the purest reflex of manners that came to her aid. Her lips curved in a politely distant smile while she performed the minimal curtsy that would recognize the obeisance without encouraging the man.

The effect was not precisely as expected. One corner of the stranger's mouth curled in a sardonic smile. He made a slight movement, as though he meant to leave his friends, perhaps approach her. For the space of a breath, Angelica felt a warm flood of anticipation, as though every inch of her skin awaited a caress.

Then the face of the man across the room tightened, darkened. He swung abruptly away. After an instant, he made some comment to the captain that caused a rumble of laughter.

"Ravishing, my dear," Angelica's father said as he came to her side. "I knew the gown would enhance your charms when I chose it, but had no idea how much you would improve the gown."

It was a moment before she could attend to his words. Then she summoned a smile and put her hand on his arm. "You are a flatterer, but I love you for it."

"I would never offer you base coin."

"And why should you indeed? Hasn't Aunt Harriet always told me I look exactly like you?"

"A gratifying observation, if inaccurate. You look like your mother."

There was a tired note in his voice which caused Angelica to give him a quick, assessing glance. His face was pale under his look of fatherly pride, and the flickering lamplight overhead made the shadows under his eyes look like old bruises. The business of arranging this wedding and getting ready for the move downriver had stretched his strength to the limit and, in his illness, he had little to spare. Her fingers on his sleeve tightened in involuntary distress.

The ghost of a smile flitted across his face. "Are you about to make a fuss? Indulge me, please, and refrain. It will only spoil the evening."

"Oh, Papa..."

"It's your Aunt Harriet's fault, your inconveniently tender conscience," he said in rallying tones. "I should never have left you with her so long. But the time sped past so quickly—one day you were a crawling babe, the next a lady with her hair up in curls and scent behind her ears."

"Rose water," Angelica corrected in dry tones. "It's all Aunt Harriet permitted."

"Was it so terrible, then, living with her? She is my sister and I respect her, but she is not, I fear, a warmhearted woman."

What could she say? To complain would only worry him while mending nothing. "She did her duty. And she is fond of me, I think, in her way."

"As bad as that?" her father said with a shake of his head. "Perhaps it's just as well that things happened as they did. You will be much happier as a wife."

Angelica made no answer. She wished that he might be right, since it seemed to give him comfort, but she was far from sure of it.

Dinner was a time-consuming production served with all the pomp of a fine restaurant. The aromas of the food hovered in the air, mingling with the smell of lamp oil and perfume and the river. The breeze over the water, laden with dampness, wafted in at the open transoms over the windows and doors on one side of the long cabin and out those on the other. The vibration caused by the laboring of the great steam engines made the water and wine shiver in their crystal glasses, and could be felt as a faint shudder through the deck and the dining chairs. The rumble and thump of the gears to the stern wheel were constant, like the steady throb of a giant heart, while the splashing of water over its paddles had the sound of distant rain. With the noise and the buzz of conversation, the music provided by an ensemble playing pianoforte, French horn, and violin was a distant, half-drowned undercurrent of melody.

Halfway through the meal, Angelica felt a strong sense of being under observation. She glanced at the captain's table in the center of the room. The man she had seen earlier was there. Paying scant attention to the animated conversation going on around him, he leaned back in his chair with his elbow on its arm and his chin supported by thumb and fore-finger. He was watching her, his eyes hooded and brooding.

Renold Harden saw Angelica Carew turn her head in his direction and was grimly pleased. It could be helpful that the lady was as aware of him as he was of her.

Fair Angelica, angelically fair. Pure and dulcet, golden as an angel done on fresco, with eyes of rich sea blue that were mirrors to hide her thoughts or reflect her joy. She really was beautiful, a possibility he had not considered. Amazing. But then he had given little heed to the daughter except as a weapon. It was an unexpected bonus. He had not thought to find pleasure in his use of her.

Renold recalled the transcendent pleasure in the face of Edmund Carew when he had seen his daughter. He loved the young woman he had sired, handled her as gently as he might a newborn, as deftly as ever he had riffled the cards. As he led her in to dinner, he had placed her hand on his arm, covering it with his fingers. Besotted, as full of news as a rooster at daybreak, he had talked for the purpose of coaxing his daughter's quick, silvery laugh and the rise of love and approval in her eyes.

It had been like watching an unreliable cur playing with a kitten. Remembering, sick rage gathered, settling its heat in the center of Renold's chest.

His stepfather, Gerald Delaup, had been a saint among men. He was seldom seen without a smile. Urbane, kind of heart, he had years ago scandalized his relatives and social acquaintances by marrying out of the aristocratic circle of New Orleans, taking an Irishwoman to wife. If that were not enough, he had also taken in the woman's bastard son. Under his protection the boy, surly, difficult, black-tempered as his black-Irish heritage, had over the years turned into a fairly civilized human being, though not, perhaps, a gentleman.

Gerald Delaup had full reason to be jovial and even kindly; life had treated him well. A man of position, he had been descended from one of the oldest French Creole families in New Orleans—those of French nationality born outside France, in this case in Louisiana. He had a sugar plantation called Bonheur on the Mississippi that supplied the wealth that allowed him to keep a townhouse for the season, a stable of horses and three carriages, a box at the opera, and to give his wife and daughter all the fripperies and fashionable nothings their hearts desired. There was also enough left over to permit himself the pleasant diversion of purchasing a racehorse now and then or sitting down to an occasional game of cards for high stakes.

One day less than a month past, M'sieur Delaup, Renold's stepfather, had traveled to St. Louis by steamboat to look at a promising Thoroughbred. The horse had proven a disappointment, but on his return he had fallen in with a gentleman of charm and address. The two of them had begun a card game which lasted from the middle of one afternoon until dawn of the next day. At the end of it, the gambler and cardsharp Edmund Carew had been the jubilant owner of Bonheur, along with its furniture, slaves, livestock, and grandeur.

Without the plantation, Delaup's livelihood and prestige were gone. The townhouse would have to be sold, the box at the opera, everything. M'sieur Delaup was grateful for Renold's offer of a loan, but he could not repay it and his pride would not support charity. Perhaps Renold would care to purchase his new carriage and matched grays? *Va bien*. That immediate sale would provide space to breathe, time to think about what was to be done. He was too old to start over, but what else was there?

Oh, and would Renold consider telling his mother that her worthless husband had beggared her? That was a humiliation too terrible for a caring, devoted husband to bear. Or perhaps he should do it himself, perhaps he owed her that much? But not immediately, not, please God, this evening. He had not the courage.

Gerald Delaup had found a different solution some time in the murky hours before dawn of the next day. Bolstered by brandy and desolation, he put the barrel of his silver-chased dueling pistol into his mouth and pulled the trigger.

Pain was something Renold denied as a weakness, but he had stood at the raw grave of his stepfather and let its aching poison seep through his every fiber. Gerald Delaup had been the first man to allow Renold his self-respect, the first to find him worthy of teaching, the only one to give him unquestioning affection. Renold had felt the fierce gratitude toward his stepfather that only a mongrel can feel toward a generous and loving benefactor.

Staring down into the grave, he had sworn to take back Bonheur, by force if need be. And no matter the cost, he vowed to punish the man who had cheated Gerald Delaup of his pride and his joy in living.

Yes, cheated, for the Delaup plantation had been lost in no simple game of chance. Edmund Carew, though known as fair and honorable as gamblers went, had played with marked cards. Gerald Delaup had mentioned the possibility before he died. Renold had confirmed it through his acquaintances and informants in the netherworld of New Orleans gambling.

Renold had thought to force a meeting on the field of honor during which Edmund Carew would learn exactly why his life was being taken from him. That was before he had run the gambler to earth in Natchez, before he discovered that Carew had a faulty heart that could stop at any given moment. It seemed pointless to kill a man already under a sentence of death.

There had to be a way to hurt Carew. Renold had found it

when he heard of Carew's daughter. At the same time, he had discovered the perfect means of regaining Bonheur.

Angelica Carew was the one thing the gambler valued, the only thing he cherished, the single avenue through which he could be reached. The man would hate it if his neat arrangement for his daughter's future security was twisted into a new form. He would cringe if he knew she was to be bedded and forced into a different and hellish marriage for the sake of the dowry he had bestowed on her. He would know the tortures of the damned if he was made to understand that she must pay the price for her father's greed and trickery every day—and night—for the rest of her life.

As he met the lady's gaze, Renold reached for his wine glass, lifting it to her in a small salute. There was no gallantry, no flirtation in the gesture, however. It was, rather, one of stark anticipation.

Angelica lowered her gaze quickly to her plate. At the same time, she caught her breath as a shiver rippled over her, leaving gooseflesh in its wake.

Beside her, her fiancé gave a loud laugh. "What is it? A goose walk on your grave?"

"Something like that," she murmured.

"Never mind," Laurence said, his light brown eyes bright with the many glasses of wine he had drunk during the meal. "Before long, I'll have the right to kill the thing for you."

Disquiet was strong within Angelica as she looked away. She preferred not to think of Laurence Eddington's rights as a husband, no matter what form they might take. The wet, devouring kisses he had pressed upon her after she had accepted his proposal made her shudder to think of them.

She was a little confused by such shrinking; she had her dreams of love and marriage and a family. More, long years of listening to her aunt's friends gossip about the misdemeanors of Natchez society and her elderly cook's salty discussions of the goings-on in the quarters behind the big houses had given her a fair idea of what was involved.

It was not as if she did not know the man she was to marry. Laurence was the son of her Aunt Harriet's best friend, someone Angelica had played with as a child, stood up with at balls, teased for his pride in being an Eddington of Dogwood Hill, one of the town's most prestigious estates. Still, she had thought of him more in the guise of a cousin or a brother than a husband. That he had transformed himself into a suitor the instant he learned she was to have Bonheur, the vast plantation above New Orleans, as her dowry was a source of distress. She felt she had lost a friend without gaining a lover.

Angelica glanced at him, at the way he reclined with exaggerated ease in his chair. His sandy blond hair was sliding into his face, his smile was loose. Her husband-to-be. Her husband in less than six weeks, since her father was looking toward a late spring wedding.

She waited for the rise of some pleasure, even some expectation. There was nothing except the uncomfortable heaviness of duty.

The problem, it seemed, was in herself. Perhaps her nature was not passionate, or she had been too long under the influence of her aunt who felt that men were creatures with nasty habits and appetites, particularly in the bedchamber. It was a dilemma she must face. Soon.

The last thing she needed was a distracting awareness of a strange man. She would not look at him again. No. She would not.

By the time the meal ended, the starched white tablecloths were limp with river dampness and scattered with stains. Both the tables and the Persian rugs on the floor were littered with the singed bodies of moths and flies drawn to dance in the hot light of the chandeliers. Insects and spilled crumbs were crushed underfoot as the diners left the room so that it might be cleared by the waiters.

Angelica, with her father and Laurence, took a digestive ramble about the boiler deck. The two men talked in a desultory fashion, Laurence complaining about the smallness of his stateroom and the insolence of the steward, her father explaining the wedding purchases he had made in Natchez before the boat sailed and how they would be shipped on after them. Neither seemed to need or want any comment from

Angelica. She let the voices of the men wash over her while she wondered if this was the way it would always be.

At one point, Laurence put his arm around her waist to steady her as the boat wallowed in a windblown wave, but also drawing her close against him. It was instinct rather than design that made Angelica pull away. She thought from the petulant scowl that crossed her fiancé's face that he was not pleased.

The moon promised by the ladies' attendant had not yet put in an appearance; the river lay dark and wide around them except for the moving glow of the steamboat's lights reflecting on the water. As they paused at the rail, Angelica grasped the polished wood with her gloved hands, gripping tight, wishing she could hold back the boat's progress. She felt suddenly as if she were being rushed toward a precipice, that soon the boat would steam over the edge and it would be too late.

Ridiculous, of course. Yet, at this time just a week ago, she would have said it was ridiculous that she would be betrothed overnight, ridiculous that she would be traveling to take possession of a plantation, ridiculous that her dear Papa could be revealed as a professional gambler.

It embarrassed her now to think of how ignorant she had been of the life her father led, the peculiar talents by which he earned his daily bread. He and her aunt had kept it from her, of course, allowing her to think that he was a man so grieved by the long-ago death of his wife, her mother, that he could only find peace in travel and the scholarly pursuit of knowledge in other climes.

Angelica had known that he drifted from one city and watering place to another, both in Europe and the United States; sometimes he mentioned Strasbourg or White Sulphur Springs, Boston or Baden-Baden. Who would have guessed that he depended for his livelihood on luck and flimsy pieces of colored paper? How could she have imagined that he would gamble for stakes high enough to gain and lose fortunes? By what means could she have suspected that he would present his greatest prize, the plantation he had won from its owner, to her? A prize hedged around with such pleas and promises and hints about his failing health that she could not refuse it or the husband he thought she needed to take care of both the estate and herself.

The wind, so fresh and pleasant at first, after the accumulated heat and smells of the main cabin, seemed to have a cooler edge. It chilled her, penetrating the India shawl she had thrown around her shoulders. When it could be seen that the main cabin was free of the debris of dinner, they moved back inside.

The whale oil lamps had begun to smoke their globes, lending the atmosphere an air of gray gloom. Elderly women in widow's weeds in various shades of lavender and purple had established one of several islands of lugubrious conversation. In the corners of the main cabin, young matrons discussed the ills of childhood and the problems of instructing servants, while middle-aged ladies kept an eye on teenage daughters who danced sedately to the music that still played or else giggled and eyed the unattached males gathered at the cabin's stern end. From the open door of the gentlemen's salon located nearby, there drifted a blue haze of cigar smoke and the slap of cards on baize-covered tables.

Angelica, glancing into that salon as they passed it, caught a glimpse of the gentleman who had saluted her. He was sitting at the faro table, absorbed in play. She looked away quickly before he could take notice of her.

"Yoo hoo!"

The hail, loud and not at all discreet, rang across the cabin. It was directed at Angelica's father by a woman of enormous girth whose embonpoint was covered with brown lace set off by a parure of yellow diamonds as large as lemon drops.

Angelica thought for an instant that Edmund Carew would refuse to acknowledge the greeting. Then, as the woman waved to them in imperious summons and a blinding flash of diamonds, the older man sighed, took Angelica's arm, and walked forward to respond.

The lady was a Madame Parnell, a widow of middle age with a jovial manner and a trace of Irish accent. She spoke in a voice husky from either constant use or the medicinal brandy she kept in a small flask in a knitting bag. The widow allowed the necessary introductions to Angelica and Laurence, then immediately dominated the conversation with a running commentary on everything from her accident with a deviled egg at dinner to the plays and entertainments she expected to attend in New Orleans.

It became obvious fairly soon that the late Mr. Parnell had also been a gambler and a crony of Edmund Carew's. The woman reminisced with relish about various journeys the three of them had made to the northeast and to Europe, of amusing incidents and hairsbreadth escapes they had made from irate losers at cards and ladies expecting matrimony from Angelica's father. Laurence, standing beside Angelica's chair, shifted restlessly from one foot to the other. Angelica sat forward, enthralled.

"Good Lord, Edmund," the outspoken lady said, breaking off in the middle of a tale involving a hay wagon, an hourglass, and some dismal female's lost nightcap, "you look fagged to death. Why don't you go to bed and leave your charming Angelica to me? I'll see no harm comes to her."

"Yes, Papa, do," Angelica said in concern. "I won't be long behind you."

"No doubt Madame Parnell wishes to blacken my character while I am not here to defend myself," Edmund Carew said.

The older woman gave an asthmatic laugh. "Only enough to make you interesting."

Edmund Carew smiled. Taking Angelica's hand, he carried it to his lips for a brief salute. "I'll say good night, then, my love. Be pleased to remember, however, that I have a certain dignity, and I am still your father." With a whimsical bow which included all three, he left them.

"Now there, my dear young friends, is a man," Madame Parnell said on a gusting sigh as she watched Edmund Carew walk away. "Oh, he has his weaknesses; he is quick to anger, and quicker to take advantage of a man who doesn't know his own limits or has no skill at cards. He has no head for money—why, I once saw him wager his last groat on which of two draggle-tailed roosters at a Spanish inn would crow first! But he is always the gentleman and has never forgotten the one woman he ever loved—your mother, Angelica, my dear."

"I'm afraid I never knew a great deal about how he spent his days," Angelica said with care.

"No doubt he meant it to be that way. Or else that sour-faced woman, your aunt, decreed it. I met her once, and a more joyless creature I never saw, tighter in her tail than alum can possibly—"

Beside them, Laurence made a strangled sound in his throat and shifted uncomfortably.

Madame Parnell broke off. Rearing her considerable bulk back in the seat so she could look up at him, she said, "Do you have a fish bone stuck in your throat, my boy, or would you be trying to tell me to mind my tongue? If you don't care for my language, you can jolly well take yourself off where you can't hear it. Maybe you'd like the card room, where you can watch the men play?"

Laurence, his face flaming at the slur on his manhood, looked to Angelica in chagrin and appeal. Angelica, however, was reluctant to abandon this opportunity to learn more of her father. She was also less than anxious to be alone with her fiancé. "I'll be perfectly fine," she said. "You need not stay."

Annoyance thinned his lips; still he inclined his head in a stiff-necked bow to Madame Parnell. "Your servant, ma'am. Angelica, I will return later to collect you."

"Like a parcel," the irrepressible older woman said under her breath as she watched him stalk away. Then she turned to Angelica with a beatific smile. "Well, now that we have rid ourselves of the likes of him, we can talk comfortably. What would you care to know about your scandalous father?"

"Everything!" Angelica said with a laugh. Then she sobered as her gaze traveled beyond Laurence to the gentlemen's salon toward which he was heading. "But first, is it possible that you may know that man over there?"

"Where?" Madame Parnell peered in the general direction Angelica indicated.

"I would rather not point him out, but he's there, at the table just inside. The dark-haired gentleman."

The older woman's eyebrows climbed her forehead. "Lord,

child, but you don't mean Renold Harden? You do have an eye for a rogue, I must say."

"He isn't respectable?"

"There are those who wouldn't allow him in their houses if it weren't for his family connections, but I can't imagine being so high-toned, myself. Lives in New Orleans, has a fine townhouse on Royal Street in the *Vieux Carré*."

"You know him well?" There was a peculiar note in the woman's voice that aroused Angelica's curiosity.

"We've met. Now what else can I tell you? No pedigree, something people set great store by in New Orleans, but he's as rich as he can stare. Got his start gambling, though he sold his gaming house just recently. They say he's the devil to cross in business—or with a sword, if it comes to that. And one lady who attracted his interest tried to do away with herself when their affair came to an end."

"Suicide?" Angelica said in a shocked whisper.

"That's how the story went. Frankly, I wonder if it wasn't a ploy to rekindle his interest. If so, it failed miserably. On the night she dared show herself in public again, at a performance of *The Barber of Seville*, Harden showed up escorting the actress who was the toast of the town."

"Oh, dear," Angelica murmured, since some response seemed required, but her gaze flickered again in the direction of the man of whom they were speaking.

Renold Harden caught that glance, saw its dubious shading. His luck at faro suffered for the moment of inattention. It had not been consistent in any case; he had been playing with something less than total concentration. Winning or losing was by no means as important as the fact that the faro table commanded an excellent view of the main cabin. He had been aware of Angelica Carew from the instant she had come back inside, was well aware that her father and her fiancé had left her unguarded.

He approved the subtle way the soft apricot of her gown enhanced her skin tones, had particular appreciation for the low décolletage. He found the tight row of covered buttons he had noticed at the back of her bodice of consuming interest; he could almost feel them under his fingers.

To watch Laurence Eddington enter the gentlemen's salon gave him virulent satisfaction. He had discovered in himself, in the last few minutes, a surprising dislike for having that young buck hanging over the lady, standing where he could look down the front of her bodice.

Angelica Carew was a lady, in spite of the man who had fathered her. The instincts were there, and the breeding. The soft oval of her face, the high cheekbones and perfectly shaped mouth gave her a look of classical purity, an impression of essential goodness. Still, there was something in her direct gaze and the humor edging her smile that intrigued him. She was not, he thought, all sweetness and light.

Idiocy, of course. As though his impressions and feelings mattered, as if her looks and personality had any bearing on his purpose. There was no question of becoming enamored. None at all.

He had, for most of his adult life, avoided permanent entanglements; he was not a good candidate for them. He realized it was only a small step from approving a female's manifold charms to falling victim to them. The risk, duly noted, could and would be taken into account.

Renold glanced toward Laurence Eddington as the fiancé made his way deeper into the room. Elaborately casual, the younger man wandered from table to table, taking note of the various card games. After a time he asked permission to sit in on a few hands of poker. Renold abandoned the faro table and moved to stand against a wall where he had a good view of the play.

For a brief moment, he contemplated joining the game. There were men at the table who knew him, however, and who might easily bring up subjects best left alone. He and Eddington had never crossed paths, but Angelica Carew's fiancé could be expected to perk up his ears at any mention of a connection to Bonheur.

Edmund Carew was a different case, of course. Renold had been at pains to avoid the gambler. Angelica's father was a familiar figure in New Orleans; the two of them had frequented the same restaurants, the same row of boxes at the opera, the same gambling dens. Carew might well know of the family connection between Renold Harden and the man from whom he had stolen a plantation.

Watching Laurence Eddington, however, proved sufficiently instructive even without engaging the younger man in play. He was a reckless gambler, one who trusted luck rather than the odds. Flamboyant in the way he placed his bets and flipped his cards onto the table, he was cocky when he won, sulky when the cards ran against him.

These conclusions, added to what he had observed earlier, gave him a fair estimation of Laurence Eddington's place in the scheme of things. The fiancé was hardly a cipher, but he stood in need of a few lessons in self-control. He lacked the courtesy that would allow him to at least pretend to prefer a woman's company over a card table, and was without the graces that might endear him to a woman's heart. His defenses would not be insurmountable or his loss to his bride irreparable.

The younger man was, in short, no obstacle. With a decisive gesture, Renold pushed away from the wall and left the card room.

He thought of walking up to where Madame Parnell sat with Angelica Carew and forcing an introduction. It was a great temptation to exchange a few words with Carew's daughter, to initiate a conversation without tears or high emotion, perhaps to let her see him as a man instead of a monster.

No, let it go. That was mere indulgence. It could change nothing and might well make it more difficult to maintain the will to accomplish his purpose.

His face set and his footsteps deliberate, Renold walked from the main cabin, going in search of the station where the ladies' attendant waited to be summoned.

Two

THE *QUEEN KATHLEEN* WAS AN AGING STEAMER AS SUCH things went; the boat was nearly four years old in a trade where snags, sandbars, storms, incompetent pilots, and faulty machinery left few afloat beyond their third year. She was a favorite of Renold's, however, mainly because she had been built especially for plying the lower Mississippi. He liked the captain, respected the pilot, and paid regular homage to the on-board chef, but his greatest appreciation was for the staterooms. Not only were they large enough to please passengers accustomed to expansive bedchambers, but were designed for cross ventilation in hot weather with both the normal inner door and also one opening to the outside deck.

He stood on the boiler deck near the outer door of Angelica Carew's stateroom. Lamplight fell through the door's closed jalousie, but little sound emerged beyond the soft, seductive rustle of silk skirts and an occasional sigh. Listening as he propped one shoulder against an ornate railing post, Renold was impatient but not at all impenitent.

The moon had come up, benign, resplendent, and shy, hiding its soft gold face behind trailing purple-gray cloud veils. The light that poured down in a shifting, shimmering track across the water had weight and substance. Renold felt it on his eyelids, his mouth. He resisted the impulse to reach out toward it, having long ago given up the struggle for the unobtainable.

Abruptly, a whistle shrilled from the Texas deck high above

him. He came to instant attention, with every sense alert. Seeing the cause of the excitement, he braced his hands on the railing to watch.

There was another steamboat plowing the water behind them. It spouted twin horns of black smoke shot with orange sparks from its torch-shaped stacks, while silver-white gusts of escaped steam were blown back from the overflow pipes. Charging forward with water rolling away from the prow on either side, the *City of Cincinnati* blasted the night with its steam whistle as it made ready to pass.

The pilot of the *Queen Kathleen*, however, had already called for more steam. It was soon forthcoming. The engines picked up their hard drive and thump, the boat surged forward. Under Renold's hand, the rail began to shudder with the faster, harder cadence. He frowned a little as he felt its unevenness.

His momentary concern vanished as there came the click of a latch behind him. Angelica Carew's stateroom door swung open. She stepped out onto the deck.

Renold turned to face her, and his breath caught, swelling, in his chest. She had taken down her hair. Soft, lustrous, the color of raw silk, it swirled around her. It shimmered in the deep waves, was tipped with moonlight on the gently curling ends, clung to the folds of her shawl and mingled with the wrap's silk fringe at a level almost reaching her knees. The palms of his hands itched to touch, to hold, and he closed them slowly into fists against his sides.

Stillness came into her face as she saw him, but she did not retreat. Her voice holding nothing more than anxious curiosity, she said, "What is it? What's happening?"

"A race," he answered.

"For heaven's sake, why?"

"Because there's a moon and visibility is good. Because the boat that reaches port first gets a full load of cargo while the next may not. Because river pilots have their pride, and then some." Renold stopped, afraid of his own volubility in the face of her considering quiet.

Her smile was a brief acknowledgment of his reasoning,

though she made no reply. She put her hand to the center of her waist, pressing as she breathed slowly in and out.

"Is something wrong?" he asked, the words carefully pitched to show politeness and consideration but no infringement.

The shake of her head made her hair dance over the silk bell of her skirt. She was still a moment before she said, "Have you, perhaps, seen the woman who acts as ladies' attendant? I've rung for her several times, but she doesn't come. I thought she might have stepped out on deck."

"I saw her about an hour ago," he answered with care. It was not a lie. He had seen the woman and given her a hefty bribe to find occupation elsewhere and ignore Angelica's bell. As if in afterthought, he added, "I believe she was on her way to look after the babe-in-arms and another tot belonging to a lady who had taken ill."

"Oh."

Renold suppressed the compunction caused by the despair in Angelica's voice. He knew the reason for it, of course, knew her dread of being confined in her clothing beyond the time she wished to be free. He had learned of it by sending his manservant to idle about the back door of the aunt's residence, encouraging chatter about the household. Advance planning was an article of faith for Renold, one of the handful he found useful. Another was to take advantage of any exposed weakness.

"If it matters so much," he said in soft reason, "I can only suppose you have need of a maid's services, or at least those of a female. Might I go in search of someone else for you?"

"No, there's no one. At least, I—can go myself in a few minutes."

He realized whom she intended to solicit for help in her dilemma. It was not unexpected, however, and he moved at once to block this interference in his plans. "You are thinking, perhaps, of Madame Parnell, the lady I saw you talking with after dinner? She has retired for the evening. I'm sure you will not want to stand around outside her stateroom while she gets back into her wig and face paint, not in your present state of dishabille."

His voice was offhand, but a warning of possible offended propriety sparked in its depths. Angelica said stiffly, "I will make myself presentable first, of course."

"There is no need. The lady travels with her own maid, I think. I can send my manservant to ask that her woman attend you."

Doubt crossed Angelica's clear features. "You don't think Madame Parnell will mind my borrowing her services?"

"I'm certain she would prefer it to the effort required to come herself."

She hesitated, then said, "I don't know. I prefer not to disturb my father since he has been ill, but perhaps my fiancé—"

"Young Eddington? I've met him. Unwise." The words were firm.

She caught her bottom lip between her teeth, then gave a reluctant nod. "I'm afraid I must accept your kind offer, then."

"It's no kindness, but a pleasure," Renold said before he could stop himself. Turning immediately, he moved along the railing to his own stateroom and stepped inside.

Tit Jean, his manservant of many years, looked up with a grave expression as he entered. Renold met his dark, liquid gaze, his own impassive. Neither spoke, for there was no need. Madame Parnell already had her instructions, which did not include sending her maid to Angelica.

In keeping with most body servants, Tit Jean knew exactly what Renold was doing and why. He disapproved, but confined his expression to a single solemn glance. This Renold could ignore.

Standing with his back against the wall, Renold closed his eyes. Pensive as a defrocked priest contemplating sin, he thought of what he intended to do. It was wrong without doubt, possibly even criminal. It was also justified. If he had ever doubted it, he had only to remember his stepfather with tears standing like warm mercury in the lines etched in his face, hear again the defeated, despairing agony in his voice.

Standing there, it came to Renold abruptly that forcing Angelica Carew to marry him for a stake in Bonheur was not the worst he could do. If he could convince her of her father's guilt and influence her to repudiate the man, it would be a punishing defeat for Edmund Carew. If she could be brought to love her husband more than her father, it would, finally, be a just revenge.

The gambler would know the desolation of lost self-respect, lost purpose for living that Gerald Delaup had known. And the knowledge would destroy him just as completely.

Was it plausible that the gambler's daughter might grow to love him, Renold wondered, or was it only a wayward inclination dictated by conscience and attraction? He could not tell. Whichever it might be, it must wait for later, after they were married.

Angelica Carew still stood at the railing where he had left her. Facing away from him as if she had been following the race, she breathed in audible gasps, plucking at the whalebone constriction at her waist. She really was in distress. He had not quite realized.

She turned, lowering her hand, forcing a valiant smile as she heard his approach. Still there was anxiety in her low voice as she said, "Is it all right?"

"I'm sorry, but there seems to be a rash of illness and accidents. Madame Parnell's maid tripped while moving a trunk a short time ago. She cut her knee, and she and her mistress are in the midst of the bandaging."

Angelica's gaze darkened, though she expressed suitable sympathy. Hesitating a moment, she said, "I suppose it will have to be my father then, after all."

"I thought you said he was unwell."

"I wish it weren't necessary, but I see no other choice."

Renold's face was calm but his voice less than even as he said, "I've given the matter some thought while I was gone. If you would accept my services, I have a certain dexterity with buttons. I can even find them without having to look—when the occasion demands it."

Her chest rose and fell as if she had been running hard. "You mean—you are offering to—"

"To act in the place of the ladies' attendant, yes. There is no one around to see, and it would only take a moment.

You may depend to the fullest on my discretion. And on my honor."

Her gaze did not falter, though her pale skin darkened with the rush of color. He thought it was caused by outrage, until he saw, in the moonlight across her eyes, the reflective gaze of consideration.

The wind of their passage stirred her skirts and carried a whiff of her scent compounded of roses and warm female into his face. It caught her hair, lifting a skein of it, turning it into silver-gold netting in the moonlight. She reached distractedly to catch the fine strands. Finally, she said in quiet demand, "Why would you suggest such a thing?"

"Concern and a willingness to please. Is it so surprising?"

"You don't know me, nor do I know you."

"An introduction is all that is lacking then?" he said, and knew, even as he gave his name and added a mocking half bow, that the tone was wrong and probably the words. She had surprised him, however, and he was not used to surprises.

"Are you known to my father?"

"I don't claim a close acquaintance." He had, mercifully, recaptured the need for care.

"I believe I saw you playing cards just now. Is that your profession?"

He tipped his head, intrigued by a shading he heard in her voice. "Would that make me more acceptable, or less?"

"All I require," she said with some astringency, "is a direct answer."

She was wary but not frightened, he saw, so could not have any great knowledge of men. It fit what he had gathered about her life with the dragon of an aunt. At the same time, he was disturbed that he was the one who must teach her distrust. He said, "I play at many things, from cotton bales and sugar to ships and land in foreign climes."

"You aren't a gambler then?"

"Not by profession, not anymore."

"But possibly by nature?"

A faint smile curled his mouth as he said, "Most men are, but not most women."

"Are you testing my inclinations?" she queried thought-
fully. "How should I tell, since I've never been invited to
play—" Her voice, even until the last, suddenly stopped.

"Except that now you have," he agreed. "To put your trust
in another person is always a gamble."

"Tell me why you should be concerned about my problems, and perhaps I will give you an answer."

It was the one thing he could not do. Or could he? He
felt his heart throb against his breastbone as he said, "There
are several reasons, beginning with the code of a gentleman
and ending with personal interest that began the moment I
saw you."

"And in between?"

She was perceptive. He would have to remember that. But
she was not, he thought, experienced enough to recognize
perfidy when it was masked by truth. His voice as fretted as a
wind-torn leaf, he said, "In between is desire."

"And you warn me? That is very candid of you."

"Isn't it?" he said. "You were going to give me an answer."

"I am my father's daughter, therefore gambling is in my
blood. More than that, my need to be released from the prison
of my garments is too great to pretend otherwise. I would
trust your promises if I could, only how am I to do that now?"

"That is, of course, the question."

She did not reply, but watched him in careful consideration.
It seemed an impasse, but one it would be best not to force.

Renold swung from her abruptly to gaze across the water
at the other boat racing along with its lights and noise and
trailing smoke. This was more difficult than he had imagined
it would be, and more disturbing. He had not expected to
care greatly what this woman thought of him, or what she
felt or wanted.

Behind him, she hesitated, then moved to the rail some
few feet from where he stood. Her gaze was turned toward
their boiling wake behind the paddle wheel. She seemed to
be watching the orange sparks that swirled backward from the
Queen Kathleen's smokestacks, drifting to wink out in blackness in the water.

After a moment, she said, "We are gaining."

"We had a fair lead," he agreed, accepting what seemed an obvious bid for time, but might not be.

"At this rate, we'll soon be in New Orleans."

"Rather, we'll soon need a wood yard," he said dryly.

She laughed a little at that. Aboard the other boat, pipes whistled and more smoke boiled upward from the stacks. Deckhands began to appear at the main deck rail, yelling across the water at the hands on the lower deck of their own boat. After a moment, she said, "I suppose it's just as well that I wasn't able to go to bed. I would have missed the excitement."

She had a point. The race in progress also increased the likelihood that their privacy would be interrupted as other passengers emerged from their rooms to watch. He must force the issue before that happened.

He said deliberately, "If it's excitement you enjoy, perhaps I have been more the gentleman than was necessary. I could, if you prefer, trade my favor for your favors."

She flinched a little as she swung in his direction, but did not swoon or strike out at him, either of which he half expected. In tones of asperity, she said, "That seems a high price for the manipulation of a few buttons and laces."

"One you might find it pleasurable to pay."

Her face took on the cool remoteness of white marble. "Possibly, if I were the kind of woman who could agree."

"All women are that kind, for the right reason, at the right time, with the right man."

She tilted her head, raising a hand to her throat. On an indrawn breath, she said, "Why? Why are you saying these things?"

"For purposes of seduction," he said with a shading of desperation. "What else?"

"No."

He watched her, his gaze measuring the troubled cast of her expression, and also the beginning of suspicion behind it. He said, "You don't believe me, do you? Why not, I wonder?"

"I have difficulty regarding you as that kind of man," she said. "Besides, I have it on the best authority that men intent on seduction are prone to seize a woman first and discuss it later."

He stood slowly erect. "I suppose I should thank you for the compliment, misplaced as it might be. If you are so sure of my character and motive, perhaps you may be able to accept my services, after all?"

"I don't think I'm quite that certain of my own judgment," she said with a trace of wry apology in her tone.

"Let me be clear, then: The answer is no."

She tried to smile and failed, perhaps because of something she read in his eyes. "I'm afraid it must be, I'll just go to my father."

Desire and violence, fueled by the urge for revenge, drummed across the surface of his mind. The most vivid emotion inside him, however, was regret. He said, "I can't let you do that, you know."

She saw her danger in that moment, and stepped away from him toward her stateroom. He surged after her, reaching to close his hand on her wrist. He heard her gasp, felt her resistance, but did not pause. With implacable will and relentless strength, he flung wide the jalousie door of her room and swept her inside.

She spun away from him in a silken whirl of skirts, coming up against the wall. Slamming the door shut, he swung to face her.

The stateroom was too confining, too crowded with trunks and bags and heavy, carved furniture to permit her to escape him. He could cover either the outer or inner door with a single long step. The bed was at his back, a lamp burning on the table beside it. He saw her note and accept these things before she raised her eyes to meet his hard stare.

Her heart was beating so hard it pulsed visibly in the long, smooth line of her neck and under the white curve of her breast at the neckline of her gown. She was braced, waiting for his next move while her chest rose and fell in a jerky and panicked motion against the merciless clinch of her corset. Yet, there was courage in her face and the race of swift calculation in her eyes.

He moved toward her. She swallowed, a convulsive movement. "What are you doing?"

"Isn't it obvious?" His voice was deeper than he had expected, softer than he had planned.

"You don't have the look of a man succumbing to temptation, much less unchecked passion."

"You, on the other hand, appear as untried as any bride can be. So how would you know?"

"Call it instinct." Her gaze slid away, then returned as if drawn.

Under her wide and steady regard, he felt heat rise along with pressure to his head. Where was Madame Parnell? She should be pounding on the door with outraged demands that he do the honorable thing by Angelica Carew. He was perfectly ready to comply. And he might, if forced to play out this little drama he had constructed, have real reason for it.

"I prefer," he said in rough tones as he moved closer to encircle his lovely captive's waist with his arm, "to call it wishful thinking."

She allowed herself to be pulled toward him, to sway against him with her lips parted and her eyelids drifting shut. She let her mouth come within a bare inch of his as his clasp slackened in anticipation.

Abruptly, she twisted from his hold and dived toward the dressing table further along the wall. Something flashed silver in her hand, an item from the box fitted with toiletries which sat there with its lid open.

Whatever weapon she had found could not be particularly lethal. With a whispered imprecation, he plunged after her. Snaking an arm around her ribs, he dragged her against him. She came easily, whirling with her hair flailing around her like a silken goad and her arm raised to strike.

Renold felt the sting at his neck where cravat and shirt collar met. Ignoring it, he sought and captured her wrist. With deliberate strength he brought her hand down, forcing her to drop the penknife she held, bringing her heaving breast hard against his chest as he clasped her wrist behind her back. Pushing the fingers of his free hand into the warm silk of hair, he tightened his grasp enough to bring immobility without causing pain.

It was necessary then to show her that he was serious in his intent. There was, in any case, such clamor and heated longing in his head that he was not certain he could restrain the impulse.

Her lips were cool and sweet, an incredibly tender incitement. He caught them half parted with the beginning of some appeal, or perhaps a cry, and hardly paused before slipping his tongue inside. She stiffened with the invasion, trying to prevent it. He would not allow it, but began to twine around her slim, smooth tongue with delicate persuasion to accept him.

It was the sound of distress she made deep in her throat that reached him. He felt as much as heard it, sensed the soft invasion of it through broadcloth and linen, muscle and bone, knew the minute it burrowed inward to encircle his heart and close around it with squeezing anguish. Lifting his head, he stared down at the woman in his arms. And he knew he had made a mistake.

The offense was grave, perhaps even fatal. There could be no pardon for it. Not now, perhaps not ever.

Renold was not egoistic; still it seemed the jolting blow that shook him, traveling upward from the soles of his boots, was no more excessive than the situation demanded. Then he heard the thunderous rumble, the vicious hiss of live steam, the throat-wrenching rasp of a man's scream.

The steamboat's boilers. They were going, bursting one by one under the strain of the race.

"Dear God," he breathed.

Hard on the words, he snatched Angelica in a bruising grasp and flung her toward the outside door. Bursting through it, he leaped for the rail, pulling Angelica with him, half lifting, half thrusting her over it.

She cried out, teetering on the deck's edge, clinging to his shoulders as she felt open space, open water below her. Vaulting the railing, he caught her close in his arms, balanced for an instant. Then he jumped with all the power that was in him.

Above and behind them, the steamboat exploded skyward in a towering mass of boiling steam, hot metal, and splintering wood. Renold felt livid pain wash over his back and shoulders, enwrapping him, searching for the woman he held.

He bent his body over her in protection, falling, falling. A crashing splash, then the river took them. It sucked them down into its cold and blessed embrace.

Three

ANGELICA LAY CONTEMPLATING THE RADIATING, SPOKE-LIKE folds of silk above her head. It seemed she had seen them many times. They formed a small part of some distant nightmare full of shouts and pain, water and fire, jolting movement and drugged fever. Still, she did not think she had recognized what she was looking at until this moment.

It was a *ciel de lit*, the gathered and pleated silk that lined the underside of a bed canopy. Fastened at the center by a gold foil starburst, the color was the pure blue of a Madonna's robe, a shade reserved for brides.

Her Aunt Harriet had an aversion for canopies and also for the bed curtains that went with them. They were, the older woman considered, Frenchified dust catchers which had no place in a Christian woman's house.

Curious.

The *ciel de lit* shone in the wavering light cast upward by the wide-mouthed globe of a bedside lamp. Beyond the lamplight's narrow circle, the room was dark, the double French doors on either side of the bed closed behind their draping of silk and gauze lace. A small coal fire burned under an ornate black marble mantel. The dainty French dressing table, washstand, and bonneted armoire that sat around the walls shone with firelight and the rich patina of constant polishing. Not a single thing in the bedchamber was familiar.

From the doorway opposite the bed, there came a soft exclamation followed by the quick rustle of clothing. Angelica turned her head with the languid deliberation that appeared all she was capable of achieving. She was barely in time to see a skirt disappearing into the darkened room, perhaps a dressing room, that lay beyond the opening.

She watched the doorway in case the woman returned. There were a number of questions drifting to the surface of her mind like air bubbles in a warm lake.

It was a man's tall, solid form that replaced the image of the flitting woman. Angelica drew a swift breath of shock. She wrenched herself upward, trying to scramble from the bed.

"Don't!"

Renold Harden's voice rang in deep and incisive command as he halted in his tracks. His face was still, stern, glazed on one side with the yellow-bronze sheen of lamplight while the other remained in shadow. Behind him hovered the dark-skinned woman who had summoned him.

Angelica's muscles locked, stopping all movement, though the command given her had nothing to do with it. She lay huddled, half raised on one elbow. Her breathing was harsh against the surging agony in her head while she clamped her hand across her eyes to hold the pain inside.

"If proof was needed that you are yourself again, it has just been provided," Renold said in quieter, more reflective tones. "If you dislike the situation you have found on waking, I apologize. It seemed best, given the circumstances."

"Where is this place? Why are you here?" She kept her eyes closed as she waited for his answer. To open them might well bring on sickness.

"You are at my home in New Orleans. I could have removed myself to a hotel for the duration of your convalescence, but it might have seemed strange behavior for a newly made bridegroom."

She stopped breathing. A long moment passed during which she gathered her strength and her thoughts. Her voice was threadlike as she said finally, "And whom did you marry?"

"Who else, my dulcet love, but you?"

She could open her eyes after all. Shock was a fine antidote for some ills.

There was alertness in his features as he watched her, and a sense of tightly strung poise in his stance. He was ready, she saw, to counter whatever response she might make to his announcement. She was capable of only one.

"No," she whispered.

"Yes," he replied evenly, "I do assure you."

She met his gaze then, staring into the dark warlock green of his eyes as she had not dared to before. There was nothing to be seen there, no hint whatever of his thoughts, not the slightest wisp of emotion.

She drew a slow breath. "Impossible."

"You want to be told how, and when, and possibly where? By all means. The where is easy: it was here in this house. When? At the time it became certain you would live, just over twelve days ago. How? By the good offices of a family friend and my mother's confessor of more than twenty years, Father Goulet—who has been known to bend a rule or two for the sake of a soul."

For an instant, she glimpsed an image in her mind to match the name he had spoken. A priest with a kind smile and a bald dome of scalp fringed with fine white hair like spider-made silk. Soft words with the sound of ritual. The smell of incense.

"You do remember," Renold said gently.

"What I recall could as easily have been absolution and last rites." The words were scathing for all their softness.

He smiled. "Those came earlier. For the other, you were not quite yourself, it's true, but you offered no objection."

She absorbed the certainty of his voice as well as his words. "You failed to say why you went to the trouble to arrange it."

"Oh, a passionate desire to bed you, of course," he answered at once.

"I don't believe you," she said in flat denial.

He watched her an instant. "No," he agreed with apparent regret, "it was, rather, the appearance of it, which is all some require."

She felt dizzy with trying to follow his swift and abstract phrases through the throbbing in her brain. She said bitingly, "Meaning?"

"I was observed doing my poor best to unfasten your buttons and release you from your corset. It was at your request. You seemed to think my touch preferable to remaining imprisoned a single moment longer—besides which, you could barely breathe. But the good people of the town where we had pulled ourselves from the river, finding us in flagrante, but not quite delicto, considered I must have some claim to future boudoir privileges, at least."

"And you let them."

"I was in no mood to be lynched," he said stringently.

"Pity," she muttered.

"Afterward," he went on, ignoring her provocation, "there arose the question of your hair. The quack brought to tend the injured from the steamboat wanted to cut it off, the better to drill a nice neat hole in your skull. I objected. He was forced to acknowledge my proprietary concern."

"Because you saw to it," she said in accusation.

His nod was prompt and definite. "After which, everyone took it for granted I would remove you promptly along with my other gear when the survivors departed."

"Your other—" she began, then stopped. Her confused gaze turned desolate. She met his watchful expression for no more than a moment before she looked into the darkness behind him. Finally, she said in husky tones, "Were there many others—survivors, I mean?"

"A hundred and three out of a passenger list of two hundred seventy-one, or so I was told." He added with quiet delibera-tion, "Your father and Eddington were not among them."

She had known how it must be from the moment she discov-ered where she was; she had only needed time to bring herself to ask. He had made finding the exact words unnecessary. For that much, and for the lack of false sympathy, she was grateful.

Tears pressed, burning behind her nose, seeping into her eyes, and running in hot tracks down her face. She ignored them. The words tight, she asked, "They were decently buried? You saw it done?"

He was silent so long that she looked up again. His face had a grim cast as he answered her. "Their bodies were not found, may never be—the Mississippi likes to keep its dead, or so the rivermen say. I would have done what was required for them if it had been possible."

She accepted that. Her father and Laurence must be gone. They would have been with her, certainly would have seen to her in her illness, if they had been alive.

"How long—?" she began.

"Two weeks and five days, to be exact. You were struck by a chunk of falling timber. For the first twenty-four hours, you seemed fairly well, but have been laid low by concussion and fever since then. It isn't surprising you have no memory of what occurred."

"I remember some things very well," she corrected him.

It was true, she did if she tried hard enough. The doctor young, sweating into his sandy hair, rank with the smell of fear as he stared across her at Renold. Herself being strapped to a door in order to be carried on board a waiting steamboat. The vile medicine Renold had tipped down her throat when she cried and begged not to go. This room the first night, quiet, cool, and immobile at last. She had clung to someone's hand, she thought, before she slept. She had felt safe, protected.

There were tears sliding over her cheekbones and into the hollows below them. She wiped distractedly at the wetness.

The dark-skinned woman, a housekeeper from her starched white apron and neat kerchief, gave a soft exclamation of concern and began to move forward. Renold stopped her with an upraised hand, then made a single, sharp motion. The woman turned with reluctance and obvious disapproval in her round face and pouter-pigeon shape. The door closed behind her.

Renold shifted his position, drawing closer to the bed with a single, careful step. Angelica stiffened, drew back.

"Calm yourself. I am no threat to you, I swear it." He moved a little closer.

"Stay where you are." She meant the words to be sharp, but they came out as a whispered plea.

"It's a little late for that, don't you think? When I've been sworn and dutifully blessed this age? Not to mention I've been lying on a cot at your feet like a faithful hound through nights longer than a saint's rosary. That's when not applying cool water to your lily white skin in places once known only to you and your nursemaid."

"You didn't." She would not look at him, she couldn't. He had a reason for saying those words, she thought, if she could only clear her mind enough to discover it.

"Someone had to relieve Estelle. Besides, it seemed I was due the privilege."

"Why? Because you had earned it?"

His smile, when it came, was wry. "Now that was almost worthy; I can see you are better. But you still need to sleep. You can annihilate me another day."

He had moved to the head of the bed where he reached to pour a dark liquid from a small green bottle into a crystal glass. His hand was steady and his gaze on what he was doing as he put down the bottle and picked up the carafe beside it to add water. Swirling the mixture, he held it out to her.

"No, I thank you."

"You prefer to keep your eyes open and your wits about you? Useless, I promise. I don't care to risk you being thoroughly sick down my shirt front."

Had she done that before? She would not ask, could not imagine being so close to him, did not want to know. Surely she had not, since he showed no sign of disgust.

"Or maybe," he went on, "you intend to tell me you have no pain. Don't, please. I've grown used to the signs. And I have no use for futile arguments."

"Or any other kind?"

"Oh, I'm as high-handed as a Turkish dey, and prone to violence, besides. Something you might find helpful to keep in mind."

"I'm not likely to forget it."

He laughed, a forced sound. "So you never overlook an injury, never forgive an error of understanding? What a lovely marriage it's going to be. I can see us in thirty years, both gimlet-eyed and scarred beyond recognition, but still tender enough to bleed." His voice roughened. "Will you take this, or is it your pleasure to make me force you?"

She was so very tired, and the stupid tears were wetting her nightgown. Or not her nightgown. Whose? And who had put it on her?

She dared not think. The best way to prevent that was, of course, the laudanum he held in his hand. Did he know that?

With lowered lashes and high color, she took the glass and put it to her lips, held her breath, swallowed. The water he immediately pressed upon her was welcome. The effort to keep the bitter draught down was so severe that she shuddered and lowered herself carefully to her pillow with closed eyes.

"I take it my shirt is safe," he said after a long, considering moment.

"Barely."

"I'll send Estelle back to you."

She made no answer. A short time later, she heard his footsteps retreating. Or so she thought. She might have imagined it or heard something else entirely. She was certain, however, that the lamp beside the bed was extinguished in silence and with dispatch.

The darkness of the room expanded, the pain receded. The night lengthened. She drifted, half woke herself with a stifled sob, and discovered she was crying in her sleep. She turned her face into the pillow, trying to control the difficult, acid anguish of loss and grief.

After a time, the mattress on which she lay sagged to accept a heavier weight. Words flavored with deep maledictions wafted above her head. Firm hands touched her and she was drawn, carefully, against a warm, hard form.

Sighing, Angelica eased closer, felt herself enclosed in a strong clasp. There was comfort in it and a measure of peace. It seemed, almost, that she had found both there before. The tears ceased.

She slept. Or perhaps she only moved deeper into her drug-induced dream.

It was a Sunday. Angelica knew that because of the bells that clanged, now silver-toned and mellow, now discordant, over the city. The sound floated through the two sets of French doors standing open on either side of her bed, one to the balcony above the street and the other to the gallery over-looking the sun-drenched courtyard. From the kitchen area below came the morning smells of baking bread and coffee, and also browning onions for a dish meant as the noon meal.

Renold lounged in a chair drawn up near the balcony doors for the light while he perused a newssheet with the swift thoroughness that was his habit. With a dressing gown thrown loosely around him, one foot propped on a stool and a cup of coffee waiting beside his chair, it appeared he was placed for some time.

Angelica had found him there when she woke. She thought he had spent the night on the cot at the foot of her bed. It had been used, for she could just see the crumpled sheets from where she lay. The narrow cot was actually an accouchement bed used for childbirth, a grim reminder of the consequences of marriage. If Renold had passed the night there, however, it was the first time in two nights, since the evening he had told her about her father and Laurence.

He had been in and out during the daytime, giving orders for her welfare, demanding that she rest, eat, take her medi-cine, cajoling her into it when commands failed. He was also out of the house for long periods, especially during the evening hours. She had heard him return the night before and thought he had slept in a bedchamber connected to her own by a dressing room.

The housekeeper, Estelle, had attended to Angelica's needs in Renold's absence. The woman had been friendly, talking easily about the household, which included Renold's manser-vant and majordomo, Tit Jean, plus two maids, the cook and her three helpers, a coachman, and a pair of stablemen who also ran errands. Regardless, she had little to say about the maître, as she called Renold, and it was difficult to say whether it was discretion or fear that held her silent.

"Where the maître goes and the things he does are for him

to know," she said in answer to Angelica's questions. "Or you can speak to him of it yourself. It could be he will tell you, depending."

"Depending on what?" Angelica asked with what she hoped was no more than normal curiosity.

"His mood," the woman said with a tart smile, "and, also, it may be, on why he thinks you want to know. A great one for thinking, is the maître, though *le bon Dieu* knows it makes him peevish."

Renold did not seem peevish this morning. Rather, he looked as content and indolent, confident and darkly handsome as a swamp panther reclining in the sun. The very sight of him made Angelica want to throw something.

She was sitting propped against pillows while she drank her cafe au lait. On a tray nearby was an empty plate that had held the flaky pastries filled with chocolate cream that were Estelle's idea for putting flesh back on Angelica's bones now that her appetite had returned. Angelica reached to put her cup on the tray and to use a lace-edged napkin. Settling back again, she folded her hands and said, "I don't understand you."

"Quarrelsome before breakfast," Renold answered without looking up. "I might have known."

"I've eaten."

He put his newssheet aside. "Oh, have you? Then tell me what it is about me that offends you now?"

She suspected that he knew the precise moment she had swallowed the last crumb. His close attention was uncomfortable, but might also be of aid in putting across a point. Pursing her lips judiciously, she said, "Now, as to that..."

His lips twisted with wry appreciation. "What? Too comprehensive a list of offenses? Tell me, instead, what it is you don't understand."

The success of her ploy was gratifying, but there was no time to savor it. She said, "Well, in your kind explanations the other day, you told me you married me because you had compromised me—"

"Acquit me, please, I said no such thing," he returned in instant repugnance. "I only explained why I assumed the role of your husband. My reasons for taking you to wife with all due pledge and ceremony are something else again."

"I beg your pardon," she said with a great show of politeness. "Perhaps you will explain the difference?"

He lifted a brow. "It's a question of will. Mine, in this case. I did not wed you because of the picayune suspicions of a pack of backwoods provincials. It was done to gain the right to order the treatment for you I felt necessary—and because I formed an irresistible impulse to see you in dishabille sitting in the middle of my bed."

She stared at him while color burned across her cheekbones and she conquered the impulse to cover her shoulders exposed by her nightgown. Not that she believed a word of what he said. She had learned enough of him to be wary of taking anything he might say at face value.

"You wanted me," she said finally.

"Something I've made amply plain, or so I thought." His gaze upon her did not waver.

She swallowed and gave her hands her studious attention. There was a wedding ring in the French style on her finger, a wide band centered by a sapphire surrounded by diamonds. She had discovered it there when she awoke from her laudanum-induced sleep the day before yesterday. She turned it for the seconds it took to recover her composure.

"Yes, all right," she said finally. "But I must suppose that I spoke my vows along with you before the priest, or at least signified my acceptance of the match. What do you think kept me from shouting a refusal at the top of my lungs?"

"Gratitude," he suggested, his green eyes turning carefully opaque. "Or at least acceptance of the inevitable."

"Because I recognized the compromising situation, whether you admit to it or not? But I had a fiancé, or I must have thought so at the time."

"He wasn't there. I was. And just how well did you know this man you were to marry? Were you anxious to be his wife?"

"That isn't the point."

"Isn't it? Marriages are arranged every day between strangers. This union between us, as awkward as it may be, has been faced by countless men and women. Somehow they overcome it and make a life together."

"Do they?" she said, and looked away toward where the sunlight slanted across the floor.

"It helps, of course, if both have the same expectations."

"I don't remember a discussion of our future life—among other things."

He leaned his head against the back of his chair. "Would it matter if you did? Or is it just more satisfying to cling to pique and revenge?"

"Revenge?" The word had a peculiar ring.

"For things better left undone. By me. For things left unsaid, certainly."

The gaze she raised to meet his was unwavering. "You think I'm annoyed now because you didn't say you hold me in affection. Believe me, I was never so optimistic. Or easily taken in."

His face went blank before he shook his head. "You hardly know me, had no reason to care—it never occurred to me you might expect it. No. I referred to an apology, properly groveling, of course, for the mistake in understanding aboard the *Queen Kathleen*. You might have had it, except I had already repented and received due punishment. If you ever realized that, however, it seems one more thing you have forgotten."

His voice stopped. Gathering himself with athletic ease, he rose from the chair. He started toward her, stripping open his dressing gown as he came.

She had been trying to catch up with his thought processes. They were wiped abruptly from her mind. Pushing herself higher on her pillows, she said, "What are you doing?"

"Don't be alarmed," he said as he put his foot on the bed steps and mounted to the mattress. Settling near her knees, he dropped his dressing gown, exposing his broad shoulders and chest to her startled gaze. "I am not bent on coercion this time," he went on, "only a demonstration. It isn't my place to pronounce the penalty for my own misdeeds, but look first, then tell me if you require more atonement. Or should I allow you to add to the scars?"

He twisted at the waist to present his back to her, then braced as if expecting the lash of a whip. Angelica almost strangled on her indrawn breath as her gaze swept across the wide span of his shoulders and down his spine to his taut waist. The livid traces of barely healed burns slashed across the ridged muscles. Deep in places, shallow in others, they were covered over with newly grown flesh that had the shining smoothness of red-shaded bronze silk.

"The steam," she whispered.

Without conscious thought, she reached out to soothe the scar tissue. Under her fingertips, his skin was firm, smooth, heated.

Angelica felt an odd, wondering regret as she realized that he had shielded her from the worst of the explosion, taking the brunt of it with his back as he jumped with her into the river. The pain must have been agonizing, both then and for some time afterward.

A shudder, not quite suppressed, twitched over Renold. Under her hand, the prickling of gooseflesh roughened his skin, spreading, running along the tops of his shoulders. Air rasped in his lungs as he inhaled with unexpected force. He turned his head to stare at her.

Her gaze flickered up to his, was caught and held. A suspended darkness came into his face. It was as if he waited, yielding, for what she would do next.

She lowered her lashes. It was then she saw one more scar. No more than a fine red line at his throat, it angled from the turn of his neck across his collarbone. It had the look of a slice made by someone careless with a small, sharp knife.

Or perhaps a penknife.

She snatched her hand away. How could she have forgotten, even for an instant? She had made that scar, that evening in the stateroom.

Her voice unaccountably thick, she said, "There was never any question of caring."

"Which is, I think, though it's by no means certain, precisely what I was trying to show you." With a swift flexing of long muscles, he removed himself from the bed, turning from her as he pulled his dressing gown back into place and fastened it.

After a moment, she said, "Am I now supposed to feel guilty, or merely reassured? You are still a stranger, a man who took me away with him as he might a kitten saved from drowning."

"Getting clawed for his pains?"

"That's always a risk, isn't it, when the cat isn't sure whether it's being rescued or pushed under, taken as a pet or shut up in a prison?" She stopped, putting a hand to her face, rubbing her forehead where her headache had returned. "I'm sorry, I don't mean to sound ungrateful. I can see that you're trying to make amends for what happened on the steamboat."

"Can you?" His laugh was short.

She barely heard, went on quickly. "I am grateful for your quick action in saving me, and I appreciate the care you have given me and the diplomacy you've shown. But the fact is that I have a home. There is an aunt in Natchez who should be contacted and told that I survived. I don't like to think how she must feel, believing my father and I, and even Laurence, were lost."

"I will be happy to send word if you will give me her direction," he said over his shoulder, "but are you certain she will want to house you now?"

"You mean now my father is—gone?"

"I mean," he said deliberately as he turned and rested a hand on the bedpost, "now that you've spent so much time under the roof of a man who is not a blood relative." He paused, went on. "Or, if your aunt hears of the marriage, won't she think it strange that you would seek shelter with her?"

"I will explain everything to her," Angelica said. "Naturally."

Grim amusement invaded his face. "I would like very much to be there for it; from what I've heard of the lady, it should prove interesting. However, I don't think I would depend on her charity. What happens if she shows you the door?"

"In that case," Angelica said with a militant look in her eye, "I have a house of my own, a plantation given to me by my father as a bridal gift."

"Yes, of course, for the nuptials which never took place. Do you think I will like it?"

She regarded him with sudden wariness. "Why should that be a factor?"

"Because," he said with watchful eyes but apparently unimpaired humor, "I have a way of becoming permanently attached to my pets. I don't expect to have them always underfoot, but I object to being separated from them for too long."

"I am not—" she began, then stopped.

"No, you aren't a pet cat but my wife. Only think," he said as he moved to the door and pulled it open, "how much more attached I may become."

The heavy door shut behind him. Angelica lay staring at it in frowning concentration.

She felt as if she had been buffeted by a strong wind. All the carefully marshaled arguments and plans she had intended to set before Renold had been blown away as if they were no more than dust. She would have been happier if she didn't have the creeping notion she was supposed to feel this way.

She didn't trust him. How could she? Not only was there his treachery aboard the steamboat, but she had little faith in men after the way her father had lied to her for years.

Married. A wife. Why did those words make no connection in her mind? Why couldn't she remember? Why did that particular episode have the nebulous unreality of a distant dream?

There was so much about the way Renold Harden had taken charge of her that she didn't understand. More, the reasons he had given did little to relieve her mind. Because of that, she was forced to wonder if her confusion on that score wasn't also his exact intention.

She couldn't stay here. Soon, in a day or two, when she was stronger, she must leave.

It was infuriating, and also saddening, but Renold was right about her aunt. Her father's sister would likely consider Angelica's situation deplorable but fixed. She had no use for a man herself, but nurtured a firm belief in male authority and a husband's prerogatives.

In addition, Aunt Harriet had shown unmistakable relief at the ending of her responsibility for Angelica. She had meant to attend the wedding; she had signified her intention of doing that much. Afterward, she had expected to return to the round of genteel entertainments given by the spinsters and widows of Natchez that had filled her days before she accepted the task of rearing her brother's motherless child. She had, rather obviously, been looking forward to that time.

There was Bonheur, of course.

Would Renold really come after her? Would he actually shoulder his way onto the property meant as her dowry? If he did, would it be from real interest or just the careless, patronizing consideration he might give an animal kept for his amusement?

She was not his pet cat, nor was she actually his wife. Self-respect and self-protection in equal measure required that these facts be kept uppermost in the minds of them both. And she would not consider injuries or regrets.

Certainly, she would not think, even for a minute, of the stroking, attention, and affectionate attachment usually felt for pets who remained close enough to receive it.

Four

THE PASSING VOICES, LIGHT AND FLIRTATIOUS, DEEP AND caressing, had a joyous ring. They called back and forth with greetings and good-natured teasing. They rose above the sound of carriage wheels, and dropped to a low murmur with secrets. The light thrown by carriage lamps and lanterns carried by linkboys or servants wavered across the bedchamber walls. Now and then there was a gust of laughter. Fragments of conversation floated up from below, drifting in at the French doors that were open to the street and the unseasonably mild evening air:

"...Hope they have something besides the pianoforte, violin, and French horn. Last time, the music was—"

"...That Alphonse, no. I don't like his mother; she said my gown was too bright!"

"...So handsome, but he won't look my way. I heard he was enamored of a lady in Paris, but I don't think—"

There was tripping anticipation in the words, and a gaiety that made Angelica feel a wistful longing. Somewhere there was going to be dancing, music, people enjoying each other's company. Perhaps it was a masked ball, since the Mardi Gras season was upon them here in New Orleans. How very agreeable it must be to join in such revelry.

She was not eligible, of course, in her state of mourning. And in truth, her spirits were not so lively that she felt able to take part in such festivities. Still, she felt a perverse urge to be out there, beautifully dressed, on her way to the ball. It was as if, lying there in the bed, she was stranded on the bank of the river of life that flowed past outside.

The door opened on the far side of the room. Turning her head, she saw Renold on the threshold. He paused with one hand on the doorknob, as if to be certain she was awake.

"Why has no one lighted the lamps?" he asked as he came forward. "Or is woolgathering better done in the dark?"

Angelica had seen no one for several hours. "I supposed," she said with acerbity, "that you were being thrifty with the whale oil."

A smile flitted across his face. "It's been a dull evening, I see. Perhaps that will make dinner in my company more acceptable."

"Dinner?" The look in her eyes was startled.

"I thought we might eat on the gallery, unless you think you might be too cool."

"I'm allowed to get up?" she inquired.

"In a manner of speaking," he said as he moved toward the bed.

A flush of anticipation rose in her face. Reaching for the dressing sacque that Estelle had laid out for her, she began to push her arms into the sleeves. She left it untied as she grasped the bed covers and flung them back, getting ready to slide from the bed.

Renold was there before her feet touched the floor. He leaned to slip one arm under her knees and the other behind her back, then lifted her high against his chest. She gasped, throwing an arm around his neck and shoulders.

As her arm struck him, he flinched, a minute stiffening that passed so quickly she wasn't quite certain she felt it. His burns. Releasing him at once, she held herself rigid. He turned his head to meet her wide gaze.

Green, green, his eyes were like melted emeralds with flecks of jasper and gold around the fathomless black of the pupils. His brows were thick, his lashes so long and curving they rested against the skin under his eyes. The bridge of his nose was strong, the ridges of his cheekbones slanting perfectly into the hard lines of his jaws. The smooth shape of his mouth was taut at the corners, while his chin had a decided jut, as if he waited for defiance.

When it was not forthcoming, he said, "Food as a sedative? If you had told me, I'd have promised you a feast long before."

She said stiffly, "If you expected me to fight you, why not give me the choice of walking instead of being carried?"

"What, and miss all your furious dignity? Not to mention testing your strength. How long are you going to lie as stiff and bowed as a plow handle?"

The tenseness in her muscles was due as much to the feel of his arms enclosing her as to her fear of causing him pain. Did he know that? With a fulminating glance she said, "I expect I can hold out as long as you can."

He hefted her. She drew a quick breath and almost grasped his shoulder again. Remembering just in time, she sank her fingers into thickly curling hair at the base of his skull.

"As restrained as a bee walking the lip of a sugar bowl," he said on a tight laugh. "Are you afraid of falling in, or just being dragged over the side?"

"Possibly I prefer not to sting the one bringing the sugar." The words were stifled.

"Charming. But what makes you think I would mind— when a bee who uses the stinger in her tail loses it?"

"Oh, I don't think it at all, but I mind enough for both of us."

"Besides which," he said, his voice carrying a softer note, "you are unprotected enough all ready. Though if I remember correctly, you prefer it that way."

He was speaking of her nakedness under the thin batiste nightgown and dressing sacque. It was quite true that she felt rather precariously dressed, but she refused to give him the satisfaction of admitting it. She said, "I prefer to offer no undue provocation, if that's what you mean."

"Having discovered the consequences? Men, as well as circumstances, are not always the same. You must learn to adjust accordingly."

"I don't understand you," she said abruptly.

"Oh, I think you do; most women recognize it instinctively," he returned. "I am suggesting that there are times when provocation is the better part of wisdom."

Irritation crossed her face. "Don't be ridiculous," she snapped. "We are neither of us in shape for it."

He laughed, a rich sound of real amusement. The tension faded from his face, seeped from his arms. Swinging toward the French doors that led out onto the gallery, he said, "Yes, well, you may be right. Sometimes it's best to leave a honey bee unmolested."

By the time Angelica was settled in a chair of woven rattan, Estelle appeared with a large dinner tray. Behind her came a giant of a man bearing a sizeable silver soup tureen which looked dainty in his enormous hands. This was Tit Jean, Renold's manservant, and it was clear his name derived, in the peculiar way of such things, from the French word *petit*, or small. Angelica had heard his deep bass voice with its West Indies lilt a few times, either in the hall or coming from the dressing room which connected with the bedchamber. However, this was the first time she had seen him.

The man gave her a smile as he ducked his massive head. There was interest in his dark eyes, however, and also quick calculation in the glance he divided between her and his master.

The housekeeper allowed the big man scant time for thought. Bustling, competent, she ordered him about, sending him after the napkins that had somehow been forgotten, for the silver stand to hold the wine that had been chilled in the cistern, and for a cloth to cover the crusty loaves of bread on their silver salver. In moments, the savory, rich aroma of seafood soup was wafting on the air, mingling with the scent of burning wax from the candles in the silver candelabra that centered the table.

Renold surveyed the preparations. Everything was precisely as he had planned it. He gave his approval and the two servants departed. He and Angelica were left alone, watching each other through the wavering candlelight.

"So," he said. "Don't let me take your appetite. By all means, eat."

Angelica picked up her spoon, turned it in her hand. She

put it back down again. Her voice shaded with quiet suspicion, she said, "Why? Why are you doing this?"

"I thought you might be ready for a little conversation with your meals." He unfolded his napkin and dropped it into his lap.

"About what?"

"Whatever occurs to us," he said, controlling his exasperation with an effort. "I have tried not to disturb your rest any more than necessary, but we must begin at some time to grow more used to each other, to take up normal married life. This seemed as good a place as any to start."

"Normal," she repeated.

"It is not a word of any great complexity or hidden meaning," he said.

"Perhaps not to you."

As she looked up at him, he saw the apprehension in her eyes and felt a brush of shame. "Is it such a terrifying prospect?" he said in quiet inquiry. "I can't promise to be an ideal husband, but I will make every effort to be accommodating. You won't find me difficult to please or ungenerous."

"Are you saying—do you mean that ours will not be a close marriage?"

"That is something that only time will show," he said with appropriate solemnity.

"What I mean to say—" she began again a little desperately.

"I understand very well what you meant. The answer is no. No, I don't mean to imply that ours will not be an intimate relationship. That would suit me not at all."

"You have some idea of an heir, then."

His gaze rested for long seconds on the hectic color in her face. He could simply agree and leave the matter as it was, or he could elaborate. The question was which course would be least alarming for her. He didn't know, so could only follow his own inclinations.

"A child in my image? Or yours? The idea isn't disagreeable, but has no great bearing. Nor do I have any use for a cool union wherein husband and wife go their separate ways, maintaining strict courtesy when they do happen to come upon each other at some public entertainment or between the sheets. What I require is someone close beside me in the night, at the breakfast table, in my mind." He stopped, appalled at the words that crowded his tongue on the verge of expression. He ended abruptly, "That is the purpose of marriage, isn't it?"

She shook her head, her gaze considering. "I couldn't say, having lived all my life with a lady who claimed to be a spinster by choice. But it appears a subject you have thought much about. Is—was there no one else you preferred to wed?"

This was safer ground. He said, "Are you asking if my past is littered with unforgotten loves? There was once a lady I considered taking to wife, but she chose another man. It was a lucky escape as matters turned out. My heart is free. And what of yours?"

"Mine?" The word had a startled sound. She met his gaze no more than an instant before glancing away into the courtyard.

"You were traveling to begin a new life with young Eddington—if you are in need of a reminder. I saw no signs of undying attachment, but it's always possible I missed something."

"You were watching?" she asked, a small frown between her brows.

"You know I was," he said softly, and had the satisfaction of seeing her blush deepen. He waited, and was surprised to feel a tightening across the back of his neck.

"Laurence was a childhood friend, since my aunt and his mother were well acquainted. I had not seen a great deal of him in the last few years, though we stood up together at dancing parties and the occasional ball. He came to call soon after my father—well, soon after he returned to Natchez. He had my aunt's approval and gained my father's permission to address me. Papa was anxious to see me settled because of his illness."

"You accepted the proposal due to the combined pressures," he said helpfully.

"I'm not sure I ever actually agreed." She looked away and back again. "I tried one day to have a conversation a little like this one with him, and he seemed to take it for granted we were discussing terms of surrender rather than the possibility of it."

He had, Renold admitted ruefully, been close to doing the same thing. He said, "The next thing you knew, you were receiving congratulations."

"After which, it was impossible to withdraw without looking like a silly female who didn't know her own mind."

"Which might have been preferable to a lifetime of regret."

"Yes," she said seriously, and was still, watching him.

He sustained that steady regard for all of ten seconds before a laugh of appreciation for her chosen method of resistance shook him. "Very well. I will undertake to exert no undue pressure. However, you might like to keep in mind that the cases are different. We are already wed, and I am not Eddington. More than that, patience is not one of my better qualities."

"No pressure," she murmured, glancing at him from under her lashes.

"Well, relatively little," he said in dry agreement. "Now if your appetite is at all improved, you should try your soup before it gets cold."

She picked up her spoon again and dipped it into the creamy broth with its tomato tint and chunks of fish and succulent shrimp and oysters. He watched with a rare suspended feeling inside until he saw the look of delight that crossed her features, then he took up his own spoon.

It was some few minutes later that he noticed her attention wandering to the sound of voices over the courtyard wall. He listened a moment before he said in explanation, "Madame Fouchet's guests for her *bal masque*; the lady lives a few blocks on along the street. The theme this year is a Venetian carnival. I'm told there's not an ounce of gold paint, a lion or flower mask, white cape, or doge's robes left anywhere in the city."

"You were invited?"

"I had a card, yes. The lady's husband is a business acquaintance."

"Then why aren't you there?"

"I had other plans," he said, smiling into her eyes. When she made no reply, he picked up his wineglass, sipped, and set it back down. "Perhaps next year you will be able to attend."

The small catch in her breath was telling. "That would be possible?"

"You may care for it, or may not," he said as he inclined his head. "New Orleans has much else to offer in the way of diversion. The social season brings everything from the grandest of balls to luncheons al fresco and expeditions to the lake. Every major European and American opera and theater troupe is booked here from time to time, as well as concert artists such as dancers, violinists, and singers like Adelina Patti. The marvels of the circus and rare animal displays are often available if such things amuse you. You have only to indicate your preference, and I will see to the arrangements. Naturally, I will also serve as your escort."

"That's very kind of you." There was a wondering undertone to the words.

"Not at all. I'm only trying to tell you what you can expect as my wife."

"As to that, I really don't think—"

"You aren't curious?" he said, smiling as he interrupted what he was unwilling to hear. "You have no interest in hearing how we will spend the days and evenings, winters and summers of our lives?" He paused, then took her silence for permission to continue. "You will inevitably make friends. Estelle and Tit Jean will help you welcome them when they call. If you wish a more formal evening gathering, you have only to tell me, and I will be on hand as host to your hostess."

"A life of gay dissipation, I perceive."

Her faintly rallying tone was, he thought, a defense against being affected by the program he was outlining. It was, therefore, a positive sign.

"Winters in New Orleans are pleasant, but the summers can be overwhelming with their heat and damp, the smells that collect in the streets and the pestilence in the air. In years past, it's been my habit to endure these things, but I would not submit you to them. We can, if you like, travel in Europe during those months. Or we might seek the more healthful air of the country." He added, as if it were an afterthought, "It could be beneficial to spend time at this plantation you have acquired; absentee ownership is seldom productive without supervision. You have an overseer, I assume?"

Her gaze was arrested. "I have no idea. I hadn't thought how it must be going on during this time."

"I could look into it for you, if you like."

She did not repudiate the suggestion, but then neither did she instantly cast the responsibility for Bonheur into his lap as would most women of his acquaintance. She was, he was beginning to see, a worthy opponent. She might have little to say, but there was a great deal going on in her mind. He would give much to know the tenor of it.

He went on after a moment. "If you care to occupy yourself with an interest in the property, there can be no objection. I would prefer to ride out with you on your inspections, or I will choose a groom for you. This is not, you understand, to burden you with supervision, but merely to have someone on hand in case your mount acts up or there is an accident. You do ride?"

She nodded. "That was one of the accomplishments my aunt considered important for a female."

"I will see to choosing a saddle horse for you, if you like. There is also the matter of a riding habit. Oh, and I should tell you, while on that subject, that I have arranged a dress allowance for you with my banker. This is not for the household account, but to be spent solely at your discretion, for whatever personal items you may need. Also, the modiste who provided your nightwear has been engaged to work up a few day gowns to your measurements—using the one you were wearing the night of the explosion as a guide. She should be visiting you in a day or two with sample costumes. If you don't care for what she has done, you have only to say so and choose something else."

"I'm overwhelmed," she said quietly. "You are remarkably generous, not to mention accommodating."

"I thought you would be pleased," he said in grave mockery for the primness of her tone.

She lifted a hand to the neckline of her dressing sacque, gathering it higher. At the same time, she lowered her gaze, focusing on the courtyard below them. There was a lock of hair trailing over her shoulder and down across her breast. It stirred with her every breath, shining back and forth along the fine filaments in glittering highlights like tiny stars riding strands of raw silk. At the same time, the long skein molded the curves underneath with lustrous fidelity.

"Do you not care for flowers?" she said.

The change of subject was so complete and his thoughts so distracted that it was an instant before he could assemble the sounds she made into meaningful words. More than that, he was caught by the desperation in her tone, which seemed to suggest a need to remove herself from his liberality. It was an indication that he had, perhaps, overplayed his hand.

His answer was made almost at random. "Flowers? I like them as well as any."

"There are none down there, where it would be so easy to make them grow," she said, indicating the stone-floored space with its protective walls covered with wild vines.

"You have an affinity for them, I expect," he said, trying to follow her lead.

She smiled for the first time without a shadow. "That's a very nice compliment, thank you, but I don't think I can make that claim. My aunt grew many kinds, all in rows, regimented as soldiers. I was never allowed to pick them. I preferred wildflowers, since they grew as they pleased."

It was the rueful, almost melancholy sound of her voice, he thought, that caused the squeezing sensation inside his chest. There was no time to voice it, however, for Tit Jean was there, bowing apologetically in the door.

"Your pardon, maître, but there is a man to see you."

A man, not a gentleman. It was not difficult to read the communication in the manservant's expression as well as his tone and choice of words. "Put him in the library and offer him whiskey," he said. "I'll be with him momentarily."

The manservant inclined his head and took himself off with offended dignity. Angelica watched that stiff-backed departure before she turned back to him.

"Is anything wrong?"

"Not at all," he said, drinking down his wine and using his napkin.

"You know who your visitor is, then, I suppose."

He might have guessed she would be adept at reading moods and attitudes. "Tit Jean has a snobbish streak. He doesn't always approve of my business associates."

"Perhaps you should pay attention to him."

He rose to his feet, smiling down at her. "Such concern, *ma chère*. I'm flattered."

"For no cause," she answered, her voice several degrees cooler.

"A shame," he said. And knew the truth of the words as he indicated with a gesture that she continue with her soup while he left her.

Angelica did not turn her head to look after Renold as he departed. It was irritating to her how much of an effort that proved.

He was a man of surprises. He was also much more considerate than she would have deemed possible. A proper gratitude was difficult, however, for she had the distinct feeling that there was a reason behind it. It seemed that he wanted to make her happy, or at least resigned, in her marriage. Why, was the question. She could not imagine that he was pleased to have a wife foisted on him, no matter what he might say.

All that was required in this situation was a decent degree of provision. The lifestyle he had outlined was staggering, and seductive, in its lavishness. The cause was difficult to see, unless it was guilt.

The services of a modiste, entertainments, his escort here and there, his presence for meals: she was slowly being drawn into his life. It was extremely beguiling in its way: the comfort, the consideration, but especially the aura of care.

Was she married to him? Was she really? Would it make a difference if she knew beyond doubting?

What was she going to do?

She didn't know. None of Aunt Harriet's strictures and maxims on correct behavior seemed to apply. What did one do about a man who threatened you in your stateroom one moment and saved you from harm the next? What rules were there for conduct toward someone who spirited you away, installed you in his bed while you were insensible, and when you awoke informed you a marriage had taken place? She was trying to be reasonable about it, but the situation was so far beyond anything she had ever imagined that she had no guidelines.

Insofar as she could discern, she had three choices: She could return to the safe and narrow obscurity of her aunt's house. She could travel back upriver to the plantation and take up life there. Or she could accept Renold Harden's care and protection and hope that his motives were trustworthy.

There was a problem with each solution.

Her aunt, as Renold had pointed out, might not be pleased to see her. She knew nothing whatever of large-scale farming methods of the sort that must be undertaken to make her living on the plantation, nor did she have the capital to pay an overseer, buy seed for planting time, or even care for the slaves who were now in her charge. As for consigning herself to Renold's keeping, every instinct warned against it.

But if she left him, how was she to go? She could not simply walk out of the house in her nightgown. She had no money to pay her way either to the plantation or back to Natchez since her father had been in charge of their funds, and whatever gold he had been carrying was lost with him. She could ask Renold for the passage money, but it went against the grain to be indebted to him, especially when she had no way of paying him back. More than that, it was entirely possible that he would refuse.

Her appetite had vanished. She pushed back her plate, then propped her elbow on the table and rested her chin on the palm of her hand.

Perhaps it was her illness, or possibly it was years of having every decision made for her, but settling on a plan of action seemed a task so wearisome it was beyond her strength. Added to that was a haunting fear of making a mistake.

It wasn't, no, not at all, that she wanted to stay with Renold. She hoped she had more strength of character than to be influenced by creature comforts and promises of a grand life. As for the man himself, how could she be attracted to someone she couldn't trust?

Married. It seemed she could almost glimpse an image in her mind to go with the word, but it shifted from her grasp like a dream on waking. If she could remember, if she knew that a ceremony had taken place, would it make a difference? Could she be bound by a legal and religious contract she could not recall making? Did she want to be?

A door closed somewhere below, and there came the scuffle of footsteps in the courtyard. Two men appeared. One was Tit Jean, the other a small man with a pinched and narrow face and thin shoulders dressed in what appeared to be nondescript gray. The shorter man was scurrying like the mouse he resembled, trying to keep up with the manservant's long strides. He was protesting every breath, though Tit Jean affected deafness. As the two men reached the iron-barred gate set within the frame of the back carriage entrance, the manservant pushed it wide for the visitor to depart, then closed it with a resounding clang after him.

The little man whipped around as if he might reenter. Then his gaze lifted toward the gallery. He stood still. Mouth falling open, he stared through the bars at Angelica's pale shape for long seconds. Ducking his head abruptly, he swung and slipped away into the shadows.

It was only minutes later that Estelle appeared. The maître, she said, sent his apologies. He had to go out and would be late returning. He instructed that Angelica enjoy the remainder of her meal, then allow Estelle to help her return to bed.

Angelica struggled through the remainder of the soup, also the slices of chicken breast in an herb sauce, the new peas, the carrot and cabbage vinaigrette, the custard and dried peach tarts. Most of the different courses were left on her plate.

Since Angelica was already up, she asked Estelle to bring a tub of water and help her bathe. It was, perhaps, a little too much; Angelica was trembling with exhaustion by the time the maid pulled a clean nightgown over her head. Within minutes after she was settled once more between the sheets, she was asleep.

Her rest was sound for only an hour or so. She roused then to some terrifying, partially remembered dream of fire and water. For long moments, she lay wide-eyed in the dark while her thudding heart slowed to a normal tempo and her breathing returned to an even cadence. Afterward, she slept only in fitful snatches.

It was toward dawn that she came awake with jarring sudden-ness. There was someone in the room with her, standing beside the bed. Silent in the darkness, he was staring down at her.

It was long moments before she could force herself to open her eyes, longer still before she could make out the shadowy form of a man.

It was Renold. She was almost sure of it. Almost.

He did not move, seemed not to be breathing for all the sound he made. She wondered if he knew she was awake; she could barely separate his body from the gray blackness around him, and she was even more concealed within the confines of the bed curtains. The urge to force some acknowledgment, to break the silence in some way, was strong. Something in his stillness prevented her.

An eternity later, he breathed a soft sigh. Turning away, he moved noiselessly toward the foot of the bed. The ropes of the cot creaked as he lowered his long form to the mattress. Quiet returned.

What had he been doing? Was he only checking on her well-being, or had there been some idea in his mind of claiming his so-called rights as a husband? She didn't know. She wished she did. Almost. She lay for a long time as the darkness crept toward dawn. Thinking about it. Wondering.

She couldn't see him from where she lay. The room was so quiet it seemed he might have slipped out. Moving carefully, she sat up in bed. She still couldn't see very well. She pushed herself higher, almost rising to her knees.

He was there, stretched out at her feet. The cover pulled over him was pale against the dark shading of his skin, so that it emphasized the broad width of shoulders above it. His hair was a dark shadow against the white pillowcase, while his face had the strong, still beauty of a death mask.

He had slept there before, but she had not been aware of it then. Even the last few nights, he had gone to bed long after she was asleep and rose before she woke. It was incredible to see him there now, so intimately near in the close darkness. It gave her a peculiar feeling of mingled safety and peril.

"I don't bite," he said without opening his eyes. "And I don't think I snore. If you should discover differently, you might shake me awake, but not otherwise. Unless you want conjugal company on that veritable ocean of counterpane you occupy?"

"No," she said after a moment. "Thank you."

"I thought not. You aren't unwell?"

"I'm perfectly fine. But are you—comfortable?"

He opened one eye, for she caught the faint glint of it. "Do I look it?"

The cot was too narrow and could have been longer. "Not particularly."

"Observant as well as wakeful," he said with dry humor. "I would advise you to sleep while you can. Martyrdom is not my style, I assure you; I don't propose to be here many more nights."

"What a happy thought to take back to my pillow," she said in acid condemnation.

"Yes," he answered agreeably. "Isn't it?"

Five

It was the misfortune of the would-be assassins that they chose a night when Renold had just come from the *salle d'armes* of Prospero, the mulatto master of fencing, in Exchange Alley.

The *maître d'armes* did not deign to cross swords with just any of his students, but was always glad to give Renold a try at besting him. Renold accepted the honor at least once per week, often enough to keep his reflexes honed and his skill with a sword at a peak, which discouraged all but the most determined challengers. On such evenings, he strolled homeward with his sword swinging at his side, his blood comfortably heated, and his muscles well oiled by exercise.

The first indication of trouble was a flutter of pigeons. Grumbling, they spiraled up out of an alleyway ahead. Renold reached out to touch the arm of the man who walked beside him.

Michel Farness had been a friend for a long time, and was no fool besides. Being unarmed, he did not hesitate, but whipped away from Renold and put his back to the nearest wall.

Discovered, and enraged by it, the hidden men chanced everything on a frontal assault. They lunged from the alley three abreast screaming rivermen's curses. The big hog-skinning knives in their hands caught the moonlight on their wickedly honed tips.

Renold's sword made a soft, silken rasp as he slid it from

its scabbard. He dropped into a swordsman's crouch with the easy coordination of warm muscles and habit.

The bricks of the narrow *banquette* darkened with heaving shadows. Grunts made puffs of clouds in air that overnight had turned frosty. Steel flashed and scraped and clanged with gritty determination. The flurry of movement was swift and deadly.

It was over almost before it had begun. As one of the rivermen fell, the other two disengaged with shouts and wrenching effort. Whirling, they broke into a run and were engulfed by the night. The body of the first remained, sprawled over the *banquette* with a thin red trickle of wetness seeping into the cracks between the bricks.

Michel moved with a graceful sweep of his silk-lined cloak to kneel beside the fallen man. Looking up at Renold, who breathed deep and hard above him, he said, "A mortal wound, my friend; you might have learned more if you had been in less of a temper."

"They were too close to home." The words were clipped, unrepentant, an explanation rather than an excuse.

"And besides," Michel said, his gaze owlishly wise, "there was an audience worth impressing?"

Renold, by an effort of will of which he was entirely too conscious, refrained from looking at the balcony of his house just down the street. Angelica had stood there seconds before, he knew, her slender form stiff and silent from—what? Shock? Disgust? Disappointment? At the first sign that he had survived the attack, she had swung in a whirl of skirts and stepped back inside.

In answer to his friend, he said, "Rather, one for which there is the need to sustain an illusion."

"Of your prowess?" There was disbelief in Michel's words.

Renold gave a short laugh. "Of my invincibility. The easiest way to prevent mutiny is to make it impractical."

"Mutiny? In a guest?" Michel asked with a puzzled frown.

"The lady is my wife."

Michel stared up at him. "You are married—you have been married this whole evening long—and I am just now hearing of it?"

Renold allowed no shred of expression to appear on his face. "She has been ill. It seemed best to defer callers and congratulations until she was able to receive them."

"Ill. And mutinous," the other man said in fascinated tones. He paused while he rose to his feet and dusted off his hands. "Mutiny in a wife is usually known as adultery."

"Or desertion," Renold answered with grim humor, "which is slightly more controllable. However, if I kill enough footpads, maybe I won't have to skewer my friends. I asked you to walk home with me for the purpose of meeting my bride. I expect she will appreciate a new face."

"I hope she won't like it too much," Michel said in pretended anxiety, "I'm in no mood for unpleasantness." His irrepressible humor rose then to brighten his gypsy dark eyes. "Then again, if your wife is as lovely as the glimpse of her leads me to believe, I may take up sword practice and call you out for the prospect of comforting the widow."

Renold, turning and walking toward his own house, said, "I don't recommend it."

"Do I detect a testy note?"

"You do. On top of which, any reward is uncertain. The lady fights her own battles, though her most formidable weapon is her sharp tongue. As I can testify. My skin is fairly whole, but my ego is as finely sliced as omelet onions."

"Taking a leaf from your book, is she?"

Renold had not considered that possibility. Words could reveal or conceal, cause joy or pain. They could also be used to construct an inner fortress from which all attackers could be repelled. He had learned that lesson long ago. Had he taught it to Angelica by example?

Answering both Michel and himself, he said, "Undoubtedly."

Michel stood where he was a moment longer, then jolted into movement, stretching his stride to catch up with him. His voice rich with amazement, he said, "Your bride doesn't worship you?"

"Not noticeably."

"She doesn't fall into a swoon at your touch?"

Renold gave him a level look that was both an answer and a warning to go no further.

"Then why," the other man said with cheerful if mystified reason, as they reached the entrance door to the courtyard, "did you marry her?"

"She owns Bonheur."

Michel stared at Renold as he followed after him into the courtyard, then waited while the door was closed and locked. "The other question," he said finally, "is why she married you."

"Simple. *Force majeure*."

"And you are enjoying this arrangement?"

"Immensely." The words were without inflection, though Renold could feel the set lines of his face.

Michel gave a short laugh. "I can see that. Enjoy it any more, and half of New Orleans will soon lie gutted and draining on your *banquette*."

"A timely reminder that I should have the body removed. Don't let me forget to tell Tit Jean to see to it."

"He probably set about that task before the misguided son out there hit the ground, as well you know."

"Very true," Renold said, and led the way up the stairs and into the salon.

Angelica was waiting for them there. She was a little pale, but magnificent in her black silk.

She had wanted bombazine, but Renold had vetoed it as too heavy for the climate. There had been some discussion over the neckline also. The keyhole affair that resulted was neither high enough to satisfy her nor low enough to please him, but was an acceptable compromise. The color had been discussed at length, but on that she had been immovable; she would have her mourning. Black on some women gave them the appearance of crows. Her it made look like a grieving angel. It was enough to put an edge on a man's teeth.

Tit Jean, apparently at her order, was just departing after bringing in a wine tray. He held the door of the salon for their entry, catching his master's eye for an expressive instant before leaving them. The message was received. Everything had gone well in his absence, and the body currently obstructing foot traffic outside would not be there in the morning.

Renold turned to Angelica, scanning her face, assessing her

mood and strength as he stepped forward with Michel. "My dear," he said, "allow me to present an old friend."

She gave her hand to Michel with a perfectly polite, if distracted, acknowledgment. She turned back at once. "Who were those men?"

Renold walked to the table where the wine had been placed, picked up the decanter, and began to pour. Watching the liquid bubble into the glasses, he said, "River scum after an easy mark. Irish Channel toughs ventured into the wrong section. Gallatin Street *canaille* with a grudge against top hats. The choice is yours, and should be as accurate a guess as any."

"Were they waiting for you?"

He did not look at Michel. "Only for my purse."

"I thought—" She stopped, said instead, "You took no injury?"

It might be possible, seeing the frown between her brows, to suppose that she was concerned. Renold did not make that mistake. "It was a sword against knives, not precisely an even contest. So, no, I was not hurt."

"Hardly uneven," Michel protested. "They were three against one, after all." He smiled at Angelica. "I would have joined the fray, armed or not, if it had been necessary. It wasn't."

"So I saw," she said, and gave his friend a faint smile.

And Renold, watching through his lashes, saw Michel succumb without resistance to the many and special charms of his wife. He was less than surprised; Michel was susceptible.

It wasn't always possible for a man to recognize what might attract a woman in another man, but he could appreciate Michel's good points. His light brown hair curled in poetic and unpomaded abandon. Liquid eyes, with a near constant sheen of incipient laughter, must be counted a definite asset. Of medium height, the other man was well made, with a stocky, muscular build concealed under rather flamboyant tailoring. His deportment was respectful, his manner interested, his smiles warm and faintly caressing. Yet the final secret of his success with the female sex was something apart from these things, or so Renold suspected: Michel was beloved by the ladies for the simple reason that he adored them all indiscriminately.

Renold had wanted to see what his friend made of Angelica. Listening to the compliments that tripped from Michel's tongue along with questions about her mourning, watching the dazed look in his eyes, he thought he had found out.

Had he also wanted to show off his wife, he wondered? Pride of possession was not a usual fault with him; still, it was possible. It was also true that no law of church or state gave him ownership of her mind, her loyalty, or her attention. It was, he thought grimly, a legal oversight.

Michel, who had taken a seat beside Angelica on the settee, glanced in his direction. He blinked as he met Renold's steady gaze, then dark color rose under his olive skin. "*Mon Dieu*, old friend, what ails you now? I thought the warning outside only a jest. You aren't actually going to be the sort of husband who glowers from corners."

"You will have to forgive me. I'm still new at the business." His voice, Renold recognized, was cooler than he had intended.

Angelica gave a brittle laugh. "In any case, there's no cause for alarm. Renold means to be the perfect husband, therefore jealousy is entirely in order as a matter of form."

"A perfect husband," he said, "might permit an innocent flirtation. I fear I am made of coarser clay."

Her gaze was direct, then, and a little surprised as she met his eyes. Still, she did not refuse the challenge. "You admit the fault? That is gallant."

"Admit the flirtation, and we are even, though the score remains at—"

"Nothing to nothing? Am I supposed to find that gratifying?" There was determined pleasantness in her voice, but no more than that.

Michel, looking from one of them to the other, said, "If you two prefer to quarrel in peace, only let me know, and I can leave."

An unfortunate intervention. On whose behalf? "Oh, this is mere practice with blunted weapons. Danger to onlookers is unlikely—unless they take sides."

"Something I would consider only if the odds were too uneven." Michel's words carried an unaccustomed edge.

Renold turned to Angelica. "You have a champion, it seems. What will you do with him?"

"I rather thought he was offering his support to the opposite side," she said with a flash of blue fire in her eyes. "He is your friend, after all."

It was a timely admonition. "So he is. Though I am always suspicious of divided loyalties."

"That's it," Michel said in disgust. "I will leave you."

"Then what," Renold said to his friend in tones intended to sting, "would be the point of the exercise?"

Michel sprang to his feet. "You can believe I need warning? If I were less a friend I really would call you out!"

"Useless." Renold walked toward the shorter man and took his arm, turning him in the direction of the door. "I've killed my man for this week, and have no use for another mouse to place before my mistress."

"Death," Angelica said magnificently, "is a matter of indifference to me."

"Unless of course it's mine," Renold answered. He paused for a bow and smile to go with that riposte.

Michel, pale under his olive skin, pulled away to make his formal adieu. On his dignity then, he strode on ahead down the stairs and into the courtyard. As Renold followed, the other man stopped and turned with his feet set and his fists on his hips.

"Well, and do you want to meet me?" he demanded.

"To salve your wounded dignity, or to impress Angelica?"

"To teach you a lesson in manners. How could you speak to such a lovely woman in that contemptible way?"

"I thought," Renold said, "that it would be better than beating her."

Michel made an extravagant gesture of repudiation. "You thought it better than ravishing her in public. If you are so entranced, what in the name of all the saints is wrong with your temper?" His face changed. "Unless—"

"Unless I am both more patient and more cunning than you suspected? These things have their price." Renold's features were grim. "Or are we speaking of the same thing?

Would you care to explain, in words suitably respectful of the lady's person, precisely what you mean?"

"You haven't taken her to bed."

It was possible to see the hot blood in the other man's face even in the dark. "Now there you are right and wrong," Renold said gently, "though I would not, myself, consider the subject one for idle discussion."

"Or else," Michel went on undeterred, "you know what you're doing is not fit, but you have charted your course and are too pigheaded to change it."

"Moral outrage? I'm amazed." He should not have been, of course. His friend, born of an Italian mother and a French father, was a legitimate member of one of the oldest Creole families in the city. Along with his birthright came a firm belief in all the higher-toned principles.

"Or maybe it's both of those reasons. In which case, there's something more than a little peculiar about this whole affair. I'm not too sure I believe in this marriage for which no announcements were made, no banns read, no invitations delivered."

"Untruthful as well as a lecherous abductor of women? What an opinion you have of me."

The shake of the other man's head sent a curl tumbling over his forehead. "I know how you felt about your stepfather, Renold, but if you are in the process of compromising the lady as a means of restitution for his death and his losses, then I have to tell you that it's infamous."

"And you actually think," he said softly, "that I am capable of this infamy?"

"Oh, I don't doubt you have other reasons. She is enough to tempt any man."

"Thank you for that much," Renold said in acid reproof.

"Yes, and before this evening, I would have said that your conduct toward a lady was always correct. But I've never seen you behave as you did toward your Angelica, not even when you were top over tails about Clotilde. You seem to me to be a very devil."

"While you would treat her with every tenderness," Renold said with malignant softness.

Michel's mouth set in a straight line. "I would certainly use common courtesy!"

"And uncommon charm."

"If you are getting ready to issue a warning again, you may save yourself the trouble; I understood it earlier. But I will tell you something to your face, Renold. If your Angelica ever stands in need of the champion you called me, I will be there."

"Against me?"

"Who else? I would expect you to protect her from every other man."

Renold stood perfectly still while his thoughts moved like quicksilver through his mind. He said abruptly, "You are perfectly right. I seem to have lost my objectivity on this subject. No matter. Interfere too much on the part of the lady, and we may wind up facing each other with swords after all."

"Pistols," Michel said. "The choice will be mine if you force me onto the field. And that's the only way I'll meet you."

"There is, I suppose, some ridiculous French Creole reason of honor which makes it impossible to challenge the man you have made a cuckold."

"Not at all. The only prohibition is something called friendship."

Renold permitted himself a brief smile. "But that," he said softly, "is supposed to be what prevents a man from trespassing in the first place."

Michel made no answer beyond a stiff bow. Renold walked with him to the back gate to see him out. Afterward, he stood for long moments with his hand resting on the iron bars. Then, still thoughtful, he went back into the house.

Angelica was standing in the middle of her bedchamber robed for bed in white lawn and lace shimmering with candlelight. As he entered, she looked up with the furious resignation he was fast coming to detest.

He paused to rid himself of annoyance, rather than for appreciation of the spectacle. It was a fine one, however, and certainly worth savoring. Not being blind or a hypocrite, he stored the more delicate points in memory for later detection.

That much he could take without injury to anyone, except, possibly, himself.

The lawn of her nightgown and light dressing sacque had a fine weave; he could see the dark apricot shading of her nipples through the material. No corset constricted the narrow span of her waist or controlled the soft roundness of her hips under the soft drape of the material. Her hair, carefully brushed and plaited, hung in a thick rope over one shoulder, an incitement to the destruction of neatness.

She was moist and fresh, the sweet femaleness of her so covered as to make peeling away the thin white layers as pleasurable as licking the frosting from a bun before consuming it in small bites. The urge to do just that was so abruptly felt and so violent that he plunged too soon into speech.

"*Sacré*," he said softly. "If I had known you were going to make a production of getting ready to retire, my love, I'd have hurried back for the performance."

Her gaze held the cool censure that he deserved. "No doubt," she said, "which is why I didn't wait. Would you care to tell me what has become of your bed?"

He glanced toward the canopied four-poster, where the cot that had been at the foot so long was conspicuously absent. His stomach muscles tightened. "Why, nothing that I can see."

"You know very well what I mean. By whose order was it removed?"

A large part of the rage in her voice was from the mortification of being forced to confront him. And that, too, like so much else these days, annoyed him.

He said, "You know it must have been mine. I take it you are concerned that I will have no place to sleep?"

"You know—"

"Yes, certainly," he took her up without compunction. "So why not simply say what is on your mind."

She stared at him for a long moment before she lifted her chin. She said clearly, "I am not sleeping in the same bed with you. I would not have considered it even before I chanced to overhear something of what you and your friend were saying down below. Now, it's doubly impossible."

Courtyards were notorious for amplifying sound and funneling it upward. He should have considered it. Was there no misfortune that could not descend on this enterprise?

He stripped off his coat and tossed it on the nearest chair. Reaching up to loosen the ends of his cravat, unwinding the folds, he said, "Eavesdropping?"

"I heard my name. It seemed best to know in what regard it was being bandied about."

Even he could not fault the reason of that. "And now you are infected by Michel's doubts. You might have shown more trust." Moving to the dressing table, he dropped the cravat onto the surface, then began to remove the studs from his shirt.

"By all means," she said with derision. "You have given me so much encouragement to bring my doubts to you, after all. Even if I did, what guarantee is there that anything you might tell me would be the truth?"

He watched the rise and fall of her breasts under the white lawn of her nightgown. Her agitated breathing was in excess of her anger. His own, on the other hand, stopped if he failed to pay attention. With the last stud removed, he tugged his shirt from the waist of his trousers and began to pull it off.

"What form," he said in stringent reason, "should this guarantee take? Ten thousand angels swearing on the Bible? An appearance of the Holy Mother with my name on her lips? A vow recorded in script at the cathedral? What?"

"A written record would be—what are you doing?"

Her gaze lingered on his bare chest. There was a compressed sound in her voice that might have been alarm, but he suspected was outrage. But he had had enough of tending the sensibilities of others for one day.

He said, "I am preparing for the bath that Tit Jean will be bringing shortly. If you care to watch the production I intend to make, you are welcome. If not, you can get in the bed and pull the sheet over your head."

"I can also leave the room," she said, and swung away in a whirlwind of white draperies.

"No."

The word was neither loud nor harsh, but had a slicing

finality that brought her up just short of the door. He followed hard on it, bunching the shirt he had removed and tossing it aside, then walking forward to brace one hand on the closed door panel. He steeled himself as though for a blow as she turned slowly to inspect him with her arctic blue gaze.

"You require an audience after all?" she said.

There was something in her quiet voice that sent a shiver up his backbone. He could drown in the clear pools of her eyes. Her lips were smooth, soft, conjuring up impulses so unreliable that it was a moment before he could think, much less speak.

He said in husky tones, "You are interested in my requirements? I want a warm presence, a willing ear, a quick and prescient smile. I would like a lovely face, an enticing form, a graceful manner. I desire tender touches, welcoming embraces, eagerness. Blame my peasant ancestors, but I refuse to go in search of all these things down cold halls and in separate beds."

"You can't force me to sleep with you." Her gaze was unblinking though her color had shifted from rose to white.

He did not raise his voice. "Your mistake. I could, easily. And in the sense that you mean when you use that polite substitute for an impolite condition. Being contrary by nature, however—and on my mettle this evening to act the gentleman husband I never claimed to be—I won't."

"You won't?"

"Don't, please, show your obvious relief just yet. Because I will force you to join me by at least playing at the part of lady wife you so disdain. And who knows? If we act our roles convincingly enough, they may become natural to us."

The silence that developed between them was thunderous. In it, Angelica stared at the man so near to her, and saw no yielding, no mercy, in his face.

She said, "You would turn this room into a stage? I see it becoming more a battlefield."

"The bed being the high ground to be taken or defended at all costs? Why not? There's at least honest hate between enemies, instead of this congealed dislike and grudging gratitude. More than that, prisoners taken in honorable combat can be honorably employed, and submit to their imprisonment honorably."

"A man's point of view without doubt," she said. "What is so honorable about the threat of superior force?"

"One side almost always has greater strength than the other. The natural counter for that advantage is surprise, guile, and superior tactics."

"Trickery and deceit, in other words. I do see."

"All is fair, and so on," he said. Not a muscle moved in the hard planes of his face.

"A convenient view. I will choose my weapons accordingly, though you won't be amazed if I fail to warn you what they may be."

"Smiles, kisses, and womanly wiles? I am more ready for them than you know."

"So I would imagine," she said, ignoring the underlayer of meaning, "since they may be so easily turned against the person who uses them."

"Not," he said, a strange sound in his voice, "so very easily."

The lamplight, flaring at some stray draft, caught in Renold's eyes. Angelica searched behind that bright flame and found an even greater conflagration there. Swallowing with a convulsive movement of her throat, she said in bald supplication, "Why would you care to have an unwilling woman anywhere near you, much less in your bed?"

"A multitude of reasons, most of them carnal, a few stupidly sentimental. Besides, there is always the possibility of a weakening of will."

The timbre of his voice set off odd vibrations in the region of her abdomen. She held her breath against them as she said, "Not likely."

"Rampant hope is a man's prerogative, and sometimes his salvation."

She looked away from him, and snagged her gaze on the hard planes of his chest. The dark fleecing of hair that concealed his breastbone looked soft to the touch. A fine tail of it plunged downward arrow-straight over his abdomen, which was made firm and resilient by taut muscle, then disappeared under the wide waistband of his trousers.

There was a glisten of wetness at that band, and a crimson

stain on the skin around it. She put out her hand as if to touch him, then jerked it back.

Her voice not quite calm, she said, "You're bleeding."

It was as if the words required translation in his head before their meaning could be understood. He glanced down, then lifted a careless shoulder. "The natural consequence of a stray blow being struck near a tender scar."

He was right, she saw, as she bent closer. There was the splotch of a bruise around the broken skin. She said in accusation, "You told me you weren't hurt."

"I beg your pardon," he said dryly. "I hadn't stopped to take a proper inventory."

"Come lie down and let me look at it. You may have a broken rib." She barely brushed his arm, urging him toward the bed.

"Sully those virginal sheets? You can't be thinking straight. Besides, how will you get me out of them again?"

She frowned at his misplaced, irony-shaded humor, fighting the guilt it brought. It was also necessary to suppress the image of him lying relaxed and lazy as some wild animal on the mattress. Idiot. He was the only person she had ever met who could send her emotions swooping like a backyard swing.

She said, "There is a towel in the dressing room; I'll get it in a moment."

"That will save the sheets, but what about you?" His voice was purest suggestion.

"I will take care not to be soiled," she said, and braved the impact of his gaze as the words reached him.

"How very brave," he said softly, "when it's so hard to touch dirt without it."

There was an inward glaze to the darkness of his eyes, the effect, she thought, of an unexpected blow. She had dealt it. "I didn't mean—"

"Didn't you?" he said, cutting across her words. "Then prove it. Touch me. Tend my wound, such as it is. Finish what you started."

All she had intended to do was check his injury in the lamplight beside the bed—and what maggot of the brain had possessed her to consider it, she could not say. If bandaging was needed, Tit Jean, when he arrived with the bath, was the person for that task. Which was well and good, except she couldn't bring herself to say it. Renold had taken care of her for days and weeks on end. The least she could do was return the favor, since she had no intention of being a wife to him.

"All right," she said, "if that's what you want."

His voice like honey-flavored butter, he said, "It's only a minuscule portion. Still, it's a beginning."

Six

She brought the length of Turkish toweling. When he lay facedown on it with his head resting on his crossed arms, she approached the bed with the care of a doe near a wolf's den.

The sheet, his body, and his eyes blurred into a haze of white, bronze, and green as, light-headed, she mounted the bed steps and sat down beside him. It was a doubly precarious perch, so near him and so close to the bed's edge. At least he could no longer see what she was doing once she was settled.

Concentrate, she told herself. Don't think of the polished sheen of his skin. Ignore the strong sweep of muscle from his lower back to his neck. Suppress the compassion for the mottled pattern of burn scars. Put aside the fear that he might obey some sudden urge of passion and roll over, pulling her down with him.

Touch him, he had said. How? Where? Her fingertips tingled and she curled them into the palms of her hands.

Concentrate.

The wound was ugly. A knife hilt perhaps, or possibly a fist with vicious strength behind it, had struck deep into one of the widest and most tender of the scars. The damage lay just behind his lower left ribs, as if he had twisted to take the blow where it would do the least damage. The skin around it was dark purple with bruising, while the center was lacerated and crusted with dried blood. There was still a slight surface ooze.

It was possible his ribs underneath had been broken. There was only one way to find out.

Placing her hands flat against his bloodstained side, she put her thumbs over the rib. Being careful to avoid the broken skin, she pressed down with first one thumb, then the other. There was no movement, no obvious break.

His lips parted for a hard, indrawn breath. She was hurting him. Yet he preferred to endure it rather than stop her.

She released the pressure, but allowed her hands to rest on his flesh. His heat seeped into her. It seemed she could feel the surging of his blood, the fiercely controlled force of him. His chest fell as he exhaled, and did not rise again as he lay still and accepting under her hands.

A soft exclamation left her. She snatched her hands away as if they had been resting on a hot stove. Drawing back, she watched him turn and sit up while she waited with dread for what he would say.

He did not speak, but slid out of the bed and walked to the washstand where he moistened a linen cloth. Returning with it, he took her hand and began to wipe away the traces of his blood that stained her fingers. "Soiling," he said then, in quiet reflection, "is a human condition, sometimes sordid, sometimes sublime. Still, it's a melancholy thing to discover that you can't, after all, avoid it."

At least he had not gloated. Without meeting his eyes, she said, "You will need to cover your wound."

"After my bath, yes. If it pleases you."

She let the words stand, neither agreeing nor disagreeing. Yet there was a strange allure in the feeling that he was content to depend on her for his needs and well-being.

Finished with one hand, he took the other. His hold was loose, warm, without confinement. There was absolutely no reason to feel as if she were being pulled toward him. The brush of the wet cloth along her fingers was like a caress; the delving deep between them, the careful scouring of the hollow of her palm was incredibly intimate. Then he tossed the stained linen square aside.

She knew, with a woman's ancient instinct, the moment

when his inclination settled and became purpose. She knew, and did nothing. Which was bad enough, but worse yet was that he was well aware of her foreknowledge. Regardless, there was only lambent light in his eyes, no triumph, no amusement bathed in irony.

His movements were studied, unhurried. Lifting her hand that he held, he placed it on his shoulder and left it there. He encircled her waist, then, and drew her to him so she slid from the bed and was caught between the high mattress and his body.

Memory was sly. It recalled what was valued, discarded what disturbed too much. She was assailed by comparisons to that other kiss. This one was the same: the mouth so firm and sure, the sweetness, the tempered questing and intemperate enticement.

Yet, it was also different. His arms cradled her closer, his lips were more tender. He was as courteous but not quite as controlled as on that first night. His hand on her cheek cupped without force, testing the texture and softness of her skin. He explored the slender curve of her neck, and also the molding of her shoulder under her gown. Sliding his fingers along the turnings of her arm, he slipped them between elbow and rib cage to span the indentation of her waist. Then, unerringly, he smoothed his hand upward and closed it on her breast with the care of a gourmet taking hold of a perfectly ripened peach.

Her lips parted to draw breath. He took instant advantage, slipping his tongue into her mouth. It was pure invasion, an intimate engagement of pebbled surfaces and warm, honey-flavored smoothness. He prolonged if inviting participation, inciting mindless acquiescence by the delicate friction of his lips on hers. Holding her in thrall, he closed his fingers on the tender nipple of the breast he held and rolled it gently back and forth until it formed a tight bud.

Her thighs were against his with only thin layers of cloth between, their bodies were welded from breasts to knees. Drowning in her own unbridled and curious desire she was not responsible, nor did she want to be. It was his play, and she had, for the moment, a compelling need to see where it would take them.

Nowhere.

There came a knock and the door swung wide. Tit Jean picked up one of the cans of hot water he had set down while he announced his presence, then stepped inside. He glanced in their direction, then paused, blinking, as he caught the look of cold temper on Renold's face.

His gaze swept to the ceiling and remained there. "Your pardon, maître, *maîtress*, I beg. I have grown used to there being no need for care as there was no need for privacy. I will not trespass again."

"Be sure of it," Renold said softly.

It was not his own modesty Renold had been defending, Angelica thought, but hers. Tit Jean knew it also, for his glance only skimmed over her as he inclined his head. He said, shifting from one foot to the other, "Shall I return later?"

Renold's lips tightened, then he sighed. "No. You have permission to finish what you have begun, even if no one else can."

The big manservant made no reply, but moved to drag a lead tub from behind a corner screen and fill it from the water cans.

With the release of tight muscles, Renold moved away from Angelica. Unbuttoning his close-fitting trousers, he shucked them down his legs. His underdrawers followed almost before she could draw breath. Turning his back on her, he stepped into the tub and eased down into the water.

Steam rose in white undulations. Water splashed over the edge of the tub, glistening in the lamplight. The surface of the water gleamed silver and reflective as a mirror, throwing back errant gleams, denying visibility. Renold leaned back and relaxed, closing his eyes.

Tit Jean moved to dump more coal from the scuttle onto the fire, then poked up the flames. He looked around, checking that toweling was laid ready to Renold's hand along with a thick cake of soap, a dressing gown was draped ready over a chair arm, the draperies were drawn.

Satisfied that his duty had been performed, he bowed himself from the room.

Angelica retreated to sit on the side of the bed once more, contemplating her hands. Estelle had shaped her nails that morning and burnished them to a smooth sheen with a kid leather buffer, so there was nothing of particular interest there. It was, however, a safe place to look.

The fire hissed. A lamp made a soft popping noise as it fluttered on its wick. The bed ropes creaked as she shifted a little for a more secure seat.

"Thinking of running?" Renold said into the quiet.

"What, in my nightclothes?" she said with a shade of bitterness. "Also, where can I go, barefoot and penniless as a nun doing penance, that I would not wind up worse than this?"

"You consider there are positions less agreeable? In a ditch, possibly, with a drunk harboring lewd designs? How gratifying."

"What did you expect? Surrender without complaint? Trembling submission? I somehow thought you would have higher expectations."

"If I did," he said meditatively, "I believe they could be met."

The smooth ivory of her skin took on a rose glow. "I am not used to—being so familiar with a man, but I don't doubt that most any woman would respond to a man of your experience."

"Don't you?" he murmured, with the brightness of silent laughter springing into his eyes.

"Human beings must perpetuate themselves," she said, frowning, "so it only makes sense that there be some reward for the effort. It doesn't mean anything. It—wouldn't mean anything."

His gaze lingered on her face. Sitting up, he reached for the soap and smoothed it over his body with brusque competence. He sluiced away the lather, then looked around for the washing cloth. Seeing where it had dropped to the floor beside the bed, he nodded toward it, stretching out his hand. "Would you mind?"

She got down from the bed to pick up the cloth, then stood with it in her hands. To approach the tub close enough to hand it to him was clearly impossible. In the first place, she did not trust the look in his eyes. For the second, she was not sure her legs would carry her in that direction.

He said, tipping his head as he watched her, "Just throw it, if it bothers you so much."

Her lips tightened at the amusement that remained in his tone. With sudden decision, she marched to the tub and extended the cloth while holding his gaze.

Admiration, unadorned and as gratifying as it was unexpected, joined the mockery in his face. He took the square of cloth, dipped it to wet it, and began to rub the cake of soap across it.

"If I should stay—" she stopped, stunned into silence by a decision made unnoticed. She was also fascinated by the moment of slippage, quickly recovered, when she saw blazing triumph behind the mask of his self-control.

Renold studied her for long seconds. With firm encouragement, he said, then, "Yes? You were about to set conditions, I think."

"I won't sleep with you."

"Then how are you to find rest? But no, you mean you will not indulge in carnal relations with me, your rightful husband. There are laws about that, though invoking them would be more embarrassing than either of us wants to endure."

"Yes," she said with feeling.

"Just so. Then you will, otherwise, share my lamentably monk-like, unsullied bed?"

"I don't know. Fighting off unwanted advances every night would also be unendurable."

He was scrubbing his face with rough economy of motion. Pausing, he looked at her over the cloth that covered his grin. "I could always cease to fight."

"I was talking about myself, as you very well know!"

"So could you."

Her eyes snapped as she glared at him. "Yes, but why would I?"

A brow lifted above the smoky green of his eyes. "For the sake of—what was it?—my experience?"

It might, in theory, be possible to light a candle at the fire atop the bones in her cheeks. "I believe," she said, "that I can live without it."

"Can you? Then do, by all means."

The words were simple enough to understand, but they gave her no confidence. It came to her, then, that there had been no agreement in them. It was possible they even held a challenge.

That problem was abruptly forgotten as he gathered himself and surged to his feet in a great, splashing fountain of water. He stood for a moment, oblivious, while rivulets ran down his chest and arms and along the hard lines of his legs. Glistening wet and rampantly naked, he stepped from the bath, then bent, twisting, to pick up the length of toweling Tit Jean had left.

He really was magnificent. The lines of arm and shoulder, wide back and lean flank, were impressive in their strength, stirring in their symmetry, like a bronze sculpture of some godlike athlete of ancient Greece captured mideffort and at the height of his glory. And yet, like many such recovered bronzes, he was irreparably damaged. The sight of those scars, and also the new injury, was an affront and also a source of distress.

It wasn't her fault. If she had not been there, Renold might still have leaped from the exploding vessel through live steam. If he had not been out on the streets in the midnight hours, he might never have been attacked.

Yet he might also have noticed the danger to the *Queen Kathleen* sooner, could have jumped with less delay and for a greater distance, if he had been alone. He might not have been out so late if she had not kept him from the comfort of his bed.

Of course, these possibilities were no good reason to permit him intimacies now. Still, it was not always possible to be strictly logical.

He had straightened and was running the toweling along his arms while his considering gaze rested on her face. He was so near that she could feel the moist heat of his body. If she reached out, she could trail her fingers through the dark chest hair with its spangling of water droplets, follow the plumb line of it lower to where…

No. Such wantonness was what he wanted, what he expected. She had given him cause by yielding to his practiced touch. So she must redeem herself, must deny him, even if it hurt to move, even if putting distance between them was like cutting a binding cord with jagged glass.

Turning back to the bed, she smoothed the covers they had disarranged earlier. She discarded her dressing sacque before climbing to the surface of the high mattress and sliding under the sheet and coverlet. Lying on her back with the long braided rope of her hair drawn over her shoulder and her hands folded, she contemplated the *ciel de lit* above her.

"You look," he said, "like a sacrificial maiden, exalted and resigned. Even if inclined, it would be blasphemy to try rousing you to passion. I believe you may depend on sleeping undisturbed."

She was grateful, of course she was. It left her charitable. "To try," she repeated in wry tones. "That was polite, I must say."

"Accurate, rather. And a craven attempt to prevent you from probing into the gash in my side while you mend it." He wrapped the toweling around his lower body, then stepped to the fireplace and went to one knee, stirring the coals Tit Jean had put on the fire.

"I forgot." The words were bald. Realizing by grace of her excellent peripheral vision that he had covered himself, she turned to look at him.

"I realize," he said with a quick glance over his shoulder. "I'm now of two minds whether to apologize for upsetting you, or sing like the lark because I can."

Her lips tightened, but she ignored that for a point that was more troubling. "But where will you sleep?"

"Did I mislead you? Infamous of me, but don't be disturbed. I will be beside you."

"I wasn't disturbed," she said distinctly.

"Good, then. It's a matter of form and covenants, you understand. I did try to explain it before."

Her lips tightened. "I thought perhaps you had changed your mind."

"My mind is not as fixed as some, but you will discover that I know it, and my heart, with some exactitude. I may scheme and barter and even indulge in bombast, but what I say I will do gets done, and my promises are made to be kept."

"That is, naturally," she said with acid in her tone, "a relief."

"It was meant to be." Turning away, he moved to the washstand where bandaging supplies were stored. He removed the wooden box that held them and walked toward the bed. Mounting the steps, he sat down, then stretched out on his good side, facing her, and placed the box between the two of them.

There was nothing to be done, then, except to execute the task given her earlier. She also kept her promises.

It wasn't easy, in spite of the fact that he said scarcely a word. He watched her, instead, his gaze steady and infinitely considering. It made her wonder what he read in her eyes when she met his by accident, what he thought of the stupid trembling that she could not prevent no matter how she tried.

She was so irritatingly aware of him. She started when he lifted a hand, twitched when he blinked, found herself breathing in cadence with the steady rise and fall of his chest. His skin felt fevered under her hands and the fresh smell of clean male and soap scented with Caribbean bay leaves made her head swim as she leaned near.

Once the heavy braid of her hair fell across his arm and shoulder as she reached over him to keep the length of bandaging smoothly wrapped. He picked it up, winding it around his hand. As he came to the end of the slack, she overbalanced, and would have fallen against him if she had not put out her hand to brace against his chest.

Her gaze, wide and dark blue, flew to his that was just inches away. She could see the emerald facets in the irises of his eyes, see herself reflected, in double miniature, in the pupils. A pulse beat in the strong column of his neck, and his lips were parted. The pressure on her scalp slowly increased to a sting as his hand clenched on her braid. She made a soft sound of protest.

Abruptly, she was released. His lashes swept down to close off access to his gaze. His self-control in place, he said, "Your pardon. My attention wandered."

She did not ask where it had been.

When she had finished, he thanked her politely and left the bed long enough to put away the box and extinguish the lamps. His shadow, elongated by the low red light of the fire, swooped and slid around the walls, then climbed to the ceiling like a demon as he rejoined her. The sheets billowed with a cool draft as he settled under them. They lay then, watching the flickering firelight on the walls, listening to the soft popping of the flames and the night wind outside.

Angelica's heart was beating so hard that she could hear its feathery resonance in her ears. She counted the strokes while she lay with every muscle tensed, waiting for a movement toward her.

The seconds and minutes thudded away into silence. There was not even a fraction of shift in position from the man beside her. Inch by slow inch, she let her guard down. Some time later, when the fire was no more than a pale orange glow, she slept.

A scraping noise followed by a thud woke her. She came awake in a single moment and sat up in bed.

"It's nothing," Renold said, "just a neighbor exercising his shovel."

Perhaps she was not as awake as she thought. "What?" she said in confusion. "But why?"

"He doesn't trust his grown sons, his young wife, or any banking establishment. His shovel, on the other hand, doesn't want his money, buries deep, and tells no secrets."

She stared at Renold, alerted by something in the bored sound of his voice. He lay with one hand behind his head, and was far too aware for a man supposed to have been asleep. She said, "But you know about it, and so could anyone else who followed the noise."

"Maybe, but he's fairly safe. He's on his own premises."

"If you say so." The activity seemed closer, but she had discovered how well sound traveled in these back courts.

He smiled in the darkness; it could be heard in his voice as he spoke. "So shall I croon you a lullaby to put you back to sleep? Or, like a kindly nursemaid, rock you after a nice dose of straight brandy enlivened with mother's milk?"

"I don't think either will be necessary," she replied with some austerity.

"Too bad."

She waited, with more anticipation than she liked to admit, for what he would say next. He lapsed into silence, however. After a moment, she lay back down and closed her eyes.

The liveliest feeling grew in her that he was watching her in the dimness. Breathing immediately became awkward, a matter of careful coordination. Her arm itched, but she did her best to ignore it; the last thing she wanted was to invite more comment by appearing restless. She wondered if the neckline of her nightgown was too revealing, for there seemed to be a hint of coolness across the top of one breast. She wished she knew the time, for it seemed this night would go on forever.

Daylight was streaming into the room when she opened her eyes again. A small sound had brought her awake, the quiet opening of the French doors, she thought. She turned her head in that direction.

The doors were thrown wide, letting in a draft of cool air and the usual smells of coffee brewing and bread baking from the kitchen, as well as an odd scent of fresh-turned earth. Renold, with his dressing gown pulled around him, was standing on the balcony. His hands were braced on the railing as he gazed out over the courtyard. The look on his face was assessing, and not quite pleased.

"Is something wrong?" she asked.

"Come and see," he said without turning.

She swung from the bed and found her dressing sacque, groping for the sleeves as she moved to join him. He glanced at her as she stopped at his side. She met his gaze and lifted a winged brow in inquiry. He nodded toward the ground below.

Swinging to look, she caught her breath with the onslaught of surprise and enchantment. The tangle of vines, fig trees, weeds, and household trash that had crowded the courtyard was gone. In its place was a floor of gray-blue slate set with a center fountain of black wrought iron stacked in a triple tier. Paths radiated from the sparkling flow of water. Between the walkways were parterre beds in geometric designs that were planted with a rich array of iris and shrub roses and herbs, all outlined with violas. The plantings were new and small, with the earth showing dark and rich between them, but the potential for fragrance and beauty was plain.

Last night there had been nothing there; this morning there was a garden. The task, with all its complications of piping water to the fountain, laying and leveling the stones, digging the beds and setting the plants, was formidable. To complete it all required a high level of knowledge, planning, and organization. To see it done in a single night needed a will of tempered steel and a consummate ability to command men.

"Astounding," she said in dazed tones. "How did you manage it?"

"You approve?"

"How could I not?" She paused, then said dryly as realization struck her, "A neighbor burying his money, was it? And I believed you."

His smile flashed and was gone. "If there's anything you want changed, please say so and it will be done. I only wanted some semblance of the finished garden installed quickly—to surprise you."

"You did that, of course," she said, watching him, "but I'm amazed at your memory. There isn't, that I can see, a straight row of anything down there."

"No regimented soldiers of blooms or greenery," he agreed quietly.

"And I can really change it as I like?" she asked.

"Anything about it, or everything if that is your whim."

There was warmth in his voice that had not been there before. They stood for a long moment, staring at each other while beyond them the morning sun struck over the courtyard wall, making patterns of bright light across the new earth and sturdy green plants, pausing to dance in the fountain.

Bit by bit, her eyes cooled, turned a deep and distressed cornflower blue. "I should thank you," she said, "and might, except that I'm waiting to hear what you expect as a reward for such a gift."

His face did not change. She might not have known of

the abrupt surge of his anger if she had not heard the gallery railing creak under the pressure of his hands. His voice as he spoke was even, however, and only slightly shaded with self-mockery. "You have so obviously divined my character and my motives. It would be useless to pretend, then, that I want nothing. More, I would not wish to disappoint you at this stage of the affair. The answer must be that, in spite of last night, I anticipate the ultimate sacrifice."

She had thought to hear a denial, or at most a vague hint wrapped up in a pretty speech. She said in disbelief, "You admit it?"

"Shocking, is it not, to hear such a depraved declaration? Especially as you so are virginal, so untouched. Still, it would give the infinite pleasure to accept that great boon and to return it in double measure, plunging in deep and remaining long."

"Don't!" She whirled away from him.

He shot out a hand to catch her arm. "Why so upset, *chérie*? Unless you are not so pure as you would have me think? Unless you know the gift I want?"

"I can guess it, pure or not," she said, twisting her wrist in his hands in a futile effort to break his hold.

"Can you? There is a name for it. Do you know it?" The words were low, suggestive.

"No," she snapped in fury, "nor do I want to hear it."

"But it's such a beautiful word, with so much of joy and happiness and bright.glory in it."

She gave a violent shake of her head. "Yes, and so much degradation."

He turned pensive. "Do you think so? I would not have guessed it, given your nature."

"You know nothing whatever of my nature!" she said, the words scathing. "All you care about is—"

"The word," he said, softly incisive, "is *love*."

Seven

Renold absorbed the blank amazement in her face, looking for what might lie beneath it. Skepticism, he thought, and a search for a motive. There was no pleased vanity that might be exploited, no melting gratification, no hint of surrender.

He wondered, suddenly, about her life with the harridan of an aunt who had brought her up and the father who had left her while he roamed the world. It was as a child that a person learned to expect love, to receive and to give it. To be deprived was to grow up malformed, that much he knew well. Bastard or not, he had enjoyed the full sun-blast of his mother's affection. There had been desperation in it that had affected him, unknowing, and later, when she had married Gerald Delaup, it had dimmed. Still, it had been there. How much had Angelica known?

"Love," she repeated.

He smiled with a twist to his lips. "A four-letter word meaning—"

"I know what it means," she said in sudden annoyance. "But I can't think why you would use it, much less expect it in return for a garden. Love has nothing to do with gratitude."

This was promising. "True. Maladroit, wasn't it? I resented, you see, the implication that everything I do has calculation behind it."

"You are saying there was none?"

He considered his answer, said finally, "None beyond a wish to show you that I take note of your likes and dislikes, that I have a care for what might give you pleasure. If such a thing can cause you to feel more kindly toward me in return, well and good. But that isn't its purpose."

"Still, you would not object if I developed an affection for you?"

His voice was not dependable for more than a simple answer. "No."

"I don't understand you. You could have left me where you brought me ashore after the accident. Or, if your conscience required more, it should have been easy enough to arrange through the steamboat line for my return to my aunt since you knew I came aboard at Natchez. There was no need to take responsibility for me."

"None whatever," he said, regaining his equilibrium and his penchant for taking chances at the same time. "I have no excuse, except that I loved you the moment I saw you, and could not resist the opportunity to take your life and your body into my keeping."

Her gaze widened while rose shading crept up her neck into her face. "But you said before that there was no question of caring or affection between us."

"It was you who said it, I think. I only agreed because I didn't want to alarm you. In any case, such mild words are too tame for what is between us."

"So now you expect my love in return, just like that."

"The game, so often, goes to the bold."

"My life isn't a prize in a game," she said. "And I have great trouble believing that you take love and marriage so lightly. You might, on the other hand, go to great lengths to make amends for a wrong."

"The wrong of pursuing you into your stateroom?" he said, cutting through her euphemisms to the crux of the matter. "I am not so noble. Believe me."

Her gaze was clear as she examined his face. "The alternative," she said slowly, "is to believe that you have a less exalted reason for keeping me with you."

"I did tell you, I think, that I want you," he said, a feral edge to his smile. "That need is as base as you may suspect, a crude desire to take you in my arms and teach you all the various ways of pleasing a man and being pleased by him. I want to see you lying in my bed clothed only in the glory of your hair. I want to see limitless passion in your eyes. I want to strip from you all modesty, all restraint, to have you cry out for me as I—"

"Don't!" she said, and put her hands to the heat in her face.

He stopped midstride and swung to look out over the courtyard until he was certain he could speak without passion. Drawling, the words in his throat dry as dust, he said, "Was that base enough?"

"Yes. But—but preferable to hypocrisy," she answered after a moment.

"It doesn't preclude love."

"Are you sure," she said in quiet reflection, "that for you the two things aren't one and the same?"

Was he? He turned his head to answer, but the words died on his lips. She had left him to step back into the bedchamber. The most astounding thing was that he had been too intent on his own reactions to her question to hear her go.

⸎

Tit Jean brought the message to Angelica just before she lay down to rest after the midday meal. A lad had come with it to the back door, he said. The maître had promised the boy a picayune for the labor of delivering it.

Angelica had been reading Dumas's *The Count of Monte Cristo*, which she had found in a *secretaire* in the salon. She put it aside and took the note in her hand.

The script was harshly black, the letters upright and without flourishes beyond the traditional scroll below the signature. The only salutation was her name on the front of the folded square. Regardless, she would have known instantly from whom it came, even if Tit Jean had not told her.

Renold had secured a *loge grille* for the evening performance of Donizetti's *L'Elisir d'Amore*. The opera, he wrote, would start late and was fairly lengthy. He suggested a long afternoon rest so she might be fit. He would be with her for dinner before the performance.

Looking up at Tit Jean, who stood waiting, she said, "What on earth is a *loge grille*?"

"A box for the theater or the opera, *maîtress*, but one which screens the occupants from view. It is much used for ladies who have been ill and do not wish to receive visitors between the acts, or else who are enceinte or in mourning."

"It's an accepted thing, then, going out to entertainments while wearing black?"

"Indeed, yes. Grief is no reason to be deprived of life's pleasures." The large eyes of the manservant were hooded as he inclined his head.

Angelica pursed her lips. "You would not say that just to convince me to do the bidding of your maître?"

A shocked look crossed the brown features. "No, *maîtress*. You must do as you feel is right. Only…"

"Only?" The word was wry.

"Only I know you would not want to disappoint him. You are a lady with a kind heart, and he is in great need of kindness."

It was a novel view. Frowning a little, she said, "Why would you think so?"

The big man smiled, and it was a transformation. Gone was the impassive correctness. In its place was worry and rich concern. "May I speak of what may be personal, Mamzelle Angelica?"

"I—yes, please." She could think of nothing the manservant might have to say that would encroach too far. Moreover, the title just given her was one of respect usually reserved for ladies of the family being served, therefore a sign of acceptance that should not be discouraged.

"Never have I seen the maître concentrate his great will and mind to pleasing a woman as he has you. He has taken you to wife, something I thought would not come to pass in my time. You have routed the bitterness of that other one, have made him believe in beauty and goodness. You could have much influence, if you wished for it."

She shook her head. "I don't know that I do, or what use I would make of it if I had it."

"Yes, yes, I would expect you to say this," the manservant said with a satisfied smile. "You have no evil in you, no petty snatching for trinkets, no desire for power for its own sake. You are true quality. After the other, and also his childhood, M'sieur Renold needs this in you."

"The other. You are speaking, possibly, of a woman who loved him?"

"She said so, Mamzelle, but she only pretended. Perhaps she did feel as much as she was able. No matter, she didn't want him. He was too different. He did not come of pure French bloodlines, was outside her circle. She thought to marry another who was all the things her kind set such store by, but to keep the maître for her amusement. He is not a man for this light frolic. No."

"He—cared for her, you think?"

"He was young, she was beautiful and, it seemed, above him. He was enamored, perhaps. It was not love or, if it was, he cut it out of his heart afterward. He does not love her now."

The deep, lilting voice trailed away. After a moment, Angelica said, "The lady's name? What was it?"

"Madame Clotilde Petain she is now, since her marriage. You will meet her, perhaps. If so, you must smile and bow, and never become her friend. If you do, she will use you."

"Why do you say Renold was not her equal?" There was diffidence in the question, but she could not prevent herself from asking.

"He came here from Ireland as a child, and to Madame Petain this means he is of an inferior race. Worse in her eyes, his father never married his mother so that he is a mongrel without a name. These things—how can I say it?—they disgusted her and excited her at one and the same time. She would meet him for a midnight ride around the lake, but not accept his invitation to dance at a ball. She walked with him through the streets on Mardi Gras while wearing a mask, but two days later married the man chosen for her by her parents."

"A strange lady." Angelica did not like the sound of this

woman at all. Nor did she care for the thought of Renold being enamored of her.

"Perhaps. Or it may be she is only a creature of her class. Yet a name, respectability, is important here where so many have endured so much for generations to achieve it. Once, it was common for the maître to hear the slur of bastard spoken of him, before he made saying it to his face too dangerous. In any case, he does not regard it, having become so secure within himself such things can no longer wound him."

The thought of these slights in Renold's past gave her a hollow feeling in her chest. He was so proud, so contained inside himself. Or was he, perhaps, barricaded there? She said, "Yes, I can see that."

"But touching on your influence with the maître—there is something troubling him, something that is occupying his mind and his time. With his attention to you as well, he neglects his business affairs. I think that he is after someone or something. I have seen this application of effort before, you understand, this sending out of spies and messages and waiting for a return. Whether he should have what he seeks is another matter. If it is as I fear, it is unhealthy, can give him no contentment. You could distract him from it, I know—if anyone could."

"Oh, I don't think that's likely."

"But, yes. You have only to offer yourself instead."

She had been wrong about Tit Jean. For him to encroach too far had been all too easy. Her head came up and the warmth faded from her features.

The manservant said in haste, "Your pardon, Mamzelle, I meant no disrespect. It's only my great uneasiness that forces me to speak. M'sieur Renold—he is not a forgiving man, and he gets what he goes after, for he never stops until it is in his hands. At the same time, he despises injustice. If he should do a terrible wrong while in pursuit of another end, I fear the deed could destroy him."

"Your concern does you credit," she said with a line between her brows, "but I'm not certain I understand what you mean."

"I can explain no further, Mamzelle, for the matter is private and I have already said too much. Only I beg you will consider what I have said. I think you will have no reason for regret."

When the manservant went away, Angelica sat staring into space. She felt so unsettled inside, so uncertain of what she should do, even what she could do.

Offer herself. Surrender.

Those words were like hammers pounding on her will. How easy it would be to give in to them, to accept Renold's name, his protection, and his presence in her bed.

"—he gets what he goes after, for he never stops until it is in his hands."

How very odd those words made her feel, almost as if resistance was of no use. Perhaps it wasn't, perhaps it was fate that had put her on the steamboat, fate and providence that had caused him to rescue her and take her into his house.

Why was she so reluctant? He was strong and attractive and generous. His intelligence and humor had enormous appeal. She responded to him as she had never thought to respond to any man.

Yet a number of things prevented her from giving her complete trust. She could not forget the terror she had felt when he had invaded her stateroom that first night. More, there was, in spite of his denials, a sense of something calculated behind his every action and word spoken in her presence. His efforts to persuade her to accept their marriage seemed excessive given the circumstances, as if he had some motive for wanting it consummated that he had not yet made known to her.

Love. That was the reason he had given. Love and desire.

How could she believe it? How did she dare?

Was it really possible for a man to fall passionately in love with a woman after only a few moments of conversation, a single snatched kiss? Could he actually decide all in a moment to marry that woman and live with her the rest of his life? Could such a tenuous attachment blossom into a lifetime of happiness?

She was not so without sense as to believe it. But she would like to, and that was her greatest weakness.

❧

The St. Charles Theatre, where the opera performance was to be held, was a plain building with plaster over brick marked to look like stone, a heavy entablature, many tall windows for air, and a line of wrought iron street lamps before it. Inside, the decor was much more ornate. The domed ceiling had gilded carving in the shapes of lyres and musical notes, the tiers of boxes, nestled between Corinthian columns, were railed with vase-shaped balusters, and gas lamps in medieval-inspired chandeliers of wrought iron flared with white-hot light.

The line of *loge grilles*, ten in number, was located opposite center stage and just above the second tier of seats. Enclosed on three sides and masked by a diamond-patterned screen, these boxes were suitably private and secluded. A row of bracket chandeliers directly above prevented them from being too dark.

Angelica's evening gown was of black silk trimmed with lavender lace. It had arrived in late afternoon, a special delivery from the modiste on the orders of M'sieur Harden, who had commissioned it three days before. With it was a cape of lavender silk lined in black and trimmed with jet beadwork. Estelle had piled Angelica's hair in curls on top of her head and fastened it with pins ornamented in jet. The maid had lamented the lack of jewelry, but Angelica could not be sorry. She felt horribly overdressed already, and still doubtful about the outing for one who was newly bereaved. What her aunt would have said about it all, she could just imagine.

It had been a novel experience, walking into the theater on Renold's arm. He was incredibly imposing in his evening wear; he moved with confidence bordering on arrogance. He nodded to greetings, but avoided any protracted conversation, perhaps out of consideration for her. It also meant, however, that she was introduced to no one. And she could not help wondering if that omission was deliberate.

He was an entertaining companion, something which was

becoming less and less of a surprise. Discovering that she was not familiar with opera, he regaled her with droll tales of mishaps during past performances and of the whims and foibles of the famous tenors and divas who had visited the city.

He spoke also of the opera's composer. Gaetano Donizetti, so he said, was prolific: *L'Elisir d'Amore* was number forty of the seventy-odd compositions the maestro had produced before his untimely death only a few years before. The comic opera had been completed in just fourteen days, under great pressure from a theater owner. Because the tenor engaged for the season had been the victim of a terrible stutter, Donizetti had tailored the part of the hero of the piece, Nemorino, to the singer by giving the character a stutter also.

As the story unfolded, Angelica began to wonder if there had not been an ulterior motive for bringing her to see the opera. She thought perhaps she was supposed to take note of the message it portrayed.

The story was one of unrequited love of the peasant Nemorino for a wealthy and much courted young woman, Adina. The peasant declares his love and is spurned, in spite of a magic potion, the elixir of love of the title, which had been sold to him by the Italian version of a frontier snake-oil salesman. Adina regrets her hasty decision, though she hides it under a flirtatious air. Nemorino sees it, however, and sings the hauntingly melodious *Una furtiva lagrima*, The Furtive Tear.

The silence in the theater was profound during the peasant's lament for the unhappiness of the woman he loves and his willingness to die for the privilege of bringing her happiness. The instant the last note died away, the theater erupted into thunderous applause and cries of approval.

Angelica, turning her head in the semidarkness that had descended behind the *loge grille* after the lamps were extinguished, found Renold watching her. She held his gaze for long moments. It was she who looked away first.

Intermission, when it came, was welcome. Nor did she object when Renold, on receiving a note by a white-coated usher, excused himself for a few minutes. It was good to have the breathing room; somehow the enclosed space seemed infinitely larger without him in the chair opposite her.

Regardless, she had a natural curiosity about who had sent the note. And it was quite impossible not to remember and wonder about Tit Jean's opinions concerning the messages Renold sent and that were delivered to him.

She searched the milling crowd in the pit with a sharp gaze, and also the groups in the boxes around her. After a few minutes, she concluded Renold had not remained in the public areas, though it was difficult to be certain with the ever-changing faces across the way and on either side as gentlemen visited ladies holding court in their boxes. The thought of standing up to increase her field of vision crossed her mind, but Angelica decided against it. She was glad she had as a knock fell on the door behind her and it immediately swung open.

"Just as I thought, all alone," Michel said cheerfully as he strolled inside and closed the door behind him. "If Renold has no more consideration than to desert you, he cannot be amazed if he finds his place occupied when he returns. That is, if you have no objection?"

"None at all," she answered, smiling up at him where he paused with his hand on the back of Renold's chair beside her. As he flipped aside the tails of his evening coat and settled next to her, she said, "You saw Renold leave?"

"Saw him in the vestibule, rather, though I don't think he saw me. He was engaged in giving one of his blistering reprimands to an individual in a paisley cravat—red and green paisley, and at the opera, too. I know you don't believe such bad taste, but I give you my word."

"I'm sure every syllable is true," she said with a smile for his nonsense. "I wonder what could have been the problem that brought the man here."

"Could be anything, a horse, a barrel of wine, a ship's cargo. Renold has some peculiar business acquaintances, most of them American—ah, I should not have said that, since you are of that race. These things slip out when you least intend it."

She shook her head without rancor. "I had always heard there was rivalry between the French and the Americans. I suppose it still exists."

"It not only exists, it thrives, it flourishes, it balloons with every election," he said frankly. "The French, I am forced to admit, are losing the battle for the city. We are too refined, too uninterested in the labor of progress. We enjoy good food, good wine, the company of lovely women; we delight in good talk and the stimulation of music and entertainment. We will fade away, it is useless to deny it. But in the meantime, we will amuse ourselves and those around us instead of working, working, and dying having never really lived."

"You are a philosopher," she said, smiling into his laughing brown eyes. "I never would have guessed it."

He assumed a look of mock horror. "Don't tell anyone, please! It would ruin my standing as a man of leisure and a budding Don Juan."

"It will be my secret," she promised.

"Yes, and now you must tell me how you are faring," he said, turning serious. "I assume you are well, since you are here." Pausing only for her polite agreement, he went on, "I ask that I may have information. You will never credit how many invitations I have had pressed upon me since I let fall, quite by accident, that I had seen you. Everyone wants to know about Renold's new wife."

"Oh, but I thought—I thought the marriage was to be kept quiet. Surely I would have been told if there had been an announcement."

"Announcement?" Michel said, lifting his brows in comical disbelief. "Who needs such things in New Orleans, when we have the drums?"

"The what?"

"Not real drums, of course, only the African grapevine, the communication between the slaves of one household and those of another. Renold's people are more discreet than most, but everyone notices when one's cook is seen buying food for an invalid—and her friends must know why. Or a dressmaker will be asked to construct a complete wardrobe down to the last unmentionable garment, and her assistants find the tale too delicious to keep to themselves. The thing spreads, you see."

Angelica looked away from him. "I hadn't realized."

"You'll become used to it in time," he said comfortably.

Would she? She wasn't so sure. She felt that her confidence had been violated. Of course, her aunt had been more stringently private than Renold, if such a thing were possible.

Her main concern, however, was for the perspective placed on her stay with Renold by this news. If she did not remain with him, then her rejection would be a public humiliation for him. The idea, and his possible reaction to it, was enough to give her the beginnings of a headache.

"So are you accepting invitations now?" Michel asked in a change of subject "Do you attend any of the masked balls that will be held on Mardi Gras day? I ask that I may solicit a dance before everyone else crowds me out."

"Oh, no," Angelica said. "I was assured it was unexceptional to attend this evening behind the protection of the grill, but a general round of merriment would not be at all fitting."

"Such sentiments must be saluted, of course," Michel said, taking her hand, barely brushing it with his lips, then clasping it loosely for a moment. "But it would be dishonest of me not to tell you that I wish you were less strict in your observance of the proprieties."

"How very cozy," came a clear and hard feminine voice from behind them. "And so compromising, too. I wonder, Michel, if Renold knows of your attachment?"

Michel sprang to his feet more in surprise than good manners. "Clotilde! How the dickens did you find your way here?"

"By following your lead, *cher*." The woman in the doorway paused a moment for effect before moving toward them. "I saw you making your way in this direction with all the exalted determination of a knight in search of the grail. Knowing you, I took the chance it was something much less holy and more interesting."

Clotilde Petain was beautiful in a highly polished, ultra-sophisticated fashion. Her brown hair with its mahogany highlights was dressed high in a sleek Psyche knot. Her gown of rose silk flared wide over an enormous crinoline, but was cut on severe lines with only ribbed cording and a few tassels for ornament.

Michel gave the woman a look of disdain. "Lord, Clotilde, don't try making me your dupe. Someone told you Renold had brought his wife, and you couldn't resist taking a peek."

"What a delightful turn of phrase, I declare I must remember it. No wonder Madame Harden was so entertained."

She turned with a look of mocking hauteur in her sherry brown eyes, an unfortunate expression since it made her look hard and older than her years. Her inspection of Angelica was slow, thorough, and designed to intimidate.

Angelica lifted her chin as she accepted the challenge. Her gaze clear, she said, "You must be Madame Petain. How kind of you to visit me when I'm sure you must be missing callers to your own box."

"Ah, forgive me, *chére*," Michel said, striking his temple with his palm. "I should have presented you."

"We don't need you for that," Clotilde Petain told him over her shoulder. "Or for anything else. Why don't you go and fetch us some punch from the supper room?"

"I don't require anything, thank you," Angelica said with a brief glance at Renold's friend that stopped just short of pleading.

Michel responded at once. "Oh, I couldn't leave Madame Harden. She has been unwell, you know, and might feel faint at any moment."

"Surely there can be no danger, since her husband has left her," the other woman said in brittle tones.

Before Michel could answer, there came the snap of the door closing. They all swung to see Renold with his hand on the door handle.

"The husband has returned," he said. "My absence, you perceive, Clotilde, was not of long duration—and an excellent thing, too. A few more minutes, and the tenor might have been forced to look here for his entire audience."

A hectic flush rose to Clotilde Petain's face while mulish irritation twisted her lips. "Are you suggesting that we intrude?"

It was an error in tactics to attempt to force Renold's hand using the lever of good manners; he discarded such handicaps without compunction when it suited his purpose. "How astute of you," he said simply.

Clotilde's bosom swelled with indignation. Michel laughed. Renold ignored them both as he strolled toward Angelica and took her hand. His gaze was steady and a little searching. She met it without evasion. A smile tugged one corner of his mouth as he bent his head and pressed his lips to her bloodless fingers.

Clotilde, her voice strained, said, "I should think you would wish to make your bride known to a few people of influence. She will require some assistance if she is to be accepted by those who matter."

"I believe," Renold said without looking at the other woman, "that my standing as a leader of commerce will be more than enough."

Clotilde's lashes fluttered nervously. "It may gain a place among the American contingent, but the French are rather more selective."

"You think so?" he said affably. "Things have changed in the last few years, as you might notice if you cared to look. Money now speaks both languages."

"Crass," she said in waspish accusation, "but to be expected."

"Honest," he corrected. "To recognize the trait, of course, you first have to be familiar with it."

Watching them, Angelica felt dizzy with the swirl of undercurrents in the enclosed space. That the three of them, Renold, Michel, and the woman, understood each other out of past experience, past events, could not be doubted. She felt shut out of that communication, though she also knew that she had changed it in some fashion.

Abruptly, the loss of all that was dear and familiar swept in upon her: her room in her aunt's house, the dull but well-known round of her days, and, most of all, her father's distracted fondness. That was gone, all gone. What did she have to take its place that was as real and safe?

Clotilde Petain's laugh was hollow and the glance she sent

Angelica virulent before she looked back at Renold. "This is a new turn for you, *cher*, dancing attendance on an invalid female. What a fierce guard you make, protecting her as if she were made of glass. One might almost suppose it a love match."

"What else?" The words were gentle.

"Well, but there are all sorts of rumors flying. They make it sound positively medieval, like a romance by Scott full of daring rescues and midnight marriages of convenience."

"I didn't know you were a reader, or that you had such an imagination," Renold said. He retained Angelica's fingers in his strong grasp in spite of her attempts to remove them.

"Of course," the other woman went on, "there seems to have been a conspicuous lack of witnesses to this extraordinary union. It crosses the mind to wonder if there was a ceremony at all. In which case, there can be no wonder that you have kept your—paramour hidden away."

Angelica stared at Clotilde Petain while she thought, incredulously, of how closely her fears matched the suggestion just made. This woman had known Renold as few others had before or since. If she felt he was capable of such shameful conduct, then it must not be beyond the realm of possibility.

"Making comparisons, Clotilde?" Renold said in silken tones. "I don't recommend it. Angelica is that most paramount of paramours, my soul mate, my solace, my savior when I am not hers—my spouse. You might, if you like, congratulate her. But you can never compare."

As the other woman stared at him in speechless rage, Michel stepped manfully into the breach. Offering his arm, he said to Clotilde, "They are lowering the lamps and twitching the curtain. Perhaps you will permit me to escort you back to your seat?"

"Yes," the woman said dazedly. "Yes, you might as well."

Angelica did not watch them go. She was looking at Renold, snared in the transparent green of his eyes. His face was still, unnervingly so. He was waiting for something, though what she could not tell. There was certainty in his features and, it almost seemed, an intimation of safety in the firm clasp of his hand on hers.

In the pit before the stage, the overture for the next act began to swell. Angelica, hearing the lovely notes of introduction like a benediction, discovered that she had not breathed in some time. Inhaling with care, she said the first thing that came into her head. "The story, how does it end?"

"Happily, with the heroine in the hero's arms. What else?" The words were quiet, even.

"I meant the story in the opera, the tale of the elixir of love."

Humor touched his mouth. "So did I. Will you stay until the end?"

"Yes, I think I may," she answered, her smile strained but her gaze steady. "How could I bear to go before it is over?"

Eight

"Masks reveal more than they conceal," Renold said. "People choose costumes for the way they see themselves, or the way they would like to be. That's why kings and queens, bishops and courtesans always outnumber the paupers and common criminals. It's also the reason you never come across a common person. No one considers themselves ordinary."

"That's all very well, but I would still rather not wear a mask." Angelica's voice was as firm as she could make it. It wasn't easy to withstand his arguments, much less resist his beguiling smile or the colorful costumes of silk and velvet and spangled netting spread out around her.

She might as well not have spoken. Lounging in his chair with his feet crossed in front of him, Renold squinted at her. "I don't see you as a queen, and certainly not a courtesan. No. A gypsy dancer in a dark wig, passionate and wild, free with her favors to the right man. Yes, I like that image."

"You would," she said shortly.

"You don't feel the part? The gypsy is there, inside you, shut up where she can never be seen. But you could let her out if you would."

Her gaze cool, she said, "You must be thinking of someone else."

"Well, then, perhaps a marionette: wooden, without emotion, pulled by strings in other people's hands." The words were acid.

"Or," she said with a tight smile, "I could be Lucia di Lammermoor." The reference was to the heroine of Donizetti's opera of the same name, a woman who stabs the bridegroom foisted upon her in a marriage of convenience. She had been reading Scott's *Bride of Lammermoor*, the story that had been Donizetti's inspiration.

"Now this is promising."

"I can't imagine why you would think so," she returned.

"There's scant difference between anger and passion, and it's at least a sign of some feeling."

She gave him a vengeful look. "You may get more *feeling* than you bargain for one day, and then what?"

"Then I will shout hosanna and hope for the strength to survive it." He leaned his head against the lace antimacassar on the chair's back.

"I didn't mean—" she began through tight lips.

"I know that, but please don't spoil the visions in my head. They are far too diverting."

"I can imagine," she said.

"Can you? Then why aren't you blushing? Or maybe there's hope for the gypsy yet?"

"For the last time," she said, her chest swelling with indignation, "I have no intention of getting into a costume and parading through the streets pretending to be something I'm not."

"You won't have to get into it," he said comfortably. "I'll be delighted to strip off what you have on and dress you in my choice. It's possible I might come to consider obstinacy a virtue if you put me to that trouble."

He would do exactly as he said; she had not the least doubt of it. She tried another tack. "I would remind you that I am in mourning."

"But you aren't dead. I'm not offering a day of gay dissipation, you know, only a walk through the streets to see what the city is like on the last day of the carnival season. You will feel more of the spirit of it if you are masked, that's all."

"And you won't have to introduce me to your friends," she said in striated tones.

Stillness closed over his face. When he spoke, the words had the clipped edges of suppressed anger. "Is that what this is all about? You think—you dare think—that I am embarrassed to be seen with you?"

"I think you prefer to keep me hidden away. Why, I have yet to decide."

"How very magnanimous of you. Did it never occur to you that my care might be for your natural reluctance to be put on display? Or was I wrong to bother? Perhaps I should have turned you into Lady Godiva today and paraded you on horseback clothed in your hair. It would have been exactly what you might expect from someone of my nature."

"Don't be ridiculous," she snapped.

"Oh, I was never more serious. Only think how much easier it would be to get you into costume."

There was heat in her brain. It almost seemed she could feel his hands on her, peeling away her gown, unfastening her camisole, loosening the tapes of her petticoats so they fell in a great billowing pile around her feet. His hands on her hair, loosening it, letting it fall around her, the freedom of being unclothed, of having nothing except air and his touch on her skin.

She wondered from the hot look in his eyes if he shared the same visions now. But she did not want to know.

She said, "Next, I suppose you'll tell me that attending one of the balls will be no entertainment, but a means of providing tone for my constitution."

"I wouldn't dream of it. There's nothing wrong with your tone."

It was an unexpected concession. Just possibly, it deserved some reward. She sighed. "All right, I'll go walking with you. But only as a nun."

"Intriguing. You feel the need for a pretense of purity?"

That jibe banished her tenuous sense of accord. "I merely thought," she said, "that you might see yourself as Christ, my savior."

"Blasphemy." His gaze was tinged with irony.

"Isn't it?" she said in bright retaliation.

Her smile dimmed, however, as he flipped aside a costume complete with train and tiara to reveal a nun's habit. She had the feeling it might have been his final choice. And that she didn't like at all.

It was late evening when they left the house to mingle with the crowds that thronged the streets, Angelica in her nun's garb, Renold dressed like a pirate. Striding beside her in his cavalier's hat, with seven-league boots and a cutlass swinging at his side, he looked raffish, darkly handsome, and more dangerous than ever.

The night was cool with a rising wind that set the street lamps to swaying on their brackets so that the shadows danced. Carriages rattled past carrying men and women wearing fantastic masks to the many balls being held over the city. Some of the ballgoers went on foot, led by linkboys carrying lanterns and followed by servants carrying dancing slippers to be put on at the ballroom door.

Music was in the air, drifting from open ballroom windows, or else played by hopeful street musicians with their caps on the *banquette* in front of them. Waltzes by Strauss alternated with the latest Stephen Foster ballads and tunes from the operettas of the season. Somewhere, a man whistled, in perfect key and with creative trills, the crying song from *L'Elisir d'Amore*. The melancholy sound of it followed Angelica and Renold as they strolled in the direction of the river.

They turned a corner and were engulfed in pandemonium. A dozen boys with faces darkened by axle grease and white capes made of flour sacking around their shoulders dodged up and down the street. They threw bags of flour to coat each other and anyone else unlucky enough to be in reach in fogging white powder. Men dressed as Arabs and Indians, wild-eyed with strong drink, capered up and down on horseback. Two women in the uniforms of sailors hung on the arms of a pair of mustachioed barmen. A pack of rivermen brawled up and down the street kicking and gouging in drunken ill-humor. From a carriage rolling past a woman in a pink gown so tight her breasts bulged above the silk slung a stockinged leg out the window and waggled it at a man staring down from a balcony. As one of the boys tossed flour at the woman, she cursed him in words slurred by drink.

It was vulgar and cheap. It was also uninhibited and exultant, free and weirdly beautiful in the half-light.

Watching, Angelica felt a curious struggle taking place inside herself. She was repelled, yet enthralled. She wanted to turn away, but could not help looking. She felt she should leave, still she longed, quite suddenly, to be as wild and abandoned as any gypsy. She wanted to fly down the street with open arms, laughing, gathering up folly and foolishness as she went.

"Look," Renold said, "here comes the street pageant, one of the things I wanted you to see."

There had been a low murmur of sound, scarcely noticed, for some minutes. Now it grew louder.

From down the street appeared a man on horseback carrying a banner of silk edged with fringe. Behind him came a dozen more men, a score, a hundred. On they came in increasing numbers, men costumed as Bedouins, as English soldiers, and as camel drivers. They came dressed as camels, as lions and wolves, as roosters and ducks and geese. Some were on foot, some in carriages and wagons. Some carried torches for light, others waved lanterns. They weaved and yelled, drunk as lords and deliriously antic with it. And they ducked a hail of flour bags and thrown bonbons, catching them and flinging them back without pausing in their march.

The last horseman passed by, but that was not the end of it. Behind the marchers came a crowd of maskers, tripping along, bowing to the applause of the people on the *banquette*, throwing kisses and handfuls of candied almonds known as *dragées*. Behind them came several carriages of women who could only be labeled as ladies of the evening. The women yelled out suggestions to men and thumbed their noses at women while shaking their bosoms and other parts of their anatomies in a fashion calculated to startle and amaze.

The maskers were spread out, overflowing the *banquettes*, pushing and shoving to make their way through the crowd. The carriages added to the disturbance, forcing an ebb and flow through the milling throng. The people watching edged close, pressing in upon Angelica. She felt herself jostled from behind. Renold placed an arm around her, drawing her closer against his side.

She could feel his hard fingers at her waist, the nudge of her hip against his long thigh as they were pushed this way and that. She did not resist, but nestled into his hold. There was comfort and safety there, and she had a fine excuse for accepting both. He turned his head to look down at her with a smile in his eyes. She sustained it only a moment before returning her attention to the spectacle before her.

The last of the marchers were straggling past. The crowd began to thin as dozens of people surged into the street to join the impromptu parade.

There was a man in front of them dressed in shapeless and dirty trousers and coat that looked as if he had been sleeping in them nightly for some time. He looked around him with a slit-eyed stare. His gaze fastened on Angelica for a brief moment before sliding away. It was an accidental meeting of eyes, yet a shudder ran down her spine as if she had touched something slimy.

It was then that she heard the sound of harsh breathing not far away. She turned her head. There was another man just off to her right, half hidden behind a Roman emperor. His grin showed blackened teeth and lips misshapen by scars. The pockmarks on his face were filled with greasy dirt, and his ears were mangled stubs projecting from his head. He looked beyond her and he winked.

Yet another man sidled closer on Renold's far side. Wiry and short, he had a round, brutish face and several teeth missing from his loose grin. His clothes were fairly new, but so tight they might have been taken from some young boy. He licked his lips in a constant motion while pushing his fist into his coat pocket and knotting it as if he gripped something he did not want to be seen.

Menace surrounded the men like the acrid odor from their bodies. Angelica's gaze was wide as she glanced from one to the other. The word compressed, little more than a whisper, she said, "Renold?"

"I see them," he answered in low tones. "Stay with me, no matter what happens. Don't get in the way, but don't let them get between us."

"What do they want?"

"Money, possibly. A fight, maybe. Or you."

"Me?" The word was doubtful.

"For the rut and bruising of joyous rape. Or the price they can get from somebody else for the same."

She didn't understand him, not completely, but there was no time for more. Stepping in front of her, he drew his cutlass from his belt with a rasping whine.

The fourth man came from behind. Robed as a friar, with his face hidden by cowl and half mask, he lunged at Angelica. A hard arm whipped around her chest, crushing her breasts, squeezing the breath from her. She gave a gasping cry, at the same time snatching at Renold. Her fingers closed on his shirt and she twisted them into the fabric.

The friar cursed in obscene rage. He brought his free hand up and around in a vicious slap. It landed with stunning force, jarring her head into a sharp throb, making her ears ring.

It did not break her hold. Instead, it sent a wave of red fury through her brain. Twisting, she struck out with one free hand and felt her nails rake bare skin, heard a satisfying hiss of pain from somewhere inside the friar's cowl. His grasp loosened.

It was Renold who broke her grasp as he swung. Immediately, he ripped her away from the other man, dragged her to his hard frame. The lamplight, wavering in the wind, kissed the steel of his cutlass with an unearthly glow of red and gold, blue and orange. The curved tip winked, ready, vicious, waiting.

"Now," he said as he gathered the men crowding toward him with a single glance. "Come on. Sacrifice of blood is an old and venerable Mardi Gras tradition. Sometimes it's a bull—other times an ass or two will do."

One moment the men crouched to spring, the next they were gone, melting, sidling, plunging into the crowd. Within seconds, there was no one near Angelica and Renold except gaily bedecked maskers with vacant, smiling faces.

The last marcher appeared, then, bringing up the rear. It was a fiddler, playing as he capered in a harlequin costume and a fool's hat set with jingling bells. He looked neither right nor left, making music only for himself. Then he was gone, and the sound of his fiddle and his bells faded into the night.

Renold made no further excuse to remain in the streets. Piercing the shadows with a stiletto gaze, wary as a dunghill cock in a pigpen, he wound his way back toward his own door. The silent curses in his mind relieved his tension if not his anxiety.

He should have known. There had been the other attack to warn him, if only he had heeded it. More, there had been his instinct; the whole thing had, until now, been entirely too easy.

Scum, the dregs of Gallatin Street. Or more likely from the swamp around Girod, that area ten blocks from the river so crime-ridden and depraved that even the police never set foot inside it. He felt sick at the thought of Angelica in their hands. Animals, unfit to touch the hem of her gown.

But then, he himself was the same.

It was no surprise to find the man waiting for him outside the gate. Small, quiet, shadow gray and thin-voiced, he stepped forward with his hands held together at the level of his top waistcoat button. His eyes caught the lamplight on their shiny surfaces, making them glisten with a hectic excitement that told its own tale.

"One moment," Renold said before the little man could speak. Turning to Angelica, he said, "I won't be long. Ask Tit Jean to bring a tray of wine and brandy to the salon, if it pleases you, while I attend to this small matter."

Her gaze as it rested on his visitor was appraising, but she offered no objection. Stepping inside, she moved away in her demure nun's garb. He watched her until she was safely in the house before he turned back to his visitor.

"So have your hounds found the scent, or was it another false trail? Tell me quickly, for my patience is not endless and I'm a little tired of finding myself cornered with nothing to do except stand and draw blade."

"You needn't wait any longer. They're found." The mouselike man's voice was so soft it did not penetrate more than a foot beyond where he stood.

"Both?" Renold's frown turned rigid with distrust.

"Aye. Two men, right descriptions. Came off the right boat, too, in a manner of speaking. Young one swam ashore, so it seems, but took a while to make his way home. The other caught hold of a log and hung on until the thing fetched up near the bank."

"Well away from civilization, I surmise."

The other man gave a bobbing nod. "Downstream, clear away from any town, nothing but bottomland and woods. The old man was sick, just about gone when a fur trapper from back in the swamp came across him, took him in. Was some time before he could get word out. T'other went after him then, brought him out."

Renold was silent while his thoughts slid swiftly through his mind. He said, "How long ago?"

"Can't rightly tell you that, your honor. You didn't say you wanted to know."

"An oversight. You have their direction?"

The little man drew air through his sharp teeth. "Did have. They left."

Renold subdued his irritation with difficulty. "It was in Natchez, perhaps?"

"Don't know why you'd think it," the other man said with a shake of his head. "Was up Baton Rouge way, dive by the wharf where they rested a day or two. They got poor taste in lodging, all things considered."

"I assume," Renold said trenchantly, "that you mean something by that?"

"Gave themselves airs, or at least the young one did, talking about a plantation, how rich he was going to be. Stupid, might have got themselves killed, what with folks thinking they had money. Except Mrs. Bowles, their landlady, knew they were nigh broke. She looked."

"You are going to tell me that such a fine, upstanding lady, the heart and soul of curiosity, failed to ask where the two gentlemen were going?" Renold drew a purse from his pocket and stood weighing it in his hand.

The other man licked his lips. His gaze jumped up and down, following the movement of the purse. He said, "Now I think on it, she did ask. The younger one wouldn't say, the older one just kept raving about his daughter. Sent to find out where she went after that explosion, was told she disappeared, hadn't been seen since. Drove him fair daft, it did. They left next morning."

"The date at the time was?"

"Better than a week ago, far as I can make out."

Not a particle of interest was allowed to invest Renold's features. His tone musing, he said, "I would expect they went north."

"You'd be wrong, now, your honor. Went south, toward New Orleans, asking along the way about a fair-haired lady. Sort of like the one here with you." The little man stared, eyes bright, face twisted with cunning.

"Could you possibly be speaking of my wife?" Each word fell in distinct clarity, lethal with warning, from Renold's lips. "I should not like to think so."

"God, no. No, indeed. My mistake." Retreating, the man stuffed the purse in his hand in his pocket as if fearful Renold might decide to take it back, and his life with it.

"Remember, then." He could trust himself to say no more. Nodding dismissal, he stood quite still in the shadows as the slight figure scurried off.

So Edmund Carew had survived after all.

He had survived and discovered, perhaps, that his daughter had departed for New Orleans in the possession of a man who could be an enemy. Too wily to confront him head-on, Carew had attempted to pry Angelica from his grasp. The men he had found for the purpose had been inferior, so he had failed.

Carew, alive. Carew, frantic over his daughter, taking a hand in the game once more.

He should be glad, Renold thought. It would still be possible to avenge Gerald Delaup's death, still be feasible to use Angelica to destroy the man who had caused it.

And yet. There was a new consideration in the game.

Angelica the fair, the beautiful, the good. She would not condone being used, would not easily forgive any punishment inflicted on her father. How was he to proceed without losing her?

That had not, in the beginning, been a part of Renold's calculations. If he had thought at all of how she would feel, he had considered that her objections could be easily overcome, by subterfuge where possible, by force if necessary.

It would not be so easy. The standards she set were high; she would accept no deviation from them. She could never give her trust, much less her love, to a man who deliberately pushed them aside.

But what was to say she would ever love him in any event? What right did he have to expect it? And if that prize was so far out of his reach, then what did he have to lose?

There was one chance.

He might, if he acted swiftly and with care, bind her to him with tender cords of passion. Desire, once roused, was a powerful bond between a man and woman. If she could be convinced no other man would ever give her the same pleasure, the same surcease, then she might remain with him. Yes, and if that passion and desire should create a child, then he would have a true hostage with which to hold her.

Yes. It was the one chance. She was fair and good, but she was also a woman capable of great passion. It was inside her, suppressed but visible in brief flashes like storm lightning. He wanted to free it, longed to be the one for that sweet task as he had never longed for anything in his life.

It was not selfish despotism, not all of it. She needed him, if she could be brought to see it—needed his help to free herself from the staid precepts and strict principles that ruled her life. She was lovely, but could be so much more that was warm and giving, sensual and inviting. He wanted to see that, could not bear that any other man should.

It was a risk. She was all instinct and febrile intelligence. She might see through what he intended to its black core of deceit. If she did, it would be over. On that point, he could not be more certain.

A child. Her child. His child. Did he dare? He was not, himself, immune to the pain of loss. Any small, fragile hostage of his blood would hold him in its tight little fist as well as its mother.

What would he do if she took his child away? What?

"God," he said, a whisper both a curse and prayer. He stood still, staring blind and beseeching into the night sky.

There was no answer.

Angelica was half asleep when she heard the bedchamber door open and close. She had waited for Renold in the salon for what seemed like hours, but he had not appeared. Every possible explanation had run through her head in that time: He might have sent her inside to keep her safe while he fought off more attackers, might have decided on a visit to another woman, might, even, have forgotten he was to join her. Fear had become doubt, doubt had turned to annoyance, annoyance had descended, by way of anger, to hurt disdain. She wanted to flounce over in the bed, sit up and demand where he had been. The only thing that stopped her was knowing that such a question must show how much the answer mattered.

Opening her eyes to slits, she watched from where she lay on her side with her head pillowed on one arm. The fire had died away; the only light was the dim glow of a moon behind the curtain. He was a blue-tinted shadow as he undressed with silent efficiency, sliding out of his coat, punching studs from the holes, stripping off shirt and trousers in a series of well-practiced motions. He bestowed his clothes neatly on a chair and turned toward the bed.

Would she ever get used to his nakedness? At least there was no need to look away now; she could hold her gaze in one place long enough to discover precisely how he was made.

Different. Powerfully male. Beautiful in an aesthetic sense that had nothing to do with gender. Threatening in an odd way she felt without comprehending the full extent of it.

He paused beside the mattress, staring down. Did he know she was awake? Could he tell?

She closed her eyes and lay perfectly still. And thought how, just short days ago, she could never have dreamed of lying there at all.

The mattress behind her gave with his weight. A draft of cool air infiltrated the covers as he slid beneath them. He turned toward her, shifting, she thought, to support himself on one elbow. She quelled a faint shiver of alarm. Or was it expectation?

"Angelica?"

His voice whispered over her. With it came the scent of fine brandy. It was strong, though not overpowering. She considered in silence what that might mean.

"Mon ange?"

A loving endearment. It was a pleasant conceit, but she could give herself no great credit. Unfortunately.

"I didn't mean to leave you so long. I just…"

His voice faded. She was still listening to the echoes of it when she felt the warm brush of his hand on her shoulder.

Her breathing altered. What to do? Recoil? Strike out? Scream? While her brain grappled with the problem she lay as still as a hunted rabbit. And waited with discomfiting anticipation for what he might do next.

He leaned over her and touched the heated firmness of his lips to her temple, feathering a line of precise and delicate kisses to the turn of her ear. At the same time, he cupped her shoulder, kneading it with supple fingers and in ever-widening circles. At the center of her back, he swept downward in a long, soothing stroke. His hand came to rest at the first gentle swell of her hips. He left it there in tacit possession. The tip of his tongue, moist, hot, flicked inside her ear.

She came up on an indignant gasp, rolling from under his clasp to face him. "Stop that."

"I didn't think you were asleep," he said in soft satisfaction.

"That's enough to wake anybody up!"

His soft laugh disposed of the evasion. "The interesting thing is how long it took you to decide to be outraged. It makes me wonder what liberties you might allow if I were patient enough to be subtle about it."

"If there is one thing you excel in," she said in scathing denunciation, "it's subtlety."

"Sneakiness, you mean? We can dispense with it if it offends. You didn't object to my kiss or my touch, only to being handled in a more familiar fashion. The question is why?"

The frontal attack left her speechless. She moistened her lips as she stared at his dark form hovering above her.

"Shall I provide an answer?" he went on, relentless. "Being human and nubile, you have a natural interest in what occurs in private between men and women. You can conceal it, but sometimes it betrays you. I may not be the man of your dreams, but I am here, and I don't repulse you—against your will, you respond to me. You sometimes wonder, if only for a fleeting second, what it would be like to accord me the favors of the marriage bed."

"No…"

"Yes. You look at my mouth and my hands and think of how they felt, how they made you feel, and you need to know the sensation again. You wonder what more I could show you, and what it would be like to abandon denial and permit me to love you."

"Love?" she said, the word tight and not quite steady in her throat. "You aren't talking about love. If we are leaving aside pretense, then you must admit that what drives you is not so far removed from the bruising rut you accused those men of tonight. Only it's worse in you because there's something in it that is—that is deliberate, of the mind instead of body or from the heart. So, yes, I wonder what it would be like to be a wife to you, but if you are thinking to take advantage of it you may stop. I prefer there to be love in it when finally I make love."

The silence was profound when she ceased speaking. Then on a breathless laugh, he said, "Amazing."

"I can't imagine why you think so." Nor could she imagine where her words had come from, though she felt their truth.

"I had the idea, you see," he said, "that you needed waking to your carnal instincts."

"There's nothing wrong with my instincts," she said shortly. That was also true, though she had once had doubts.

The problem, she now saw quite plainly, had been the wrong man, the wrong time.

"Suppose I said that I—"

"Don't!" The single word had an edge of panic that she could hear in her own ears.

"No," he said in pensive agreement "You would never believe it, would you? Love isn't that convenient. Usually. What a pity."

He rolled away from her and rose from the bed in a single swift movement. Gathering his clothes, he moved toward the door. The latch snapped closed behind him.

Staring after him, Angelica shook her head. She lay back down on a long sigh.

She did want to believe him. That was the real pity.

Nine

WHEN MICHEL WAS ANNOUNCED, ANGELICA WAS LYING ON A chaise in the salon with a cloth soaked in rose water on her forehead for headache and a tisane at her elbow. She was happy to have the company; Renold had been gone all day and she was feeling low and thoroughly sorry for herself.

She had been thinking of her father, also, and of how he had been taken from her just as she thought she might come to know him. In spite of his illness, she had looked forward to long hours at Bonheur in which the two of them could explore the past and plan at least a brief future. Gone, all gone.

Michel was just the tonic she needed to bring her out of her doldrums. With his comic, teasing ways, and uncomplicated interest in how she felt and what she thought on any and everything, he soon had her sitting upright and even laughing.

Tasting the tisane of brewed herbs sweetened with molasses, Michel pronounced it undrinkable. Very much at home in Renold's house, he bullied Estelle into bringing wine and rice cookies for them. And when he learned Angelica had refused to eat at noon, he commanded also a savory plate of olives and cheese and tiny fried fish spiced with lemon.

"So why are you shut up here alone?" he asked as he popped a purple, ripe olive into his mouth and followed it with a sip of wine. "Has Renold turned tyrant?"

She shook her head with a smile. "No more than usual."

"So you don't require rescuing?" He heaved a sigh of mock

disappointment. "Well, then, you must have been listening to gossip. Fatal, I warn you."

"Has there been gossip that would disturb me? I'm glad I didn't hear." She shielded her expression with her lashes as she reached for a piece of cheese.

"Only Clotilde, but most know her malice toward Renold, so disregard what touches on him."

Angelica hesitated, uncertain of the wisdom of what she was about to ask. She spoke anyway. "If the lady married someone else of her own will, why is she so spiteful?"

Michel shrugged. "Injured vanity, possibly. Renold was supposed to waste away for love."

"I heard a tale," she said, playing with her wine glass, "of how he appeared at the theater after she was wed with another woman on his arm."

"An actress, rather," Michel said, his gaze amused. "A minor liaison, on the rebound; I promise it's long over. The lady became demanding, which is a fatal tactic with Renold."

Angelica accepted that, and said with a frown, "Even if Madame Petain disliked having Renold's new interest flung in her face—and even if she expected to continue their affair—her resentment seems excessive."

"She is a woman of excesses," Michel said, choosing another olive.

He was hiding something; Angelica knew it. She considered what it might be while she drank wine and reached idly for a cookie. She ate a small bite before she said, "Perhaps there were promises exchanged, so that she feels betrayed?"

"Renold would not pledge himself falsely, nor give his word where it could not be kept." The words were positive.

"Well, but I still don't see—"

"If you must know what is between them, then you will have to ask him. He will tell you if it pleases him, but he would not care to know that I talked behind his back. This much I will say: Clotilde did him a great wrong, and it was this rather than mere hurt pride that caused his retaliation. And it sometimes happens that the very person who does someone the most harm is the one who harbors the most ill will against them."

It was possible that she might have persuaded Michel to say more, possibly to defend Renold if for no other reason. She was given no opportunity. There came a clattering of wheels in the street outside, then the bell on the courtyard gate clanged like a clarion.

Michel got to his feet and moved to draw aside the drapes at the French door and look out. From that vantage point, he reported the presence of a carriage down below. Tit Jean had apparently admitted the passenger, then emerged to deal with the brass-bound trunks that were piled on top of the vehicle.

Michel turned to stroll back toward Angelica with a quizzical frown on his face. "I swear, if I didn't know better, I would think—"

The door swinging open cut off his words. A young woman sailed into the room, unfastening the frogs of a fitted coat of black velvet as she came forward. Handing the coat to Estelle, who followed her, tearing at the strings of her chic little hat composed mostly of velvet and violets, she launched into speech.

"How do you do? You must be my new sister-in-law. You won't mind, I hope, that I have descended upon you? Really, sitting at home hearing news secondhand, and by post at that, was too much to be borne. Mother agreed someone must come and see if what everyone is saying is true. I can see that it must be, indeed."

Michel said in dry tones, "Permit me, Angelica, to make known to you Renold's sister, Mademoiselle Marie Lena Frances Deborah—"

"Just Deborah, if you please," the girl interrupted with a smile as she handed over her hat to the housekeeper, revealing light brown hair streaked with gold, then began to draw off her black kid gloves. "Michel always makes a fuss over the fact that I was Lena for years, but prefer the last of my four given names, now that I am old enough to choose for myself. Men despise change; have you noticed?"

"The problem is that Deborah is so Biblical, and you are not," Michel returned with an unaccustomed edge to his tones.

"And a good thing, too, or I might smite you!" The girl

held her bare hand out to Angelica with frank friendliness in her hazel eyes. "Please say you won't throw me out, now that I'm here. I promise to be an exemplary guest, not interfering in the least. That is, if you will only permit me to stay."

"Yes, yes, of course," Angelica said, almost at random as she clasped the other girl's hand. "I'm sorry to stare, only—I didn't realize Renold had a sister."

"Half sister, to be perfectly correct," Deborah said with a quick, rather odd glance at Michel. "But how very peculiar of Renold not to tell you; he must be quite besotted to let such a detail slip his mind. Or perhaps he was saving it for a surprise?"

"Speaking of surprises," Michel said with an air of grim determination, "he will certainly be amazed to walk in and find you here. He thought you intended to stay quietly in the country this season."

The look on the piquant features of Renold's sister was derisive. "No one catches Renold off guard, as you must know if you gave it half a thought. I expect Tit Jean sent a boy off to inform Renold I am here the instant he clapped eyes on me. As for remaining in the country, it's now Lent, so the season is over. I can hardly be accused of discarding my mourning for gay dissipation." She turned her back on Michel, speaking to Angelica. "I see you are also is black. You have had a bereavement?"

"My father," she said briefly.

A shadow crossed the other woman's face like a shutter closing out the light. "Mine also—how very strange life can be. In any case, I give you my condolences."

Angelica said everything that was suitable and polite in answer. As she fell silent again, an awkward silence developed. In the midst of it, the woman known as Deborah locked glances with Michel across the room.

Angelica was a little perplexed, wondering if the two were at odds in some manner that went beyond the good-natured bickering of those who have known each other from child-hood. A moment later, she dismissed the idea. To expect ordinary behavior in this situation was foolish when there was nothing else ordinary about it.

Falling back on her duties as hostess to ease the situation, Angelica offered her sister-in-law refreshment, then rang for Tit Jean to bring the orange flower water requested. She also directed the manservant to place Deborah's trunks in the room Deborah always used. It was amusing, considering her sister-in-law's protestations, to discover that not only had this already been done, but that the maid Deborah had brought with her was even now unpacking her mistress's belongings.

Michel waded manfully into the breach then, by inquiring if Deborah had noticed the new courtyard garden and soliciting her opinion of it. They had not quite exhausted the subject when Renold appeared.

He came into the room with a smile and an easy greeting for his sister, but his gaze went immediately to Angelica. She was not certain what he saw in her face, still he came at once to take her hand and go down on one knee in front of her.

"Tell me the worst at once," he said in wry pleading. "You and my sister have discovered my perfidy between you and decided to rend me limb from limb in tandem."

"Now there's a thought," Deborah said pleasantly.

"Actually," Michel said, "they haven't come to that, quite. They have only established that you treat all your relatives, wife or sister, in the same cavalier fashion when it comes to sharing information."

"Just so," Deborah said with a nod that sent a sun-kissed curl to the center of her forehead. "Mother had the news of your marriage from old Madame Mignot, and a more lurid piece of gossip you never heard! There has, supposedly, never been a more romantic rescue. You saved your Angelica from fire and drowning and the dangers of the surgeon's knife, then married her secretly in the dead of night. Now you keep her hidden away like some beauteous Rapunzel in case she should try to escape you!"

"What a blackguard I must be," her brother said pleasantly.

Deborah pursed her lips. "I wonder. I didn't believe half of it, but felt compelled to come and see so as to set mother's mind at ease. Now that I am here—"

"Yes? Now that you are here?" There was an edge to Renold's voice that had not been there before.

His sister's eyes softened. "I think perhaps you had your reasons, whatever you may have done, and I congratulate you most sincerely."

"Thank you." The words were sardonic.

"Oh, that's quite all right. Only, I want very much to be there when you explain yourself to mother."

"Which I am expected to do with all haste?"

"Absolutely. She asks that you bring your bride to—to be presented to her." Deborah glanced quickly at Angelica, then away again as she stumbled over her words.

"Ever the autocrat," her half brother said, smoothly filling the tiny gap. "You will tell her, when you write your report, that I live to obey?"

"With pleasure, though she won't believe it."

It was disturbing to Angelica, looking at Michel, to find compassion in his gaze. It was more disturbing to listen to intimations of unspoken understanding in the voices of Renold and his half sister.

There had never been a time in Angelica's life when she had been able to communicate with another person in that fashion. How many shared confidences and kept secrets did it take, how many hours of casual rambling from subject to subject? She longed for such closeness, but despaired of achieving it. Especially with her husband. He had his sister, or half sister, for understanding; a wife was scarcely necessary. Certainly not one he had failed to inform that he had a sister, and a mother.

Yes, but then she had not asked, Angelica realized. She had assumed, like an idiot, that Renold had been whelped in some ditch and left to make his own way in the world. Her aunt's influence, of course. Or perhaps that was only an excuse. It might be closer to the truth to say that she had been so wrapped up in her own fears and griefs that she had given little consideration to the manner in which Renold lived. She had accepted what he told her and what she heard from others, and not looked beyond it. It was her fault if she did not have his confidences.

Or was it? She understood him enough to realize that, though she might have asked for kisses and been given them, confidences from him had not been encouraged. The question then was why. And what did it have to do with communication between brother and sister?

It was later, after the passage of a grindingly slow afternoon and a dinner notable for its interminable length, that Renold was cornered by Deborah in his study. There was no welcome in his face as he looked up to see her standing in the doorway. Tossing aside his silver-nubbed pen, he leaned back in his chair, laced his long fingers together over his waistcoat buttons, and waited.

"You remind me," Deborah said as she closed the door behind herself and came forward to settle gracefully in a chair across from him, "of the hound we used to have when I was girl. Old Bellows, remember? Every time he ran down a deer for Papa, he would go off and take a rabbit for himself. Since this is conduct unappreciated and unbecoming in a deer hound, he hid his prizes in the most cunning places. Mother once found one, quite dead, behind the sofa cushions. She felt for old Bellows, but she was not pleased."

"Angelica," he said with some acerbity, "is not a rabbit, quick or dead."

"But she is a prize, I believe. Don't you think she has the right to know why you have taken her?"

"She will discover it in time; that's inevitable."

"When you're ready, I would imagine. Do you want her to hate you?"

Not a muscle in his face changed. "That, too, may be inevitable."

She studied him with her head tipped to one side, almost as if the weight of her hair was too heavy for her slender neck. "I can see why you're doing this—at least, I suppose it's to keep Bonheur in the family, so to speak, since a husband controls his wife's property. But was there no honorable way to go about it, no way to woo and wed her that did not smack of deceit?"

"What, offer my heart, my hand, *my name* like some callow,

beardless boy?" he said with bitter emphasis. "She would have thrown all three in my face."

"Not all women are like Clotilde," his sister said with heat. "Besides, you had saved your Angelica from death. Surely that would have weighed in the balance."

"Are we speaking of a wooing before or after the explosion of the steamboat? Before, she was betrothed and had the protection of her father who would not, you can be certain, have entertained my suit. Afterward, she had the memory of attempted assault." His gaze held self-incriminating revulsion that he made no effort to hide.

Deborah lifted a hand to her lips as they parted on a gasp. "When? On board the—you didn't!"

"No, I didn't, and I thank you for that much," he said on a soundless sigh. "But I could have, easily; there are few things in my wild careering that I have wanted more. The plan, rather, was to be caught in a compromising position. I would then agree, with great reluctance, to do the honorable thing. An old friend, a Madame Parnell, was primed to walk in upon the sorry scene. The explosion of the boilers made hash of the plan."

"That explosion. I'm so glad mother and I did not know you were on the *Queen Kathleen*."

"If you had known, you would have been apprised of my survival," he said evenly.

"Would we?" Deborah said, opening her eyes wide with amazed and entirely false surprise. "You are all consideration. But you might have 'apprised' us of the wedding before half New Orleans took up pen to twit us about it!"

He looked away toward where the candelabra shedding light on his desk sat stolidly supporting triple flames. "I thought to allow Angelica time to regain her strength. I thought repair a little of the damage I had done. I also thought," he added deliberately, "to consummate the marriage before celebrating it."

"How very—interesting," his sister said, her hazel gaze concentrating as she stared at him.

He said shortly, "I'm not without some consideration."

"And at what cost," she said with a spurious sympathy. "I understand now why you're crabby as a bear with a sore head."

"Do you indeed? Now how is that?" To admit she was right would not add to the conversation, and might increase his own awareness of his condition to something above its current bearable level.

Her smile was saucy. "Men talk, and aren't always careful who might hear. I listen. It's a useful trait."

"A dangerous one, if you aren't careful."

"Dear Renold, don't try to change the subject from your felonies to my misdemeanors. I want to know what you are going to do."

He heard the censure as it seeped into her tone. It was intolerable, as was her interference. "I am going to have Bonheur again," he said in quiet savagery, "with my dear wife's will or without it."

"Renold!" It was a cry of shock.

"It's what you expected, isn't it? What you came—or were sent here—to know. There must have been some doubt about my intentions, or you would have waited, busily preparing the wedding feast, for me to appear with my bride in tow."

"That wasn't it at all," his half sister protested. Her face was turning from pink to pale at something she saw in his eyes.

"What then? To save me from myself? I don't require it, just as I don't require supervision. Or advice on the care and handling of a wife. You will oblige me by returning to Bonheur as soon as possible, before you do more damage than you have already."

Deborah sank back in her chair, considering him with wide, steady eyes. Finally she said, "It isn't like you, Renold, to be so abrupt or so brutal. There is something you are afraid of. What is it?"

"I am casting a hazard at the future. A man who treats that lightly is a fool."

"Yes," she said in tentative agreement, "but that isn't all, is it? Estelle tells me you were badly burned in your escape from the steamboat, worse than need be had you not paused to rescue Angelica. More, in your single-minded determination to make her well again and bring her around to your purpose, you have not been sleeping."

As his face tightened, she lifted her chin. "No, you will not scold Estelle. I badgered her into talking of the past few days. Besides, she spoke only because she was troubled. As I am. I love Bonheur as much or more than you; I was born there, it's my home. But it's only a house and a piece of land. It isn't worth destroying another person over. Or yourself."

"Melodramatic and presumptuous," he said in acid condemnation. "My marriage is a union based on practical considerations, with no place in it for such heart-burnings."

Her piquant features were serious, her tone remained reflective. "Is it? Then why didn't you tell Angelica of your connection with Bonheur? She is tied to you by bonds both civil and religious, bonds it is almost impossible to sever. What reason can there be to keep her in ignorance, then? Unless you want the additional guarantee of ties of affection? And you are doubtful these can be implanted if she learns of your—what did you call it?—your perfidy?"

"This is my supposed fear, that she will not love me?" he said, voicing the words she did not quite dare say. "I will agree that a modicum of affection would be convenient, will even admit it could be pleasant. But it isn't necessary for my ends and I am unlikely to fade into a decline without it."

"It isn't your aim?" she said, as if in clarification.

"Should it be?"

She gave him a dour look. "You always did enjoy answering a question with a question, a trait that shows a lamentable lack of forthrightness. Very well. Assuming you mean what you say, I expect you would still object if Angelica formed an attachment elsewhere?"

"Now I am to be tested for jealousy, I suppose. You might remember, while you are taking my character apart, that I am a possessive man. I would certainly object if this attachment was a threat to our union, therefore to Bonheur."

"How very reasoned. Then why in the name of common sense do you allow Michel Farness to visit your wife while you are from home?"

"Michel has been warned," he said succinctly.

She was momentarily dazed, but recovered. "I don't imagine he was impressed. It's easy to see he is captivated."

Renold smiled without warmth. "Concern heaped upon concern; what a thing it is to be a sister. But are you certain it's all for me? If you want Michel's attentions turned in a different direction, perhaps you should undertake the task yourself."

"I don't want—!" She stopped, drawing a hard-pressed breath, before she said, "I had almost forgotten how devious you can be. You won't involve me that easily, however. I am not going to distract your friend for you."

"A talent for deviousness runs in the family," he said, "through the distaff."

"You must tell mother that, when you see her. She will no doubt be delighted."

"Or you can report it, with the rest, on your return."

Her gaze as she met his across the highly polished desk was clear and candid. "Oh, I've decided to stay awhile in New Orleans. The season may be over, but the shopping is still marvelous."

Renold absorbed the challenge in her eyes. Behind it was audacity and determination, and the memory of a hundred such encounters wending down the years. He had won, more often than not, by exerting superior authority and will and even, on occasion, strength. He said in soft threat, "I could see you off in the morning."

"Yes, you could. Perhaps I should go and have a little discussion of a family nature with Angelica tonight."

He laughed, though with no great amusement. "Do. If you want to be sent home with your pretty neck rung like a pullet's and a rosary in your hands."

"Murderous as well as lecherous, anxious, and seething with husbandly vigilance. I believe you need me near to keep you from doing, or being forced to do, something you may regret."

It was, in its way, an explanation. It was also a bargaining counter. He said, "You are agreeing to undertake distracting Michel after all?"

Her smile was pure sweetness. "It will be my sacrifice on the altar of family duty."

Renold kept his satisfaction to himself. It was better that way.

The bedchamber, when he stepped inside it a short time later, was lit by a single candle guttering low in its own warm wax. The light gave a soft gold sheen to the blue silk above Angelica, and danced with molten gleams upon the thick wheaten braid that lay over her shoulder. It caught the pure angle of a cheekbone, the snowy, linen-covered crest of a globe-like breast, the burnished satin length of her lashes sealed together where her eyelids met. Wavering, backing from his swift approach, the uneven flame made it difficult to tell if she was still breathing.

She was. More, the pulse that stroked his fingertips as he placed them against her neck was steady and even as a metronome.

The crystal glass that sat on the bedside table had a quarter inch of water flavored with laudanum in the bottom. He drank it, then stood holding the glass against his heart.

She had been troubled by one of her headaches earlier; he had seen the discarded cloth damp with rose water, the barely tasted tisane. Was that why she had sought oblivion? Or had it been the charged atmosphere of the first confrontation with Deborah in the salon?

It could also have been something else entirely, something she had read into what was said, something sensed without words or deeds. She was capable of it, he knew that too well. More, she might or might not feel the need to face him with discovered sins.

She was an enigma.

Most people were fairly easy to read: their simple joys and angers, their impulses of generosity, venality, humility, and causeless pride were there in their faces. A few were more difficult because their deeds were darker. There were not many who defied understanding.

Angelica was different. Her face was beautiful and clear and expressive, but her thoughts were at a level far deeper. She saw more than was on the surface, considered beyond the obvious, and what she discovered was filtered through a screen of intuition and experience to remove the dross.

If he was afraid of anything, it was her understanding. Not what she might learn, but what she would make of it once she knew. What she would make of him.

She could, he thought, given time, see through everything he was and had been, and look into his naked soul. He didn't like it.

At the same time he was drawn to it. There was a terrible seductive power in being finally, completely, understood. Even if it meant being destroyed.

He had lied to his sister, barefaced and without compunction. Some things were absolutely necessary. Angelica's affection was fast becoming one of them.

Reaching with a steady hand, he pinched out the light. He stripped off his clothes, tossed them aside, climbed into the bed. With careful strength, he drew Angelica to him until she lay with her gentle curves fitted against his every possible body surface, every heated inch of his skin. Then he was still, his breathing shallow while he stared into the darkness.

His arm, where he had pillowed her head, grew bloodless and numb. He did not move. And in time, by dint of will and concentrated purpose, his breathing grew even and his body lost its heat.

He dozed. But he could still feel the throb of her heartbeat under his palm.

Ten

THERE WAS THE SOFT FEEL OF SPRING ON THE MORNING AIR AS Angelica and Deborah left the house. They were going marketing, or rather Tit Jean was going and they were joining him. The three of them strolled in the direction of the river, the two women abreast and the manservant following with a large rectangular basket on each arm.

The hour was early; a shopper who did not reach the market before nine o'clock was too late for the freshest meats and vegetables. It was the first time Angelica had been out of the house without Renold. It was also the first time she had been completely free of headache since the explosion.

The exertion of walking warmed her and brought a sparkle to her eyes. She felt free and lighthearted, and inclined to smile at all passersby. After a time, she allowed her shawl, a soft Indian cashmere in the inevitable black, to slip from her shoulders to the bends of her elbows. She had been doubtful about the lightweight muslin gown that Estelle had laid out for her, but it was proving a good choice after all.

A Lenten quiet hung in the streets. Gone were the maskers and the music, the loud laughter and shouts of drunken merriment. Instead, children played on the overhanging balconies; maids scrubbed steps with brick dust and a dog scratched fleas as he lay in the middle of the street. Now and then a gentleman passed with a polite lift of his hat, or a pair of nuns, with starched caps flying and crucifixes banging at their knees, hurried along on some errand. Just ahead of them a gentleman nearly as wide as he was tall, obviously a frequent visitor to the market, carried his own basket in the same direction they were heading.

Deborah chatted with ease and humor, keeping up a running commentary on the people who lived in the houses along the way and on the recent political improprieties in the city. She also complained, as she tripped over the uneven flagstones of the *banquette*, that most of the money for civic improvements was going uptown to the American section while the French Quarter was left to rack and ruin.

Angelica enjoyed listening to Renold's half sister and appreciated the information gleaned from her observations. She also laughed often at the dour but pithy comments Tit Jean interjected from time to time.

The French market was situated along the levee near the *Place d'Armes*. There were steps leading from the levee to the river for the use of the market boats that drew up there in the early hours every morning. The building had a low-pitched roof of red tiles and arcaded sides open to the movement of air and the coming and going of buyers. Inside, there were more than a hundred stalls along a length of some three hundred feet.

There were other markets in the city, according to Tit Jean; the Americans frequented one on Poydras Street. The French market, *La Halle des Boucheries*, was of course superior.

As a beginning, since Angelica had never been to the market before, they made a circuit of the stalls. Tit Jean consulted them about their preferences and took careful note of their responses, since a lady did not bargain or carry money for purchases. The manservant soon wended his way back to the meat stalls, however, since that was the commodity most likely to disappear early. The two women were forgotten as he greeted friends and butchers and haggled over the price of a fat goose and a huge slab of pork loin.

Angelica and Deborah wandered here and there, threading their way between sellers of cheeses and sausages, onions and cabbages, greens and strawberries, ground peppers and cinnamon, strings of garlic and bouquets of sweet peas, and a thousand other things. They eased past the lines of free women of color ready to hire themselves out as laundresses and scrub-women. The next moment they were stepping over the feet of Indian women who sat weaving baskets, grinding sassafras leaves to the thickening powder known as *filé*, and nursing, openly and unashamedly, babies with enormous black eyes.

Around them was a hubbub of voices speaking in Parisian French and also the French-based African-Indian patois used by servants; in Spanish, English, German, Gaelic, and a smattering of some half dozen other languages from the seaports of the world. The noise rose in a dull roar under the market roof, disturbing the gray rags of spiderwebs and nesting sparrows clinging to the cross beams, and forcing the two women to lean close to hear each other speak.

It was exhilarating, fascinating; Angelica did not want to leave. Still, it would not do to let the fresh meat Tit Jean had bought spoil. After a short time, she and Deborah turned back to look for the tall black man with his huge baskets.

Angelica was glancing at a tray of dried figs as she moved past it when she felt a firm grip fasten on her arm. "Don't look just yet," Deborah said in low tones near her ear, "but I think that man is following us."

"Which man?" Angelica pretended to study the figs.

The other woman barely tipped her head to the left behind them. "Over there."

"I don't see any…" Angelica began, then trailed off as she saw only too well. It was the small gray man she had seen at the townhouse. "Oh."

Deborah lifted a brow. "Don't tell me you know the creature?"

"I believe," came the slow answer, "that he works for Renold in some fashion."

Confusion followed rapidly by chagrin crossed Deborah's face. "*Mon Dieu*, don't tell Renold I pointed the man out to you."

There was only one reason it could matter. "You think he sent him to watch us?"

The color in the other woman's face deepened. "Something like that."

What Renold's sister apparently thought was that Renold had sent the man to watch his wife. Was it possible?

"Please don't look like that," Deborah said in a rush. "I'm sure Renold is only concerned for you. You are very important to him."

Angelica gave her a fleeting glance before moving on again. "He told you so, I suppose."

"If you are wondering if we discussed you behind your back, the answer is no. On the other hand, some things are obvious if you know how to look for them."

"Which you do?"

"An acquired habit. Renold, you will have noticed, says a great many things but doesn't give much of himself away."

That was too true to be denied. Angelica thought, however, that it was merely an introduction to something more Renold's sister wanted to say. Slipping past an elderly black woman with a tray of pecan confections on her lap, she gave Deborah a frown by way of discouragement.

Undaunted, Deborah said, "Renold has been solitary for so long that I despaired of his ever taking a wife. He keeps so much to himself that I felt—as did our mother—that he could never break free to love. You have no idea how intriguing it is to see him with you now. It's as if years have fallen away, as if he never left home, never embarked on his quest for power and riches."

"You mean he didn't have those things from his step-father?" Angelica asked.

"As if he would have taken them!" Deborah said with a quick shake of her head. "No. What he has, he earned himself, by methods conventional and unconventional, by buying and selling and taking chances."

"On cotton bales and ships, sugar and land and cattle," Angelica said, stirred by a memory.

"And warehouses and investment in the construction of railroads, not to mention a considerable interest in at least one house of chance."

"Gambling," Angelica said in laconic tones.

"You don't approve? There is nothing illegal in it, and men

will seek risk somewhere, whether it's with their lives or their money, in a gaming house or out of it."

"My father was a gamester," she said. "It—took him from me."

"Mine also," Deborah said with a thick sound in her voice.

They had wound their way back to the vegetable stands where the aisles were wider and quieter and they could again walk side by side. Passing the new green peas, Angelica said in stifled tones, "Why do they risk so much? What can it give them that they can't find elsewhere?"

"For many, I think, the feeling of being alive and of winning against the odds. For others, those who cannot afford to lose, it gives them the hope of something, anything, better."

"You've thought about it."

"I never said I approved of all Renold's methods of gaining wealth. Anyway, he sold the gaming house just recently, you know."

"So I was told."

"I think he had never considered how destructive gambling can be, having few such weaknesses himself. The moment he realized it, he acted. But that is his way, to make amends for his mistakes without counting the cost."

Angelica gave the other girl a close look, her attention snared by some shade of meaning in her tone. She was given no time to question her, however, for Deborah turned abruptly away to wave to Tit Jean, who was coming toward them.

"Ah, mamzelles, here you are," the manservant exclaimed, looming up beside them with a full basket in each hand. "I thought you had lost yourselves."

Deborah and Angelica exchanged a humorous glance. As they turned to accompany the manservant homeward, it occurred to Angelica that Tit Jean made a formidable guard. Why on earth, then, should Renold require another to keep an eye on her?

There was, of course, no answer.

The carriage that came hurtling in their direction when they were halfway home was handled with verve and dash and a reckless lack of control. An expensive equipage, it was pulled by a pair of glossy blacks and had a shining ebony body perched high on slender wheels. The interior was of burgundy leather with silver appointments. The driving costume of the woman on the seat matched to perfection, as did the tailored suit of the boy who sat at her side and the livery of the frightened groom who stood up behind her.

The carriage splashed muddy water from a pothole as it pulled up beside the *banquette*. Watching Angelica and Deborah brush the droplets from their skirts, Madame Petain gave them a cool smile, "My apologies, ladies," she called down without noticeable remorse. "Deborah, how nice to see you; I heard you were in town. I left my card just now, as I was told you weren't at home. This is much better."

Renold's sister made a polite answer as she surveyed the woman above her. She added, "How daring of you to drive yourself, Clotilde. Are you setting a fashion?"

"You know, I believe I am. It's quite the thing in Paris. Soon all the ladies will be tooling their carriages as women did thirty years ago. Besides, it gives one a certain independence of movement." She turned toward Angelica. "Perhaps, Madame Harden, you may be able to persuade Renold to indulge you."

Angelica had been somewhat interested until she heard the suggestion. Suddenly, she conceived a preference for being driven. "Oh, I don't think I shall bother. I wouldn't want Renold to worry."

"How considerate of you," the other woman said sweetly. "Perhaps as you have his interests so much at heart, you will give him a message?"

"Yes, of course." Manners required no less.

"Tell him, please, that Bernard is well and sturdy, and grows more like his father every day."

"Bernard?" Angelica looked instinctively at the boy next to Clotilde. He was a handsome youth of perhaps ten years, slender and well made, with dark, curling hair and wide-spaced eyes of soft, indeterminate green.

Clotilde reached out to smooth the boy's hair. As he flinched away from the gesture, scowling down at his hands on his knees, her lips tightened in irritation. Still, there was cool pleasure in the glance she gave Angelica as she said, "Bernard, yes. My son."

Angelica flinched as surely as the boy, though she had been expecting it. The behavior of her heart, knocking back and forth against the walls of her chest, was sickening. Her head began to pound with the same heavy beat. It took two deep breaths to steady her voice before she said, "I will try to remember."

"Do," the woman said on a laugh. With a careless farewell, she whipped up her horses and sent the light carriage spinning away down the street.

Deborah turned an indignant face in Angelica's direction. "That woman lives to make trouble. You won't let her do it, will you?"

"You think I should forget her message? Then what if she asks Renold if it was delivered? He will think I was either jealous or afraid to mention it."

"She won't do it, she wouldn't dare!" The words were scathing.

Angelica frowned as she met the gaze of Renold's half sister. "She did mean what I think, that the boy is Renold's son? If he is, then why wouldn't she dare anything?"

Deborah stopped and looked around her. There was no one near. Even Tit Jean had developed a sudden intense interest in the cramped window display of an apothecary shop down the street. Still, Renold's sister lowered her voice to just above a whisper.

"I am not supposed to know of this, but was told by Estelle—who learned of it from the downstairs houseboy at the Petain house and who had it in turn from Clotilde's personal maid. It seems Madame Petain was very much enceinte at the time she was wed to M'sieur Petain. After the baby was born, she received a visit from Renold, during which he demanded to know why she had chosen to allow another man to play father to his child. The answer had to do with money and prestige and birthrights. He left. But this much I know because I saw it with my own eyes when he returned: Clotilde hurt him as he had never been hurt before. He has not forgiven her for it, nor will he."

Was Deborah right? Angelica, turning and walking on toward the townhouse in dazed confusion, wished that she might be sure.

The problem remained at the back of her mind all the rest of the day. It was there while she and Deborah pored over the dress plates in a copy of *La Mode Illustrée*, while she lay down in the afternoon to rest, and when she dressed for dinner. It stood white-hot in the forefront of her mind during the meal, and afterward while she and Deborah and Renold sat drinking sherry in the salon, alternately talking, reading, and listening to the ticking of the French ormolu mantle clock.

By the time Renold came to her in their bedchamber, she could bear it no longer. Sitting up straight in the bed the moment he closed the door behind him, she said, "Deborah and I saw Madame Petain this morning. She entrusted me with a message."

Something flickered in the depths of his eyes, but the look on his face remained perfectly pleasant. "Am I to guess what it was? Or are you waiting to see if I am able to bear its weight before you burden me with it?"

"Actually, I've come to think that the information was for me, while you were merely to have a reminder." She continued with the exact words that Clotilde Petain had given her to say.

He studied her a moment before he said, "You are taking the fact that I have a son with remarkable calm."

She wasn't, but it was some consolation that he thought so. "I can't change what's already done, and he appears to be a fine, strong child."

"I see. Assessing my worth for breeding purposes?"

"Hardly." She ignored the inevitable sweep of color into her face. "But I would not blame you for being interested in his welfare."

"No? How magnanimous. Unfortunately, his mother is not of the same mind. I am not permitted to visit, therefore any report is in the nature of salt in the wound. You, of course, are the salt cellar, a bit corroded around the edges from the contents, but effective."

In all the turning of her thoughts during the day, she had not considered that she might be used to hurt Renold. It was an indicator of the selfish turn of her mind, and of her uncertainty with him. She said abruptly, "I'm sorry."

"Don't be. Tit Jean told me you were accosted, though not what was said. I have been impatient to discover if fear, rage, or simple embarrassment would keep you from coming to me with whatever poison the lady might have seen fit to administer. I am honored by your show of confidence."

All her vacillating and anxiety had been for nothing. Through tight lips, she said, "I might have known."

"Next time you will," he said, his smile crooked, "and then where will I be?"

He turned from her, striding toward the door. His hand was on the knob before she found her voice. "Where are you going?"

The glance he gave her over his shoulder was no longer amused, nor was there light in his eyes. He said softly, "Why do you want to know?"

Did she dare tell him? Why not, when honesty had served her so well? "I would rather not be the cause of you visiting Madame Petain to demand an explanation for her conduct."

"Now which is it that troubles you more, my love, the visit or the explanation?"

She blinked rapidly, her composure all but destroyed by the endearment in that caressing tone. "I just see no reason for either one."

"Don't you? The lady has upset my wife, meddled in my marriage, and involved my son in her petty revenge. Tolerance is a virtue, but it has its limits. She has reached them."

"You won't, that is—"

"Are you concerned that I may use methods which require physical coercion? No. Those I reserve for you alone. Aren't you gratified?"

"Not," she said, "especially."

He might not have heard, of course. He had already gone, snapping the door shut behind him.

Angelica lay awake, watching the shadows cast on the

ceiling by the bedside candle and thinking, endlessly thinking. Until it occurred to her that it might look as if she were waiting up for a report on his meeting with Madame Petain. She heaved up on one elbow, then, and blew out the candle. Lying down again, she settled herself so that it might appear she was relaxed and on the edge of sleep.

She wondered if Renold would join her in the bed, as he had the night before. She had not known when he arrived, but had been awake when he left her, rolling from the mattress before dawn. And the space next to her had been warm, while she seemed to have some vague memory, like the remnants of a dream, of being held close with a hard arm across her waist.

To doze was not her intention, nor did she recognize the line between waking and sleep, and yet she jerked and opened her eyes as a sound came inside the room. She lay listening, trying to place the clicking noise that had roused her.

There was a faint glow behind the draperies at the French doors giving onto the balcony, one coming from the street lamp further along the way. In its light, she saw the heavy folds shift, wavering as if from a draft. And suddenly she recognized the noise. It was the quiet snap of the latch on the doors.

Had Renold come in, then decided to step outside for a moment? He might have used a certain stealth if he had thought she was sleeping.

Or perhaps Estelle or Tit Jean had discovered some errand on the balcony overlooking the street? They might also have been reluctant to disturb her.

No. Renold moved so quietly he would not have awakened her, while Estelle and Tit Jean would never have risked disturbing her at all.

There was one other possibility.

"Deborah?" she asked.

The dark shadow of a man swooped from behind the draperies. He barreled down on her. Hard hands snatched at her and she was dragged against a damp, smelly form. An arm clamped her throat, closing off her scream.

She was lifted, swung. Her head swam dizzily and gray darkness crowded her vision. No air. She couldn't breathe.

Choking, she kicked at the man who held her. Reaching back toward him with fingers curled into claws, she raked tough, bearded skin.

The blow came from nowhere, a reverberating thud that sent sickening pain through her head. Blackness rose like a thundercloud behind her eyes. Golden sparkles lit it, raining around her as she fell with them into the dark.

∽

Diligent in his cold rage, Renold traced Clotilde Petain from her Italianate mansion on Esplanade to the home of a lady friend who resided on Dumaine Street, and from there to the house of a woman known for her card parties, her oyster suppers, and her racy style of living. Clotilde had apparently told her husband she was going to a meeting of her sewing circle. Renold's advantage was that he had not believed the story for an instant.

The butler who took his hat, cape, and cane was burly and sharp-eyed, the kind who might be expected in an establishment where trouble sometimes erupted over losses. Otherwise, the house was perfectly ordinary, with brightly lighted rooms and pleasantly ornate furnishings. The music coming from the double parlor was competent and the company excellent.

Renold nodded to several male acquaintances as he strolled through the main salon, made a circuit of the smoking room, and paused for a moment in the gentlemen's card room. He did not linger in any of these places, however, but made his way to the ladies' card room at the back of the house. He ran his quarry to ground there at a polished table covered by a cloth of green baize. With her were two dowagers in the worn black and purple of old mourning, and a young married lady who appeared to be in trouble from the quiver in her upper lip and the hunted way she looked at him as he entered.

Clotilde faced him with the malicious dignity of a Chinese empress, sitting stiff in her chair and gowned in crackling taffeta of a reptilian green. She wore emeralds on her fingers and held cards that were painted on their backs with gaudy

Brazilian parrots. She did not wait for him to speak, but attacked at once.

"My dear Renold, I thought you disdained play for high stakes these days. Or has a few short days with your bride driven you to seek excitement at any price?"

"I came," he said evenly, "to take you away from your pleasure for a few short minutes. If that's possible."

She laughed. "I don't think it is, you know. If you wish to speak to me you may do it here."

"What, air the dirty linen? Shock the ladies with a tale of vice and greed and licentious coupling? Not to mention the consequences." He gave the openmouthed dowager in purple an acid smile. "I'm sure they would find it agreeable, but it's doubtful you would."

"You villain!" Clotilde said in disbelief. "You know there is nothing of the sort between us."

"Did I say it was about us? No, no. I am a newly married man with an angel for a bride; what need do I have for such things? Now, you—but I must not be indiscreet. Yet."

Twin spots of hectic color appeared on either side of Clotilde's nose. "This is blackmail."

"Undoubtedly," he said, putting his shoulder to the door facing and crossing his arms over his chest. "Shall I continue?"

Clotilde Petain flung down her cards with such temper that they spilled across the table and fluttered over the edge to the floor. Her chair scraped as she pushed it back and rose, rustling viciously, to her feet. The look in her eyes was murderous as she pushed past him and led the way to an upstairs sitting room where she turned in a tornado of stiff skirts.

"Very well, now we are alone," she snapped. "What do you wish to say to me?"

His voice quiet, almost reflective, he answered, "I have no wish to say anything whatever to you on any subject, and haven't in some time. But you knew that, which is why you spoke to Angelica this morning."

"So now you are overheated because your bride knows you have a son. Did you expect to keep it secret forever?"

"My expectations," he said with definition, "as well

as my needs, desires, wishes, dreams, and most fervently held hopes, are no concern of yours. If you make them so, ever again, you will discover regret such as you have never known. This I swear to you by whatever poor, pitiful saint you may still revere."

"A threat?" she said with a cool smile. "I suppose you mean to beat me?"

"I would not give you the pleasure; for that you must apply to M'sieur Petain," he said quietly. "What I will do is drag your name through every puddle of filth and degradation to which I can lay hand and tongue. I will make of you such a pariah you will be hounded from place to place with no city in the world, no country, no single spot on earth to find the respect and social acceptance that seems to make your life worth living."

"You would do that to the mother of your child?" she said, flinging up her head. "I think not, since you would make him a pariah, too."

His smile was cold. "I neglected to tell you how that would be prevented, didn't I? First, I would take my son."

Her face turned pasty so that the red stain of the Spanish papers she had rubbed on her cheeks stood out like fire. She clasped her hands at her waist to prevent their sudden trembling. Her voice not quite even, she said, "Petain may have something to say to that. He thinks the boy belongs to him."

"Does he? Ask him. Petain is an inbred idiot, but even he must be able to count. Certainly he can see the line of a nose, a brow." His voice hardened. "And if he still proves stubborn, I believe he may be persuaded to relinquish his claim at sword point."

"That's your answer to everything, isn't it?" she said bitterly. "The sword, a duel. You may discover one day that some things can't be taken by force."

"Or by chicanery? There is an additional lesson for those intelligent enough to give it heed."

She turned her head. When she looked back again there were tears shimmering in the sherry brown of her eyes. She took a step toward him with her hand held out to grasp his arm. "Don't do this, Renold, not to me. Only think of what we have meant to each other, think of the love between us."

He removed himself from her reach with a smooth step. Finding himself near the back of a carved rosewood chair, he traced the pattern of vines and leaves with a fingertip, then lowered his hand. His voice even, he said, "That wasn't love. It was calf devotion on one side and wild cupidity on the other; it was nose-thumbing, fire-juggling, and the effect of hot nights on a frigid heart."

"I loved you!" she cried.

"You enjoyed thinking so," he replied without hesitation. "What you loved was the reflection of yourself you saw in my moonstruck eyes."

"Nothing is worth anything without you," she said on a miserable gasp. "It's all so dull and empty."

He considered her. "What you miss is the risk, the excitement of playing with the forbidden. But you got caught, Clotilde. The game is over."

"I hate thinking that this is all there's ever going to be," she said with an aimless gesture that took in the room, the house, the city, and her life. "But at least you're also caught, now. That's some consolation."

It was a more telling blow than she knew. He was still recovering from it when he heard a commotion in the front of the house. It was heading his way. And his sword cane was in the custody of the butler.

A gray and spare figure appeared in the doorway, looking around wildly. Close behind was the big butler with a snarl on his lips and his face an enraged purple. The two skidded to a halt as Renold stepped forward.

"House cat and a mouse, it seems," he said politely. "You were looking for me?"

"That I am, your honor," said the little man. "I been searching high and low, up one side and down the other, and a rare ol' time I've had of it. Now this here baboon's trying to put me out of this fancy house before I tell you what you got to know—hey!" He ended on a yelp as the butler grasped the collar of his coat and hauled him up on tiptoe.

"That will do," Renold said.

The butler paused. An uneasy look passed over his face as he absorbed the slicing sound of the words addressed to him.

"Better back off, bucko," the little man said, "or he'll have your gizzard for a watch fob."

The butler released his grasp and dusted his hands. He retreated to the door but no farther, taking up a stance there with the same look of disgust on his face that he might have assumed if guarding the portal of a privy.

"You wanted something?" Renold said to his confederate.

"I have to tell you about the lady. All was right as rain after you left, then along about an hour later, I hears this wagon. It goes along, then it stops somewhere in front of the house. I don't think much of it, at first, then it gets to worryin' me, see. What's a wagon doing there that time of night? I ain't too sure 'bout leaving the back gate to go look. But I goes, and that's when I comes across these two jokers letting a bundle down from the balcony that looks on the street. They plunks it in the wagon and drives off like the fiends of hell are after 'em. Comes to me the bundle had the look of a body. And all the doors into the house was shut tight—except the one in the lady's room."

Renold stood in total stillness. "Yes?"

"So I climbs up to have a look. Not there. The bed was empty, bedcover gone. She was took, all right."

Renold turned a speculative gaze on Clotilde. She blanched under the force of it and stumbled backward a step. "No, dear God, no," she cried. "I wouldn't. Really."

He swung back to the smaller man. "It did not, I suppose, occur to you to follow the wagon?"

"Sure, and it did, fast as I could go. Happens I had seen the two in it before, so figured the direction they would take. Caught up with them down to Gallatin Street. Saw them take that bundle of bedclothes into the back door of a barrelhouse."

If he was to be useful to Angelica, he could not rave and curse. Or, like an avenging Greek king, kill the messenger. Renold said softly, "Give me the direction. Then gather three men and meet me at the barrelhouse in fifteen minutes."

"But your honor—!"

Renold looked at him. "Or less."

The man swallowed, a convulsive jog of his skinny throat. "Right," he said, and tore from the room.

Renold followed him with swift strides, leaving his hat and gloves behind inside the house because they were like too many others left on the rack and there was no time. He was on foot, but it would be faster to walk than to return to the townhouse for a carriage.

Clotilde hurried from the door of the gaming house in a crackle of skirts, calling out to him. He did not stop, nor did he look back.

Eleven

THE SMELL CAME IN WAVES, A FETID, SOUR MIASMA THAT clogged the nose and rose to the brain to trigger nausea. Angelica turned her head, trying to find air that was free of it. There was none. She moaned, a sound she stifled instantly as it jarred her into wakefulness.

There had been furious argument going on in the room; she realized it as the sound stopped. Until then, it had been no more than the undertone to a cacophony of sound somewhere nearby: the drone of male voices, hysteria-edged laughter of women, drunken shouts and screams, all underscored by the far-off grinding of a barrel organ.

Abruptly, the soft coverlet wrapped around her and covering her face was twitched away. The smells grew stronger. She kept her eyes closed and breathed carefully against a strong urge to be violently ill.

"Still out. Gawd, Clem, why the hell you have to hit her so hard?" There was contempt in the coarse female voice, as well as a noticeable lack of sympathy.

"She was all set to screech. Anyways, I barely tapped her. Can't help it if I ain't used to dealing with her sort."

"You might a killed her, and then where would we be? The gent won't pay for dead meat."

"If the gent shells out at all, you'll be lucky."

The words were a sullen jibe. Hard on them came the sharp crack of flesh on flesh.

"Aw, Ma!"

"Git on out there and git to work with the other good-for-nothings. I might a knowed I'd have to do all the thinking."

There came a low muttering and a curse from the man, but no defiance. A creak sounded, as if weight had been removed from a wooden stool. Footsteps scuffled, followed by a brief flare of light that appeared as a dull glow behind her eyelids. The noise rose and fell as a door opened and shut.

There was a moment of unnerving quiet. A draft of air, strong with the odor of an unwashed body, was the only hint of warning. Then something wet and foul splashed into Angelica's face. She strangled and heaved away from it with her eyes flying open.

"Playing possum; I thought so." The words were spoken with a satisfied grunt that retreated with much groaning and squeaking of the rough plank floor. "Have to get up earlier in the day to fool Ma Skaggs."

The liquid in Angelica's face smelled of raw spirits and something unidentifiable but less wholesome. Angelica tried to lift a hand to wipe it away. It was impossible; she was trussed up like a Christmas goose.

Turning her head, she squinted in the direction of the woman's voice. She could just make her out in the dimness lighted only by a lantern with a pierced tin shade which sat on the floor. She was grossly fat, a tub of a woman with great rolls of flesh ballooning under her neck and carried like a twelve-month pregnancy beneath the voluminous folds of a filthy skirt. Her greasy hair was thin and brown and pulled back so tightly in its knot that it gave her a slit-eyed look. Returning to a bench on which sat a wooden keg, she began to stir the contents with a short-handled boat paddle held in ham-like fists.

In the darkness just beyond the lantern's glow were barrels and boxes stacked to the ceiling. A rumpled bed sat in the corner with a pile of men's clothes reaching waist-high beside it, the coats, waistcoats, shirts, trousers, and crushed hats wadded together without order.

Bewilderment making her voice husky, Angelica said, "What is this place? Why am I here?"

"Lord, dearie, what cabbage wagon did you fall off that you don't know a barrelhouse when you see one? As for why, just you think about it. I'll warrant you can figure it out."

"I heard—it sounded as if you expected to be paid for bringing me."

"My boys, they be handy at odd jobs that way. Clem, he's my oldest, had him a yen to toss up your skirts, but I figure you're worth more without that kind of wear and tear."

Angelica took painful note of the information offered. She also considered the careless way it had been given, as if the woman called Ma felt herself beyond reprisal, or else never expected to hear from her prisoner again.

Angelica swallowed hard. After a moment she said, "This gentleman you spoke of, you saw him? You know what he looks like?"

"Handsome devil, I'll give him that. Nice way of talking, smile to melt the heart of a brass monkey. Wouldn't trust him, though, not if I was young and pretty again."

Angelica lay quite still. It sounded like—but that could not be. Why would Renold have her kidnapped from his house? If he had wanted her that badly, all he had to do was reach for her across the width of a mattress. She could not have been any more unwilling then than now.

Yet, he was a devious man. On top of that, she learned something about him every day that she had not known before, and not all of it to his credit. If he meant to rid himself of her, he might hire someone to see that she disappeared. He could then say that she had wandered off in the delirium of illness. Such things had been known to happen when a husband had no more use for a wife.

No, she would not think such things. There must be another explanation, if she could only find it. Pushing herself up on one elbow, she leaned against a whiskey barrel. The position gave a better view. She watched as the other woman dumped something black and sticky into the barrel she was hovering over, then began to stir it in with motions that shook her whole body like a blancmange.

Angelica said, "I don't think you're washing, not in pure

alcohol, and it isn't the season for pickling. Unless, of course, it's meat. Is it meat?"

The woman guffawed. "That's a good one, dearie, that it is. The only meat-pickling on Gallatin Street would be to souse a body in a barrel to get rid of it. Which would be a fair waste of good alcohol when the dead ones can be dumped in the river easy as can be. No, what I'm doing is making a miracle like in the holy book, turning water into wine. When I gets through with that, I'll make up a batch of good Irish whiskey."

"Water into wine. Very profitable, I imagine," Angelica said, talking to keep her fears at bay, and also to establish some kind of rapport that might allow her to ask a pertinent question or two.

"Well, you don't expect me to sell the real thing for a pica-yune, do you, now? My wine is better'n most, I can tell you. I uses real burnt sugar and a bit of dried cherries and prunes, and only one part alcohol to three parts water, instead of one to four. And my whiskey has just the creosote in the alcohol, no horse dung, because I purely couldn't stand to be around that kind of rotgut."

"Your principles," Angelica said dryly, "are amazing."

Ma Skaggs eyed her with a twist to her thick lips. "You might say so. I don't never add enough knockout drops to kill. A man can have three or four drinks in my place, and maybe even a good time upstairs, before he loses his purse."

"But he will lose it eventually, I expect." There was a morbid fascination for Angelica in the things that came out of the big woman's mouth, almost like listening to a creature of another species.

"That's the chances. Them as don't like it can go some-where else." The woman banged her paddle on the side of the keg to knock off the excess alcohol, then flung it down. She went to open the door, then returned to the bench. Stooping, she picked up the keg in her massive arms and waddled out of the room with it.

The rumble of the barrelhouse's customers was louder through the opening. Male voices, loud and boastful, low and conniving, thick and slurred, were pierced by the predatory sharpness of female tones. Curses and raw, pithy phrases could be heard, some of which had meaning, some that could only be guessed at, but most with ugly emphasis. There were sounds of carping and complaint, the boasting of the braggart and the sniveling of the broken of spirit.

Then, floating above it all, deep and fluid, incisive with irritation, came another voice. It complained with the others, boasted and was profane with the others, still was instantly recognizable.

Renold.

It was not possible that his presence was an accident. He had come for her.

He had come for her, yes, but in what capacity? Was he there to find and remove her? Or had he arrived to ensure that she was never seen again?

A pulse beat with sickening strokes in Angelica's head. Her sight feathered at the edges with grayness, then began to dim.

No. Dragging air into her lungs, she fought the darkness. No. She would not believe the man who had held her and made a garden for her and explained to her the story of the elixir of love could plan to kill her. He might strangle her in fury or in possessive rage, but he would not send a thief to take her from his house, nor would he deal with scum from a barrelhouse for so paltry a reason.

If he was here, he meant to take her home. Somehow, in some incredible fashion strictly his own, he had discovered where she had been taken. He was in the common room out there, rubbing elbows with the drunks and derelicts and desperate men, trying to find his way to her. And he was drinking.

He was drinking the foul brew stirred up by Ma Skaggs. The brew that was laced, liberally if not lethally, with knockout drops. How long he had been there, she did not know. How many drinks he had taken she could not tell.

Did he suspect, or know, that the concoction in his glass had been designed to render any mortal man unconscious? She had no idea, and would not until he managed to come to her. Or fail to come.

There was only one thing to do. She drew in her breath to scream.

"Here, now, none of that," Ma Skaggs said, blocking the door with her huge form, then slamming the door panel shut. Advancing on Angelica, she fell to her knees with a solid thump and dragged a dirty rag of a handkerchief from her bosom.

The struggle was furious, but brief. The big woman put a knee in Angelica's abdomen, shifting her horrendous weight. Hampered by roped wrists, Angelica had to open her mouth to drag in air. The rag was pushed in so far she thought she would suffocate.

Ma Skaggs climbed, huffing and groaning, to her feet and moved to resume her mixing. Angelica lay breathing in and out of her nose in winded rage overlaid by terror.

Long minutes passed. She grew calmer, her brain more clear. She could not just lie there and wait for whatever was going to happen.

She fastened her gaze on the lantern of pierced tin. She might be able to upset it as a means of drawing attention, preventing Renold from drinking, even if at the risk of self-immolation. However, there was no way to reach the lantern without running afoul of Ma Skaggs.

She thought she might, if she were quick, trip the old woman next time she carried a keg into the main room. The crash when she hit the floor should be spectacular; the commotion should attract some notice. It would not be particularly useful, of course, if she herself were crushed by the fall.

The best thing she could do for the moment, it appeared, was to concentrate on her bonds. They were so tight her fingers and toes had no feeling; Ma Skaggs's Clem was an expert at such things, doubtless for good reason. As she worked her wrists back and forth, she searched the room with her eyes at the same time, trying to find some other way to help herself.

Ma Skaggs had not reached her current place on Gallatin Street by being unwary. She gave Angelica no opportunity to trip her, but sidled around her each time she came and went. After the third trip, she carried a keg away and did not return.

The voices from the front room grew louder and more coarse. Now and then a man was ejected into the muddy street for buying no more than a single drink. Frequent fights broke out with the patrons shouting encouragement that consisted of helpful recommendations such as "Bite off 'is ear, Jack!" or "Yank out 'is other eye!" Two women fell to pulling hair and bets were placed on the outcome. On three separate occasions, the Skaggs brothers dragged unconscious men into the back room where they relieved them of their valuables before taking them out a rear door into the alley. The last time they stayed longer than before. There came from that direction the sound of a strangled cry, suddenly cut off, before the brothers returned, passing through to the front room again. While the two men were near, Angelica pretended unconsciousness until all was quiet again and she could renew her frantic efforts to release herself.

Her ankles grew raw and her wrists wet with blood and the fluid of broken blisters. Her back ached from lying on the hard floor. Strangely enough, the pain in her head faded away, vanquished, perhaps, by anger and concentration. Her spirits were flagging, however. The barrelhouse was such a den of corruption she could not see how she was ever to escape it. More, she was beginning to think that Renold's appearance had been a fluke after all, or else she had imagined his voice out of the fervor of her need.

Lying there in the dimness and the stench, Angelica recognized that she had fully expected he would rescue her as he had before. She knew, too, that she longed to see him, to hear his voice ringing in humor and anger, in desire and persuasion. She wanted to be held close by him, to feel shielded and secure once more. He had in such a short time made her a part of his world, had come close to filling hers. It was startling to realize how close.

Light slashed into the room. With it came the forms of three men. Two were burly and upright while the third sagged between them, head hanging, feet barely moving. He wore the impeccable clothing of a gentleman, though he was minus his hat. The dark waves of his hair hung forward over his forehead, trailing across his closed eyelids.

Renold. Unconscious.

Angelica smothered a cry of dismay. At the same time, she shut her eyes to the barest slits and lay perfectly still.

The two Skaggs brothers kicked the door shut and flung Renold to the floor not far from Angelica. Crouching over him, they rifled through his pockets, taking purse and watch, gold chain and signet fob. Silent, efficient, they stripped away coat and waistcoat and flung them on the pile against the wall. They stooped to take hold of his boots, smearing fingerprints on the polished leather.

"Clem! Danny! Gent's here!"

The screeching yell came from the front room. It was Ma Skaggs summoning her sons, perhaps to make sure they would be paid for Angelica.

The older brother known as Clem gave the man on the floor a rough kick and waited to see if he would move. When he remained inert, they exchanged a low rumble of comment that Angelica did not quite catch. Swinging around, they plunged from the room.

Angelica waited a few minutes, fearful the two might return. She then dragged herself across the planks to where Renold lay. She raised above him on her braced arms, but could not free her hands to touch him or search for a heart-beat. Hovering over his face, she lowered her cheek near his mouth to see if she could feel his breathing.

Abruptly, his warm lips pressed the soft contour. In a single swift movement, he caught her shoulders and rolled with her, ending on his elbows above her as she lay on her back. His eyes in the dim light were bright with drink, large-pupiled, and frenetic with laughter. "*Damnable* jade," he said with great cheer, "all worried care and with tangles in your hair. What in the name of heaven do I have to do to keep you out of trouble?"

The sound she made was indignant, if somewhat muffled. It would not have been particularly coherent even if plainer. The hard length of his body was pressed against her from breasts to ankles. He was not especially incapacitated by the liquor he had taken; there was an extraordinary firmness nudging like a wedge at the line of her closed thighs.

"Well, yes, I know you may be a bit overwrought," he said as if she had made perfect sense. "And you're right, I might have found you sooner. Only I didn't feel capable of taking on all of Gallatin Street single-handedly, and there seems to be some difficulty with the arrival of reinforcements."

Drunk. Not profoundly so, but enough to be loquacious and confiding and inclined to recklessness. Enough to account for the caress in his voice. She did her best to make him understand that it was urgent that her gag be removed.

He gave her a considering glance as he levered his weight from her, then began to work at the knots at her wrists. "Speech," he said, "can be a blessing or a curse. I'm not sure how far your voice travels, or what kind of maledictions you may call down upon my head."

She begged him with her eyes because it mattered so much. She gasped with relief, coughing, as he pulled the noxious gag from her mouth. Ignoring his abrupt oath caused by the nature of that rag, she said, "How many drinks did you have?"

"Three more than I wanted, two more than I needed, one more than I dared. How many is that?"

"Don't be so glib," she snapped. "There were—"

"Knockout drops in them. I know. So the faster I can get out of here and rid myself of what passed as liquor but tasted like cow—anyway." His smile was crooked. "It would not improve your current condition to have me throw up in front of you, but I well might if I am forced to think—God, the stupid bastards!"

There was more, all of it lurid, inventive, and specifically accurate. He was holding her wrists with their bruised and swollen flesh smeared with blood. She said in abrupt embarrassment, "Never mind, I did it myself. We have to get out of here."

"If you managed to truss yourself up that tightly one-handed, you have unheralded talents," he said, his gaze suddenly hooded as he began to release her ankles. "The question that exercises my curiosity is why you tried so hard to get free."

"There is a man coming, the man who paid to have me—stolen."

"And you were afraid you would miss him? Is he worth mutilating yourself over, or did you do it to earn his sighs?"

"I did it because I heard you out there and knew you were drinking yourself insensible," she said in a heady rush of anger. "I had the odd idea that it might be a good thing to stop you. I failed, but that's no reason to suppose I am now all a-twitter at being sold to a stranger. I think he's here now, but if you could hurry just a little, we might avoid him and the others. Unless you would enjoy being sat upon by Ma Skaggs."

"The mind boggles," he said as he unwound the last of the rope from her ankles and dragged her to her feet. "Do you really think she would?"

"She would adore to," Angelica said, and stopped, gasping, as she found she could not stand.

"Not as much as I'll enjoy this," he replied, and scooped her up in his arms.

She grabbed for his neck, holding tightly as he stood with his legs spread for balance and his arms slowly tightening around her. She looked into his eyes, and saw such insouciance and undisguised pleasure that it curled the edges of her heart. Then he swung with her, striding toward the store-room's back wall.

The door to the alley, barred from the inside, was easily opened, though the hinges squealed in protest. Renold paused, listening. After a moment, he shouldered out into the dark. There he paused once more, quartering the night and the confined space with his eyes. Nothing moved. He stepped out along the alley toward the noise and light of the cross street a short distance away.

He stopped again almost at once. A soft exclamation left him.

Angelica was deposited against the wall of the building, placed on her feet to lean there. She watched as Renold moved into the deeper shadow beside the wall.

"Open the door," he said in soft command over his shoulder.

She stretched out one arm to do as he asked. Her fingertips barely reached the door panel; still she pried it open. Light spilled in pale yellow gleams into the alleyway.

She turned back toward Renold, then drew in her breath.

In the dim illumination, she could just make out the body of a man with a black-red blotch of drying blood on his throat. As Renold shifted out of the light, going to one knee to feel for a pulse, she realized she knew the dead man. It was the mouselike creature who had come to the townhouse to see Renold, the same one who had followed her and Deborah at the market.

The noises in the alley. She must have heard the man being killed. A shudder moved over her at the thought, gripping at the back of her neck.

"So much for reinforcements," Renold said, the soft words barely stirring the air.

"He worked for you," she said in the same barely audible tone.

"Among others."

"Surely you weren't depending on him alone?"

"He was to bring help. They must have broke and run at the first sign of trouble—if they came at all. My fault. I should not have rushed the job."

She heard the guilt in his voice. "You could not have known what would happen."

"I should have."

The words were curt and carried dismissal. Rising with decisive swiftness, he swung in her direction.

"I think I can walk now," she said in objection.

He might not have heard. Moving closer, he bent as if to take her in his arms once more.

The three men came from the cross street, turning the corner into the dark alleyway. Two were broad and heavy, looking like giants with the light behind them throwing their shadows into the alleyway. The other was more slender, with the swirl of a cape around his silhouette. Catching sight of movement, they stopped.

There was time for Renold to steady Angelica against the wall once more. He stepped apart, then, facing the men, drawing the attack away from her.

"Here now, what's going—you!"

There was shock and wariness in the rough voice. Clem Skaggs, the man in the lead, dragged a knife from his belt, at the same time motioning his brother to swing wide to come up behind Renold. The younger brother did as he was told, sidling along the wall of the next building. The third man drew back into the shadows, waiting.

Renold and Clem circled each other, crouched and with hands held wide, ready to defend. As Renold moved into the light, it could be seen that his hands were empty.

"How now, buck," Skaggs said in harsh triumph. "This time we'll see how you do without that fancy sword of yours."

Hard on the words, he lunged. The knife he held whipped through the air with a sibilant rush. Renold leaped aside. The big man cursed, then growled at his brother who was creeping close enough to join in. "I got him. You watch the girl."

The other man hesitated, but stepped back out of the field.

"You're very sure of yourself," Renold said in tones of contempt as his gaze clashed with that of the riverman. "You just may need someone to back you."

Skaggs let out a belly laugh. "Lord, man, I'm half bear and the son of an alligator. I can howl like a dog and run with the wolves, and I'm champeen on the river with a knife."

"But you are afraid of your mother," Renold said, cutting off the typical riverman's boast with sarcastic brevity.

The other man cursed and swung, a clumsy move fueled by anger. Untouched, Renold drifted away like smoke before swirling into a new defensive posture.

Now the purple of rage congested the riverman's face. His style of fighting was without finesse, relying on bluff and might and animal ferocity. Yet he was dangerous in his power there in the narrow space between the buildings. There was a limit to how many times Renold could avoid the crude blade in his hand.

Angelica, standing with wide eyes and her fingertips stopping her mouth, could feel the roughness of the wall biting into her back. Hot horror curled in her mind. She did not want to watch, yet could not look away. Her stomach contracted with every plunging attack, every move Renold made counter to it. At the same time, she was aware that the second man had edged around to the wall where she stood.

Renold, retreating in smooth coordination, spared no more

than a flickering glance for Angelica and the man closing in on her. His concentration was reserved for the knife point that dipped and swayed and drove toward his vitals. Instinct sharpened to a razor edge, he watched for an opening, a weakness, a moment of inattention.

Skaggs was forcing Renold farther down the alley. The riverman's teeth gleamed with his brutish grin and sweat ran in runnels down his face. His breathing was a harsh rasp in the enclosed space.

Then a flash of low cunning twisted the riverman's face. He swiped at Renold again in a bull-like rush. As Renold leaped back, the big man feinted, then tossed his knife to his left hand in a dull gleam of honed steel. Striking backhanded, grunting with effort, he put the entire force of his huge body into a roundhouse cut.

Renold should have been caught on the wrong foot, unable to avoid the blow. He wasn't there. Clem Skaggs could not stop his hard swing. Renold stepped behind its arc, caught the man's knife hand in a grinding hold. They swayed, grunting. Then with an abrupt, wrenching effort, Renold brought Skaggs's arm down across his knee. There came the sickening sound of breaking bone. The knife went flying. Clem Skaggs gave a hoarse scream and fell to his knees with his arm dangling.

His brother whipped around. The flung knife spun to a stop near his feet. He sprang to snatch it up. Arms spread, he faced Renold. Then in a sudden about-face, he swung on Angelica, reaching for her. His grime-encrusted hand closed on the front of her nightgown.

Renold did not hesitate, but bent in a single smooth movement to sweep his hand along the top of his boot. He came up fast with a gambler's silver-chased pocket pistol glittering in his fist.

The small firearm boomed out, drilling red-gold fire across the alley. Skaggs gave a hoarse yell as he was flung backward. Falling in an ungainly sprawl, he lay with red spreading over the dirty white of his shirt front.

Immediately, Renold swung toward the third man. No

more than a gray shadow, he swung around in a billow of his cape to slide into the night, disappearing around the corner.

Renold looked to Angelica. His face was pale, with a white line around his mouth. "Let's go home," he said.

Twelve

THE TOWNHOUSE BLAZED WITH LIGHTS AS RENOLD AND Angelica approached. Angelica's absence had been discovered, the alarm given. The house servants were up and standing in hushed groups in the courtyard. Their outcry as they saw their master and his wife brought Estelle and Deborah hurrying onto the gallery.

Tit Jean was not there. He had sent runners in every direction in search of Renold, and was himself out looking for him. Estelle was nearly incoherent in her relief at seeing them safely returned, though she was horrified at Angelica's scrapes and bruises. Deborah, eyes sharp, demanded to know where they had been and what had happened.

Renold had no time for explanations. Handing Angelica over to the two women, he shut himself into his dressing room where he was extremely, if usefully, sick.

It was not going to be enough. He had never been quite so completely drunk or drugged to near insensibility in his misbegotten life. Careless hilarity waned in his veins with an overwhelming need to lie down somewhere and sleep like a dog. He could give in to neither, but had to keep moving, force himself to think, to plan. There was too much to be done.

If he had been more in control there in the alley, he might not have killed the younger Skaggs brother. To risk leaving him alive and able to follow after them was something he could not afford at that particular moment. Besides, the man had been about to put his filthy hands on Angelica.

There had been that other one, the man who had paid to have Angelica taken. He had retreated, a more cowardly move than expected. Most fathers would have fought to prevent leaving a beloved daughter in the hands of an enemy.

His hands. God help him.

He could not afford to think of Angelica as she had been, bound and helpless, in that back room. He would not remember the feel of her in his arms and the degrading need to take her while she was grateful to him, while she might not, could not, resist.

No.

No. But neither was anyone going to take Angelica from him.

Reeling from the dressing room, he struck the door, then clung to it, breathing in harsh gasps. He put a hand to his face, fighting the disorientation, the hovering stupor. His fingertips were slippery with the sweat seeping from his hair. A violent shudder rattled his skeleton and made his teeth chatter. He clenched his jaw, bracing against it.

It passed. Somewhat. Enough that he noticed voices coming from the courtyard. He pushed erect, swaying until he found his balance. Fastening his gaze on the French doors to the gallery as a goal, he made toward them.

Tit Jean had returned. He was there below, surrounded by a half-dozen people, all trying to give him the news that he might end his search, that the lost were found.

Matters could now proceed. Renold summoned purpose and authority, injected it into his voice as he called out to the manservant:

"Yes, maître?" Tit Jean's voice, mellow, concerned, obliging, floated up to him out of the dimness.

"Pack," Renold commanded. "With all speed. We leave for Bonheur within the hour."

At Tit Jean's side, another face swam into view. Michel. No doubt he had been alarmed enough to join in the search when Tit Jean came to him for news. He looked as if he had dressed hurriedly, leaving his hair in a tangle of rough curls and merely wrapping his cravat twice around his throat.

Hands on his hips, his friend called up to him, "Bonheur, Renold? Have you given this serious thought?"

"Not a great deal," Renold answered, his voice wavering as he was shaken by a sudden, helpless laugh. "It doesn't matter. The alternative is—unacceptable."

"I see," Michel said, and perhaps he did. He went on, "If you must go, can you bear to have company?"

Renold felt an odd coolness brush the back of his neck. Shivering with it, he said, "You have also discovered an urgent need to be gone from New Orleans?"

"I only thought you might have need of companionship in your exile," he answered.

The look on the other man's face was sincere, and only a little cajoling. Renold wavered while his thoughts moved with something less than their usual precision.

Another figure separated itself from the group in the shadows. Deborah's clear tones assailed him. "If you insist on this ill-considered course," she said with some acerbity, "then you may as well have as much support as possible, not to mention the extra right arm."

"Pleading his case for him, chère?" Renold said in carrying tones. "It doesn't seem like you."

His half sister put her hands on her hips. "I would be less inclined to increase our forces if you appeared more able."

"Flattering," he answered after no more than an instant. "Also amazing evidence of forethought. One would almost think you care."

"I care about Angelica and what she has been through, both tonight and all the other nights with you."

He tilted his head. "She has been complaining?"

"Not at all," came the short reply. "She is as private in her way as you are in yours, dear brother. But I don't have to hear her complaints in order to understand how she must feel."

"Your fellow feeling, then, leads you to think she requires Michel in her entourage. But for what purpose? To prevent her recapture by kidnappers, or to protect her from me?"

"You are her husband; it's your job to protect her," Deborah said. "However, Michel may be required to protect you from her when she discovers what you have done."

"Yes, I take your point," he agreed in haste, then added, "Where is she now?"

"Taking a bath in the kitchen. She felt the need, and couldn't wait for it to be brought to her dressing room."

She had felt the need because she had been mauled and handled and left trussed up in a barrelhouse like some sordid parcel without worth. Who could blame her for wanting to remove the stench of it? He had a strong urge in that direction himself, and would attend to it when time permitted.

Coming to an abrupt decision, he said to Michel, "There is something in what Deborah says. The upriver steamer leaves at dawn. We will be on it with or without you."

"Fair enough," Michel said, his face creasing in a grin as he began to back toward the courtyard gate. "I'll see you at the wharf."

Renold lifted a hand in acknowledgment. The moment the gate clanged behind his friend, he swung back toward those waiting below. His voice quiet, yet with the sting of a rebuke, he said, "Well? Is there nothing any of you can do to make ready for departure? Or do you require detailed instructions?"

They scattered.

Renold stood where he was with his hands clamped on the railing. Listening to the receding scuffle of footsteps and murmuring voices, he arranged in his mind the various tasks he would need to see completed before the night was over. The first of these was to inform Angelica of their departure. It was not a task he relished.

Finding exact words, however, much less convenient excuses, proved unnecessary. Angelica emerged from the kitchen a few seconds later. With her hair trailing in wet, wheat gold strands down her back and her dressing sacque pulled around her, she paused to stare up at him.

As he drew breath to speak, she shook her head so that water sprayed from the dripping ends of her hair in silver droplets. "Never mind, I heard," she said in clear, bell-like tones. "Wait there. I'll come up to you."

It was odd, and oddly affecting, to be the recipient of her concern. If he had been more himself, he might have assessed the difference. As it was, he could only seek to minimize the disturbance it caused inside him.

He was waiting inside the bedchamber when she came through the door. His trenchant glance at Estelle, who followed, was enough to recall to her the many tasks she must accomplish elsewhere. Muttering something about clothing left in the laundry, the maid whirled and went away, closing Angelica in with him.

"You have no objection to leaving here?" he said abruptly.

The look in her eyes was speculative. "I don't know, I haven't considered. But what of you? This is your home."

She considered Bonheur as her property, and why should she not? Hadn't he kept all other knowledge from her? His thought processes were so muddled, however, that the adjustment to her manner of thinking was an effort.

He said, "I am at home anywhere. I believe it will be better for you at the plantation. Certainly there will be less disarrangement."

"I suppose that's as good a description as any for what happened," she said with a wan smile. "Regardless, I will admit I'm surprised. I would have expected you to stay in order to go after whoever is behind it."

"Brandishing a sword and dire threats? I might, if there was only my own safety and convenience to consider. It's different with you involved."

She looked away from him, hesitating before she said, "Why am I in it at all? Can you tell me that? Is there someone who has a grudge against you and might consider that you could be reached through me? Or am I an obstacle in some other way I can't begin to guess?"

He felt a burning constriction inside his chest as he recognized the source of her second suggestion. What had he done that she could entertain the notion he was behind her abduction? Why should such a thing occur to her?

He said with considerable force, "I am capable of many

things, but hiring waterfront scum to dispose of my obligations is not one of them."

"I'm sorry," she said as a flush flared across her cheek bones. "I only, that is, you—"

"I treated you with some violence and a complete lack of the respect due a lady, which makes you consider that I might have a tendency to murder."

"You have been saddled with me against your will when you thought, perhaps, that I would die and leave you as you were before I accosted you on the *Queen Kathleen*."

"Now that is an appealing conceit, but we both know who accosted whom. Moreover, you should understand by now that I do nothing against my will. I thought I had made it clear that you are here because of the strength of my desire to have you near me. Why in the name of God's holy hell should I act contrary to my own interests?"

"I don't know, but Ma Skaggs said—"

"Tell me," he demanded as she paused, then listened carefully as she complied. He watched her face, analyzed the quiet timbre of her voice, but could discern nothing to show that she realized her abduction might have been planned as a rescue.

Shrugging when she finished, he said, "As flattering as it may be, the description of the man who paid to have you brought to him is hardly exact or meaningful. To an old harridan like that, any well-spoken man of reasonable cleanliness would have to appear a paragon."

"Yes, I suppose." She lifted a hand, running her fingers through the long, wet strands of her hair. Encountering a mass of tangles, she frowned a little as she worked through it.

"Allow me," he said, stepping to the dressing table and picking up the hairbrush that lay there. At the same time, he indicated the stool before the mirror.

Her manner took on a certain wariness. "I'm sure you have other things to do, if we are to leave so soon."

"It's being taken care of." That was true only up to a point, but there was no reason to admit it.

She sent a doubtful glance toward the stool. As he remained politely adamant, she moved to settle upon it. He stepped behind her, gathering the long silken weight of her hair in his hands, lifting it free from where it clung to her dressing sacque. It had begun to dry, but was cool and damp to the touch. With care and attention, he chose a section and began to ply the brush on the ends, working upward.

In drawing her hair away from her face, he uncovered the dark shadow of a bruise along her jaw. He paused, his gaze lifting to its reflection in the mirror before them. It was necessary to control his sudden rage before he said, "Estelle saw to your wrists and ankles for you?"

"She applied some kind of salve. It smells of carbolic and something else not exactly medicinal."

"Or pleasant?" he suggested. "I thought I recognized it. Contrary to what you might think, it helps."

"I never doubted it," she said with a wry smile.

He contemplated the curve of her mouth while he worked at a snarl with more delicacy than effect. From there, his gaze drifted to the shadows under her eyes. Abruptly, he said, "I apologize for not allowing you to rest before we go. But you are not to disturb yourself, all will be taken care of for you. You should be able to sleep once we are on the steamboat."

"You think so?" she murmured without meeting his gaze.

"The journey upriver will take some time. From what I know of the plantation, we should not arrive for something more than twenty-four hours."

She looked at him, then away again. "I don't know that I can even board the boat, much less sleep there. The mere idea of it makes me feel—peculiar, as if I can't get my breath."

"As if you were drowning?" he said, narrowing his eyes.

"Something like that. It may seem foolish, but I would so much rather stay here."

"It's a natural fear, perhaps, but will pass. You'll be fine once you are in your stateroom and we get under way."

There was a skeptical lift to her brow, though she made no direct answer. After a moment, her expression turned thoughtful and a little sad. In husky tones, she said, "I'll be glad to see Bonheur. It meant so much to my father to own the place; he had such plans for it, and for living there."

"Did he?" That comment was the most he could manage.

"It was supposed to be my security when he was gone. I think, too, that he enjoyed the thought of leaving something behind for his grandchildren, and their children after them. He so wanted to see them before he—"

As she stopped, her voice closed off by grief, compunction moved over Renold. He said, "He must have cared a great deal for his daughter."

She tried to smile as she wiped at the moisture under her eyes with the edge of her hand. "All he wanted was to see me settled and happy, to know that I needed for nothing and had a firm and proper place in life."

"There was some mention, I think, of a grand wedding." The tangles had melted away under his slow strokes. Her hair lay like a shining shawl across her shoulders and down her back. A few contrary and shining filaments clung to his fingers, however, as if permanently attached.

"Oh, he intended to make a great to-do about the affair, but it wasn't because he cared for it. Rather, he wanted to get off on the right foot with his neighbors."

"Now everything is different," Renold said softly. The words tasted bitter in his mouth because they were so false. She was in pain because of the loss of her father, pain he could banish if he would. Guilt was not an emotion with which he was familiar. He accepted it now with grim recognition.

"Yes," she whispered, then sent a quick look at him in the mirror before lowering her lashes and reaching to adjust the position of a jar of hand pomade which did not need it. "He would have approved of you as a son-in-law, I think. You are very like him in many ways."

Both the shock of the suggestion and the impulse to repudiate it had to be suppressed. Renold's voice was still rigid with the effort as he said, "In what particular can that be—unless you mean that we are both not quite reputable?"

A frown creased her brow, but her voice was even as she said, "My father cared very little for what other people thought and was ready to risk everything for what he wanted. His intelligence was fearsome, and he had an affinity for words and phrases which said more than was readily obvious."

Careful, careful, he told himself, even as he felt his conceit expand. To counteract the unwanted gratification, he said, "And he had the devoted love of his daughter."

"Yes, of course," she said, then stopped, her gaze flashing up to meet his again. She went pale as she saw where her answer could lead her if he so desired.

The temptation was overwhelming. Perhaps for that very reason, it had to be resisted. He said, "Unlike his son-in-law."

It was a release for her from her fear, even against his best interests and best judgment. He gave it because he did not have the nerve to force the thing to its natural conclusion. He lacked the nerve because he feared that she would say, plainly and without hesitation, that she did not love her husband. Without waiting for a reply, he leaned to place the brush he held on the table before her, aligning it precisely with her comb and mirror. "I will send Estelle to help you dress."

He had nearly reached the door before her answer came with a soft sigh. "Yes."

The need to turn back, to demand which of his three comments she might possibly be answering, was almost more than he could bear. Logic insisted that it must be, had to be, the last, yet he was in no condition or mood to be logical. It was, perhaps, a good thing that time was pressing and imperative duties awaited him. Forcing himself to continue walking, he let himself out of the room and closed the door quietly behind him.

Dawn hung like a gray shroud over the city when they reached the wharf. There was the glow of lanterns up and down the water's edge, either hanging from docking poles or gleaming from the decks and windows of the steamers pulled up to the levee. Most of the boats wallowing in the river's wash were quiet, with gangplanks up and guards posted. It made the activity around the *General Quitman* seem noisy and even frantic.

Angelica, glancing at the boat as she was handed down from the carriage, felt a shiver run down her spine. It almost seemed she could smell scalding steam and hot metal, could hear the crackle of flames and screams of women and children. Perspiration garnered across her upper lip. Her hand in Renold's grasp felt clammy, and it was a moment before she could force herself to release him.

"Are you all right?" he said, his gaze resting on her face with concern.

She gave a brief nod. She would not complain. She had voiced her objection without avail, and now it was too late to turn back. Besides, she was tired of being weak and sickly and having allowances made for her. Her apprehensions were the result of overwrought sensibilities, that was all. She would conquer them.

The distraction of a light carriage rattling up to the dock was welcome. It was Michel who piled out of it and came toward them while his manservant and driver began setting down bags and boxes. He was greeted with a sally by Deborah on the amount of his baggage. Renold, dealing with the unloading of his own party's luggage from the dray which had brought it, merely gave him a salute. Still, the general atmosphere of the departure became lighter.

The trunks and bags were carried on board. Up the gangplank after them went the boxes containing spices, oils, and wines to enliven the plantation table, the linens and pillows and fine soaps for making up the staterooms, the bolts of cloth and ribbon Deborah had purchased from the drapers, and various other crates of goods. Attended by Estelle, Angelica stood talking with Deborah and Michel while Renold went aboard with Tit Jean to see that everything was stowed away and the paperwork was in order.

At last the smoke drifting in a gray pall from the *General Quitman*'s smokestacks turned black and was shot with sparks. The deckhands gathered at the gangplank, ready to hoist it aboard.

"Well, ladies," Michel said with a whimsical smile and a brief gesture toward the vessel, "Shall we?"

"I expect we had better," Deborah said, "before Renold decides we have deserted him."

"Permit me, then." Michel offered an arm to Renold's half sister. As she took it, he extended his other elbow toward Angelica.

She wanted to accept Michel's laughing escort, to make some gay quip and march up the gangplank with the others. She wanted to be sensible and brave.

It wasn't possible. She just couldn't do it.

Her knees felt as if they might give way if she took a single step. Her hands were shaking and her stomach uneasy. She issued firm mental orders to herself to move, to behave, to stop acting like a senseless ninny. Her body paid no attention.

"Angelica, what's the matter?" Deborah said with a look of sharp concern.

"I-I can't go," she whispered, her voice jerking in the middle. "All I can think of is the last time, the explosion. I don't know why I feel like this, I wish I didn't. I wish—"

Deborah, her eyes dark with sympathy, broke in. "Oh, I should have realized! I'm so sorry, *chère*; I wasn't thinking. Would it help, do you suppose, if I held your hand?"

Angelica gave a quick shake of her head that turned into a shudder. "Nothing will help. No. I can't do it. I really can't."

"But we can't leave you here," Deborah said with a worried frown toward the steamboat where the deckhands were untying the gangplank ropes. "Everything is ready; it's too late to take our things off." Suddenly her voice changed, becoming silvery with relief. "Oh, good. Here is Renold."

"I hesitate to interrupt the party," he said, "but it's time to go. River pilots wait for no man, or woman, when the mood is on them."

"Don't be ridiculous," Deborah said with a sharp look at her brother's flushed face. "Angelica is frightened, as any one would be after such a harrowing accident. Tending to your wife will be much more useful at the moment than chiding us as if we were children."

"When did you become her protector, *chère*?" Renold said with a crooked smile. "Never mind, I expect she has need." He turned from his sister toward Angelica. "Do you?"

"No," she answered, hardly knowing to what she replied.

"Please, couldn't we go back to the townhouse? The pilot will wait for you to unload our things."

"Your faith in my influence is touching, but misplaced," he said, his eyes keen on her face. "What is this? Perhaps a sudden premonition of disaster? Or have you suddenly realized that we will be duplicating the circumstances, incendiary as they might have been, of our first meeting?"

"Don't!" she cried, her nerves rasped by the mockery in his voice with its gently slurred consonants. "I just don't want to go!"

His voice soft, he said, "Not even if I ask it? Or can it be because I ask it?"

"It has nothing to do with you or the way we met," she said, the words tumbling out as if shaken from her by her shuddering. "The thought of being shut up inside, of steaming away upriver, makes me feel sick. I think—I think I'll die if I have to endure it."

"Overemotional," he said, "and highly unlikely." He took a step toward her with purpose in it, and the hint of a threat.

Estelle stepped forward then, a deep frown between her dark eyes. "Maître, if you will permit, perhaps I could give her a calming draught?"

"No time," he said, his gaze so forbidding the housekeeper blinked. With a panther's grace, he moved closer to Angelica.

"You have to believe me," she cried, panic and tears rising in her eyes as she backed away from him. "I can't do it!"

"You must," he said, "because the penalty for going back is the same as for going forward. Caught between two devils, which do you choose?"

She knew the answer, but that did not mean acceptance. A sharp denial rose in her throat, but it was too late.

"The devil you know," he said, his voice soft and his eyes a bright, daring green. Immediately, he swooped upon her and caught her high in his arms.

Her scream was thin, instantly extinguished by her own disbelieving horror. Rigid with shock and dread, she sank her fingers into his coat, snagging a wrenching hold on his lapel. She pressed her forehead against the hard line of his jaw and squeezed her eyes shut so tightly she felt the prickle of her own long lashes against her eyelids.

The gangplank swayed under them, the deck seemed to dance and swing around them. The main cabin was cavernous and filled with people, all exclaiming, whispering. The iron hold of Renold's arms was painfully tight, yet he was her only security in a formless world of terror. Her breath was rough-edged, tearing in her chest, sawing at her throat. The shivering that wrenched through her in violent waves clattered her teeth together so that she could taste blood where she had bitten her tongue.

Hide, she wanted to hide, needed darkness and oblivion, and something, anything, to stop the pain of betrayal. She had thought Renold of all people must understand. He had been there. He had known, had felt the fire. He was part and parcel of her nightmare, yet her refuge from it. How could he push her back into it and hold her there with his hard arms?

The slam of the stateroom door was muffled and far away, yet it reverberated through her mind. The strides he took to reach the bed were uneven, almost staggering. She felt the soft mattress come up to meet her back. Crying, she twisted away, but he landed beside her in a hard jounce of the bed ropes.

"Don't, don't," he said in a low supplication as he reached to drag her close. "I didn't know, was too busy to see. God, I-I am as drunk as a politico and only a step away from comatose. Drive and necessity blinded me, but are no excuse. Another time, any other time, I would have known, seen. Curse me, hit me, but don't cry. Please don't cry."

His remorse pierced her despair, sundered her self-absorption. She was not the only one in pain, not the only one lost in a fog of confusion. And if he was less than himself, then for whose sake had he drunk the rotgut whiskey that made him so?

The resistance left her muscles. With a small, convulsive movement, she flung herself against him, offering comfort as well as taking it.

His hands upon her were gentle; he caught her closer. Their faces touched so that she felt the faint scrape of his beard stubble against her cheek.

The steam engine rumbled, began to hiss and thump into movement. With an inarticulate murmur in her throat and her eyes tightly closed, she burrowed nearer Renold's hard, male form. Her lips brushed his chin.

Awareness did not come in an instant, but stole in upon Angelica like the creep of the morning sun through an open window. Her lashes quivered. Stillness and heat suffused her from head to slippered heels. As Renold shifted, getting an arm under him for leverage, she did not draw away. When his lips touched hers, she drew in a deep breath, but remained quiescent, unresisting.

He smelled of soap from the quick bath he had managed and starch from his fresh linen, tasted of the cloves he had chewed to remove the alcohol's vile flavor. Warm, his mouth was warm and silken smooth. There was passion and competence in his kiss and a yearning that went beyond the moment. Against her thigh she felt the hard ridge of his arousal, and an odd pleasure shifted through her that she could stir him to it.

What would it be like to be his wife indeed?

It was not the first time the thought had fluttered through her mind, but it was the only time she did not immediately turn away from it. Embarrassment, doubt, and fear had stopped her before. Now, they hardly seemed to matter beside the urging of the moment.

To be with him always, to be wrapped in his concern, to be cherished and kept safe—what more could she ask? If there were children, she would have someone to hold and to love, someone to love her unconditionally and forever.

It was not so different, really, from the marriage her father had planned for her. Renold might have chosen to keep her with him without her consent, but she could also choose him now, couldn't she? One thing did not prevent the other.

And if she must be initiated into the rites of love, then she might well be in better hands with Renold than she would have been with Laurence. Experience was not necessarily of tremendous value in a lover, but care and consideration, patience and delicacy of touch certainly were. Intelligence might also offer untold advantages.

There was only one way to find out. What, after all, did she have to lose?

Her virginity. Her heart.

Well, yes. But how much were these worth when everything else was gone? How much, when in Renold's arms was the antidote for fear, the cure for loneliness?

A soft sound came from Renold's throat, as though he had been touched by a hot iron, as she relaxed against him and allowed her lips to part. His reaction was instant. His tongue slipped, swirling, into her mouth.

It was a shocking yet heady invasion. She made a soft, startled sound, but did not draw back. Warmth licked somewhere deep inside her, leaping into vivid heat. She shivered with it and reveled in the boldness of her own acceptance. What she was doing seemed so right, so necessary.

He lifted his head to stare down at her. She could see herself reflected in the darkness of his eyes with their too wide pupils. There was soft desperation there also, and something that was almost like pain.

There was no threat, nothing to fear.

As her eyelids drifted closed, his mouth came down on hers once more. She met it, her own lips tingling, ready. As she felt the probe of his tongue, she allowed herself to be enticed to sinuous testing of its velvet and satin, to be drawn into delicate explorations of the rich inner textures and tastes of his mouth. The intimacy was absorbing, fascinating. She savored the incredible pleasure in silent wonder even as she felt the slow expansion of her heart in her chest.

He shifted, placing a hand at the narrow, corseted turn of her waist. An instant later, he slid his grasp higher to cup the soft mound of her breast. His thumb brushed across the nipple under its layers of thin cotton and silk.

A current of exquisite sensation flowed through Angelica, coalescing in the center of her body. She gasped at its deep internal pulsing. A soft sound, like a cross between a laugh and a groan, left him as he caught her soft breath of wonder in his mouth.

The grainy stroking of his tongue over hers made her senses

spin. She slid her arm along his shoulders to his neck, holding tightly. As sensations uncurled, threatening to sweep her into their vortex, she threaded her fingers into his hair at the base of his neck, closing them on the crisp curls.

Once he had kissed her, and the night had erupted in scalding steam and fire. It seemed it might happen again, only this time from within, from between them, because of the terrible internal heat and pressure of their two bodies. She didn't care. Murmuring incoherently, she pressed closer to him, closer to the danger.

"Angelica, my angel and sweet incubus, take care," he said, bracing his forehead against hers as he spoke in husky despair. "My need for you is strong, and restraint isn't possible. What I do now, I may not recall or believe in the morning. Stop me, or it will be too late."

"Stop you? But why?" The words were so soft she was afraid he would not hear. She need not have worried.

"To prevent accusations of strength using unfair advantage over weakness. To preserve the status quo. To guarantee whatever vestige of freedom you might once have claimed, since I hold what I take, keep what is mine."

"Take me then," she whispered. "Keep me." And the essential desire and wanton intent in her words sent such a rush of sensation through her that she caught her breath with it.

His laugh was surprised, but rich with something deeper than mere satisfaction. "Depend on me," he said, and lowered his mouth to tug with his lips at the tight nipple under the material of her dress, making her shiver with the hot wetness of his mouth.

Disoriented, drowning in languor and unimagined urges, Angelica hardly noticed when the buttons of her dress parted from their holes. She felt his hands at her corset and the tapes of her petticoat, but his tongue was abrading hers, and she twined around it, enticing deeper penetration.

She inhaled with the release of the corset's tight clasp, but also with the feel of his hands upon her, soothing the indentations left by whalebones, turning the sweeping movement into an endless caress. Stretching under his touch with the abandon of a kitten, she reached out to tug his coat open and push it from his shoulders. Nimble-fingered, she loosened his cravat and began to slip the studs of his shirt free.

He was still for suspended moments, then he moved to help her. Together, with myriad kisses and growing impatience, they stripped away petticoats, stockings, and slippers; trousers, underdrawers, and half boots, seeking beneath the layers for bare skin. Splendidly naked, they lay enjoying the lack of confinement, and the view.

Angelica looked with unabashed curiosity at the width of his shoulders, the hard planes of his chest and the flat surface of his abdomen, before reaching to thread her fingertips through the fine dark hair that glistened across his breastbone.

He caught his breath on a low laugh and rolled to cover her with his body, allowing her to feel his weight by slow degrees. She took it, reveling in it, needing it with a deep hunger such as she had never dreamed. Her breasts swelled, tingling, to meet the rough surface of his chest. She let her eyes drift shut while she closed her hands upon his shoulders, smoothing their ridged hardness under the mottling of scars, taking their power deep inside her.

She felt so vulnerable with the heat and hardness of him pressing against her softness. At the same time, she had never felt stronger. The desire racing in her veins was a glory she could not contain, one she wanted to share. The need was overflowing inside her, filling her, mounting to her head with a passion so acute it might, if she were not careful, be mistaken for love.

Love. Did she love him? Was it possible?

Or was the physical act between a man and a woman designed to counterfeit that deeper emotion? Was it a sham to trap the unwary into being fruitful and multiplying the species?

Did it matter, while her heart was battering against her ribs and her mouth burned for his kiss? When his hands upon her were seeking the very center of her being and closing it in his gentle hold?

His fingers as he opened the tender folds were careful and not quite steady. His eyes, how dark they were, and shadowed. She could not see what he was doing, but she could feel it.

Yes, she could feel, and the force of it took her breath, caused her to writhe upon that slow and careful penetration while liquid delight overflowed like broached champagne.

He made a sound deep in his throat. Stopped. She felt the sting of his invasion even as he spoke.

"Tight, tender, repelling the impaling as only a virgin can. Why? Why was there no experimenting on some lonely road while driving in the country? No fumbling on the front veranda while your aunt read in the parlor? Why is it left to me?"

"I told you—"

"So you did. So you knew Eddington as a child. Even children are sometimes more forward."

She could hardly think straight with his hand still in place. Her voice was strangled as she said, "I didn't mean to disappoint you."

"Disappoint? A paltry word. I am appalled, incensed. And with these, as fiercely glad as any doubting barbaric chieftain with a stolen bride. But it makes it more difficult."

"Does it? But how?"

"You will hate me more." The words were so soft they barely disturbed the air.

"No, why should I?" she said with something beseeching in her face.

"Some things are less forgivable," he said, even as he pressed deeper, stretching the fragile, offending membrane.

"You are making me afraid again." She turned her head, unable to bear his despairing gaze or his detachment. She was shaking, so finely poised on the edge of some unknown hazard or pleasure that she could hardly bear it.

"It's nothing to my terror," he said.

It was true. There was a fine trembling in his every limb. His hair and the surface of his skin were damp with perspiration. In his eyes was the reflection of lamplight and torment and an inner desolation beyond comprehension.

"Come, then," she whispered, "and let's give each other courage."

He complied. Easing his way with the emollients of care

and intimate caress, he parted the tender folds, introduced his silken hardness to the petal-soft opening. Carefully pressing, he eased deeper. The barrier was reached and breached with hardly a pause. Then she encompassed him, taking his hardness, his throbbing fullness, into her internal heat.

Abandoned, that was how she felt. Transfigured. Incredibly alive. Her heart expanded in her chest, filling it to overflowing. She wanted to laugh, to cry, to jump up and down. Her hands closed upon him in a hold so tight her bones ached, and still it was not enough.

"Am I hurting you?" he whispered.

He was stretching her; she could feel the long length and power of him with every breath he took. But he was not hurting her. She shook her head, a quick, positive movement.

A low laugh shook him. Gathering himself, he began to move in a slow, deliberate rhythm. It rocked her, sounded her, sent the blood surging to her head. She gasped, holding to him. A moment later, she caught the motion and joined it, panting, her skin prickling with sheer, fathomless delight. He bent his head, kissing her forehead, her eyes, tip of her nose before taking her mouth. There he mocked the sensual cadence with his tongue and invited her to do the same.

It was wild grandeur, it was fascination. It was a deep erotic exploration. Time was obliterated; effort had no meaning.

He lowered himself over her, entangling his legs with hers before rolling with her to draw her on top of him. Setting her free, then, he let her take the pace. She shifted, finding comfort, sitting upright. Flinging her hair that had loosened behind her back, she rode him with a gentle rocking.

The pleasure was inside her and outside, within him and between them. It came in waves, and also in a sharp, sudden onslaught. It gripped them, rolled over them, washed them in its wake, before returning with renewed strength.

Effort made their bodies gleam with heat and moisture as they slipped upon each other. Their breaths rasped in their chests. Hot-eyed, they strained, reaching toward a goal neither could bear, quite, to reach.

Merciless magic, white and black, dark and light, Angelica

could feel it rising inside, feel its pressure and force. Her muscles ached, her lungs burned, but she could not quite find its release.

Once more, Renold turned with her, pressing her down into the mattress. She took his deep internal invasion, his surging power.

Escape, abrupt and uncontainable. It was a searing completion, a silent inner eruption that mounted upward like the boiling of live steam. Lost in its power, she let it take her while with sobbing breaths she clung to him. Shuddering, racked by paroxysms that bunched his muscles and arched his back, he pressed her down, down into the glory.

Afterward, they held each other, staring into the lamp's glow with wide, unseeing eyes. Disaster or stupendous success, they did not know which they had found.

Of one thing only were they certain.

They had barely survived it.

Thirteen

"VOILÀ, LE CAFÉ!"

The cheerful greeting woke Angelica from a sleep so deep it was like swimming upward through heavy darkness. Opening her eyes required a considerable effort.

It was Estelle who stood holding the tray with its silver coffeepot and basket of napkin-wrapped rolls. There was a wide smile on her face and a twinkle in her eyes. Placing the tray within reach on the bedside table, the woman bustled around, throwing back the lid of a trunk, drawing out a dressing sacque. She brought the wrap to the bed and leaned to help Angelica slip it around her shoulders as she sat up. And if the maid found it in the least unusual to tend a mistress who was naked under the twisted and rumpled covers, she gave no sign.

Angelica was alone. Renold had gone. She reached out to touch the place where he had lain, but there was no trace of his body heat remaining there.

Estelle looked up from where she stood pouring out a steaming cup of coffee. "The maître has been out and about for some hours. It was he who sent me with your breakfast."

Angelica removed her hand without undue haste. "Is it so late then?"

"Near noon, Mamzelle. But it's a gray day out with drizzling rain, and he would not allow you to be awakened earlier." The maid's lips curved in a faint smile. "He said you had need of rest."

Angelica could feel the flush that worked its way up to her hairline. She said with as much composure as she could manage, "That was considerate."

The maid tilted her head, her round face bland. "Everyone knows you were much upset earlier. They were not surprised."

The purpose of the comment was to prevent embarrassment when she emerged from the stateroom. It was a thoughtful gesture, even if it added to Angelica's discomfort now. With an inarticulate murmur, she took the cup the maid offered and buried her face in it.

The maid moved away back toward the trunk where she fell on her knees and began searching out a gown for Angelica to wear for the day. Over her shoulder, she said, "It is a fine thing you have done. The maître has need of a woman who will be a real wife to him, who will give him children, a family, all the things that make living good."

It had been hopeless, of course, to think that Estelle, and probably Tit Jean also, would not know just how things were between Renold and herself. She said with resignation in her voice, "I can't think why you would say so. He has given no sign of it."

"Men don't always know what they need. The maître has been too much alone in his life. He is like a boat floating empty on the river. He requires an anchor, needs to be tied to someone, to be useful to them, before he can be happy."

Angelica sent a wry smile in Estelle's direction as she leaned her head back on the pillow. "I wish that might be true."

"Only wait, you will see," the maid said comfortably. "So. You are all right about being on board now? You feel well enough to get up?"

Amazingly enough, the constant rumbling and thumping of the engines gave Angelica not a qualm. She was tired, her wrists and ankles were still bruised and sore, and she was aware of some internal tenderness, but she had seldom felt physically better in her life.

"Yes?" Estelle said at her assent "Excellent! Then which will you wear, the blue twill, or the *tan d'or* velvet?"

The rain still fell when Angelica emerged from her

stateroom. She was attired in blue twill, with a small shoulder cape against the dampness and her hair braided and looped and fastened to the crown of her head to defeat the wind on deck. It was her intention to walk on the boiler deck, under the shelter of the Texas deck above, to blow the cobwebs from her brain. If she also wanted to test her courage and new sense of invulnerability to steamboat accidents, it was no one's business except her own.

The boat was buffeted by a light wind that made its course less than arrow-straight and blew the fogging drizzle under the overhang to wet the decks on the windward side. On the lee, it was possible to stand and watch the misty green shoreline ease past. Smoke from the stacks overhead whipped around the deck, tainting the air with its smell. The rain had increased, slanting down to dent the gliding, metallic gray surface of the river like silver arrows striking a great iron battle shield.

"So here's where you are hiding? Are you contemplating jumping, or have you developed a sudden passion for what once repelled you?"

Angelica swung at the soft yet caustic tone. She had intended to be serene and self-possessed when she saw Renold again, giving not the least indication that she remembered the night before and the things they had done. It was impossible.

More, the hidden meaning in what he had just said was enough in itself to discompose her. As with steamboats, she had once been afraid of the physical consequences of marriage. She had also once considered that she might have a cool nature. How very foolish she had been.

She laughed, a throaty, knowing sound she hardly recognized. "No," she said. "And yes, perhaps."

His smile was brief. "I take it you are as well as you look?"

"Shouldn't I be?" The glance from under her lashes was not meant to be provocative. Quite.

"I thought I might have taxed you unduly. It isn't so long since you were injured."

There was a grim, satirical tone in his voice that troubled her. With heightened color, she answered his suggestion rather than his words. "I seem to have taken no harm."

"Then possibly it will be as well if you come and convince the others. They seem to think I am an ogre for carrying you aboard. And they aren't too certain you haven't been confined to your cabin to conceal bodily damage suffered at my hands."

Her eyes widened. "You can't mean it!"

"Can't I?" he said with a twist of his lips. "Those who know a man best are apt to believe the worst calumny of him."

He had exaggerated, perhaps, and yet she was greeted with such cries of relief and gladness that she had to wonder. She was also warmed by them, finding it pleasant to think that she had been missed. It seemed that she might one day gain a sense of belonging again. Renold was not the only one in need of a family.

Yet it was Renold who gave her the least confidence in her prospects for the future. Withdrawn, pensive, he took no part in the exclamations and sympathetic comments that made her welcome. His glance, when it happened to turn in her direction, was as impenetrable as a window glass with darkness behind it; it reflected everything but gave no indication of what lay beyond.

The steamboat *General Quitman* was not the equal of the *Queen Kathleen*. Even if Angelica had not been able to guess as much from the Spartan nature of her stateroom, a brief sojourn in the main cabin would have made it plain. The open room was utilitarian, with simple oak tables and chairs. The overhead lamps had no embellishments of brass or crystal, but were simple globes shielded by red-painted tin. There were no rugs on the unpolished wooden floors, no draperies at the windows. The posts that supported the ceiling down the long length were plain wood cylinders unburdened with ornamentation or even paint.

Among their fellow passengers, the preference for calico and challis for the ladies and short coats, flat-crowned hats, and shapeless trousers of linsey-woolsey for the men marked them as country farmers or small town tradespeople. These travelers kept to themselves, the men lounging in knots of three or four near the well-used spittoons, and the women gathered in family groups where they talked with their heads close together. Their interest in the elegantly turned out members of Renold's party was high, judging from their stares, but it was difficult to make direct eye contact.

The noon meal was heralded by the invasive smell of hot oil and overcooked food. The menu recited by the waiters was simple to remember as it was made up of fried items, from fried chicken and fried ham to fried apple pies for dessert. The beverage served was not wine but whiskey that was brought out without ceremony and slammed down in front of the diners in earthenware jugs. That the fare exactly suited the tastes of the majority of the passengers was evident, for they dug in with flying elbows and clashing forks, scarcely waiting to tuck their napkins under their chins.

The steamboat's captain presided at the head table where Angelica and the others sat. A jovial man of corpulent shape and high color, which suggested he found no fault with the food and drink, his uniform made up for any deficiencies in his boat. Of the finest black broadcloth, it was bedecked with a ludicrous excess of epaulettes, bouillon, stripes, and braiding.

"I see, Madam Harden," the official said, leaning toward her and putting his hand over hers where it lay on the table, "that you do not partake of the fine beverage there before you. Understandable, perhaps, I'll warrant you are not used to spirits. If you would care for it, I can supply you with wine from my private stock."

"You are very kind," Angelica replied, removing her hand from under his grasp before he could quite close it, "but I couldn't put you to that trouble."

"No trouble at all for a lady of your quality. I can't remember when I've had the pleasure of transporting such a fair flower. You must allow me this one gesture."

"Some gestures have unforeseen consequences," Renold said. He did not raise his voice from where he sat at the foot of the table, studying the glass of whiskey in his hand. "I have ordered wine for my wife. My manservant will arrive with it shortly."

The captain reared back in his chair, his face taking on an alarming purple color. "My good man! I intended no impropriety."

"You intended to create an obligation, and therefore a reason for encroaching," came the answer in tones of stinging censure. "You have been prevented. My advice is to let it pass."

"You're a damned unpleasant fellow!" The captain clearly resented the affront to his dignity, but was as yet uncertain what to do about it.

Renold lifted a dangerous gaze. "You have no idea."

"Please," Angelica said, looking from one man to the other. "There is no need for this."

She was given scant attention. The captain's nostrils flared. Scowling heavily at Renold, he said, "I've a good mind to put you off my boat."

"Try," Renold recommended succinctly.

Here and there other diners had raised their heads to listen to the exchange. Anxious to avoid anything that might interest them further, Angelica said, "I'm sure the captain meant no disrespect, nor is he likely to address his gallantries to me under your very eyes."

"Ah, but keeping you under my eyes," Renold said, turning his acerbic gaze in her direction, "is not always easy."

"If you are referring to last night, I am at a loss to see how I could have prevented my absence!"

His gaze rested a moment on her breasts, which rose and fell noticeably with her indignation. He clenched his jaws so that a muscle stood out before he said with biting irony, "Permit me to suggest intelligence and attention to unlocked doors."

Deborah made a small gasping sound. A frown gathered between her fair brows as she stared from Angelica to her half brother. On her far side, Michel tilted his head. "Here, now!" he said. "That's hardly fair, and you know it."

Renold turned his head slowly to meet this new defense. "I know, my friend, that your interest in my darling wife's welfare is only a cut above the captain's. I am giving you the advantage of supposing that at least a small portion of your interference is motivated by sympathy."

"Why should she need sympathy, unless she stands in danger from you?" Michel demanded.

"I thought we had settled that," Renold replied, "or would you care to inspect her for bruises?"

Michel's pleasantly handsome face took on a look of serious affront. "You know—"

"I know that you have the presumption to disapprove of my conduct while knowing full well the reasons and goals. You might remember, however, that my concessions in the name of friendship are not infinite."

Michel made a movement as if he meant to rise. Deborah reached out to touch his wrist below his sleeve with the tips of her fingers. A stillness came over Michel's face, though he did not turn in the direction of Renold's half sister. He was quiet for long seconds while he held Renold's hard gaze. Finally, he said, "We will discuss this later."

"Unproductive and unnecessary," Renold said. "Also unlikely."

Michel's lips tightened, but he made no response. Tit Jean arrived then with two bottles of the wine they had brought with them, a welcome distraction. Her voice brisk, Deborah put a question to Angelica which changed the subject and created some degree of normality. The incident was allowed to pass.

However, the repercussions from it lingered. One direct result was that Michel remained near Angelica's side for the remainder of the afternoon, therefore was nearby when the steamboat stopped at the wood yard. It may also have been responsible for the fact that he offered his escort when she expressed a desire to leave the boat long enough to stretch her legs. Certainly it was in a spirit of leftover defiance that she accepted.

The wood yard was a thriving enterprise, still something less than impressive. Run by a man and his two older sons, it consisted of a four-square log house surrounded by open ground dotted with the stomps of trees felled to stoke the steamboats that passed. The wood, dragged now from farther afield by a pair of skinny oxen, was stacked in long ricks near the bluff above the water. At the cabin's door was a slattern of a woman who sat piecing quilt scraps while keeping an eye on the half dozen ragged children playing in the mud and misting rain.

An air of impermanence hung over the place, showing in the rough door through which daylight must shine when it was closed, the sagging shutters that took the place of window glass, and the absence of such niceties as steps, porches, or curtains. When all the trees within a reasonable distance of the river were gone, the owner of the wood yard would leave also.

The woman in the doorway sat staring at Angelica and Michel as if they were beings from another world. It was not often, perhaps, that someone got off the boat, much less strolled the track leading up from the water. Angelica, nodding in her direction with a brief smile, wondered about the life the woman led, if she was happy in her rough existence or sometimes longed for something better, if she loved her husband or was merely resigned to her lot.

Love. How very strange it was, how hard to recognize, to capture and hold. It was possible to feel it and accept it in any given moment. Yet, short seconds later, anger and hurt could banish the warm generosity and singing heart of loving and leave emptiness in its place.

She had thought she loved Renold last night. She had been so certain that only love could make her feel such wondrous pleasure, that only love could engender the incredible tenderness and ardor she had discovered in her marriage bed. Today, she was plagued with doubt. Was it possible the pain caused by his distance and anger was also a measure of love? It might, but there was no way to be sure of that, either.

Angelica paused to stand huddled into the rain cape she had borrowed from Deborah, looking back down the muddy slope she and Michel had climbed from the river's edge. The deckhands were loading wood at a leisurely pace; there was no great hurry about returning.

Above them, the leaden sky hovered close. The rain spattered with soft, tapping sounds against the cape's hood. It also made her skirts hang limp and heavy so the hem brushed in the mud, though she couldn't bring herself to care.

Beside her, Michel pulled his hat lower over his eyes and adjusted the collar of his coat, which was waterproofed with gutta-percha. The fidgeting was a sign, perhaps, of his discomfort when making remarks of a personal nature, for his tones were gruff when he spoke. "You must not take too much notice of Renold. He has a fiendish tongue on him at times, but he doesn't mean half what he says."

"You think not?" she said with more than a little skepticism.

"I don't mean to suggest that he makes idle threats—far from it." He looked away from her out over the river. "Nevertheless, I think Renold sometimes savages people when the person he's most enraged with is himself."

She gave him a small smile. "You're a very forgiving man."

"Not at all," he said with a shake of his head that sent collected raindrops flying from his hat brim. "In fact, I wanted to smash his face back there at the table." A wry laugh shook him. "Not that it's likely I could unless I caught him off guard. But I'm doing my best to make allowances, first because I know he has the grandfather of all hangovers today, and secondly because I can see his jealousy is eating him alive."

She was unimpressed. "I thought we settled once before that he has no cause where you are concerned."

"He doesn't particularly need a reason, not any more," Michel said flatly. "And it certainly isn't restricted to me, but includes any man who looks your way. Renold isn't sure of you, you see, because he knows—"

"Yes?" she said as he paused. She could not begin to see where what he was saying was leading.

"Well, the way the two of you met wasn't exactly the usual thing, was it? Oh, it was dramatic and all that, but he took advantage in his regular high-handed fashion, and now—well, now he can't be sure you want to be with him."

"No more can I be sure he wants me."

"Yes, but that's different, you're a woman. Naturally you expected to marry where you were directed, and for reasons having more to do with financial and social standing than affection."

She gave him a blank stare. "I don't know that I expected that at all."

"It's the way things are done," he said pityingly, as if that answered everything. "Anyway, you can assume as a female that Renold wanted you, otherwise he wouldn't have gone to so much trouble."

"It isn't the same," she said in low tones.

He gave her a quick, considering glance. "Perhaps not. But the thing is, Renold knows that he has done wrong, and he can't be easy in his mind until he is more certain that he has a firm hold on you."

The words he had used were unfortunate, the result of nervousness, she thought. Regardless, they sent a chill along her spine. Was the reason Renold had come after her in the barrelhouse merely because he meant to hold what he had gained? Had he established his husbandly rights now, after being so patient before, merely because he thought it would be easier to retain his grasp on her? Had he used the power he could gain over her with his skill in bed to control her? Was he, with his gardens and gifts and kisses, trying to make her love him?

Michel, his gaze on her face, said, "I've upset you and that is not what I thought to do at all. I'm sorry."

"Don't be," she said tightly, "it isn't your fault. I just don't understand him."

"Nor do I, exactly, and I've known him far longer." Michel paused. "I think a lot of it has to do with Clotilde and what she did to him."

"Jilting him for a man with more money?"

"The money wasn't as important to her as the family name, the social position—all the things Renold could never change. But that wasn't the worst of it. There was also his son."

"Yes, I saw him. She made sure of it."

Michel's lips tightened. "She does love to twist the knife. She knows, you see, how much ties of blood mean to Renold. She keeps that boy away from him deliberately, yet flaunts him in front of him, taunts him with being the father. She does it to punish Renold because he wouldn't play her aristocratic game of love outside marriage. She took his son from him and he hasn't forgiven her for it. He won't, ever."

"He is not a forgiving man…"

Angelica said, "So he doesn't trust women."

"He can't. He has been betrayed too many times, beginning with his mother."

"His mother?"

His gaze was doubtful. "You know about his birth?"

"That he is illegitimate? Yes, he told me."

"Did he also tell you that his mother loved him extravagantly, until she met his stepfather, who was rich and respectable? Afterward, she loved Renold no less, but he was an embarrassment to her, a constant reminder that she would never be as respectable as her neighbors."

Angelica shook her head. "I wondered why he never spoke of her, or visited."

"Oh, there is no estrangement, if that's what you're thinking," Michel said without quite meeting her eyes. "The lady never tried to hide him away or deny him. Regardless, I think she was relieved when he left to establish his own household in New Orleans. He knew it. It hurt."

"I think I see," she said slowly, then gave the man beside her a straight look. "You are a good friend to be so concerned."

"Not just for Renold," he said simply as a flush darkened his olive skin. He glanced down at his boots, then out at the river once more. "Yes, well, all I wanted was to let you know that it wasn't anything you did that set Renold off at luncheon. It was just—everything."

She looked away across the sodden land and the ugly, decapitated tree stumps, considering the things he had said while the chill of the day seeped into her. Finally, she said, "He was right as usual, wasn't he? You do pity me." She turned her clear gaze once more to Michel. "Why is that?"

He hesitated, his lashes flickering. Whatever he might have replied, he apparently decided against it, perhaps out of loyalty to his friend. He gave her a wan smile. "Renold suggested I was sympathetic, I think, a different thing. You are lovely and a victim of tragic circumstances, also a little mysterious." He shrugged. "Renold knows me well enough to understand that I find that combination irresistible."

What, exactly, did he mean? She was too disturbed to consider it beyond the face value of the words. She said, "You have been kind, and I do appreciate it."

"You are very easy to be kind to," he said with his singularly sweet smile. Taking her hand, he lifted it to his lips.

It was a brief gesture signifying a friendly meeting of the minds, hardly more familiar than a pat on the shoulder. Yet as Michel lifted his head, he drew a harsh breath. Angelica, following his gaze, stiffened.

Bareheaded in the rain, Renold stood with his hands braced on the railing of the steamer's forward deck. He was watching them.

To appear casual, unconcerned, and innocent as she strolled with Michel back toward the boat was difficult beyond words. Her knees were stiff, her face set, and her hand on his arm felt as if carved from ice. She stumbled once, and felt foolishly clumsy. Her skirts dragged in every possible mud puddle and flapped in dirty wetness around the tops of her shoes. Rain collected on her face and ran to drip, disconsolately, down her nose. Their progress had all the grace and style of a cheap funeral procession.

Ahead of them on the boat, another figure joined Renold. It was his half sister. As much to ease the strain as anything else, Angelica said to the man walking beside her, "Deborah did her best to come to your aid at luncheon. I hadn't realized she has such a fondness for you."

Michel gave her a startled glance. "She meant to protect you, rather. Me, she considers frivolous and hardly worthy of her attention."

"I doubt that."

"Do you? Then you can't have noticed that she measures all men against her brother. I stand too much in Renold's shadow to attract notice."

"But you would like to?" Angelica tilted her head in order to see under his hat brim.

"What man wouldn't?" He shifted his shoulders in a hopeless movement.

So much for her fears that he might have too much feeling for her. In practical tones, she said, "You must do something to gain her favor then."

"If she is ever abducted, I'll be sure and rescue her," he said with a wry grimace.

She laughed and they tripped up the gangplank in fine spirits with each other. Which was not, she realized belatedly, the best way of soothing her husband's annoyance.

"If you had told me you were feeling the confinement of the boat, my dear," Renold greeted her in slicing accents, "I would have seen to the problem."

Angelica, abruptly, had little regard for her husband's feelings, justified or not. Michel and Deborah might be unaware of his meaning, but she had no doubt of it. Several answers suggested themselves, but had to be discarded as too revealing. Chest swelling, she said, finally, "Quite impossible. You were not available."

"Oh?" he said softly, as he walked forward to take her arm. "I am here now."

Fourteen

ANGELICA ALLOWED RENOLD TO DETACH HER FROM THE others and lead her in the direction of their stateroom. What else could she do? He was her husband, and she had no wish to cause a scene.

That did not prevent her from resenting his high-handed methods. He thought he could blow hot and cold, kiss her one moment and leave her the next, and she would accept it and be satisfied. He felt she should sit twiddling her thumbs, all meek and mild, until he decided to notice her or see to her entertainment.

It was possible he had married the wrong woman.

She had not until now felt able to oppose him in any material way. The situation had been so peculiar, she had been so disoriented by injury and grief, that she had drifted like an uprooted sapling in the fast-moving current of his will. That was at an end.

They had reached the boiler deck and circled to the starboard entrance, which was closer to their stateroom. They were alone; the other passengers were either inside, out of the damp, or on the landward side watching the top-heavy craft pull away from the wood yard.

"Stop," Angelica said, dragging her gloved hand through the bend of Renold's elbow as she came to a halt. "This is far enough."

He wheeled to face her, a movement that effectively

shielded her from the windblown rain. His voice soft, he said, "Feeling combative? I'd like to indulge you, but this isn't the time or the place."

"Indulge me? I am not a child to be indulged—or to be led away to my room because I've behaved in a manner that doesn't meet with your approval. What on earth is the matter with you? Why would you subject me, much less Michel, to such ill temper? If it's jealousy, let me tell you that you owe Michel an apology." She felt light-headed with the swift beat of her heart, but it was wonderful to say exactly what she thought.

"What a lovely sight, you rising to Michel's defense; I'm sure he would be grateful. Or perhaps he would expect no less since the two of you seem to have joined forces."

"That's absurd! I barely know Michel, and then only as an acquaintance met in your home. If you had not invited him to come with us, there would have been no occasion for us to walk ashore. And if you would refrain from attacking the two of us, we would have no need to band together against you."

"So logical," he answered, his gaze penetrating, "but there are several flaws. One: Time is an inconsequential factor in the relationship between a man and a woman; either can love in an instant. Two: I did not invite Michel, he invited himself. Three: I am not attacking either of you, only trying to protect my wife. You will agree, I hope, that I have some right to do that?"

"Your protection bears a strong resemblance to imprisonment." She stopped, then released her hard-drawn breath in a sigh. "Oh, all right, I realize you feel some responsibility. But if I am in danger because of your business affairs, I fail to see why I am left to depend on Michel for my escort."

A faint smile touched his lips. "Complaining of neglect? Now that is unexpected, especially when you object to being taken to our stateroom where I can keep closer vigilance."

An odd frisson ran along the back of her neck, caused directly by the look in his emerald green eyes. "I am merely saying that as Michel is your friend I can't imagine why you object to him as your deputy. Surely the real danger has been left far behind us, and whatever might happen at a wood yard is within Michel's capacity to handle."

"Undoubtedly, but you see I object to his usurping my role as your savior."

She gave him a furious frown. "If you mean—"

"What a quick imagination you have, my love. I do mean. And so would he, given the opportunity. He is fascinated, rather than in love, but would, I suspect, be charmed to accept your gratitude, however you might express it."

There was an undercurrent in his voice that gave her pause. She said in a different tone of voice, "Is that the reason you think I—"

"Failed to repulse my husbandly advances?" he finished for her when she paused to search for words. "Yes, though I don't make the mistake of thinking it the only one."

This was uncertain and also uncomfortable territory. She shifted her ground by reverting to the previous subject. "I can't imagine why you think you understand what Michel feels. He has given no sign of anything other than the greatest respect."

"He wouldn't, being a gentleman. But you are beautiful and alone in the world and persecuted. How can he resist you?"

Michel had said much the same thing. With a twist of her lips, she said, "So I am an object of gallantry."

"Among other things."

"And you? Is that why you married me?"

"Not being a gentleman," he said deliberately, "I have no use for mere gallantry."

It was ridiculous to feel gladness, but that was the principle reaction that seeped into her. She almost allowed a smile to curve her lips, she almost let him see the elation inside her.

Then he drew a concentrated breath, spoke again. "I married you for your dowry."

She felt her heart knock against the wall of her chest. Her head came up sharply and she stared at him with wide eyes. "That can't be. You didn't know of it until I told you."

"You are mistaken. The nature of it was common gossip in Natchez."

The beat of the engines was increasing as the boat gathered speed. Above them, the wind whistled around the jigsaw work of the superstructure. It burrowed under her rain cape and she clasped her arms across her waist against its chill. "It makes no sense," she said. "You are a man of wealth and, I would have sworn, no great regard for such mundane arrangements."

"True," he said evenly, "but I have a tremendous interest in the return of family property. You see, my stepfather was Gerald Delaup."

It was enough. The name was not one she was likely to forget: Gerald Delaup was the man who had owned Bonheur, the man who had lost the plantation during a game of cards with her father.

Rain swept in a blowing mist across the ship's bow and along the deck. The unpainted cypress boards gleamed with it, while the long stretch of railing next to them dripped. The smell of the wet wood was heavy in the air, blending with the muddy scent of the river. Angelica drew moist air deep into her lungs before she said, "You married me to regain your inheritance."

"Not mine, but my mother's. Also Deborah's."

She said, "But as my husband, you will have use of it, control of it, be owner in all except name. How very—clever."

"I would have preferred to wait a little longer before telling you. That became impossible the instant the decision was made to go to Bonheur."

"Everyone there would recognize you, greet you by name." The droplets of rain that dampened her cheeks were hot. She felt as if a weight had been draped around her shoulders, as if it were pressing her down into the deck.

"Including my mother who is in residence," he said in brief agreement.

"Deborah and Michel? They know?"

He inclined his head. "You will be happy to learn that they join you in considering my methods arrogant and manipulative."

Deborah. Somehow, Angelica had assumed her last name was Harden, like Renold's. Looking back, she could remember Michel stumbling over the introduction, never quite pronouncing the surname. She had thought it an over-sight in the midst of the excitement of her arrival.

It took strong resolve to turn her head in her husband's direction again. Her voice strange in her ears, she said, "Do they also consider you unprincipled and a—depraved devil?"

"Oh, that goes without saying." He was perfectly still, his face without expression.

The rain was wetting him; she could see it trickling through his hair and dripping from the lobe of his ear. She had an almost overpowering urge to draw him away from the wet, to dry and comfort him. A typical female weakness that was in no way personal.

She said with tight irony, "No wonder you have been so out of sorts, having to confess to such a thing before you were ready."

"I had actually hoped that in time it would make no difference."

The sound she made was less than polite. "What might have changed things, do you think? The conceiving of a child? Take heart, you may have accomplished your objective already. You did manage to ensure that there was at least a possibility."

"Depraved indeed," he said, softly. "I could tell you the consummation of our marriage was something I had avoided, against my best intentions, until last night. I could point out that there was neither planning nor cold blood in it. But I wouldn't expect you to believe a word."

There was a tearing ache inside her that nothing could mend. "That's fortunate, since the odds are extremely low."

"Spoken like a gambler's daughter. Which reminds me that you have no monopoly on grievance, or indignation."

Anger gave her voice strength. "If you are suggesting that my father was in any way at fault in the death of your step-father, I would remind you that there is no law against playing cards, or winning."

The color receded from under the skin of his face, leaving the bones prominent. His eyes blazed and his lips parted. Then abruptly he closed them again.

There had been, she thought, something he intended to say before he had been prevented by—what? Manners? Some

vestige of concern for her feelings? Considering all the things
he had found it easy to put into words, she could not imagine
what could possibly be so terrible that compunction would
hold him silent now.

Or perhaps she could, after all.

Suddenly afraid that he might be able to overcome his
reluctance, she said, "Why didn't you simply ask? You once
mentioned arranged marriages based on practical considerations; you could easily have presented such a proposal."

"After the fiasco aboard the *Queen Kathleen*?" he said in
mirthless irony. "I had no faith that you would see reason
once you were completely yourself. I also had the distinct
feeling that you would expect more from marriage. No.
There was too much at stake, and it was not I who would
lose if I failed."

"If you are speaking of your mother and Deborah, I would
think that you are perfectly able to provide for them."

His fingers curled into a fist and he thrust them into his coat
pocket to conceal them. "Oh, perfectly, if all that mattered
were a roof and a few gowns to spruce up their wardrobes for
the season. But there is Bonheur, the plantation that has been
under cultivation by the Delaup family for a hundred years.
It's the place where my mother arrived as bride, and which she
has made her personal responsibility, giving it all her energy
and resolution. Without it, she would have no reason to live.
Then there is Deborah. Rant and rail as she may about the
dullness of life in the country, Bonheur is in her blood; it's a
part of who and what she is, and nobody is going to take that
from her."

She watched him while her heart swelled inside her.
Having no heritage of his own, he was guarding that of his
mother and half sister as if it were something golden and
irreplaceable. She honored him for the impulse, but could not
condone his methods.

She said quietly, "In spite of all that, I would have said
a gambling debt to you would have been a debt of honor,
something that must be paid. Or is that, perhaps, the real
reason you married me? You discovered, with your peculiar

ingenuity, a way to pay your stepfather's debt while leaving his family in possession."

His eyes were hot, but he made no reply. Was that because she had guessed his motives, or only because the one she suggested was no more acceptable than the truth?

She couldn't stand it. She had to get away, needed desperately to think, to decide what she was going to do. Or decide if there was anything at all to be done.

Her voice strained, she said, "You will forgive me, I'm sure, if I don't join you in our stateroom just now. I somehow prefer my own company." Turning with a heavy swing of damp and bedraggled skirts, she began to walk away.

"At least come into the main cabin," he said. "You'll be chilled out here."

"Unlikely," she said over her shoulder. "Anger creates a great deal of heat."

"And hurt pride even more? I could have whispered words of love. Perhaps I should have, after all."

She paused. Her muscles ached as she forced herself not to turn. Moving forward again after a moment, she spoke in commendably even tones. "Not for my sake."

"Certainly not," he said, the words following after her, almost lost in the wind and the rain. "For mine."

There was a place near the stern on the lee side of the steamboat where the wooden grid of a ventilator shaft was set into the wall. It was apparently connected to the kitchen, for warm air flowed from the opening along with the smells of chopped onion, rancid grease, and stale dishwater.

Angelica stopped on the far side of it, standing with her back to the planking of the boat's superstructure. She could feel the vibration of the boat's engines and the steady thumping of the paddle wheel's beam as it made its turn. Trailing black wisps of woodsmoke stung her eyes. Darker veils of it wavered out over the water to mingle with the rain. She narrowed her eyes against the tiny particles of soot and ash falling from the smoke, ignoring the bits that caught on her damp clothing.

Her mind turned endlessly; she wished that she could stop it. Too many possibilities presented themselves, too many emotional disasters. Poking around among them for the truth was like foraging barehanded through garbage heaps.

Renold, watching her in the dining room of the *Queen Kathleen*. That night in her stateroom, before the explosion. The wedding she could not remember. Last night, or rather the early hours of this morning, behind the shutters of the stateroom of the *General Quitman*.

Suspicion. It was inescapable.

Balanced against these memories were others just as strong. Renold sitting beside her while she slept. A garden appearing magically where none had been before. The magic of an operatic aria. His appearance in the back room of a sleazy barrelhouse, bringing hope.

She was an optimist by nature; she preferred to look for the better side of people. Look for the good, and you found good. If you looked for the worst, that was what you saw more often than not. Did that mean she was naive, or was it only proof that everyone had their bad and good sides? Was character a matter of moral fiber or just a question of timing, degree, and circumstance?

Her father had not been a man of evil character. Genial, erudite, he had been a good and kind person, a loving father in his way. He had enjoyed a certain style of living. If he had a weakness for gaming in all its forms, there were many who had the same.

Regardless, what he had done had been wrong. He should never have accepted the wager of a man's home. Certainly, he should never have cheated at cards, not even for the sake of his daughter's future.

That was the cause, Angelica knew. He would not have done so otherwise.

Edmund Carew had cheated to win Bonheur, and Gerald Delaup, losing it, had died. This base deed was the thing Renold had kept silent about just now, rather than flinging it in her face in anger. This was the shameful thing that compunction, and respect for the memory she held of her father, had made him withhold from her.

She was grateful for that impulse. It had been gallant, in its way. At the same time, it hurt that she had needed his reticence.

A man stepped from a doorway a short distance down from where she stood. He glanced out over the river while rocking on his heels with his thumbs hooked into the pockets of his florid tapestry vest, idly scratching. Catching sight of her, he stared with a narrowed gaze. Then he lowered his hands and turned to swagger in her direction.

Angelica hoped that he meant only to walk the deck for air, passing her by. That was not his intention at all.

"Troubles, little lady?" he said, his voice low and insinuating as he bowed with a lift of his hat. Lowering the flat-crowned headgear to his side, he added, "Perhaps I can be of help?"

"No, thank you." The words were cool. She did not look at him.

The gentleman was offended. "Surely you don't think I mean you harm, here where an outcry would bring half the passengers running? It's true that most would arrive in a lather of curiosity, but come they would. Not that there would be the least need. I wouldn't hurt a hair on your pretty head, and so I promise you. Come, tell me what is making you cry?"

"I assure you, I'm perfectly all right. Please don't concern yourself."

He threw his head back, gazing at her with admiration. His hair, in oily black strands streaked with silver, was dislodged by the wind so it flopped over his forehead. He pushed it back, then smoothed his fingers along a slack and inexpertly shaven jaw. Showing yellowed teeth in a practiced if some-what loose smile, he said, "But my dear, how can I leave you here, alone? You look quite forlorn." He moved a step closer. "Perhaps I should stay and engage you in conversation; it's the least I can do. Are you, perhaps, traveling alone? But no, I think I saw you not so long ago in close conversation with a gentleman."

"My husband," she said shortly.

"Indeed? How shameful of him to leave you to the elements. There is, perhaps, some problem between you?"

"Nothing of moment. I must ask you to leave me to my privacy, sir, if you will." She could not imagine how she could put the matter more plainly.

"How very distressing it is to refuse the wish of a lady, but consideration for a fellow creature requires it. If you don't care to return to your stateroom or the main cabin, possibly I might offer the use of my own poor accommodations for your shelter. The door is only a step away."

The offer was so transparent as to be insulting, a thinly disguised invitation of a kind that would only be accepted by either a total innocent or an experienced woman ready to enjoy the aging roué's company. Regardless, there was something disturbingly familiar about the man and what he was saying.

Then she knew.

It wasn't the man at all, but the circumstances. She had stood on the deck of a steamboat alone once before. Then, as now, a man had accosted her with an intent in his mind quite different from the words on his lips.

But this time she was not in need of aid. This time she understood far better what was being offered. This time she was not attracted to the man.

Renold had been more dexterous. At the same time, he had been more direct. He had given her plenty of warning, though she had failed to heed it. Had she, just possibly, been more willing than she knew?

Could she have been searching, without realizing it, for an excuse to end her betrothal and a way to avoid the marriage planned for her? Had she wanted to be seduced?

The last thought bloomed in her mind with such horrified self-recognition that she brought her hands to her mouth to hold back a cry.

Alarm appeared in the roue's face. "Here, now, I didn't mean to upset you. Shall I fetch your husband to you? Will that help?"

She gave a violent shake of her head.

"You don't want him, huh?" he said, his expression turning shrewd even as his language deteriorated. "Maybe what you'd like is to get clear away." He considered a moment "I tell you what, we'll be pulling into a town here before too long—I know because I make this run a couple of times a season, being a drummer by trade. What I'll do is bundle you up in my long coat and walk you off the boat. We can go to a rooming house, wait for the next boat. Go anywhere you want, north, east, south or west, you name it. Woman like you can call the tune any way she wants with Josiah Fothergill."

There it was, a way out, another escape. All she had to do was accept this man's help. Afterward, she could leave him and go her own way.

Yes, but where? And how? To leave Renold while still laying claim to Bonheur was clearly unacceptable. It would not be fair or right to take what had been gained by her father's error. What, then, would she do to live? What if the future she ran toward was worse than the one from which she was running away?

There was no real escape. There never had been any.

"No, thank you," she said quite clearly. "No doubt you mean to be kind, but you cannot help me."

His laugh was very like a snort, "Snooty aren't you? If you're so high-and-mighty, how come you're out here by yourself? How come you've not got yourself a maid on hand as a watchdog, or else hightailed it back inside where people can watch out for you? It's my belief you're waiting for something or somebody. Might as well be me."

He moved in closer and reached out to catch her arm. She put out her gloved hand and her fingertips dented his tapestry vest as she held him off.

"I was waiting," she said, "to learn the course I must take. You seem an unlikely guide, but may have shown it to me. Now I must ask you to leave me alone."

His look was pitying. He shook his head, and pushed forward to press her against the wall. "You think that's going to happen?"

Angelica opened her mouth to reply. Before she could speak another voice sounded. It was stringent with control, deadly in its softness.

"I believe it will," Renold said. "At once."

Josiah Fothergill blanched. His eyes glazed. His mouth opened, but no sound emerged. Releasing his grasp on

Angelica's arm as if he had clutched a hot steam pipe, he lifted
his hands by minute degrees and held them wide.

"Step back," Renold said. The hard grip he held on the
back of Fothergill's collar did not slacken.

"Listen, it's not what you think," Fothergill began in a
rapid undertone. "The lady—"

"Refused. Twice over, and then some. If you cannot
understand her then perhaps I can explain it." In Renold's
face was hard purpose and a detachment that was frightening
in its coldness.

"You're the husband."

"Astute, however belated." There was no relenting in
the words.

"She's a rare prize, that she is. I don't blame you for being
het up. All the same, you shouldn't have left her alone."

Bravery or stupidity, it was difficult to say which moved the
drummer. Renold was unimpressed. "She was not alone. Not
even for a moment."

The other man laughed. "Which one were you testing
then, old son? Her or me?"

Renold released the man with a flick of his fingers.
"Neither," he said. "Only myself."

The other man nodded, replaced his hat on his head as he
took a backward step. "Congratulations. You win either way."

"Do you think so?" Renold said, his gaze on Angelica's
still face.

Fothergill bowed, retreating another pace. "You're still
married to her, aren't you?"

Renold's eyes had no more expression than the gray-green
reflective surface of the river. Turning his back on the other
man in flagrant contempt, he gave his arm to his wife. His
hand covered her fingers, chill even inside her gloves, as he
led her away.

There was warmth and the buzz of conversation in the
main cabin. They did not pause to savor them, did not look
for company. Too soon, Angelica and Renold reached the
door of their stateroom with its painted scene of a bison herd
on its transom.

She moved inside ahead of him. While he shut the door, she busied herself removing her gloves.

The chamber, barely noticed the night before, was more drab than she had thought. There was a high window for air and only one door. The brass bed was in need of polishing. The pitcher and bowl on the shelf which served as a washstand were both chipped, and only a rag rug protected against the splinters of the plank floor. The small amount of space that was left was crowded with their trunks and bags. With barely room to move, there was certainly nowhere to hide.

Angelica put her gloves aside, then reached up to push back the hood of the rain cape. Glancing at Renold, she saw that he was locking the door. Her movements stilled. She watched with a wide gaze as he turned and leaned against the narrow panel.

The light in the closed room was dim with the gray day. Only a faint gleam came through the transom from the main cabin. However, it was enough to show her the determined set of his face and the steady sheen of his eyes.

"Martyrdom or dislike for your deliverer," he said, "I wonder which kept you from leaving the boat? I don't make the mistake, you see, of thinking it was a preference for your present situation."

The breath she drew was shallow. "I saw nothing in the gentleman's invitation to attract me."

"You could have eluded him, deluded him, run rings around him, or put one through his nose to lead him where you wanted him to go. Why didn't you?"

"You overestimate my powers of persuasion."

"But not your talent for duplicity. So I ask again, why?"

Swinging from him, she dragged open the frog closure of the cape she wore and slid it from her shoulders. In a pretense of distraction, she said, "Now what was your other choice? Oh, yes, martyrdom. If that is yet another instance of a choice of evils, then I still prefer the devil I know. Does that qualify?"

His face changed and he pushed away from the door and started toward her. It was then that she realized exactly what she had said.

Panic flared along her veins, leaping with the sudden throb of her blood. As he stepped within reach, she put out her hands to stop him.

He caught her wrists in a loose but powerful grasp. Carrying them behind her back, he brought her close to his hard form. The cape fell, unheeded, to the floor as she leaned back within the taut circle of his arms. She tilted her chin to give him a defiant stare.

"My darling wife," he said in soft exasperation, "I think you have come to enjoy prodding and poking to see what you can rouse. There are consequences for that game. Will you take them?"

She should have known better than to bandy ripostes with the master. *I still prefer the devil—*

The words, those stupid, flippant, thoughtless words that exposed her innermost soul. She had not meant to say them. Or had she?

Did it matter, when her heart was hammering in her chest and her head spinning from a cause that had nothing to do with anger or embarrassment, betrayal, or past wrongs? She wanted him, needed him in all the ways that he had shown her the night before and that she had elaborated upon with imagination and goodwill. The good had gone, but the will remained.

"This is no game," she said in quiet despair. "The stakes are far too high."

"It happens, when the play matters. That doesn't change the rules. You are either in or out, win or lose, stay or fold. And if you fold—if you leave the game—you lose by default."

"Don't," she said, looking away over his shoulder. "I require no reminder."

"I do, I think. Or else I would not ask, quite humbly if with little hope, if you haven't been confined in your wet clothes long enough, if you don't require freedom in this regard if no other? And if you don't wish for the services of a husband who has a certain dexterity with buttons and corset laces?"

"I am—a little damp," she answered. It was as much as she could bring herself to say.

With slow care, he turned her so that her back was

presented to him. His fingers on her buttons were warm, deliberate. They moved down her back with unerring precision. The brush of them against her sent a shaft of purest sensual awareness to the center of her body.

It was incredibly intimate, that service, a prelude to greater license. He reached to hold her steady, his strong fingers sliding around her waist, spanning across her abdomen with his thumb nudging the soft lower curve of one breast.

And suddenly her mind was spinning backward to another dim stateroom, another time, so soon after another attempted seduction. To Renold, holding her just this way.

Reminders.

It was all so clear. She stood quite still, aghast that it had taken her so long to see it.

By his own admission, Renold had known who she was and why she had been on the *Queen Kathleen*. He was a man who left few things to chance; it could have been no accident that he had been standing outside her stateroom that night.

How easy she had made it for him with her desperate need to be released from her corset, her dissatisfaction, her trusting nature. Oh, yes, and she must not forget her willingness to be fascinated.

He had meant her seduction, perhaps from the very moment he had arrived in Natchez. He had intended, by fair means or foul, to force her into marriage so that he could regain Bonheur.

Dear God. Tears pressed in a painful knot against her throat, but she swallowed them back. She wouldn't cry, she wouldn't. Not any more.

So many buttons, but not enough. Her gown was already open to below her waist. His lips brushed warm and smooth across the top of her shoulder, his breath was gentle on the nape of her neck. Then she felt a tug at her waist as he began to loosen the tapes of her petticoats and crinoline.

What was she going to do?

So alone. She had no one now, no one except Renold. Faith had conspired to give him everything he wanted; he had only to open his arms to it.

He had taken risks, of course.

No wonder he had tried so hard, ventured so much pain to save her. She had prided herself that it had been some slight personal interest which had moved him. Such conceit.

Then there was the marriage. What promises of church contributions, what donations for roofs and altars had it taken to persuade the priest to unite him in wedlock with a woman who was practically comatose?

Renold had gambled heavily on that ploy. To go to such lengths, he must have thought she was going to die. He had felt, no doubt, that it was his only hope of retrieving Bonheur.

If, of course, there had ever been a wedding. He had known that her father was dead. Who was there to question the ceremony or ask for proof? Who had the right, if it came to that, to demand that the marriage be proven in a court of law?

She could do those things now. She might have done so in the beginning, if she had not been so weak from her injuries and in awe of her new husband.

How plausible he had been, how utterly sincere and reassuring. Words, just words. A torrent of explanation and defense, generosity and concern designed to keep her docile, dependent, and, yes, enthralled. Like the devil he was, he had said all the things she needed to hear.

And yet. And yet. Hadn't he also, as far as he was able, tried to be the perfect husband?

She breathed deep as the constriction of her petticoat tapes eased. His fingers at her corset, loosening the laces so that the front hooks could be released, sent gooseflesh rippling over her. He paused to smooth away that roughness, at the same time slipping his hands under her corset cover to stretch the laces wider and soothe the indentations caused by the under-garment. Light-headed with the release, she let her thoughts wander again.

Renold had his reasons for what he had done. Yes, she had to admit that. The death of a good man, the loss of a way of life and a priceless heritage: these were enough to set any man on a course of retaliation.

Still, why should she be the one to pay? She had done nothing wrong.

Why did he have to lie to her? Why did he have to make her love him?

Her mind, skittering away from that thought, found another. Jealousy. That was what Michel had said was troubling Renold. How very mistaken he had been. It was almost laughable how mistaken.

No. It wasn't funny. She had come close to believing it. It was enough to make her want to hide in shame.

No. She wasn't going to do that.

"I could have whispered words of love…"

She had to know what he meant, why he had said that to her. She had to separate the lies from the truth, the real from the false, the right from the wrong.

She could not do that by demanding answers, she had discovered that much already. Nor could she do it by running away.

No, indeed. She would stay, and she would use whatever it took, including—what had been the phrase, her talent for duplicity?—to arrive at the full truth. She would be the perfect wife, smiling, pliable, loving, until she knew exactly what he wanted of her.

Loving, yes. That part was important, she thought, for he felt desire for her. She knew he did because he had told her so in plain words. Perhaps that desire was a weakness which could be used as a lever to open his heart and mind to her.

And if in the loving she could discover some comfort for her pain, if she could find some basis for a future that did not require too much compromise, then why should she not accept these things? There was everything to gain, and so little to lose.

Her gown was held up only by Renold's arm now. At the urging of his hands, she turned slowly. He made short work of the corset hooks, so the undergarment lay open. She was left vulnerable without its encasement, exposed in her softness with the curves of her breasts gleaming above the low neck of her chemise. Resolution and relief brought a faint, trembling smile to her lips.

He met her gaze, his own dark and constricted. He bent his head toward her, hesitated, touched her mouth with his own.

Sighing, Angelica let her lashes flutter closed and parted her lips to allow his entry. She lifted her arms and closed them around his neck.

Fifteen

BONHEUR WAS AT ITS BEST. FLUSHED WITH THE SUNRISE, IT rose dreamlike from a drift of morning fog. Every individual leaf of the oak trees lining the drive was edged with diamonds of dew. Roses nodded their fragrant pink heads from where they twined around the slender columns lining the front gallery. Above the *pigeonniers* that flanked the house, gray and white pigeons circled the high rooftops uttering glad, piercing cries of welcome.

Renold loved the place, had from the moment he first saw it as a boy, as it appeared while he clutched the back seat of a carriage driven by his new stepfather. It had seemed magical to him then, a place of bounty and beauty where there were always delicious things to eat and his every wish had been granted.

Substantial without being massive, grand without being formal, the house was four-square and solid. Sitting on a raised basement of handmade bricks, the second floor was the main living area, while a dormered sleeping attic provided room for spillover guests. Wide eaves spread over expansive galleries, like outdoor salons, on all four sides. French doors opened from the galleries into the basement and each room on the main floor to take advantage of every breeze. Constructed of heart cypress from trees felled in the swamp that was a part of the acreage, it was filled with all the furnishings that made life gracious as well as comfortable. It stood as the perfect embodiment of the word "home" to Renold, as close to that ideal as he had ever seen, or ever would.

Mounting the steps, he looked around him with an appraising eye. The rain had stopped during the night, but evidence of it lingered in the puddles on the drive, where robins scratched and fluttered in the litter of twigs and tender new leaves scattered on the lawn and across the gallery floor. However, there was a crew clearing away the debris already. His mother must be up.

There had been no one to meet the steamboat at the small river town near the plantation where his party had been deposited. He had expected no one, of course, since their departure had been unplanned, their arrival unannounced. Leaving Angelica and Deborah having coffee at a pastry shop under the protection of Estelle and Michel, and Tit Jean guarding the baggage, he had come on ahead. Tit Jean had been scandalized at the idea of the maître renting a stable hack and riding the five miles to the house to summon a carriage and baggage wagon, but Renold had insisted. He wanted to speak to his mother in advance of the rest of the party.

She was in her sitting room overlooking the garden. There was a tray in front of her holding coffee and toast and a boiled egg, though she ignored it while she perused a newssheet. He must have made some slight sound as he paused in the door, for she looked up. The paper fell from her hand. She rose quickly to her feet.

She was one of those people that passing years touched with gentle hands. Her shining brown hair was abundant and marked by only a few strands of silver. Slender as a girl, she moved and thought and spoke with quicksilver grace. The oval of her face was clear, while the fine lines around her eyes and the corners of her mouth spoke of warmth of character rather than age. She had been some weeks short of sixteen when he was born, so she was barely fifty. She looked still less, even in the unrelieved black of her mourning.

He moved forward with long strides, covering the space between them before she could move to meet him. As she held out her hands to him, he took them and carried them to his lips, then caught her in a close hug, swinging her gently so that the keys and scissors and other attachments hanging from the silver chatelaine at her waist banged against his thighs.

She laughed a little with a tremulous sound as she released herself. Smoothing a wisp of loosened hair, she said, "You came on the steamboat, I suppose; I heard the whistle. Have you eaten?"

It was typical. He smiled down at her. "Not yet. I only paused long enough to give orders about the others."

"I am to entertain my successor, then," she said, the gladness fading from her face.

"If you please," he answered simply.

"More correctly, she will be entertaining me," Madame Margaret Delaup said. Moving away from him, she walked to the window and stood staring out at the garden with unseeing eyes.

"Yes. Will you help her?"

Something in his voice snared her attention. She turned with a quickening in her gaze. "You expect there to be a need? I rather thought from the tone of the report sent to me by Deborah that you meant to shut up your new wife like Peter Pumpkin Eater."

"In a pumpkin shell? Inadequate, don't you think?" He watched her, and waited.

"I wouldn't know, never having met her. She might tear it to pieces. Or she might make a pie."

"And force me to eat it?" he suggested tentatively. "Is that what you would like, or only what you fear?"

She lifted a brow. "Does it matter? I will not involve myself in this affair. New widows, having lost the purpose of they lives, are notorious for meddling in the affairs of their children. I am determined to embrace my widow's weeds with a stranglehold. I will not interfere."

"Masterly," he applauded softly. "An expression of loving reproach and dismissal in one short speech. But do you mean it?"

Her lips thinned. She said, "Don't, please, practice tricks on me that were learned at my knee."

"Don't talk nonsense, then. Consign yourself to a nunnery, and then I might believe you mean to wash your hands of me. Otherwise, I will expect to hear daily reports on my lack of finesse as a husband, and hourly requests for news of my continued health."

"Very well, I am concerned," she said, flinging up her chin. "What I really want to know is if there is a possibility that you will be able to find peace, if not happiness, in this marriage."

"I can't tell you that." A prickle of perspiration was damp-ening his shirt between his shoulder blades. His brain felt sore with all its recent twists and turnings.

"Meaning that temper and audacity have landed you in a situation you cannot predict, much less control?" Her lips twisted with irony. "I am all amazement."

"If you are trying to make me aware that what I have done is arrogant and depraved, I have already heard it."

A suspended look came into her face. "Your wife told you so?"

"Among other things less complimentary."

"Yet she is still with you, or so I suppose?" Her gaze was intent, infinitely measuring. It rested for several seconds on the dark shadows under his eyes.

"Fortunately," he said with some satisfaction, "she has nowhere else to go."

She moved to pick up the coffee pot and pour out a cup. This she handed to him. Taking up a piece of toast, she nibbled at it, then brushed a crumb from a corner of her mouth. Her eyes hooded, her words carefully considered, she said, "I expect she is attractive."

A corner of his mouth lifted in a smile, though his gaze remained on the coffee's dark surface. "Angelically fair."

"She is a lady, so Deborah says, in spite of her father's habits."

"Her manners are refined, her voice well modulated, her mind agile. She speaks well, but doesn't gossip or make personal remarks."

"And on top of everything else, she is smart enough to induce you to speak for her. If she is such a paragon, why does she require intercession?" His mother's voice was caustic.

"She doesn't. It was my idea to come first and prepare you for our arrival."

"I am a widow, my dear son, not an invalid. I assure you I can still withstand a surprise or two. I can also tell when I am being inveigled into suspending judgment."

He gave an abrupt nod. "Not judgment, but prejudice. It would not be amazing if you despised Edmund Carew's daughter before you ever set eyes on her. That would be a mistake."

"One you have already made, perhaps?"

He hesitated before he said deliberately, "As you say."

"So you want me to befriend her, smooth her way, perhaps even step aside for her as if she were any carefully nurtured young girl brought home as your beloved bride."

"It would be a kindness." His expression did not change.

"Indeed. Yes, and then we two women could close female ranks against the self-important male who caused the awkward position in which we find ourselves."

"If you rant at me for my many faults, perhaps it will leave her nothing to complain about."

A double line appeared between her brows. "Matters are that difficult? What have you done?"

He met her gaze, unsmiling. He did not answer.

She searched his face, drew a sharp breath. "And she hasn't knifed you in your sleep?"

"Her methods," he said deliberately, "are more subtle."

The clock on the mantel measured brittle seconds. Somewhere well behind the house, a rooster saluted the morning. The scent of hot coffee and toasted bread became a stench in the air.

"Congratulations," his mother said. "If you wished to arouse my curiosity and sympathy, you have succeeded. The new mistress of Bonheur intrigues me greatly, in fact. By all means, bring her at once."

The horse Renold saddled to ride back to the dock was a Morgan gelding with three white stockings. Gerald Delaup's favorite mount, the animal had more than his share of spirit. He expressed his equine resentment of the short canter down to the river and the sedate trot back again beside the carriage by tossing his head and caracoling sidewise three yards for every one he went forward.

The horse wanted to run hard and far and ramble home again at his own pace. So did Renold. Duty and tradition prevented it.

Like returning royalty, he had to be welcomed by the people of Bonheur. More, Angelica, as his new consort, had to be seen, approved, and anointed by the blessings of one and all.

The bell began to clamor to announce the gathering as they drew near the main house. It was old news to most of the servants of Bonheur by that time. The drive was lined with the dark, smiling faces of the field hands, while the house servants waited in a row on the steps, lined up in order of ascending importance.

He wondered what Angelica thought of her new domain, wondered if it was what she expected, and if she saw it as he did. Did she see the neatly scythed spring grass beneath the spreading oaks on the lawn, the winding drive with the comfortable old house at its end with kitchen and *garconniere* extending in a wing to the rear? Did she recognize the overseer's house and the infirmary beyond, the stable and barns, the cooperage, blacksmith shop, smokehouses, corn cribs, and distant slave cabins, all in their fresh coats of whitewash? Could she identify the fine crop of cane waving in the fields? Could she tell the industry and good husbandry that had gone into every detail?

Did she guess that these things were there because the late owner had cared about his land, his home, his family, and his people? Gerald Delaup had abused nothing, keeping all in good condition, good health, good tilth. It had taken diligence, vigilance, and the constant outlay of funds, fat times and lean, to keep it in such fine order. It had also taken time. Bonheur had known the footprints of Delaup feet, that most effective of fertilizers, for generations.

Gerald's grandfather, Pierre Delaup—so Gerald had liked to tell on winter evenings—had been a restless younger son of a minor noble house. Getting into hot water in Paris due to his attentions to the mistress of a minister to Louis XV, Pierre had been forcibly placed on a ship bound for Louisiana. He had adjusted well to the new land, and soon found employment on the king's plantation. Only a little later, he contracted a marriage to the daughter of a planter possessed of a huge grant of land along the river. Acreage and a house had been the girl's dowry. She had planted the oaks for the drive, dropping the acorns from a supply gathered in her frilled mock apron. Pierre Delaup had done the rest.

Gerald's father, and Gerald, had followed Pierre's example. They had planned, schemed, and labored in their shirtsleeves alongside their hands to build something worth keeping. That a place that had taken so long to bring to perfection could have been lost on the turn of a card defied belief.

Turning his head in Angelica's direction, he found her watching him. Her face was sober, her eyes as full of sadness and grace as those of a Madonna. If she felt any sense of home-coming, any pride of possession, she was courteous enough not to show it.

Politeness and something that might be good breeding also carried her through the next hour, he thought. It was not sangfroid, he knew, nor was it carelessness, for he felt the tremors that rippled over her as he led her from the field hands to the artisans and their apprentices, then on to the yard boys and girls, the cook's helpers, the housemaids, and from there up to the butler, his mother's personal maid, and the cook. Angelica might be nervous, but she took it in stride, smiling and giving each person a pleasant greeting or appropriate answer to their comment.

Margaret Delaup, waiting at the top of the stairs, was last. Deborah had gone on ahead, running lightly up the steps to hug her mother and stand beside her to exchange quick, half-smothered comments while they waited. The eyes of both women were suspiciously intent as Renold and his wife reached them.

"Bonheur welcomes you," Margaret Delaup said, an odd, impersonal phrase conveying little enthusiasm. "I hope you will find your new home agreeable."

Angelica smiled, though it was no more than a mechanical

movement of the lips. "You're very kind," she said with great politeness and no discernible inflection.

Margaret lifted a brow. "I would turn over the keys to your domain to you at once, except I understand you have been unwell, and I am sure you are tired from your journey. I would not want you to be burdened with trouble and responsibility too quickly."

"You're quite right," Angelica said, her voice even. "I expect I will be better in a few days. Perhaps we can settle things then without too much fuss or ceremony."

Renold, listening to the ultrapolite exchange, felt the hair rise up on the back of his neck. As soon as he was able, he steered Angelica toward the suite of rooms, including bedchamber, dressing room, and sitting room, that they would occupy. Leaving her to direct the unpacking and settle in, he escaped to the stable for a tour of inspection.

The air inside the long, low building was heavy with the smell of hay and horses, and acrid with ammonia. Standing in the open run, he made a mental note to speak to the stable boys about the consequences, general and personal, of the failure to muck out the stalls thoroughly and often, beginning today.

The quiet fell gratefully on his mind. He could hear the crunch of a horse eating oats, the snuffling of another around a water bucket. However, the approach of one of the barnyard cats was noiseless.

The cat stopped beside the open doorway where the sun cut across the floor with a wedge of golden light. It surveyed him with an unblinking gaze, then, unimpressed, sat down and lifted a leg to groom itself.

Renold skirted the cat, walking along the row of stalls. He passed a hand over the low gates, feeling the wood where bored horses had chewed chunks from the planking, stopping now and then to pat an inquisitive head or scratch a twitching ear. Most of the horses seemed in fine condition, in spite of the dirty litter in the corners.

He wondered if Angelica would permit him to choose a mount for her. If she preferred to do it herself, he would see to it that the range of animals was restricted and excellent, so that the final selection made no real difference.

Manipulative, she had called him. He was that, and then some.

A memory of the night before, of Angelica in his arms, drifted through his mind. He stopped abruptly. Turning to put his back against a heavy upright, he stood frowning at the dust turning in pale gold motes in the shafts of sunlight streaming through the cracks in the walls.

Something in her response disturbed him. It wasn't that she was unwilling or cool. She had moved into his arms with perfect naturalness each one of the three times during the evening and early morning that he had reached for her. Her innocence wasn't a factor; he was charmed by it, and also by the assiduous way she dispensed with a little more of it each time they made love.

No, it was something less obvious that was lacking. She was cooperation itself as she moved and turned under his hands, and yet she never made a sound. She did not evade a caress, but neither did she volunteer one. Her skin flushed, her heart throbbed under his hands, she held him at the peak of her pleasure with near desperation, but she never opened her eyes, never looked into his. Afterward, she lay close in his arms, staring into space while she fingered the burn scars along his ribs as if telling her rosary, but she did not try to hold him when at last he turned to sleep.

Silent, always silent, that was a part of what troubled him. The sweet, beguiling prelude to love and its thunderous cataracts of joy were miracles she kept to herself. It was as if she held them close inside her because she could not afford to share them. Or else had no one to share them with, especially not him.

His fault. It must be.

She didn't trust him.

Possibly his scars repelled her, were reminders of things she shuddered away from in her mind.

Or maybe it was only that he was expecting too much of a less than ideal marriage, and the problem was simply that she didn't, couldn't, love him.

But she might have, if things had been different, if he had never embarked on his program of retribution and restitution. The first time they made love, she had been—loving.

He had that memory. It was a part of his punishment, self-inflicted and obsessive, that he had that memory.

That wasn't all.

Several times this morning, he had caught her watching him. The look in her eyes gave him the same wariness he felt when hearing footsteps behind him on a dark street, the same inclination to look to his weapons.

Danger came in many forms, and he had learned to recognize most of them. Instinct told him this was a new one, though his brain had trouble accepting it.

What was going on in her mind? Was she concocting a revenge of her own? Had she, just maybe, begun already?

It was all too likely. She had not reacted to his confession of his misdeeds as he had expected. Tantrums, tears, even cold rejection: he had looked for these things, had decided how he would manage them.

Instead, she had expressed her pain and scathing anger, given him her opinion of his tactics and his morals, then accepted the situation. She had made no threats to dissolve the marriage, never mentioned barring him from Bonheur, had made not the slightest attempt to deny him her bed. She had smiled and been polite and held her mouth for his kiss.

If he was as arrogant as she seemed to think, he would consider the thing over and done, would expect matters to go along smoothly from here on out. He wasn't. He didn't.

She had thrown up barriers to her heart and mind, locking him outside. Within that fastness, she was plotting in her diabolically quiet woman's fashion. He knew it, he could feel it. Whatever she was up to, he would have to guard against it as best he could.

But if she was in the mood for vengeance now, what would she be when she discovered that her father and Eddington were alive? He did not dare think of it.

So intimate an enemy. It was the last thing he had expected.

Let the battle be joined, then. The skirmishes should be

remarkable, if he managed to live through them. And if he went down in defeat, well, he could think of no one to whom he would rather surrender.

A stunning thing, that, to recognize at this late date.

A shadow fell through the stable doorway, stretching toward where Renold stood. Michel followed his own dark image. He stood a moment, allowing his eyes to adjust to the gloom, then, catching sight of Renold, walked toward him.

"Hiding?" his friend inquired, his voice rich with amusement. "I can't say I blame you."

"Rather, seeking a respite."

Michel's smile faded. "Shall I go away again? I saw you come this way, and thought to speak to you in private, but I would not intrude."

Renold sighed and rubbed a hand over his hair, clasping the back of his neck. "You are always welcome, as you must know, since otherwise you would not be at Bonheur. What is it?"

Unease was plain in the other man's face. He swung away, moving to the empty stall nearby where he put his back against the gate and thrust his hands into his pockets. He studied the tips of his shoes for long seconds before he looked up in sudden decision.

"I wanted—" He stopped, took a deep breath, and started again. "I would like your permission to pay my addresses to Deborah."

Renold had expected many things, from a homily on the duties of a husband to a decision to return to New Orleans on the next boat. This request he had not foreseen. Surprise and the instant leap of suspicion made his voice abrupt. "Why?"

"I've known your sister since she was a child, have watched her grow up and turn into a lovely woman. I always had an affection for her, but thought I didn't have a chance. Your family has always been a bit better off than mine. Then, I expected M'sieur Delaup to have her future planned and settled."

"He tried it," Renold said with dry emphasis. "Deborah set him straight."

"She knows her mind," Michel said with a smile. "It

seemed she might consider the idle and lacking in ambition compared to her brother. I was fine for teaching her to waltz or as a harmless male to use for practicing her flirtation, but nothing more serious. Lately, I've come to think—that is, Angelica suggested that I might have a chance."

"Angelica." The word was expressionless. To keep it so required startling effort.

"She was kind enough to listen to my doubts and problems."

"I'm sure. She is nothing if not kind."

A frown gathered in the other man's dark eyes. He dropped his head, then looked up again. "God, Renold, I don't know you any more. I thought you would be happy to hear that I am entranced by your sister, regardless of whether you wanted me for a brother-in-law or not!"

"I might at that," he said softly, "if I didn't have to worry that courting my sister might make an extremely useful excuse for staying close to my wife. Especially if she is going to be your adviser in love."

Michel squared his shoulders. Dark color invaded his face, turning his olive skin to a gray hue. His mouth set in a straight line, he said, "That's finally enough. You will oblige me by naming your seconds."

"No." The word was as quiet as the request had been.

"Friendship, I suppose, prevents it," Michel said bitterly.

"Rather, a disinclination for exertion at the moment. And the certain knowledge that a dueling injury would make you picturesque and appealing, while I would be cast once more in the role of villain."

"If you are the one injured, what then?" Michel said with justifiable irritation.

Renold shook his head, his gaze level. "Then I would have gotten what I no doubt deserved—in the view of both ladies, of course, not to mention their defender." He added, "I can't win either way, therefore I refuse to fight."

"You are afraid you'll kill me in your ridiculous jealousy," Michel charged, lifting a clenched fist.

"I am afraid I will be tempted, yes, and afraid I will try. I'm afraid that if I do try, simple fairness will require that I give you the privilege of retaliating in kind. And I greatly fear that you will not be able to resist the opportunity to make Angelica a widow."

"I can see you allowing it." The words were stiff. Michel followed them with a different tone. "But it's just talk, isn't it? I have a feeling that the thing you fear most is that Angelica might be there to watch you kill again, as she did once before when you dispatched one of the thugs who attacked you in New Orleans. It's my belief you would rather not test the tenderness of her heart."

"Can you be suggesting I am in love with my wife?" he said in mocking accents. "Calumny. Worse, it's blasphemy. Possibly tragedy. Or is it a comedy? I think it must be the last, though I'm not laughing."

"Neither am I," Michel said. "When you decide which it is, perhaps you will tell Angelica. She isn't laughing, either."

Swinging around on his heel, Michel left the stable. Renold stood staring after him, while his mind turned over thoughts of death and dueling and honorable impulses. He contemplated the workings of revenge, and how easily one man could be set against another. In that context, he also considered the nature of women and their inclinations, some honorable, others murderous.

Was it possible that Angelica, chafing at his hold upon her, had found a way out? Could she have set Michel against him with gentle encouragement, hoping that his friend would kill him? To do that, of course, she would have to understand her husband's motives and feelings almost as well as he knew them himself. Or better.

No. She was not that intuitive or that vengeful. Was she?

She could not hate him that much. Could she?

With a low sound in his throat, he turned to the post behind him and struck it a hard, sharp blow. The post shuddered under the impact. Renold pressed his fist against the vibrating wood, then rested his forehead on it. He closed his eyes.

Sixteen

"WHY ARE YOU MOPING OUT HERE, MAMZELLE?"

It was Estelle who put that question, standing in the garden path with her hands on her ample hips and a belligerent look overlaying the worry on her round face.

Angelica sat up straighter in the teakwood chair placed under the rose arbor, and hastily retrieved the book turned down in her lap as it slipped. Summoning a smile, she said, "Just reading. What else is there?"

"You know well what else. You could be talking to Cook about dinner tonight, consulting with the gardener about what vegetables you want planted; maybe checking the dairy to be sure they are making butter the way you want. You might be having the salon swept and dusted and the rugs put up in the attic for summer. There's plenty—if you want to worry with it."

Angelica looked away to where a bee invaded a full-blown pink cabbage rose near her left shoulder. "But my mother-in-law sees to all that, and so well, too."

"Because you let her."

It was true, and Angelica knew it. It was almost a month since she had come to Bonheur. The weeks had come and gone, and still Madame Delaup had not given up the keys to the household.

The keys were central, a symbol of power. So many things were kept locked away: the sharp knives in their polished wooden boxes; the tea in its special caddy; the spices in a many-drawered chest; sacks of coffee, barrels of sugar, flour, ground corn meal, and crocks of preserves and jellies in the pantry; the smoked meats hanging in the smokehouse. Each of these things had to be parceled out by the mistress of the house as needed. It was an onerous duty to many women, but a source of pride and responsibility to others.

Madame Delaup appeared to be among the latter. Angelica had not, in the beginning, realized quite how attached Renold's mother was to her position. She did now.

If the situation had been more normal, Angelica might have forced a confrontation. With the passing days, however, she had come to see to what an extent she would be usurping the only place the other woman had, taking away the one thing that filled the emptiness of her life. So much had been stolen from Renold's mother already that Angelica found it difficult to take the rest.

Excuses were plentiful. Madame Delaup had a headache. It was wash day, and Madame was too occupied to show her daughter-in-law which key went to what. Madame had visitors, or was expecting visitors, or was just leaving to pay a charity call on a needy family of country people. It went on and on.

At the same time, Angelica had grown increasingly irritated with her position. The house servants of Bonheur, not unnaturally, looked to their longtime mistress and to her son for their orders. No single request that Angelica made was answered instantly. If she asked for a cup of tea and a piece of toast between meals, Renold's mother must be the one to send to the kitchen for it. If she wanted the sheets on her bed changed, Madame must approve. If she decided to ride, Renold must relay the order for her horse to be saddled. If she wanted the furniture in her bedchamber shifted, both Madame and her son must be consulted. Nothing was so trivial that achieving it could not be turned into a drawn-out procedure.

Then there was the insolence. It was not overt, of course, nothing that could be seized upon as a cause for punishment. It materialized in a crooked smile, a glance from the corners of the eyes, the tone of a voice. Added together, it showed plainly that she was considered negligible, someone to be neither respected nor feared. In the manner of servants everywhere, the people of Bonheur had looked her over, noticed the attitude of their master and mistress toward her, tested her, and decided she was powerless.

The exceptions were Estelle and Tit Jean. These two had become more partisan as the days slipped away. It was as if they felt she was being persecuted and were rallying to her defense. Angelica was grateful, since it meant at least a few of her needs were seen to without complications. More than that, it was good to have someone on her side.

Her side. As if she and Renold's mother were in some kind of tug of war.

Part of the problem was that she could not blame Madame Delaup for resenting her, even hating her. If she was made to feel like an interloper, she could hardly complain, because that was precisely what she was.

Still, the strain of it was beginning to wear on her patience. Twice in the past week she had snapped at Deborah. Only this morning, she had come very near to lashing out at Renold because he had suggested that his shirts were not ironed to his satisfaction and she might speak to the laundress about it.

The worst of it was that the petty infighting was preventing her from coming closer to Renold. He had ridden out with her once in the first week, and seemed to take pride in showing her the acreage belonging to the plantation, the fields in cane and food crops, the lay of the lands along the river. Since then, she had barely seen him at all during daylight hours. He always had so much to do: talking with the overseer about new plantings; having land cleared, ditches cleaned, or rubbish burned; looking after repairs and even doing them himself so that he came home hot and tired and disinclined to talk.

If these labors did not fill his time, then he went fishing on the river with Michel. Or he rode out to visit with local planters and talk sugar and cotton and land, along with more interesting tales of local misdoings. Coming home, he brought the news he had gleaned to discuss with Michel and Deborah and his mother. An occasional comment was directed to Angelica, but since she knew neither the places nor the people involved, she had little to contribute to any discussion.

It was only at night that she saw him alone. Sometimes, he was too exhausted from his labors, perhaps purposely, to do anything else except sleep like the dead. Other nights, he reached for her the moment the lamp went out and made love to her with such desperate skill that all else was routed from her mind.

She said to Estelle now, "It isn't as easy as it may look."

The other woman shook her head. "But it won't happen at all, Mamzelle, if you don't try."

It occurred to Angelica, as it had before when some request created a standoff in the kitchen or laundry and her helpers came flying to her in high dudgeon, that Estelle and Tit Jean might have other motives for being biased in her favor. It seemed they would gain supremacy in the servant hierarchy with her elevation—particularly Renold's former housekeeper who had been appointed as her personal maid—and were interested in seeing she assumed her rightful place for that reason. There was no point in saying so, however.

Shading her eyes against the sun's glare, she said in an attempt to change the subject, "Is anything wrong in the house? Did you need me?"

The maid clapped a hand to the side of her face. "Oh, Mamzelle, I almost forgot. You have a visitor."

There had been visitors before in plenty. As with Angelica's aunt in Natchez, receiving and paying calls took up a major portion of the time of the ladies at Bonheur. They came in various forms, from the fashionable call in which a lady merely left her card to the formal call which lasted a carefully calculated half hour and usually included taking some refreshment. There were also informal calls between family and close friends which might take up an afternoon or extend to several days. The practice was a means of renewing the ties of both kinship and friendship. It was also a favored way of keeping abreast of events in the neighborhood.

The advent of a bride at Bonheur would always have been sufficient to bring forth numerous visitors. That the bride was the daughter of the man who had won Bonheur at cards had caused a stampede.

In no sense, however, had these many women riding up and down the drive been considered to be visiting Angelica. They had come, rather, to pay their respects to Madame and Mademoiselle Delaup. They expected, in fact almost demanded, to see the bride, but had little to say to her. They wanted to inspect her, assess her qualifications as a wife, then go away to discuss her shortcomings among themselves.

"A visitor for me?" Angelica said doubtfully.

"She calls herself Madame Parnell," Estelle said, and handed over the caller's card between two fingers in a gesture that was a totally unconscious judgment on Madame Parnell's status, or lack of it.

Angelica stared at the card. Madame Parnell. That was the name of the woman who had been on the *Queen Kathleen*, the former actress who had known her father. The lady had survived, then. But how had she found her way here?

Angelica rose to her feet and shook out her skirts. Consideration in her eyes, she said, "Where did you put her?"

"In the back salon, Mamzelle. It seemed best."

"Yes. I'll join her there. Could you bring coffee and whatever else you can find by way of refreshment?"

Estelle agreed, still she stood staring after Angelica with a frown as she moved toward the house.

Bonheur boasted a double salon, a long room divided in the center by tall sliding doors. The front salon thus formed was larger and more formal, the place where important visitors were received. The back salon was considerably less important, a relaxed space used by the ladies of the house for reading and sewing. At this time of the morning the French doors opening from it were closed against the sun, so the room was cool and dim.

Angelica, sweeping inside from the gallery, left the door standing open while she placed the book she still carried on a side table. "Madame Parnell, what a pleasure to see you again. But you have been left in the dark, and that won't do at all. One moment, while I open the other door to let in the light."

"Lord, child, no need to worry about that," came a familiar gravelly voice. "Light or dark, it's all one to me now."

Something in the words, the tremor of them, or perhaps the resignation, reached Angelica. She turned from pushing open the second pair of French doors. She stood perfectly still.

Gone was the brassy-haired, loud, comfortably embonpoint woman from the boat. In her place was a thin, frail creature with graying hair slicked back under a bonnet, livid scars on her face, and a swath of bandaging across her eyes.

She was not alone. A plump young woman with snapping black eyes and a belligerent chin sat beside Madame Parnell. She kept the older woman's hand in hers and her expression was as grim as a bulldog on guard.

Madame Parnell's lips curved in a tremulous smile. "You're shocked, I think, my dear, and who can blame you? I know I look a fright, for all that my niece Gussie here tells me different. But it's you I'm worried about. I heard you were bad off after the accident, that you were taken away by Renold Harden. I had to see that you're all right. I must say you sound it."

The concern was warming. Infusing her voice with lightness, Angelica said, "I had a head injury, but am perfectly recovered now."

The blind woman sighed, a sound of infinite relief. "Yes, and I hear he married you too, after all. I'm so glad. I thought while I was lying half alive, shut away in this awful dark, that what happened was God's judgment on me. If I'd been tucked up in my bed like a decent woman should, instead of traipsing along on my way to your stateroom, I'd have been no where near the steam that blinded me. Maybe all I'd have had to get through was being near drowned."

"You were on your way—?" Angelica paused, said in a different tone. "I don't think I understand."

"Don't you? Oh, dear. Renold will be in such a rage. But I can't help that now. It was wrong, what he planned. I knew it at the time, but I had such gaming debts run up in his place of business, and he offered to relieve them if I would do this one small favor. It seemed worthwhile, in its way, especially after

I talked to you. You weren't happy, and I did feel for Renold and his mother and sister."

"What was it Renold asked you to do?" Angelica said, cutting across the floundering explanations.

"I—oh, it sounds so very wicked if you put it into words. It wasn't meant that way, you must believe me. I would not have been drawn into it at all, except for the circumstances of having once known your father. Renold assured me that the wrong we were doing was only to right another wrong far worse. And anyway, that young man of yours seemed not to value you as he should."

"Please, Madame Parnell."

The older woman began to fumble at her bodice. The woman with her, apparently her niece, reached into her drawstring purse and pulled out a handkerchief, pushing it into her aunt's groping hand. Madame Parnell wiped at her nose, and touched the bandages over her eyes as if habit was stronger than need.

"Well, it was like this," she said in half-strangled tones. "I was to wait until a certain time, then come to your room. No one would be around, for it would be late and Renold said he would pay the ladies' attendant to find duties elsewhere. I was to open the door, then pretend great shock at the sight of the two of you—that is, at the fact that you had a man not related to you in your stateroom."

As she faltered, her niece put a square, work-roughened hand on her back, soothing her. "You don't have to say any more, Aunt Dorothy."

"Yes, I do," Madame Parnell said on a gasping breath. "It's important. What Renold intended wasn't—wasn't your ruin; he said he would be honor-bound to offer for you, and so he would. He said—he said he would not hurt you in any way, and that he would make you a good husband and always behave toward you as a gentleman should. Oh, dear, oh, dear." She rocked back and forth while a sob caught in her throat. "He was so handsome and seemed taken with you, as well as determined to get his stepfather's place back. I thought you might—that is, I thought it would not matter so much, after all."

Questions, cries, demands crowded Angelica's tongue so quickly that she could not untangle them enough to speak. It was then that Estelle, knocking once, came into the room with the coffee tray.

The maid was not alone. Hard on her heels was Renold's mother.

Madame Delaup surveyed the visitors with a critical eye. Watching her, Angelica realized for the first time that Madame Parnell and her niece were wearing the simple homespun and plain straw bonnets without ribbon or frills that marked them as being something less than gentry.

What had happened to the jewels and fine clothing the actress had worn on the steamboat? Lost in the explosion, perhaps? Or could it all have been as false as her pretense of friendship on that night?

The smile Renold's mother gave the women was cool, her greeting a shade too gracious. She went on, "How very pleasant it is, to be sure, to meet friends of Angelica's. Do you live nearby?"

It was the niece who answered, bristling visibly as she spoke. "My aunt is acquainted with your son, ma'am. His wife we barely know. As for where we live, I don't see it matters, but my husband and I have a place downriver. My aunt stays with us now."

"I see." Madame Delaup glanced around, then moved to take a seat behind the coffee tray which sat ready. Picking up the silver pot, she said, "Coffee anyone?"

But Madame Parnell's niece was rising to her feet. "I don't think we care for any. My aunt has said what she came to say, I think. We had best be going."

The former actress, following the exchange, put on dignity as if assuming a costume for a role. "Quite right," she said, elevating her chin in a gesture made pitiful by her bandaged, sightless eyes. Her false hauteur dissolved, however, as she turned in the direction from which Angelica had last spoken. "I am so sorry, my dear, truly, I am. Ask Renold to forgive me, will you? And perhaps you will forgive him—since it seems to have turned out for the best?"

"Yes, certainly," Angelica said. "Please don't concern yourself any longer. Everything is fine."

What else was there to say, after all? There was no purpose in telling the blind woman that the plot she had been involved in had turned into a disaster.

Avoiding the eyes of her mother-in-law, Angelica walked her visitors to the front steps and saw them into their wagon. She stood staring after them as Madame Parnell's niece, competent at the reins, sent the ramshackle vehicle away down the drive.

She was not aware that Madame Delaup had followed her out onto the steps until she spoke at her elbow. "Attacks of conscience," the older woman said, "should be repelled at all costs. They usually harm more than they help."

"You heard," Angelica said without surprise.

The other woman's face was impassive, though there were tiny lines of tension at the corners of her eyes. "I was arranging a bowl of roses for the dining table. The door between the dining room and the back salon was not shut well."

Angelica let her breath out in a small sigh. "I'm sure she had the best of intentions."

"They always do." Margaret Delaup glanced at her. "I was about to turn out the linen closet. Would you care to join me?"

It was either a bribe or an olive branch, Angelica was not certain which. There was, of course, no question of refusal.

"It would be a pleasure," she said as she turned and walked back into the house with the other woman.

The linen closet was a large armoire of handmade cypress which took up most of the end wall of the bedchamber used by Renold's mother. She was serious about inspecting it.

The armoire seemed bottomless, disgorging linen sheets, pillowcases, shams, and bolster covers without number, most of them monogrammed or else embroidered in flower designs in colors or white on white. There were piles of toweling in bird's eye weave, also tablecloths of damask and jacquard from sizes to fit a tea table to those large enough to cover a banquet board, and all with napkins to match. Bolts of cloth took up one whole shelf, including fine linen and cotton to be made up into men's shirts, lawn for handkerchiefs and ladies under-garments, and even soft flannel for baby diapers. Nothing in the nature of linen had been overlooked.

Angelica and the maids stacked everything on the bed, then unfolded and inspected each piece, checking them for rips, tears, and stains. Those that needed attention were set aside. The others were refolded and handed to Madame Delaup, who counted each piece off against a master list before putting it back in its proper place. From a basket nearby, the older woman took pieces of vetiver root, slipping them between the items to scent the stacks and keep out insects.

When they had finished, the several hundred pieces were neatly stacked in a fresh-smelling and impressive display.

Angelica had often helped her Aunt Harriet with the same task. However, the collection of linen had not been nearly so impressive. Reaching to smooth the intricate drawnwork and hemstitching of a pillowcase border, she said to Renold's mother, "You have some wonderful pieces. I've never seen such beautiful needlework."

The older woman's smile was wry. "The credit isn't mine. Almost everything was here when I came, the result of several generations of brides arriving at the house with twelve dozen of every useful item. My contribution is to keep them in good condition for the next mistress of the house. You, as it happens."

It was a concession of some magnitude, especially as it was made in front of witnesses who would be certain to carry news of it back to everyone else at Bonheur. Angelica might have thought it inadvertent, except that she had lived with Renold's mother long enough to understand that, like her son, there was a purpose behind most of what she said and did.

Her gaze sea blue and clear, Angelica said, "In that case, I thank you for your care. I only wish that I might have added to the supply."

"There's nothing to keep you from it, eventually, since you have an interest in it and talent with a needle." Madame Delaup closed the doors of the armoire and glanced at the maids. To them, she said pleasantly, "That will be all. Perhaps you will inform Tit Jean that we would like fresh coffee? Tell him also, if you please, to find M'sieur Renold and ask him to join us here."

There was a small table sitting near the French doors which stood open to the morning air. As the maids left the room, Madame Delaup moved in that direction, indicating with a graceful wave of her hand that Angelica should be seated. She took the opposite chair, then settled her skirts around her feet before she leaned back, resting her wrists on the arms of the chair. She studied Angelica's face for long moments before she spoke.

"My son," she said, "is very much his father's child—I am assuming you are aware Renold was not fathered by my late husband?" At Angelica's brief nod, she went on. "Renold's father was the son of a small landowner in County Kerry; his name was Sean Dominick O'Malley. Sean was sent to school at Douai in France, since education was difficult for Catholics in Ireland. Revolutionary ideas were in the air, and he listened to them. When his studies were interrupted by the Terror, he returned home, but brought his ideas of freedom and equality with him. Sean became involved with me, then, but also with Daniel O'Connell and the Catholic committee, and the agitation for Catholic rights. His skill at organization and opposition brought him into conflict with the authorities at Dublin castle. A decision was made to remove him and he was charged with smuggling—he had an uncle who was a free trader, and Sean may actually have given the man a hand from time to time. He was arrested the day before our wedding, hanged on the day itself. Fate enjoys its little ironies."

"I'm sorry." Angelica did not add to that. It was inadequate, she knew, but nothing else seemed likely to help.

Madame Delaup gave a small nod. "I was expecting his child, of course. I could have stayed in Ireland; my family would not have disowned me. But I suppose I had heard too many speeches about freedom; I hated the thought of Sean's child being born into the same narrow world that had killed him. One night I packed my bag, stole the money from my father for my passage, and took ship for New Orleans."

"It was a brave thing to do."

"It was foolhardy," the older woman corrected with a wan smile. "Renold and I almost starved—I thought for a long time that I was being punished for my sins. Sometimes, I still think so."

The gaze Madame Delaup bent upon Angelica was searching, as if she wondered how much of the story Angelica might have heard. Sitting forward in her chair, Angelica said in encouragement, "You and he were alone for some time, I think."

"I was so young. Renold was my playmate, my toy, and my mainstay in one. We were close, so close. Then I met and married Gerald Delaup. Renold saw it as a betrayal, and also an admission that he had failed me. M'sieur Delaup he forgave for taking me away. For me for allowing it there can be no forgiveness."

"A harsh judgment, and untrue. He cares for you greatly."

"Love and forgiveness are two different things. One can love from afar, half fearful of the feeling, but to forgive you must come close and take many things on trust. He remains apart, locked inside himself in fierce isolation. I wonder, then, if I am not to blame for his treatment of you."

"I hardly think so. Renold is not a child hanging around his mother's petticoats." It wasn't easy to find words to say what she meant, but she trusted that the other woman would understand.

"No, indeed. Yet he has grown hard and mistrustful, and with no great respect for a woman's word or her feelings."

Angelica searched the older woman's face. "That may be, but everything he did was to keep Bonheur for his half sister and for you, mostly for you."

"Yes, and what, precisely, has he done? In spite of everything, I would have said that my son would never misuse a lady. Apparently I was wrong." Lips stiff, she added, "You are, of course, under no obligation to disclose the extent of my error. Still, I would like very much to know what he did to you."

There was a warm breeze wafting in at the door. It fanned Angelica's flushed cheeks as she returned the other woman's steady gaze. Finally, she said, "Perhaps it would be best if you applied to Renold."

"Depend upon it, I shall," his mother said. "However, it's possible your perception of what took place may be different from that of my son."

"Nothing happened," Angelica said in abrupt decision. "The boat exploded."

"And later?"

Angelica looked away from her. "Later, we were—married."

"I see. After this thing that did not happen, then, you accepted my son's proposal and entered into matrimony with him with an easy mind and heart?"

"The occasion was somewhat unusual," Angelica began.

"Which means that you did not. Were you asked?"

The words, sharp-edged as razors, were irritating, and perhaps meant to be. "Being insensible at the time, there was a little difficulty there, also."

"Insensible? You mean he—" Renold's mother drew a quick, uneven breath. "No. He would not do that. What do you mean?"

"She means," came a hard voice from the door, "that joyful as the event may have been, she has no memory of it."

His mother sat forward in her chair to face Renold. "But you do."

His smile as he came forward was sardonic, his bow a model of courtesy in spite of hair that was wet from the exertion of riding and clothes that reeked of horse. He said in answer to her question, "The occasion is chiseled on mind and heart."

"We can dispense with the melodrama, thank you. Unless the engraving is self-inflicted, a reminder of ill-considered plans."

"You suspect me of not knowing my own mind?" he asked pleasantly.

"Rather, to borrow a phrase, of correcting in haste a mistake made at leisure."

He tipped his head, said softly, "There was no mistake."

"I have watched for years," his mother said with grayness in her face, "while you broke the rules that annoyed you and rejected every canon of gentlemanly conduct that seemed

likely to prove a barrier to fortune. No!" she said sharply as
he opened his mouth, "permit me to finish. I never interfered
because it seemed you had a code of your own more stringent
in some areas than the one that you rejected. That code seems
to have deteriorated. Let me inform you that depravity in the
treatment of females is an inexcusable trait."

Renold's eyes were steady and darkly green, but he did not
look at his wife. He said, "Who accuses me?"

"Not Angelica, though I would imagine she could."

"Her visitor then," he said. "Who would have thought
Madame Parnell, of all others, would live to tell about it?"

He stood straight and a little pale, as if facing a tribunal.
A slow bead of perspiration trickled from his hair and disappeared under his shirt collar. Angelica, watching him, felt her
heart begin a hard, sickening beat.

"You admit it, then. You intended to ravish a young
woman and have yourself discovered in the act in order to
force her to the altar with you."

"The appearance is sometimes enough." He let the words
stand without amplification. He had lost his verbosity along
with his color.

"And sometimes the appearance precedes the deed," his
mother said, her voice inexorable. "Are you quite certain the
explosion aboard the *Queen Kathleen* was not the only thing
that prevented you from forcing yourself upon Angelica?"

"Quite sure," he drawled. "There was also her resistance."

Madame Delaup's eyes dilated. It was a moment before she
could speak, and then there was loathing in her voice. "Her
resistance? It was necessary for her to fight you?"

It seemed Renold might not answer. The fingers of his
right hand closed tightly, then opened again to hang lax. He
looked down at it, said softly, "Yes. Desperately."

"No!" Angelica said, rising to her feet so quickly her hoop
skirt swung, bumping against the chair behind her. "He
stopped of his own accord. He was about to apologize when
the boiler exploded."

Madame Delaup rested her gaze on the face of her son,
where all reaction had been wiped away as if with a damp

cloth. To Angelica, she said, "You could not have known what he meant to do."

"I have had a great deal of time to remember every second of that night. More than that, I've come to know Renold and how he thinks."

"You absolve him, then? Charming, but unreliable since your future comfort depends on his temper."

It was a motive Angelica could not accept. "I also know that he would not have been in my stateroom at all that night if I had not—encouraged him."

"Not so," Renold said with a sharp gesture of denial. "I had every intention of joining you there."

Angelica gave him a look of annoyance. "I could have gone inside and locked the door, and then where would you have been? I might have done just that if you had not been so—"

"Persuasive? There were other methods in reserve if that failed."

"They were hardly needed, since I practically begged you to take off my clothes!" She gestured toward her corseted form in indignation.

Renold glanced at his mother while a frown crept into his eyes. "She has a horror of being trapped in her undergarments, and I had sent away the ladies' attendant who should have helped her out of them."

"I know," his mother said without expression.

"Anyway," he went on, "Angelica had no intention of allowing me the slightest liberty. What I gained, I took by force and subterfuge, and do not regret."

"I don't doubt it; you always accepted responsibility for your misdeeds even as a child. The question here does not concern your feelings, but rather what Angelica might or might not regret."

What did she feel? Angelica hardly knew. Then, noticing the intent, considering light in the eyes of Madame Delaup, she realized abruptly that it made no difference, after all.

Renold's mother had, perhaps, intended to make a point to her son. Her main purpose, however, had been to undo the damage brought about by the visit of Madame Parnell.

Toward that end, she had forced a confrontation with Renold, castigating him in such terms that she had encouraged Angelica to play devil's advocate. In that guise, Angelica had been persuaded to review in her mind the night on the *Queen Kathleen*. In the process, she had come to the conclusion that as reprehensible as Renold's purpose might have been, his reason for it was unselfish. More, the method he had chosen to attain it, compromising her without physically possessing her, had been relatively humane.

The only question in Angelica's mind was at what point Renold had caught on to the trick.

She said quietly, "I regret, Madame, that I did not recognize sooner where your son acquired his ruthless habits. What you just did was—what was the word? Oh, yes. Inexcusable."

Swinging from them, she moved toward the door. She had almost reached it when she heard a soft laugh and the sound of quiet, deliberate applause.

"Bravo," Renold's mother said as she clapped her hands.

Hard on the syllables, there came a cutting remark in her son's voice. The words were too soft to be understood, but the tone was perfectly clear. It carried hot, consuming rage.

Angelica had had enough. She ran, not from the angry confrontation taking place behind her, but from the things she herself had said, from the knowledge of how close she had come to exposing how she felt.

She ran because she knew how perceptive Renold could be, and was afraid of what he might say or do if he should put his mind to understanding. She did not stop until she slammed the door of her bedchamber behind her.

Seventeen

THE FARO GAME IN THE SALON HAD BEEN GOING ON SINCE JUST
after dinner. It was fun at first, with Renold keeping the bank
against Deborah, Michel, and Angelica. The four of them
laughed and joked and placed their bets with careless disregard
for winning or losing. The piles of chips in front of them
shifted back and forth as fortune smiled on first one and then
the other.

Madame Delaup remained with them for a while, looking
up with dry indulgence from where she sat working a Berlin
stitch pattern in shades of rose and peacock blue silk on a chair
seat. As the evening lengthened, however, she put her needlework in its bag, bid them good night, and went off to bed.

With his mother's departure, Renold tried to catch
Angelica's attention. She pretended not to notice, since she
had the distinct feeling he meant to convey his own readiness
to call it a night. Being alone with him was something she had
managed to avoid since the contretemps that morning. She
hoped to use the late hour as an excuse for postponing any
discussion still further when they finally did retire.

It was perhaps a half hour after Madame Delaup's departure that the luck began to run exclusively in Renold's favor.
The easiness died out of their play. The atmosphere took on
a sense of strain. Michel settled down and kept careful track
of the cards laid out. Deborah sat frowning over the place-
ment of her chips for much longer than Renold thought

necessary. Angelica, who had never played anything more exciting than piquet with her aunt, felt her nerves mounting to a painful pitch.

Faro, according to Michel, who had explained the rules, was a card game brought to Louisiana from France where it had been played since the time of Louis XIII. The name came from the original cards, which had featured the picture of an Egyptian pharaoh on the reverse side. A folding board marked with the different suites was laid out on the table, and players placed their chips on the cards they thought would turn up in the deal. Two cards were drawn from the dealing box each time, the first losing, the second winning. Play was made against the bank, which was held by the house when played away from home, but by any person good at numbers when in private company. Though the bank enjoyed a slight advantage, it was so small as to be unimportant—unless the banker was a cardsharp. Perhaps because of faro's long history, there were more ways for the banker to cheat at the game than at almost any other.

Deborah, as she continued to lose, grew upset. Out of deference to her feelings, Renold relinquished the bank to Michel. Michel later gave it up to Angelica, but she was too distracted by her own play to do it justice. It was Deborah who was in charge when the cards began once more to run in the bank's direction.

The game had long ago ceased to be fun. Angelica searched her mind for some reason to stop the play that would not also bring the evening to an automatic end. A late supper might be acceptable.

It was just as she opened her mouth to make the suggestion that Renold leaned back in his chair and flung his cards face down on the table. "If you are going to deal from the bottom, Deborah," he said in exasperation, "at least wait until you are good at it."

A flush rose to Deborah's face, though the look in her eyes was rueful. "I only wanted to see if I could do it without being caught."

"Now you know," her half brother said. "I would advise you not to try it away from home."

"I wouldn't! Honestly, Renold!"

"You should know Deborah better than that," Michel said, coming to her defense. "It was just high spirits."

"The kind of spirits that can gain her a reputation for being fast and free with money, if not with a great deal more." Renold's gaze was hard as he met his friend's across the table.

"Of all the unkind things to say!" Deborah exclaimed in indignation.

Michel, rising from his seat, said, "I think you owe your sister an apology. There is not the slightest reason to suggest such a thing."

"I was issuing a warning which she apparently needs," Renold countered, his face implacable. "If she can't accept that, then she has no business going out in company."

Bewilderment surfaced on Deborah's face. Angelica could sympathize with it. At the same time, she felt the stir of suspicion. She herself had been at a similar loss when Madame Delaup attacked Renold earlier.

Michel displayed no such ambivalence. His face set and eyes hot as he glared at Renold, he said, "You are setting yourself up as an authority on the proper conduct in company? That's rather farcical, don't you think?"

"No, rather a matter of experience," Renold returned. "It takes a thorough knowledge of improper behavior to recognize it when it occurs."

"And of improper women? Where does that leave Angelica? Or does your conduct with her not count?"

"We will leave my wife out of this discussion." The words were edged with raw steel.

"By all means. It wasn't her conduct that was in question." Michel's answer had a slicing edge of its own.

"You don't care for my behavior?" Renold said softly.

"Renold! Michel! Please stop," Deborah said with tears of dismay rising in her eyes.

Her half brother barely glanced at her. "I believe," he said, "that my honor has been called into question."

"I would have said your common sense," Michel returned instantly, "but you may take it however you like."

Renold's smile was chilling. "I would advise you to take care. The fact that I have refused your challenge before doesn't mean I will every time."

"That is, of course, your choice," Michel said, his face flushed under his olive complexion.

Renold considered his friend, then gave a slow nod. "So it is, and also my choice of weapons in that case. As you well know, I prefer the sword."

"No! You can't!" Deborah cried.

The two men paid no heed. Michel got slowly to his feet. His gaze on Renold's face was steady, his bow stiff. "As you please."

"Exactly."

Angelica, watching them, made not a sound, though her heart felt too large for her chest. Farcical, that had been a good description of what was going forward. She could not believe that this sudden spurt of temper was actually going to end in bloodshed.

"I'm sure," Michel said, "that we can find seconds among the neighbors. If you will be good enough to send Tit Jean with a message now, it can be arranged for the dawn."

Renold pushed back his chair and rose to his feet with casual grace. "You think I intend to leave my wife's loving arms at first light just to go dancing about in the dew? Imbecilic. Here and now will do."

Michel stared at him. "There are ladies present."

"They can go or stay, it's all one to me." Stepping away from the table, Renold pulled the cord beside the mantle that would bring a servant.

"You don't mean this. We should at least move out onto the gallery." Michel remained stiff and straight beside the table.

"An excellent suggestion. My mother might have a few words to say if we damage the furniture."

A frown appeared between Michel's eyes. "You are pleased to make light of this meeting. No doubt you have reason; I will grant you the greater degree of skill. But I assure you, there is nothing light about it in my eyes. I will defend myself as long as possible and draw your blood if I'm able."

"Spoken like a gentleman," Renold said in dry approbation.

Then, as Tit Jean appeared at the door, he turned to the
manservant. "The dueling swords, if you please."

Tit Jean's eyes widened an instant before his usual impas-
sivity closed in again. He turned without a word and went
away to do Renold's bidding.

Michel said in answer to Renold's jibe, "I hope that I
deserve the title of gentleman."

"So do I," Renold said, "otherwise the effort will be wasted."

A frown appeared between Michel's brows. "I am to learn
a lesson, I suppose?"

"The duel as a guard to ensure civility and courtesy. There
is that, but no."

"What then?"

"I prefer to call it a demonstration."

"Of what?" Michel inquired in rough tones.

As Tit Jean returned soft-footed with a long case of
polished wood in his hands, Renold turned away to open it
and lift a slender sword from its velvet bed. This he presented
hilt-first to Michel.

"What is this gloom?" he said in sardonic humor. "Surely
the purpose of a meeting is to settle a point of honor by might
in the hope that truth and conviction will lend strength to a
man's arm? Honor is satisfied by a mere show of blood unless
a man is vindictive or tempers get out of hand. Supposing,
of course, that you have not joined the Americans in their
insistence on death as the final outcome."

"Not so far."

Renold's smile was affable. "What we have here, then, is
mere sport. Why should we not enjoy it?"

"Oh, by all means," Michel said dryly.

The eyes of the two men met for a long moment. Then they
turned as one toward the door that opened onto the gallery.

That long open space was swept by a pleasant night wind. It
was also dark, but that was soon remedied as Tit Jean brought
lamps and set them in the corners made by the railings and
the house walls.

Renold stripped off his coat and began to roll his sleeves to
the elbow. Michel had just shrugged from his own coat when

he looked up to see Angelica and Deborah emerging from the house. He stopped with his arms still confined. "No, ladies, really. I know what was said, but surely you can't wish to watch such a sorry spectacle."

"What is it you don't want them to see?" Renold inquired, his gaze satirical. "Your bestial nature, or only your manly physique?"

"Neither," Michel said with a snap in his voice, "but I would think even you would feel the distraction of their presence."

"Oh, assuredly, though there are compensations. I fight best before an audience."

"What if your audience goes into hysterics?"

"Unlikely, since it would require an unconquerable fear over the outcome." Renold looked toward Angelica, his smile twisted. "You won't cause a disturbance, will you, my love?"

"Not," Angelica said, "if I can help it."

He held her gaze a moment longer before turning to his sister. "Deborah?"

"I'm staying if Angelica is staying."

The words were not quite steady. Angelica glanced at the other girl. Deborah's face was pale and her hands tightly clenched at her sides. Her brother appeared not to notice, but turned away with a lift of a brow in Michel's direction.

The other man's lips tightened, but he made no further objection. Pulling off his coat, he loosened his cravat, then leaned to pick up his sword.

The two men took up their positions, right sides facing, sword tips lowered to the floor. They watched each other there in the flickering light while grim concentration settled over their features. Their shirts were silvered with the lamp's glow, which also cast oblique shadows across their eyes. The shifting brightness made a stage of the gallery and closed out the dark reaches of the night. Quiet descended, in which the lamp flames sputtered in their chimneys and the whisper of the wind in the trees on the drive was soft and impatient, like the far-off murmur of a crowd.

"Deborah," Renold said with a ringing quality in his voice, "you may give the office to start."

It was an honor and, perhaps, an indication of other things.

Angelica heard the inrush of the other girl's breath. Deborah paused so long it seemed she might refuse the office. Then she spoke.

"En garde!"

The blades swept up in salute, then down again, in perfect unison. The two men settled into position. Light glimmered in brief lightning along the lengths of the matched swords as they crossed at the tip, steadied with points touching. The first searching tap chimed with a delicate, musical sound.

Their initial moves were used for testing only. The quick, shuffling feet as they circled, the supple revolving of taut wrists, the swift feints and half-completed maneuvers ended as often as not with a laugh and an easy comment. Slowly, however, the cadence increased, the click and chime of the blades took on a more challenging resonance.

Abruptly, orange sparks blossomed, showering down as sword edges scraped. "Oh!" Deborah exclaimed as the two men strained together, hilt to hilt, then sprang apart to stand breathing deep. She clapped her hands over her mouth at once to prevent another outcry.

The wind ruffled the men's hair and billowed the fullness of their shirts about their waists. Narrowing their eyes against it, they plunged forward in attack again.

Back and forth, their feet shuffled on the floor. The swords clanged like tolling bells. Hard-muscled, determined, they advanced and retreated, lunged and parried, extended to feint so their trousers clung to the muscles of their legs, then leaped back again to avoid a sudden defensive charge. The sheen of perspiration appeared on their faces and made their shirts cling across the shoulders.

Renold's hair was curling with the dampness. He flung it back from his eyes, then grinned as he parried Michel's attempt to make use of that second of inattention. Keeping his guard, he recoiled with the smooth competence of iron muscles and perfect control.

"Hold," Michel said in hard tones. He stepped back and dropped the point of his sword toward the cypress boards of the floor.

Renold eased his stance, resting his blade tip on the floor also. Placing his hands on the sword hilt, he said, "What is it?"

"Have you forgotten how many times I've watched you at the *salle d'armes*—not to mention standing as second while you fought for your life? This is child's play."

"You're suggesting I'm being too easy on you?"

"I know it." Michel's eyes were shaded with disdain.

Renold moved his shoulders as if shrugging off responsibility. "Then guard yourself well, my friend."

It became plain in the next few minutes that Michel had been right. The contest took on a faster pace, a sharper edge. The two men plunged back and forth over the length of the gallery in incisive offensive and counteroffensive while their footsteps made rough thunder on the boards. The feints were quicker, the parries more desperate. The clanging of the blades jarred on the ears and scraped nerves.

Michel's hair became wet with his exertions. His breathing took on a rasp. A grim cast closed over his features, turning them into a mask of endurance and determination while his gaze grew fixed on the tip of his opponent's sword. Pressing, withdrawing, he displayed a competent knowledge of swordmen's tricks and a willingness to use them. His blade slithered and slipped against Renold's, searching for an opening.

Still, Michel was cautious by nature, and it showed in his swordplay. He took no chances, tried no exotic ruses or strategies.

Renold was more flamboyant. His feints crackled with power, his parries and ripostes were not only dexterous but wickedly effective. In his advances there was subtlety and glittering grace. Michel, sweating, retreated before him.

Yet Michel was not overwhelmed. He might lack Renold's brilliance, but he was not to be despised as a swordsman. His form was excellent and there was force and stamina in his hard shoulders and firm leg muscles. Above all else, he had heart.

"I make you my compliments," Renold said to Michel with a tinge of surprise in his voice as he leaped back from a whistling cut that should have sliced his arm open to the elbow. "I didn't know you were quite so able."

"That's because you would never try me," Michel said

through his teeth. He surged forward with a blacksmith's hammering of steel on steel.

"It's too easy for practice to become real when pain is inflicted." Renold danced back from Michel's offensive, deflecting it without apparent effort.

Michel recovered before he answered. "But a small injury or two can teach self-knowledge."

"Something you think I am in need of?" Renold essayed a ruse that almost succeeded, but was flicked aside with a scream of blades and a spray of sparks.

"It's possible, though I had myself in mind." Michel lunged into a classic effort that was countered with such a nimble device that he had to stumble backward in hard-pressed defense.

So the fight continued, back and forth, with neither of the two men in perfect ascendancy over the other. Yet. It still seemed that Renold was holding some measure of skill in reserve, waiting for the moment when it would be most useful.

Angelica thought after a time that she saw what he intended. She could be wrong; it was so dangerous. Michel did not know, could not guess the hairsbreadth escape that loomed, the clever manipulation that could, and just might, prove fatal.

Her eyes burned as she followed the thrust and parry without blinking. Her chest rose and fell, still she could not get enough air. In the center of her body was a piercing ache, as if she could feel the thrust of a sword in her own vitals. She made a soft sound of distress.

"It's awful, awful. He'll kill Michel," Deborah moaned, clasping and unclasping her hands. "They've got to stop."

"Impossible. They can't." The words were no more than a whisper. Angelica would not turn her gaze toward the other girl for fear Deborah might see her terrible fear.

"There must be something that will put an end to it. There has to be." The other girl clapped her hands together in sudden inspiration. "The lamps! They can't fight without light We could put them out."

"We don't dare!"

"You might not," Deborah said.

"What if it doesn't work?" Angelica objected. "What if they don't stop?" For the two men to slash and thrust at each other without being able to see would be murderously risky.

"What else is there?"

There was no answer to that. In any case, Deborah did not wait for one. Running to where the nearest lamp glowed, she bent to cup her hand over the globe and blow it out. Spinning around, she ran toward the one in the opposite corner.

Renold uttered a soft imprecation. His gaze flicked to his half sister and away again. His face hardened.

And abruptly, his blade became a whirl of slicing proficiency. It sang, snicked, screamed, beating a tattoo of incipient injury against the sword in Michel's hand. Feinting, Renold swirled into an attack with such blinding speed that it dazzled the eyes and numbed the brain. He extended in fluid strength and deliberate intent, wrist turning in an artful tactic which no doubt had some renown and a name bestowed by Italian fencing masters. Michel plunged to meet it with a wild upswing and blank eyes.

"Oh, no," Deborah moaned as she saw that her action had accelerated the fight. "No," she said again. Then closing her eyes tight, she swung and ran with outstretched hands toward the flashing blades.

"Dear God," Angelica breathed in horror, and sprang after the other girl.

Her feet skimmed the floor. She felt her hair slide as her hairpins jarred loose. Close, so close. She shot out her hand with her fingers spread to grasp. They closed on the sleeve of Deborah's dress, ripping, dragging her to a halt.

But they were both within the arc of attack, with the clatter of steel ringing in their ears. They had interrupted the rhythm of the fight.

Renold, nimbly sidestepping, avoided them. Michel, defending still with a desperate riposte and finding no opposition, stumbled into a desperate lunge that sent his blade straight at Deborah's heart. It hissed toward her with the glint of blue fire along its length, too fast to follow, impossible to deflect.

Almost impossible.

Renold leaped forward. There was a flurry of action too swift to follow. A harsh breath, a soft grunt. Michel gave a short, shocked cry and drew back. His sword shimmered in his hand with the sudden tremor that ran over his body. Its point, upraised, gleamed a bright, jewel-like red in the lamplight.

The clank of a blade falling to the floor brought Angelica around in a whirl of skirts. Renold's sword rolled against her skirt hem and lay still. He clasped his shoulder with his good left hand while his right arm hung at his side with his fingers slack and useless. Blood seeped from under his palm, creeping black-red into the white of his linen shirt.

For a fleeting instant, Angelica felt light-headed with the muddled clash of horror and relief. Then she stepped quickly toward Renold and closed her hands on his arm. Her voice much calmer than she expected, she said, "Come inside at once where we can see the damage."

Michel flung his sword from him so it whipped the air, spinning into the night beyond the gallery. He sprang to Deborah and pulled her into his arms. "Sacred mother of God," he said, "are you all right? Tell me you are all right!"

"Yes, yes," Deborah said on a sharply indrawn breath, then buried her face in his shirt front.

"What did you think you were doing? You could have been killed." Michel gathered her close, rocking her in his arms, though his color above her head was waxen pale.

By then Tit Jean, never far away, was at his maître's side. But as Renold was urged toward the salon between the manservant and Angelica, he pulled away from them.

"Well done, my friend," he said to Michel in dry tones. "Though I think you owe me a return match."

Michel, facing him with Deborah in the curve of his arm, shook his head. "No credit whatever is due; I'm well aware it was an accident that I touched you. But you were right before. This isn't necessary between us."

Renold's glance touched his sister, then returned to mesh with that of his friend. "Apparently not."

"Try it again, and I'll kill both of you!" Deborah interjected with fervor. "I've never been so frightened in my life."

"Or I," Angelica agreed.

"In that case," Renold drawled, "I suppose it may have been worth it after all."

"What!" Outrage leaped into Deborah's eyes as she met her brother's gaze.

"Never mind," he answered, smiling before he swung away and moved into the house.

They remained in the salon only long enough to make certain that nothing vital had been touched by the sword thrust. It seemed to have merely pierced the hollow below his collar bone and slid through to the back. Clean and uncomplicated, it was Tit Jean's opinion the wound would be stiff and sore, but cause no great incapacitation unless blood poisoning should set in.

The manservant was not entirely satisfied with his diagnosis alone, but wanted to send for a doctor, then rouse Madame Delaup. Renold refused to allow it. He was, he said, in no mood to be prodded and poked, nor was he interested in hearing strictures on his conduct more lethal than the sword thrust itself. All he wanted was to repair to his dressing room and have his wound bandaged with as little fuss as possible. Collecting Angelica with a tilt of his head, bidding Michel and Deborah a casual good night, he moved off in that direction.

In the dressing room, he took the bandage box from Tit Jean and put it in Angelica's hands. To the manservant he said, "I believe we forgot the restorative. Would you find brandy and bring it here? Oh, and afterward, go along and see if Michel has need of a bottle."

"But maître, who will tend you?" The manservant stopped. His head came up and he looked at Angelica with intent interest.

"Exactly so. You are supplanted. If you hear no yell for help from this direction in the next quarter hour, you may go to bed."

The words were dry, Renold's manner casual, yet Angelica felt an odd catch in the beat of her heart.

The ghost of a smile came and went across Tit Jean's coffee brown face. Inclining his head to Renold, he indicated his understanding. He left the room, then, closing the door quietly behind him.

Angelica turned away to set the bandage box on the washstand. Lifting the lid, she said, "I've bandaged a cut foot and a few sliced fingers, but nothing like this."

"You'll manage," Renold answered easily. Looking around, he pulled a chair closer to the washstand and sat down on it.

She considered the rolls of linen, the scissors and needles and strong-smelling salves in the box, trying to concentrate. After a moment, she set out what she thought she would need, then turned to the pitcher and bowl on the washstand. A brass can of warm water sat ready to be used for their ablutions before bed. She poured a generous amount into the bowl and dropped a cloth into it before she turned back to Renold.

His face was bland, but his eyes were bright. She thought she knew the reason. He had achieved what he had set out to do, which was to increase Deborah's interest in Michel. Taking his cue from his mother, he had sought to make his friend an object of sympathy by forcing him into a fight and then wounding him. It had not worked out quite as planned, but the results had been much the same.

She said, "I suppose you're happy."

His gaze was sapient, but he was not inclined to be confiding. "Should I be?"

"Your try at playing Cupid by making Michel a martyr appears to have succeeded, even if you were felled by your own arrow."

"Are you disappointed?"

"Disappointed? I can't think why I should be." The words were spoken almost at random. She put her hand on his wrist, removing his fingers from his injury. The flow of blood had slowed, almost stopping. Her movements quick, she began to strip his shirt from the waist of his trousers. It was, unfortunately, one made in the old style, without a front opening. It would have to come off over his head.

"You appear to have lost a devoted admirer, while being forced to patch up a mere husband." He reached to pick up a fat silver-gold curl that had rolled forward in front of her shoulder and sat rubbing it between thumb and forefinger.

"There is no question of force." In fact, she was glad to have something to do so she would not have to think about the moment the sword had plunged into his flesh. She also prized these moments, however brief they might be, when he needed her.

"Lift your arms, please, as much as you can."

He released her hair to do as she asked, ducking his head so she could pull the bunched shirt off over his head. The movement left his hair rakishly tousled, but he made no move to smooth it. Watching her while she discarded the shirt and picked up the cloth in the bowl to squeeze the excess water from it, he said, "There was also no question of making him a martyr."

She met his clear green gaze, her own startled. "You mean you picked a quarrel with Michel because he—because you thought he was an admirer?"

"Not precisely, though I had my reasons."

She absorbed that as she moved nearer to him and reached with her cloth to wipe the edges of his injury. He rested his left hand at her waist, halting her movements while he shifted one long leg out of the way. He then drew her between his knees so she had better access to his shoulder. He did not remove his hand, but settled it more firmly on her hip.

The position was practical, and more comfortable than leaning forward to reach him. It was also disturbing in its familiarity. Though she slept beside him in the night, and often woke lying against him, she was not used to casual intimacy during the course of the day.

She kept her eyes lowered while she attended to the task at hand. As the seconds ticked past, however, a feeling of strain invaded her senses. It was not helped by his thumb moving in a slow circle around her hipbone.

"These reasons," she said in an effort to maintain some degree of normality. "I don't suppose you mean to tell me what they might be."

"I am waiting with bated breath," he said, inhaling sharply as she came too near the quick, "to see if you can puzzle that out for yourself."

A frown drew her brows together. There was no time to answer, however, for Tit Jean reappeared with the brandy tray.

There were two glasses, and the manservant poured out two measures of the fiery liqueur. Angelica, at his insistence, sipped a little of the one that he pressed into her hand. She nearly choked on it, though after a moment, it did seem to help melt the knot of lingering disturbance inside her. Nevertheless, the best use for the brandy, she thought, was to clean the sword cut.

The fumes rose to her head as she tipped the glass to wet a clean cloth, then used it to sponge the deep stab injury. With the utmost care, she allowed a little to seep into the center.

Perhaps the alcohol did something for her mental processes, for it was as she was reaching for a pad of linen to cover the wound that abrupt enlightenment came to her. She met Renold's eyes an instant, then returned to what she was doing as she considered it.

The purpose of the duel had never been to elicit compassion for Michel, or to draw out his half sister's feelings for his friend; that was not Renold's way. His intention, rather, had been to make of Michel a hero, a man who had stood up for Deborah in argument and carried that argument to its extreme, a meeting on the field of honor.

She said with a trace of wonder, "You planned for Michel to win. You intended to be injured."

"In a manner of speaking." The lids of his eyes curtained his expression. Tilting his head, he gave his attention to a one-handed operation at the front fastening of her gown.

He meant, Angelica realized, that his objective had been to fight just well enough to make it a fair fight, then allow his friend first blood. A slice on the upper arm, a small cut to the face or body would have been sufficient. Honor would have been satisfied. Renold had not meant to allow himself to be injured quite so bloodily.

Asperity was strong in her voice as she said, "Don't you

think making a pincushion of yourself over Deborah's affair of the heart is going a bit too far?"

"My sister is a darling girl, and it's my pleasure to aid her in so far as I am able. But Deborah's heart had nothing to do with it."

Her gown was growing loose at the waist; he had been assiduously releasing the buttons. Distracted by the warm brush of his fingers against her, she could not think. Yet it seemed obvious that if Renold was to have been the martyr, then he was the one intended to arouse compassion.

Whose compassion did he want? Whose heart was involved? Hers.

So what benefit was he to gain? What had actually happened out there on the gallery?

She had shown clearly her fear and concern. He had gained a greater knowledge of how much she cared.

But why would these things matter to him, unless he valued how she felt, unless he wanted to prove for himself the loving concern she had shown in answer to his mother's probing earlier?

There were two possible reasons why he might like to know that she cared. The first was to bind her closer to him, to make certain that Bonheur was his because she was attached to him by ties of love.

Then there was the other one, the one she hardly dared consider, much less believe. He just might want to know she loved him because he cared for her.

Eighteen

"Have you no interest in any other heart?"

She felt the vibration of his voice under her fingers as he spoke. It took an eternity to turn her head and meet his gaze.

The lamp on the washstand was reflected in the dark green surface of his eyes. It burned so steadily in the close room that the twin spots of golden light did not waver. His skin was burnished bronze, his hair caught the lamp's rays in a blue-black shimmer.

In the bedchamber beyond the door, the carving of the high bed had the rich patina of age. The gilded and lacquered crucifix above it, image of a more exalted martyr, shone red and gold. A leather-bound book with a clasp and latch of silver lay on the table beside the bed, resting on a crocheted cloth that looked like a fragile spiderweb. Roses, full-blown and sweet-scented, were arranged beside the book, drooping over the edges of an alabaster vase. In the warm silence, the sudden shattering of a pale pink blossom was loud, the petals rustling down in their inevitable destruction.

"You might have been killed," she said, and despaired as she saw that the words gave her away. Or maybe she had meant that they should.

"It's impossible to calculate the reactions of every person around you, each with their own needs and fears. You do what you can to achieve what you must."

"And what did you hope to achieve?"

"An epiphany," he said. "What else? The manifestation of perfect love. A nadir of blessedness in married bliss. I wanted," he added deliberately, "to see if you were content as my wife."

She was still an instant before she leaned to wrap the linen band around the back of his shoulder, smoothing the strip. She said, "It would have been considerably less drastic to ask."

"Yes, and to discover what? Lukewarm politeness, or possibly a ladylike assurance that all women are fond of their husbands on principle and as a matter of convenience. I required something with more passion."

Passion. It was a melodramatic word by its very nature, and could never be less. It could, however, be more. It was her task to prevent that. High drama would not help her. She said, "Then I'm afraid you may have been disappointed."

"I never expected you to fling yourself between the swords like Deborah; that would have been mere loss of confidence. So no, I wasn't disappointed." He leaned forward to make it easier for her to wrap the bandaging around the back of his shoulder. At the same time, he slid both hands inside her gown. He spanned her corseted waist so his fingertips met at front and back, then skimmed higher to cup her lawn-shrouded breasts.

She caught her breath on a small gasp. Closing her eyes, she swallowed quickly, then forced them open again. Her fingers not quite so nimble as before, she brought the roll of bandaging around to the front for the last time, tore the end in half lengthwise to form two strips and tied a flat knot. Placing her hands at the firm column of his neck, she tested the pulse which beat there with her thumb. She gathered courage, then looked into his eyes.

"Epiphanies require faith," she said, "faith comes from trust, trust is the result of truth. I might be more content as a wife if I could be sure I was ever a bride."

She watched the wrath darken his face, felt its rise in his blood under her touch. She also saw it fade almost immediately, settling into thoughtfulness.

"If it matters so much," he said tentatively, "there may be a way to manage it. We could repeat the wedding ceremony before a priest here at Bonheur."

She drew back a little. "You would do that?"

"Why not?"

"It would be a great deal of trouble." There was amazement in the words.

"It doesn't matter if it will ease your mind and make matters as they should be between us." His thumbs brushed the crests of her breasts, turning the nipples into tight buds of arousal.

"Even if you have already spoken the vows?" she said without a great deal of coherence.

"Saying them again won't make them less binding, and may make them more so." Busy under her clothing, he released the tape of her petticoats so that her skirts sagged against his knees. He smiled into her eyes as he said, "But I hope you wrapped my shoulder up well, for I don't intend waiting to exercise the more pleasurable of marriage rites."

Surely his willingness was proof he had not lied? Or perhaps she only wanted to be convinced of it. In any case, she could not deny the gladness rising inside her. And if passion was what he wanted, it was within her also, a passion of appreciation for his generosity, of thankfulness that his injury was no worse, of spirit that he desired her now.

More than these things, she wanted him with a rich, burgeoning need that had nothing to do with promises, past or future. The heat of his skin under her hands was an incitement, the hard muscles of his legs around her made her weak with longing. She wanted to be held close against him, to feel his mouth on hers and his hands urging her to fulfillment. Yet she couldn't bring herself to say it for fear he might condemn her for wantonness or discover more passion in her than was proper or needful.

She did not have to speak. He was so near it was only necessary to lower her gaze to the firm curves of his lips and sway a little closer. His smile faded as he released a hand to cup her face and draw her mouth against his own.

Clothes, there were so many clothes. Maddening in their weight and fullness, they clung and billowed, resisted removal with knotted ties and recalcitrant hooks and binding seams. Renold made a game of divesting her of them, however, placing a kiss in the bend of her elbow as he drew off the long sleeve of her gown, demanding the reward of a kiss for every hook undone on her corset, tracing the line of her chemise over her breasts as he pulled the cap sleeves down her arms.

He castigated the designer of pantalettes and suggested lascivious compensations if she should decide to dispense with them in the future. And so impatient was he with her garters after he tugged off her slippers that he left them and her stockings on as he bent to carry her to the bed.

"No, don't," she said in startled objection. "You'll start your shoulder bleeding again. I can walk."

"Backward?" he inquired. Without waiting for an answer, he rose from the chair and held her against him, mouth to mouth, while he stepped carefully toward a goal she quickly lost all sense of, certainly could not see.

A soft edge nudged the backs of her thighs. It was the low, single-width accouchement bed that sat against one wall of the dressing room. She sat down on it with more suddenness than grace.

Renold went to one knee before her. His voice rich with amusement and purpose, he said, "I used to think about having you on the bed like this in New Orleans. Constructing elaborate fantasies of what I would do, and what you would say, kept me sane while I tried to get at least a little sleep."

"You—wanted me then?" she said, the words jerky as he smoothed the calloused palms of his hands up her thighs and around her to clasp her hips.

"I wanted you from the moment I saw you, a desire—you must believe me—which had nothing to do with Bonheur or your father. Every time I wake and find you in my bed, every time I watch you brush your hair or look at you across the table, see you mount the stairs, walk across the floor, smile, frown, yawn, sneeze, I want you more. You fill my waking moments and walk naked through my dreams. If a time should come when I can no longer have you, I will go slowly, inevitably insane."

She wanted to believe it, could think of no reason for doubt. It was enough for the moment. She allowed her gaze to move with painful pleasure over the planes and angles of his face, though she avoided the emerald fire of his eyes. Inside her, a great pressure of longing rose, bringing with it the slow heat of a flush that had nothing to do with anger or embarrassment.

She felt voluptuous in her nakedness, wanton and wicked with only her jet earrings in her ears and black silk stockings to just above the knees held with blue silk garters embroidered with roses and studded with ribbon knots. She wanted him to be naked and wicked with her.

Reaching out she made trails with her fingertips through the curling hair of his chest, touched the copper coins of his paps. The soft hiss of his indrawn breath was an incitement and she rubbed slowly back and forth across the small taut knots of his nipples.

"Wait," he said, the deep timbre his voice like a caress. Rising, he stared down at her for long moments, his warm gaze touching the line of her throat, the pearl-like sheen of the globes of her breasts, the smooth white perfection of her thighs. Slowly, he put his hands to the waistband of his trousers.

She had never watched him undress before. He had come to her naked or in the dark, or else she had turned her head in modesty or to allow him privacy. Her lashes fluttered now and she swallowed, but she did not look away. Her pulse leaped as she realized she need not, that he would not mind her interest. She was more than merely interested, she acknowledged in newfound honesty. There was fascination for her in waiting for his body to be revealed.

A faint smile touched at his mouth. His movements became deliberate. Watching her with a tantalizing gleam in the depths of his eyes, he released the buttons at the front flap of his trousers, then made short work of the row that closed the concealed opening. Underneath, he wore linen drawers, and he unfastened these also. Without faltering, he spread the vee-shaped opening wide, exposing the flat, hard expanse of his abdomen and the narrow line of hair that dived down to a darker shadow. Then in a single, supple movement, he stripped off trousers and underdrawers together.

Splendid in the lamplight, rampantly naked, he turned from tossing his clothing aside. Facing her, he tilted his head, lowering his hands to his sides. The amusement vanished from his face, to be replaced by still watchfulness. A trace of darker color appeared under his skin.

Graceful, yet powerfully masculine, he was beautiful in the perfect proportions of his body, in the sculpting of muscle and the cording of the veins across them. His days without a shirt in the sun of Bonheur had given him a definite demarcation line between torso and lower body, so that he seemed like some mythical creature, half lusty inhabitant of the heated day and half ethereal being of the moonlit night. His male organ, strutted in arousal, was silken, enticing, yet foreign, a lure and also a threat. Angelica felt the compression of the muscles of her stomach, and also the contraction of deeper, more vital muscles and nerves.

She moistened her lips, held out her hands. Her voice soft with doubt and entreaty, she said, "Renold—"

He returned to one knee, taking her fingers and pressing them to his lips. Eyes shuttered, head bent, he turned her palms upward and laved the sensitive surface with the wet heat of his tongue. She shivered, her body inclining toward him so that her forehead touched the crisp waves of his hair.

With a hand on either stocking-clad knee, he inserted himself between them, holding her legs wide. He bent his head to kiss the tops of her knees, then follow the encircling garter with his tongue. At the same time, his hands spanned her slender waist, tested the satin surface of her skin at her abdomen, the tops of her thighs and between them. Faithfully and with slow precision, he followed the same path with his lips before moving inward.

His touch at the delicate, many petaled opening of her body was tender, careful, impossible to avoid in her position. She caught her breath with the wonder of it, then closed her eyes and stifled a low moan as with lips and tongue he traced and tasted her. Drifting in perfect delight, she discovered how wanton she could be. Her most secret recess was open to his gaze; she knew he looked and did not care. At the center of her being there was a hot, melting sensation and a tense emptiness that only he could fill. Nothing mattered except that he not stop until that was done.

He didn't. Imperious, exact, maddeningly expert, he teased and tested with mind-stopping deliberation. At the same time, his hands cupped and held and caressed, spreading the pleasure until it flowed in endless tides inside her, until her senses reached such a vibrant pitch that she writhed with soft sighs, half-stifled moans.

Her blood seethed in her veins and she could hear it thundering softly in her ears. Her chest rose and fell with the force of every breath. Her skin glowed with heat, while the muscles of her abdomen and her thighs tightened, quivering. She turned her head from side to side, her hands trembling as she clutched his shoulders, though she released him swiftly with a cry of self-reproach, afraid she had hurt him.

She raked her fingers through his hair instead in the mindless need to touch and hold. Smoothing the crisp strands back from his temple and over his ear, she dipped the tip of a finger inside his ear opening.

With a soft sound in his throat, he caught her hand, placing it on his shoulder, then moved inside her arms to gather her close. He buried his face between the tender mounds of her breast, placing a kiss there, then reached to twine his fingers in her hair and draw her moist and parted lips down for his kiss. He plunged his tongue into her mouth to probe the sweetness of her arousal, abrading the raw-silk roughness of her tongue with his own, applying gentle suction while he eased closer against her.

The press of his maleness against her abdomen and pelvis was hard, exciting. She moved nearer still, holding herself against it, reveling in the firm heat while her blood simmered in her veins. Inside, she waited, liquid and suspended.

He kissed the sensitive corner of her mouth, brushed his lips across her cheekbone, then feathered across her eyelids to taste the slight saltiness at the base of her lashes with his tongue. His voice quiet and a little rough, he said, "Open your eyes, Angelica. Look at me."

It was hard, so hard. Such an exposure of the soul. Her lashes quivered with the strain, lifted. Her eyes were dark blue and liquid with the desire that suffused her, so brilliant with loving emotion that their pupils were black and fathomless with it. His own gaze was devouring and glazed with such deep longing it had the look of pain.

His chest rose and fell with a long, difficult breath. "I love you, my angel."

The gladness that rose inside her swamped thought, encompassed the world, glittered in her eyes. "And I, you, my very own devil," she said.

Savage joy flowed over his features. His arms hardened around her. "Then take me inside when you're ready. It shall be as you wish."

She needed no more. Sliding her hands down the long, muscle-ridged line of his back, she grazed his hipbones with her palms, collected the silken length of him and set it in place. Then closing her hands slowly upon his hard flanks, she drew him close so he penetrated her engorged flesh in a slow and heated slide. A soft gasp left her, and she took him deeper, embracing him with spasmodic internal contractions.

He drew a hissing breath of tested control. Then in answer to her tentative movements, he set a rhythm with the steady throb of a heartbeat. He filled her, stretching, fueling the hovering rapture. It suffused them, spreading over the surface of their skin in a rippling of gooseflesh and the dew of perspiration. They rocked with it, gasping, spiraling higher, then higher still.

The apex caught them abruptly, in a frenzy of bliss and gladness and desperate longing. They surged upon each other, grasping, holding with panting breaths and tender flesh, seeking to deny the wisps of doubt that clung to them.

He picked her up, tumbling her to her back while he hovered above her. She cried out with pleasure for his deeper plunge, the deeper joy. A moment later, he shifted her with her hair coiling around them, drawing her on top of him on the narrow cot for the deepest possible penetration.

It was pulsating and sensual ecstasy, a primary indulgence

that vanquished time and place. They hovered, striving, mouth to mouth, their limbs moist and locked. Inside her, there gathered a shivering, dissolving sensation. Her hold grew rigid while a soft sound of distress escaped her.

Renold heaved above her once more, driving into her with shuddering impacts that ignited a brilliant internal explosion. She arched upward, welcoming the violent strokes, wanting them, needing them. Bracing on the cot's edges, he gave her what she required, throbbing and powerful inside her, his every movement fueling the wondrous rush sweeping through her.

It was consuming glory, a miraculous upheaval that transcended fear, banished thought, and could surely forge bonds of the flesh past all severance. Stunning, bursting, it held her, and with it she gave him all she had of herself, offered every vestige of her love.

With a final, wrenching lunge, he joined her in the perfect bond. Surrendering to it, they clung, drifting. And were hardly conscious of the moment when it left them and they were divided, separate, again.

He eased down beside her, settling her into the curve of his body. The steady burning lamplight burnished their skin with tints of yellow and gold, pink and peach, bronze and ivory. It caught the glint of their eyes as they lay, each staring wide-eyed, seeing nothing in the dim room.

Angelica grew cramped and uncomfortable, still she didn't move. There sifted into her mind a vague disturbance over Renold's offer to renew his wedding vows. The suggestion had been made so readily. He seemed comfortable with the idea, ready to do whatever pleased her. And yet, he had quickly turned to more personal matters without discussing it in any detail. It seemed odd.

A wedding at Bonheur. It would be a quiet affair, no doubt, as became a simple reaffirmation of vows that had supposedly already been made. She didn't want a great many people around her, did not care for the special decorations or a fine new dress, could not face a lavish display of food and drink. Her mourning made it impossible, of course, but more than that, it would be a reminder of everything that her father had planned for her.

She wondered what he would think if he could see her, if he would be horrified or pleased. Certainly, he would be worried, she knew, for he had loved her in his way, and must be concerned that she was living with a man so much his enemy. It was possibly just as well that he would never know.

She had accused Renold of self-sacrifice, of martyring himself on the field of honor to prove a point. Yet, wasn't she doing the same by marrying Renold in order to return legal claim to Bonheur to those from whom her father had taken it? Was it martyrdom if she wanted the consequences with all her heart?

But perhaps Renold was also sacrificing himself by marrying her. It was his choice, one she could not remember being given the opportunity to refuse. Still, it might be wrong to accept that gesture from him now.

Did he mean it? Would he go through with another ceremony? And if he did, would it be as he said, a concession to ease her mind? Or could it be just a clever ruse to legitimize their union, their first and only wedding? She wished she knew, but saw no way to discover the truth.

Renold stood with his shoulder braced against the column of the gallery, staring down the drive. Tit Jean was approaching from the steamboat landing, coming on his mule at a fast trot. It was plain the manservant had news. Pray God, it was what they all waited to hear.

It was. Father Goulet would be arriving on the steamboat tomorrow morning, following after the note the priest had sent accepting Renold's invitation to Bonheur. The wedding could proceed.

Renold was relieved. He had been afraid his whim to have his own priest, his mother's old confessor, would cause considerably more delay. He wanted this over and done; the sooner, the better. They would have the ceremony tomorrow evening.

Everything was ready, he thought. His mother had seen fit

to approve the decision when he told her of it, and had thrown her considerable talent for organization into the preparations. The thing would be a bit more grand than he had planned, but it made no difference so long as Angelica was pleased.

It had been touch and go two days ago. Tit Jean, in the small river town on an errand, had watched the arrival of a steamer from upriver. The boat had landed several crates and barrels for Bonheur. The manservant had naturally seen to it that they were brought up to the house. Following after them, he had begun to unpack them. Angelica had walked into the middle of the operation.

Renold had heard her cry out as he walked from the stable. Cold sweat drenched him, and he broke into a run. He found her standing in the middle of the litter of straw and broken crates, her hands to her mouth as she stared at the carefully stacked china and crystal, the burlap-wrapped hams and sides of bacon, the boxes of raisins and crocks of pickles and curious shell-shaped pottery jars of olive oil. Tears had spilled over her lashes as her gaze rested on the silk gown that spilled from a special box. Of lustrous pale blue, it was embellished with cobweb lace, draped with ribbon loops and streamers, and set with pink silk rosebuds.

It was, of course, the bridal gown commissioned in Natchez for Angelica by her father. With it were all the rich meats and other confections for the wedding feast. Standing there, staring at it, Renold had cursed himself for his lack of forethought. He should have known the things would come, should have done something to stop them.

He had stepped toward her, meaning to take her in his arms. Turning away as if she had not seen him, she walked to her bedchamber and closed the door behind her. He had listened shamelessly outside, afraid he would hear her crying. There had not been a sound. That had, somehow, been worse.

When she appeared later, she had been quite composed. She would wear the bridal gown, she said. Torn between a need to see her out of the black of mourning, if only for a day, and reluctance to have his wife dressed by the man who had stolen Bonheur, Renold had said nothing. Wearing it had some meaning for her, he thought, a gesture toward what was past. He had no objection to that so long as she looked toward the future. With him.

"Maître?"

The manservant was still standing before him, patiently waiting to be noticed again. Renold said, "My apologies, Tit Jean. There was something else?"

"The men you have been expecting? I think they may have come. Two strangers got off the steamboat on the day of the blue dress, one young, one older. They have been asking questions."

"Hardly conclusive," Renold said. "Unless you have a more exact description?"

"Indeed, maître," Tit Jean said, "but it is, I think, unnecessary. The watch posted along the river road reports that these two rode past the house late last night. They stopped to look, then went on."

"No one disturbed them?"

"No, maître."

"The watch wasn't seen?"

Tit Jean shook his head. "They think not, though they can't be sure."

"Instruct them to look sharp. They will be back, and they may bring friends."

The manservant inclined his head, then moved away into the house. Renold turned back toward the front lawn with a frown between his brows.

It was Carew, of course. What was he doing sneaking around? Why didn't he just ride up the drive and demand his daughter?

Scorn rose inside Renold as he considered the question. He could not believe his reputation as a swordsman was so fearsome it would keep a loving father at bay. That it apparently could only strengthened the low opinion he had of Edmund Carew.

What was the man up to, then? Would he try another piece of trickery like the one that failed in New Orleans?

Let him. Bonheur would be ready.

Twilight was the time chosen for the wedding. The sun set

across the fields, edging the blades of the long rows of cane with gold. It swathed the sky in gauzy clouds of pink, rose, mauve, and lavender before sinking behind the saw-toothed line of the trees. The evening settled into the melancholy half-light known as *l'heure bleu*, the blue hour.

Doves called with a mournful note across the lawn. The scent of honeysuckle hung on the warm air, drifting in at the open French doors. Blended with it were the smells of woodsmoke and roasting meat from the wedding feast that waited. The rich fragrances joined the sweet lemon scent of the magnolias that banked the altar erected at one end of the front parlor. Branched candelabras stood there also, their candles casting a soft glow over the fine damask altar cloth, the silver chalice, the worn cassock of the priest who stood to one side.

Deborah, softly and with precise fingering, played a Beethoven sonata on the pianoforte. The notes flowed around the long room—the doors between front and back parlors had been thrown wide—then drifted out the French doors into the evening. Michel stood at Deborah's side, turning the pages of her music. They glanced at each other now and then in silent, half-smiling communication.

As if drawn by the scents and sounds, the people of Bonheur approached the house, the house servants crowding into the back of the parlor, the field hands lining the gallery. Estelle and Tit Jean, as was their right, took their places in the forefront of the gathering near Renold's mother.

All that was needed was the bride. She was late.

Renold stood in a pretense of ease beside the bedchamber door where Angelica would appear. He kept his face impassive with an effort while he waited, though his heart was beating so hard he could hear the links of his watch chain rattling against a waistcoat button. So much had gone wrong in what might be called, with some irony, his courtship of Angelica. He would not be surprised if something prevented this last step.

Yet if she did not mean to emerge, surely she would have had Estelle tell them. The maid had left her over half an hour ago.

He himself had not seen Angelica since dinner the evening before; she had kept to her room all day as was the tradition. She had been composed and cheerful last night at least. If she had had second thoughts since then, there had been nothing to indicate it.

The doorknob in front of him rattled, turned slowly. He exhaled slowly in soundless relief. Then she stood in the opening, and he forgot to breathe at all.

Sublimely perfect in her wedding gown, she was lovely in a way that tore at his heart. She met his gaze, her smile serious, searching, then moved forward to take his arm.

The silk of her skirts made a soft, whispering sound as she walked beside him toward the altar. The nudge of her hoop against his ankle was incredibly sensuous. Pride was a curious thing to feel, yet it surged up inside him along with a wild and reckless desire to take her away somewhere out of all this and make love to her the whole night long.

But the priest was waiting; the look in his old wise eyes a bit severe, as if he knew the impetuous thoughts that raged within the bridegroom. Renold steadied Angelica as they genuflected. The priest stepped forward to receive them.

"My child," the priest said, smiling at Angelica, "it isn't often that I must unite a man and woman in matrimony twice over. Still, your scruples become you well, and it is my great pleasure to perform this service. I pray that the devotion you share with Renold be doubly blessed as it is doubly sanctified."

Renold had not expected such a confirmation of the first ceremony from the priest. He had thought, rather, that seeing Father Goulet, hearing the same vows spoken in the same way, might spark some useful memory. If it had not, he had expected to turn the conversation later to draw it from the priest. He was intensely grateful that it had come without his urging.

The gaze of wonder and sweet, spreading joy Angelica turned up to him made the waiting for the priest's arrival as nothing, the time spent worth the effort and the hazard. Taking her hand, he pressed his lips to it, smiling into her eyes. Together, then, they turned toward the altar.

There was comfort in the ritual. The response had as much to do with the sounds of the Latin, the smells of the incense and burning candle wax, the movements of kneeling and rising as the meaning of the words. Yet the words themselves had a grandeur that transcended place and intent to bring an upsurge of pure exultation.

So Renold spoke his vows without faltering, and felt them inside where pledges become a matter of honor. Angelica's responses rang in his ears with soft fervor. The sentence of mutual and inseparable bondage was pronounced. Renold placed the loving kiss of a husband on Angelica's lips, and they turned to face their well-wishers.

It was then that the voice struck through the sound of applause and the chorus of felicitations. The words were quiet, gently chiding.

"Congratulations, my darling daughter," Edmund Carew said from the doorway of Bonheur. "I am delighted to wish you happy. I have just one concern: Who gave the bride away?"

Renold stood perfectly still while Angelica turned with the soft stuff of her skirts brushing his legs under his trousers like the stinging silk fluff of nettles. Her eyes burned with blue fire and condemnation.

Her voice was quiet as she spoke, yet he felt every word like a lash on his unprotected heart. "You said he was dead. Did you think—but no, you knew. You must have known. You might have married me once, otherwise, but never twice."

She turned then and ran from him, flinging herself into her father's open arms. Above her head, Edmund Carew stared at Renold, the deserted bridegroom, with dark disdain.

Renold knotted his hand into a fist and walked to where the two stood. He might have done more if not for the priest who moved swiftly after him to place a hand on his arm. He spoke for Angelica alone.

"The reason for the excess nuptials, you think, is to make sure of the dowry? I would have married you," he said, "if you had ten fathers living, and nothing to bring me other than your sweet bare self."

"Words," she said, turning in her father's hold, "always

words. They may be pleasant to hear, but how can I tell what they are worth?"

"They are worth what I make them, like the vows just sworn between us."

Carew's voice cut between them. "There is such a thing as annulment."

Renold gave the man no more than a single glance. "Ineligible."

"Something you saw to with your usual thoroughness," Angelica said, the words acidly accusing.

"And with all the attendant joy and mindless rapture," he agreed because he couldn't help it.

"Swine," her father said, breathing hard through his nose that was pinched white around the nostrils. "I would like to call you out."

For a brief flicker of time, Renold evaluated the man as an opponent. Edmund Carew was gray of face and his body skeletal from the effects of the accident and his illness. There was no strength in him. It was difficult to see what held him upright other than pride and concern for his daughter. Renold felt his contempt leavened by a fleeting admiration.

"Do," he said in provocation, though he hoped the older man would ignore it.

"No!" Angelica cried with the color receding from her face. "No," she said again as she looked from one to the other. "Neither of you is in any condition to fight."

"More than that," Carew said simply, "the game isn't worth the ante. Come away with me, Angelica. Laurence is waiting outside. We will go to New Orleans where we will appeal to the law to put these people off our property. There is no need to stand here bandying words with the man who took advantage of you."

Laurence was not outside, Renold saw, but waiting in the shadows of the gallery beyond the door. The younger man was following the exchange with a look of gloating satisfaction on his weakly handsome face.

Ignoring the former fiancé, Renold said, "No, no need at all to bandy words, unless they are tokens of love." His gaze sought and held Angelica's as he went on. "You are my wife.

This time there is no denying, no doubt, no looking back. Bonheur is only bricks and boards and fallow fields without you by my side. I need you, and I can't live without the promise of forever we made short minutes ago."

"Love?" Carew said. "What makes you think you know the meaning of the word?"

In the affairs of men there was a rough justice, Renold recognized. Once, in his arrogance, he had pledged himself to make Angelica love him, then to force her to choose between her father and himself. He had wanted by that means to show Carew what it felt like to lose the thing he valued most, the love of his daughter. Now Carew had put that choice to Angelica, and it was he himself who must fight to keep her.

To his left, his mother was on her feet, her face strained as she watched them. Deborah, who had moved from the pianoforte as the ceremony began, was standing next to Michel. Anger and dismay was mirrored in the faces of the other guests.

"I know love," Renold said in vibrant certainty. "It's in a smile, a glance, the sound of a sigh in the night or laughter at noon. It's the touch that takes ugliness from a scar, that gives and seeks warmth and does not flinch from bleeding wounds. It's the sharing of pain and comfort in need, company in sunshine and rain. It's bright beckoning hope, and also the unguarded meshing of hearts and minds that makes words unnecessary, or like alchemy, turns them to rich, indestructible gold. Love is the single person without whom nothing else has meaning. Love is Angelica."

A strained quiet fell. It almost seemed, as Edmund Carew stared at him, that there was sympathy in the older man's face.

Still, Angelica's father shook his head. "I am aging and ill, and can make no pretty speeches. All I have to say is this: I cannot live without my daughter, and I will not try."

Simple, yet devastating.

Renold saw the pain and pity and love the words roused in Angelica, and stilled himself to face what must come. And because he was fair and preferred a swift end to prolonged agony, he spoke in quiet inquiry. "Go or stay, my love? Which will it be?"

She was no coward. She faced him and met his gaze more squarely than expected, also with more understanding and meaning than he might have wished. "You are my savior and my comfort, Renold. I love to laugh with you, and love with you, and to reach out with some thought and find that you have taken it, turned it, and made it more than I expected. You gave the desire, I gave you the passion you asked, but that isn't enough. You lied to me for gain, you let me think my father was dead when he needed me. Now his need is greater, while you are so locked within yourself that you need me not at all."

"That might have been true once," he said, "but no longer."

"I would like to believe that, but I can't. And so the question you asked has only one answer. You know what it must be; you have always known, or you would have done things differently from the start."

Yes, he knew. But accepting was another matter. He took a swift step toward her.

"Stop," Laurence said as he strode forward into the double parlor. "Didn't you hear Angelica? She has no use for you now that we have found her."

"Laurence!" Carew said, spinning around so quickly he staggered. "I asked you to stay out of this."

"It looks to me like you might need some help. Come on, Angelica, let's get out of here." A faint sneer flitted across the younger man's face as he glanced at Renold, then he reached and closed his hand on Angelica's arm.

She gasped at the bite of Laurence's fingers. That soft sound snapped Renold's tenuous control. He shot out his hand to grasp the other man's wrist.

Carew wavered on his feet "Here now. No rough stuff, I told you, Laurence—"

He broke off, his face twisting. Clamping a hand to his chest, he crumpled his shirt and coat in a hard grip. He swayed, gasping. Then he caved at the waist, pitching forward.

Renold saw him falling, spun around in time to receive the

older man in his arms. He eased him to the floor and knelt beside him.

Edmund Carew stared up at him. His fine old eyes were mirrors of pain and doubt. They held also the same abject despair that Renold felt inside.

Nineteen

ANGELICA SAT IN A CHAIR IN THE DIMLY LIGHTED BEDCHAMBER and contemplated, wakeful and desolate as an orphaned owl, the ruin of her wedding night. Only it would not actually have been her wedding night, of course. Renold had, amazingly, told her the truth.

She did not want to be here, still, at Bonheur. Her instinct was to get away. She required distance between Renold and herself so she need not see him, need not hear his voice, need not have any reminder of all the things he had done, the things he had said. She needed nothing to weaken her defenses. Most of all, she wanted her father well away from anything that might upset him.

Impossible.

Did Edmund Carew mind that he had been put to bed at Bonheur? Did he even know it?

His collapse had been brought on by the strain of the confrontation in the parlor on his weak heart. His condition was the same as that which had caused him to be set on seeing her married and secure in the first place. Yet, it was worse now, aggravated by all he had been through in the past weeks.

He had stayed in the water for hours, Laurence said. The two men had been separated. Her father, who had tied himself to a floating log, had been swept to the bank far downstream. It had been touch and go for several weeks; he had been out of his head, among strangers. He had finally sent word back to Natchez. Laurence had gone to get him, at the same time telling him of Renold's message to her aunt indicating that Angelica was alive.

Angelica could not get over it: He was alive. He was here at Bonheur where he had so looked forward to being. Here, finally, with her.

Her father had been desperately ill, near death, and she had not known, had not been there. Her own injuries would have made her useless, she supposed, but she should have been there.

At least she was with him now.

Heart failure. There was nothing that could be done for the problem. Rest, quiet, an easy mind and a pleasant future, these were the only things that could be prescribed. None of them seemed likely.

Her father was determined to wrest Bonheur from Renold and his mother. She could not permit that, knowing as she did that he had no right to it. What was left, then, except to go back to Natchez and live with her aunt? There, her father would fret and scheme over her future just as he had before; it was inevitable.

How long could he live in such a stew? A few weeks? A month or two? Perhaps a year? She could not bear thinking of it.

There came a soft rustling from the direction of the bed. She was on her feet instantly, moving to stand beside it. Her father was awake, his head turned toward her. There was doubt in his face before it was replaced by a slow smile.

"I thought I… might have dreamed that I found you," he said weakly.

His face was so gray and drawn that it hurt her to see it. She said softly, "I'm here, and it's no dream. Could I get you something? Water? A little broth? Another pillow? Or perhaps you need Tit Jean to help you?"

"No, nothing. I just—want to look at you."

It seemed a little of his usual force had returned to his voice. Regardless, she said, "You need to rest and regain your strength."

"In a moment." His gaze roamed her face and he shifted his hand, opening the fingers, so that she reached to clasp them in her own warm grasp. He said, "I should have stayed away. It would have been... better, I think."

"No. Never."

"You have a home, someone to care about you. It's what I wanted."

"It was built on lies. No, we'll go away as soon as you're strong enough, just as you said last night. I don't want Bonheur, never want to live in this house. There are too many things here I would rather forget."

"Can you do that?" he asked, his gaze open, steady.

"I can try," she answered, unblinking. "Maybe—maybe we could find a little place, a cabin somewhere off to ourselves, just the two of us. We could have a garden and keep a few chickens, I could take in a little sewing. It wouldn't take so much to live—"

"That's no life for you," her father said in revulsion. "I wanted—I wanted so much more. Divorce is difficult, ugly, but can be arranged. Afterward, you and Laurence can be together."

"No," she said before he even finished speaking. The word was final, her tone without compromise.

"He won't hold this marriage against you."

"It doesn't matter. Laurence and I—it just isn't possible. Please, we can talk about this another time. You should rest."

"I can't. What will become of you after I'm gone? You'll be alone, all your life long. I know what that is, you know. After your mother—no, it isn't good, isn't right."

"You weren't alone," she said quietly. "You had me."

He looked away. "Yes, and I love you dearly, but still."

"It isn't enough? I do understand; you never remarried." She went on quickly, afraid the reminder might upset him. "Anyway, I was trying to tell you that I may not be alone. If I'm right, you will have to stay around a long time, after all, to see your grandchild and watch him grow."

"What are you saying?" There was doubt and incredulity suspended in his face.

Her smile trembled at the edges. "The ceremony last night was not the first; Renold and I were married some weeks ago." She hurried on to explain as best she was able.

"And you think there may be a child." Excitement burned bright in the depths of her father's eyes.

"I would rather not tell anyone yet, especially Renold, but the chance is there. Do you think it makes a difference?"

He watched her face while he gave a slow nod. "It may, yes, a great deal of difference."

Uneasiness touched her. "It's far from certain. My—my monthly courses are only a little late, barely more than two weeks. It could come to nothing."

"You are a healthy young woman, your body has regained its tone since the accident." He paused, "I suppose all was as it should be with you the month before, just after you were injured?"

She nodded in agreement, though she was a little flushed. These were not matters she had ever discussed with her father.

He pursed his lips in consideration. "Women have an instinct."

"I would still prefer to be sure before it's mentioned to anyone."

"Yes, yes. This is news, indeed. It requires thought." He closed his eyes as if suddenly exhausted. At the same time, there was much more color in his face.

Angelica stood for long moments beside the bed. It appeared her father had fallen into a sudden light slumber. She turned away at last.

The dusky light of dawn was edging around the draperies that were pulled over the French doors. She pushed the long silk panels aside, along with their lace undercurtains, then opened the door.

The air was fresh, clean, and cool. She breathed deep of it, even as she wrapped her dressing sacque closer around her. Obeying a strong impulse, she stepped out onto the gallery.

The quiet was pervasive, broken only by the distant crowing of a rooster. It was welcome; the celebration of the wedding in the quarters, with the music of banjo and fiddle and shouts of laughter and enjoyment, had gone on far into the night. At least someone had wrung some pleasure from the proceedings.

She wondered what had become of Laurence. She had looked around for him while the doctor from town had been with her father. He seemed to have disappeared, perhaps going back to the boarding house where he and her father had put up when they arrived. She had thought to offer a bed at Bonheur, but was relieved that it had not been necessary.

No doubt he would return some time during the day to check on the older man, since he had been looking after him. It would be convenient if he did appear; she wanted to talk to him. She was curious to hear more about how he and her father had found her. Most of all, however, she owed him the courtesy of an explanation and a formal release from any obligation he might still feel toward her.

There was a movement at a doorway farther along the length of the house. Nerves jumping, Angelica whipped around in that direction.

It was Deborah, also in a dressing sacque over her nightclothes and with her hair spilling down her back. The other girl smiled and walked toward her. As she came closer, she asked after the patient. Angelica answered her with guarded optimism.

Conversation ground to a halt. They stood in awkward silence, staring out over the dew-spangled fields of cane that rolled away from the edge of the lawn beyond that section of the gallery. A flock of pigeons wheeled above the house and lit in a silver-white flutter of wings on the roof of the *pigeon-nier*. The morning breeze stirred the two women's wrappers, lifting the folds and dropping them again.

Deborah glanced at Angelica, hesitated, then said abruptly, "You aren't really going, are you? I mean, I've grown used to having you here and seeing you with Renold. Even mother thinks you are good for him now, though she had her doubts at first. Isn't there some way to make it work?"

The concern in the other girl's voice made Angelica's throat close for an instant. She swallowed before she said, "I don't think so. There are too many things between us. If they were not enough, there is the fact that I was about to leave him, go with my father. Renold is unlikely to overlook that. I have been told that he—*he is not a forgiving man.*"

She had heard those words in New Orleans. She had good reason to remember them.

"What things?" Deborah demanded. "What can matter so much?"

"He told me my father and Laurence were dead so that I would be forced to depend on him, to stay with him."

"He thought they were at first. I know because Michel told me so. Renold would not have given you the pain of thinking them dead if he had not believed it himself. Later, when he learned they were alive, the damage had already been done, and he wanted time to win your love."

"Time to see to it that the marriage could not be easily dissolved."

"Oh, please, Angelica! Renold is many things, but I don't think you can accuse him of being cold-blooded. If he had wanted to do what you are suggesting, he could have accomplished it the moment you regained your senses. Or before. What was to stop him except common decency?"

"He always intended it; he said as much." The words were defensive.

"Yes, and what could be more natural in a husband? What else did you expect?"

She hadn't expected anything because she had never been certain she was wed. She still had only the most vague recollection of that first ceremony. And yet, her heart must have known what it wanted and needed.

She said, "Renold set out from the first, even on the steamboat, to use me to regain Bonheur and avenge your father's death. He did that. He need not have carried it so far, unless—unless the intimacy of marriage was a part of his plan."

"He loves you; he said so in front of everyone. And you love him. Surely that changes matters?"

"Love, the panacea for all ills?" Angelica lifted a hand to press her fingers to her tired eyes. "It isn't, you know. There are some things nothing can mend."

"Maybe it can't, maybe it can," Deborah said, "but do you really think, knowing Renold, that he will give up so easily?"

Angelica was afraid he would not, which was why she wanted to get away the instant her father could travel. "Do you think," she said, "that I will give in so easily?"

Deborah sighed. "I suppose you can't," she said, "but oh, how I wish you would."

The morning advanced. The brazen ball of the sun rose higher in the sky, laying its furnace heat across the galleries of Bonheur, raising the temperature inside the house so that all the doors were flung open except those keeping out the direct rays. Summer had arrived.

Angelica, dressing for the day, stood in indecision. Her armoire was filled with black which she no longer needed, having no one to mourn. A single colorful gown hung on the hooks, her blue silk wedding gown. It was difficult to say what was more inappropriate.

There was no real choice, of course. The black gown with the shortest sleeves, lowest bodice, and most white trim would have to do. Wearing it was a potent reminder, if she had need of one, of exactly how things stood.

Her position at Bonheur was as muddled as her wardrobe. As neither the mistress of the house nor a guest, she once more had no place, no duties, no right to order her father's sick-room or even request a cup of tea or coffee for herself. It was disconcerting. She had not quite realized that she had come so far toward being the lady of the manor. All that had been lacking were the symbolic keys. Madame Delaup had hinted lately that these would be forthcoming after the wedding. Now it was too late.

She kept mainly to her father's room, where she read or did needlework while he dozed. Even her breakfast and luncheon were served on a tray in the bedchamber.

Now and then, she stepped out onto the gallery for air and to stretch her legs, sometimes even making a full circuit of the house. She never lingered, however, since she did not like leaving her father alone for any length of time.

It was on her return from walking in late afternoon, as the sun's heat began to fade, that she heard voices in the sickroom. She stepped inside, then came to an abrupt halt. It was Renold who stood at the end of her father's bed with his hands braced on the footboard.

Her heart throbbed in her chest. The others had come and

gone on courtesy visits, but it was the first time she had seen her husband since the night before.

His gaze stabbed, his hands were clenched on the wood, but his voice remained polite. "Good evening, my dear," he said. "We have just been having a pleasant chat about various things of no particular importance, your father and I. Squabs for dinner, the waters and gaming at White Sulphur Springs—the mathematical odds of my wife's first child being a son or a daughter. I have my money on a boy, but will pay up gladly for a daughter in her mother's image."

Angelica turned on her father, her hot gaze accusing. "You told him!"

"I have given it much thought while lying here today," Edmund Carew said, his head turned toward her on his pillow. "It seemed best."

"You don't know what you have done."

Her father's pale lips curved in wry acknowledgment. "I have tried to right a wrong, or perhaps several of them."

"And I am grateful for the consideration," Renold said to the older man. "I would be even more grateful if you will give me leave to speak to Angelica alone."

Edmund gave him a straight look. "The time has passed when you might have needed my permission for anything."

"Still." Renold waited.

The older man gave a slow nod. "I see no reason to object. I was about to ring for Tit Jean to help me dress for dinner in any case. I do—have my standards."

Recognition and something more that might have been appreciation flickered in Renold's eyes. He inclined his head before turning to Angelica. "Shall we walk outside?"

"I don't believe it will benefit either of us." She held her head high as she gave her answer.

A line appeared between Renold's brows and his mouth took on a hard set she had never seen before. He said bitingly, "There can be no benefit for us in a shouting match guaranteed to attract friends, relatives, and the entire complement of house servants, either. But I am willing to oblige if that is your whim."

"My whim," she said with emphasis, "is for solitude."

"It is, of course, the best milieu for sulking, but my indulgence does not extend quite that far."

"Or your consideration?" she said. "What point is there in discussion if we only run around in circles and return to the same place?"

"We won't do that," he said with frightening resolution. "There's too much at stake." He walked past her to the French door where he turned. "Coming?"

She had time to think as she followed him, time to marshal her arguments while they skirted the house, descended the steps, and moved out under the spreading oak trees. It was his error that he insisted on going so far away from the house.

As he turned to face her in the deep shade, she said, "This is about your son by Clotilde Petain, isn't it?"

"It's about my weakness in preferring to have the people I care for near me, if that's what you mean." He moved to put his back to the wide trunk of the oak.

"Possessiveness is hardly an attribute of a good parent," she said. "And being responsible, however noble it may appear, is no substitute for integrity."

"I only want any child of mine to know its father and be acknowledged by him, to have a place in the world where he belongs without question. I understand, as you apparently do not, the importance of it." His hands were behind him, pressed hard into the woody bark so that his fingertips gleamed bloodless in the fading light.

"So because you were baseborn," she said, "you have suddenly decided that you can't let me go, after all. Or is it guilt that moves you, guilt that your vengeance and unbridled desires may bring another soul into the world who must always yearn to belong? Well, you need not trouble yourself. If there is a child, it will belong to me, and will have all the love there is in me."

"Your love and my name? I will never allow you to dissolve this marriage, but will stand squarely in the way of any move you make to do it. You will never have another husband." The last was spoken deliberately, as a pronouncement.

She was grimly amused. "A horrifying threat, but you will forgive me if I don't shrink from it. My experience of marriage has not been so rapturous I yearn to repeat it."

"Rapturous, no," he said, lifting his hands, storing at the perfect pattern of bark indented on the palms. His voice dropping to a lower note, he added, "But it was not without its moments of joy, or so I thought. What did I do that was so terrible you must leave me, taking my child for revenge?"

The evening was deepening around them. The haunting perfume of honeysuckle drifted on the still air. She thought the fragrance would always be a reminder of a candlelit ceremony on a summer evening, and also this moment when she was forced yet again to test the untold limits of pain.

She could go, taking his unborn child, or she could stay while her father went away to die alone. That was the choice he was forcing on her. She could not have them all, father, husband, child. Of the three, Renold was the one to whom she was least necessary for existence. And if he could force her to choose, it was he who would be the least worthy of the loving.

Turning her gaze to the dusk beyond Renold, she said, "What did you do? Nothing. You were the perfect husband. Oh. Except for one or two small failures. Such as attempting to compromise my good name. Abducting me so that I lost contact with my father and my fiancé. Marrying me when I was too ill and drugged to know what I was doing in order to gain possession of Bonheur. Telling me my father was dead when you had no proof. Making love to me under the guise of banishing my fear of steamboat travel. Spiriting me away to Bonheur when, if I remained at the townhouse, there might be a chance I would be rescued, or worse, discover that you lied."

"No, Angelica," he began.

"Yes," she insisted. "And we must not forget the worst crime of all. You made love to me in order to gain a hostage to keep me with you. For these small joys, I am supposed to love you and reward you by allowing you the honor of being a father to that child?"

He thrust his hands in his pockets and turned his head to look at her. He said, "So it really is for revenge?"

She had thought he would defend himself, was momentarily confounded that he did not even try. All at once, she was tired beyond imagining. She said slowly, "Perhaps it is at that, though I thought it was self-preservation."

"And the words of love you spoke last night? Was it only the passion of the moment, or is it simply that you hate me far more than you ever cared for me?"

She opened her mouth to deny it, thought better of it. The currents of emotion surging inside her ran both ways, in all truth.

"I thought so," he answered. "Deborah told me you said that I am unforgiving. It's possibly true. But I am not alone in that fault, Angelica. God help me, I am not alone."

He pushed from the tree and left her then. She watched him walk away and a cry rose up, aching, inside her.

She did not make a sound.

That was some consolation.

Twenty

HIDING WAS COWARDLY, POSSIBLY CHILDISH, CERTAINLY useless. Angelica didn't care. It soothed the edges of her jangled soul to be alone there in the deepening darkness while lamps were lit inside the house and around her the fireflies began to sparkle like earthbound stars. To stand with her back pressed against the tree where Renold had stood gave her a peculiar comfort, almost as if some essence of him remained in the wood. How she longed to be closed in his arms, to rest her head on his chest while she allowed him to do whatever he wished with her, for her.

Never again.

Her throat ached. She swallowed against it as she gazed unseeing into the lavender-gray dusk.

She was perfectly capable of taking her destiny into her own hands. She could order her life, decide where she must go and what she would do, care for her father, provide for her child. She had the strength and the ability.

Yet, how much easier it would be if there were other hands to help with the tasks, other shoulders to share the burdens.

She had made her choice. Or had she? Had there ever really been a choice? She had done what was required by circumstances and the tenets of right and wrong by which she had been taught to pattern her life. That was all.

What would she have said to Renold if she could have answered only according to the dictates of her heart?

What was the use in contemplating something so impossible? It was done. There could be no going back.

She heard the footsteps, saw the flitting shadow, and her heart swelled. Renold. He must be returning to escort her back to the house. It was like him to extend that courtesy to her even now.

The man stepped from behind her, around the trunk of the tree. His voice light and without depth, as he spoke.

"You knew I would come, didn't you? That's why you waited."

"Laurence," she exclaimed, whirling to face him where he stood so close. "What are you doing here? Where did you come from?"

He stepped nearer, the man she had once been engaged to marry, a tall, slender figure in the night shadows. "I've wanted to see you, to talk to you, for such a long time. But Harden was always there. It's been maddening."

The anger in the last words surprised her. She said, "Why didn't you stay last night, or call at the house today?"

"Oh, sure. I can just imagine the welcome. The truth is, Harden doesn't want anybody near you, hasn't from the minute he pulled you out of the river."

She stared at him a moment before she said, "How do you know that?"

"Oh, I saw him with you after the explosion. He was like a crazy man, threatening the doctor and anybody else who tried to take you out of his sight. Besides, there have been rumors all over New Orleans about how he quarreled over you with Farness, a man who had been his friend for years."

"How could you—no, that's right. You said you weren't hurt in the accident or swept away like Papa."

Laurence shrugged, his gaze moving past her shoulder. "I had a few bruises. Actually, I made it to shore pretty quickly; I've always been a strong swimmer." There was uneasiness in his voice.

"But then—where were you when I was injured and unconscious?" she said in puzzlement. "I don't understand why it was Renold who took care of me."

Laurence gave her a petulant scowl. "Everything was so confused, some people taken to one house, some to another, the dead and injured laid out in rows together. Harden was the man of the hour; he not only brought you to the bank, but went back in after a bunch of other people—a couple of women screaming bloody murder and an old gent, a couple of kids. Then he took over, had people jumping every which way, snapping to his orders right and left. Whatever he said was the law; nobody was going to listen to me if I stood against him. Besides, you were soon out like a candle, and I didn't have the faintest idea what to do for you."

Excuses, self-justification; she recognized their sound. She said, "You thought I was going to die."

"But you didn't. Harden took you to New Orleans and, after a while, you got all right. I followed along, but soon found out what an expert he is with sword and pistol. I found a man to keep a watch on you, and he did, though it turned out he was a double-dealing little rat who sold me out when it came right down to it. Anyway, there wasn't much else I could do. It was pretty plain you wouldn't be allowed visitors, and it would have been suicide to try forcing my way into the house."

A double-dealing little rat. The idea triggered a memory that made her scalp tingle in horror. In an effort to banish it, she said, "You didn't tell Aunt Harriet where I was?"

"I intended to, really I did. But she was half out of her mind with grief over your father, and I didn't see what help she would be at getting you out of Harden's clutches. Besides, she would have got together with my mother, and the two of them might have decided the best thing would be to let you go, leave you to him. I couldn't do that."

He had not said why he couldn't. Was it from duty and affection, or could it be that he could not relinquish the prospect of Bonheur? But he was speaking again.

"None of it matters now, not really. I've found you, and that's the important thing. We'll go to Natchez, stay with some people I know while we see about getting you out of this stupid marriage. It's bound to be expensive—trips to appear before the legislature, gifts and money to the right people—but you can stand the price. Once it's over, you may not be accepted in society any more, but we'll be so busy traveling to the watering places in the summer, to New Orleans in winter and Europe in spring and fall that we won't care for that. What do you say?"

She turned away from him. Over her shoulder, she said, "I don't think you quite understand how matters have developed these last weeks. I mean between Renold and myself."

"Do you think I can't guess?" he said, his tone just a little snide. "So you are no longer pure and innocent, I don't mind; I'm perfectly willing to forgive any little lapse of that nature. You know I will always love you exactly as I did before."

Which could mean anything, she thought, even that he had never loved her at all. No, that was unjust. He was young and it was not his fault that he had been afraid of Renold. And if the picture he painted of their life together failed to appeal, if she was put off by his unconscious assumption of worldliness mixed with moral superiority, well, she knew whom to blame.

She said quietly, "I am grateful for your concern, and deeply appreciative of the favor you have shown me by asking me to be your wife, but circumstances are not as you seem to think. It's difficult for me to tell you this, but I—may be going to have Renold's child. I could not impose that burden on you, nor can I think you would wish it. In truth, you have been embroiled in my problems long enough, and I feel it's best that I set you free. Please don't consider yourself bound any longer by our betrothal. It is at an end."

"His child."

The loathing in his voice, as well as the point he chose to emphasize, touched her on the quick. Facing him squarely, she said, "It's the natural consequence of losing one's innocence."

"Yes, especially if you enjoyed the loss," he sneered.

"Did you think this lapse of mine, as you called it, occurred only once?" The anger rising in her veins was cleansing. She discovered that his opinion of her mattered not at all.

"You allowed me no more than a chaste kiss!"

It was his pride, she saw, that was injured. She said with some recklessness, "That was different."

"Oh, yes," he said, lifting a fist to her face, "I am not Harden, am I. But I am the man who is going to be your husband, so you will come away with me now, like it or not." His upper lip lifted. "Since you have developed a taste for lovemaking, I expect you'll settle down once you are in the right bed!"

"That's a disgusting thing to say," she said in scathing tones. "If you think I'm going anywhere with you after hearing it, you must be quite mad."

She swung from him in a whirl of skirts. He shot out a hand to clutch her arm, wrenching her around so she slammed back against the tree. Pain burst inside her head as her temple struck the rough bark.

Laurence moved in closer, pressing his hard groin into her. His breath was hot in her ear as he said, "Oh, yes, I think you will go with me. Harden isn't here, and I have you myself this time instead of leaving it to gin-soaked half-wits."

Outrage and certainty transfixed her. "It was you. I knew it! You were the man in the alley on Gallatin Street, the man supposed to pay the Skaggses for abducting me. I've thought all day it must have been my father. I should have known he would never put me in such danger."

"I had to get you away from Harden," he began.

"Yes, and how you went about it or what happened to me afterward didn't matter, did it?" she said in low, trembling fury. "You never felt the slightest degree of affection for me, much less love. You killed that mousy little man who worked for Renold, didn't you? And you would have let Clem Skaggs do whatever he pleased. All you ever wanted was Bonheur. I thought that was the way it was back in Natchez, and now I know it."

"Did you really expect me, an Eddington of Dogwood Hill, to marry a gambler's daughter if there wasn't good reason?" he demanded. "I was staring ruin in the face. As it is, I'll be lucky to stave off my creditors until I can wade through the mess of a divorce and marry you."

"That is something you will never do," she said with satisfaction as she snatched her arm from his grasp. "Neither will you see a penny from Bonheur. Renold has a legal hold on me and the plantation, and will do everything in his power to see that it stays that way. He swore just now that he will never allow our marriage to be dissolved. I would advise you to believe it."

"In that case," Laurence said deliberately, "I will have to see about making you a widow. It may be faster and easier, anyway."

Something hard and hot closed around her heart, but she refused to be overcome by it. "Yes, indeed. And just what do you intend to do, send hired thugs to strike him down in the dark? You tried that once before, I think, but it wasn't so easy."

"He has the devil's own luck, but it's bound to run out," Laurence said with vicious bravado. "I'll get him."

"Even if you do, can you really think I'd go with you like a mindless sheep? Never!"

"I think," he said, catching her face in his hand, squeezing the delicate bones, "that you will do exactly as I say when I get through with you. You will marry me and be glad of it. You will jump at my every command. You will fetch and carry for me. You will hold yourself ready to serve me as my whore. And if I allow you to produce Harden's brat, you will keep it out of my sight and hearing if you want it to live. Then when it is old enough, it, too, will be taught to obey me."

There was no sound. One moment there was nothing but the night, the next Renold was there, a shadow lunging out of the darkness. His voice preceded him, exact, hard, slicing in its contempt. "Such dastardly threats, Eddington. I would be in a sweat of alarm if I were in skirts or unweaned. But I seem to recall that the last time I faced you in the dark, you ran."

Laurence rapped out a curse. He released Angelica as if she were a hot poker.

"Exactly so," Renold said dryly. "I would ask why you are on my wife's property, but it seems obvious. You were in search of something you lost through carelessness. I don't believe it's to be found here, but will let you know if it ever comes to light."

Laurence shifted slightly. Something hard and cool and blunt-nosed pressed against Angelica's side. "Don't bother; I may have found it," her former fiancé said. "Stand back out of the way, or I will blow a good-sized hole in your darling wife's side."

"Take care," Angelica said quietly across the distance which separated her from Renold. "He intends to kill you."

"A kindly warning, sweet Angelica, if unexpected," Renold said. "Also unnecessary. I have known since the moment I saw your father that he could not have been behind the crude attempts to take you from me. He has more finesse, and more manners."

"You mean me to understand that I have neither?" Laurence said, snorting. "It won't matter when you're dead."

"No, but it goes against the grain to be bested by a flashy coward," Renold said with a contemplative tip of his head, "a companion of sneak-thieves and cutthroats. I don't think I can allow it."

"Prevent it, then," the other man suggested with a coarse laugh near Angelica's ear.

"Good," Renold said with satisfaction, "you will understand if I do what I must. The waterfront scum you hired to come with you will be no help, you know. Tit Jean and my men had them in their sights from the moment they set foot on Bonheur. They are now under guard."

Laurence's grasp tightened. He lowered his head, scowling toward where Renold stood. "And I've got Angelica. Now what?"

"I was hoping to interest you in a little practice at swords, if you have the stomach for it?"

The offer was lightly made, yet carried a dangerous undertone. It chilled Angelica to the bone. "No," she said, "you can't do that."

"Now, why can't I, my love?" her husband said in caressing tones.

She moistened her lips, which were suddenly dry. "Your shoulder, you aren't fit for swordplay."

"Probably not, but it will give me great pleasure to try. Though it was unwise of you to point out my weakness to

Eddington. Unless you are looking forward to the delights he promised."

There was bite in the last words. She shook her head so quickly the coiled ringlets of her hair bounced against her face. "Never."

"But neither do you crave my delights. Who can fathom the heart of a woman? Who would even attempt it when the prize is already won?" He turned to Laurence. "Bonheur is mine, by right of a husband to direct his wife's property. If you want it, you will have to take it from me. There is no other way."

"Renold, don't," she said, with the pain inside her creeping into her voice. But he had removed his attention from her like wiping a column of sums from a slate.

Laurence stared at Renold with calculation. "What will keep your men from jumping me the minute you hit the ground?"

"My word," Renold said, and waited expectantly.

The other man laughed. "I think I would rather leave now and take Angelica with me. You can't stop me. Try and I'll kill her."

"Showing a total lack of skill at negotiation," came the answer in tones of contempt. "If she dies, there ends your hope of marrying her dowry; you lose by default. So why shouldn't I force you to end her life and have done with it? I could then order you shot before you have taken two steps, and enjoy Bonheur as a happy widower, without the bother of a wife I never wanted."

A wife I never wanted.

It was a bluff. Or was it? Angelica could not tell. The blood pouring through her veins felt as if it carried bits of broken glass. Her hands were cold, but her face was hot. The binding of her corset made her ribs ache and constricted her breathing so that the need to be free of it beat silently at the back of her mind.

Laurence appeared to have no trouble taking Renold at his word. The press of the pistol against Angelica's side eased a fraction. In tones of malevolent frustration, he said, "Bastard."

"That is hardly news." Renold's voice took on irritation. "Will you stay or go? Fight or run away? You had best be quick about your decision. There are others in the house who might take serious offense at finding you threatening Angelica."

"Old Carew is not likely to stop me."

"Not in his present condition, no." Renold shifted a shoulder, his shirt front glinting in the dark. "But Michel Farness has appointed himself her knight-protector, and would welcome a chance to earn his spurs. And possibly a place as her next husband if we both should fall."

Laurence relieved his feelings by a steady string of curses. As he shifted a little, the acrid smells of sweat and fear wafted from inside his coat. He said abruptly, "All right, then. Swords or pistols, which do you want?"

"The choice," Renold said softly, "is yours by custom."

"Yes, and just where are we going to find these weapons?"

Renold raised a hand. From the darkness beyond the nearest oak, Tit Jean stepped forward. He placed two wooden cases on the ground, one long and narrow, the other square. There could be little doubt about what they contained.

Laurence gave a rough laugh, staring through the darkness at the other man as if he could gauge his strength by his indistinct shape. "You've thought of everything, haven't you?"

"It's a habit."

Laurence watched Renold a moment longer, as if weighing alternatives. His eyes narrowed and he gave a hoarse laugh. "You think I'll choose swords because you've got that bad shoulder. But there are some who can handle a blade with either hand, and I seem to remember hearing that you're one of them. Anyway, I'm not a New Orleans dandy used to practicing in Exchange Alley, so I don't intend to fall for that trick. With pistols, now, it happens I'm a fair shot; I've met my man and put him down. But I heard the tales about you using a single shot to take the flame from the top of a candlestick. Shooting in the dark is something I've never tried, nor have I handled one of your fancy dueling pieces, so pistols would be a foolish choice."

"Yet you must pick up one or the other."

"Must I?" Laurence gave a snide laugh. "The people I've been around lately settle their differences with hog-skinning knives."

"Crude sport, or so I found it." In Renold's voice was dry disdain. Angelica, with memories of a dark alley and a vicious, whining blade in the forefront of her mind, could only agree.

"It may be, but I have a knack for it," Laurence said. "It's what I favor. Of course, if you can't lay hands on suitable knives, we might talk compromise."

"Compromise? Rather like letting a rattlesnake bed up under the front steps, there are some things too chancy to risk. In any case, there is no problem with weapons. It happens that we took enough bowie knives off the men you brought to outfit a small army." Without turning his head, Renold added, "Tit Jean?"

"At once, maître." The big manservant melted away into the night.

Renold turned back to the other man. "I take it," he said, "that you have no objection to this as a dueling ground?"

"It will do," Laurence said shortly.

"Well enough." The reply was spoken with judicious calm. "I don't like to suggest that you are unfamiliar with the dueling code, but you must know that no apology or excuse can be accepted on the field. The night before, yes, or even on the way to the meeting, but not on the field."

"You aren't likely to get either."

"My mistake. It must have come from your mention of compromise." Renold went on lightly. "You are allowed a second to see to your interests while you are actively engaged, but I don't believe Angelica qualifies; women are usually exempt, besides which, she is hardly impartial. You could, of course, keep her in front of you as a shield, but I feel she would be more handicap than asset."

Laurence snorted. "You want me to let her go now so you can snatch her for yourself. Then for all I know, you may have some of your hands set to take me."

"Your sort of maneuver, I believe. I assure you I will let nothing interfere with our meeting."

"Fine talk. I'd rather be safe."

Renold shrugged from his coat and threw it aside, then began to unfasten the cuffs of his sleeves. His gaze on the other man, he said with derision, "The phrase having to do with hiding behind a woman's skirts has just taken on new—bloody hell!"

His abrupt descent into ill temper was caused by the appearance of his half sister on the gallery of the house. Silhouetted by the lamplight spilling through the open door behind her, she scanned the darkness. As she caught sight of them there under the trees, she snatched up her skirts and hastened down the steps. Michel, stepping from the front door just behind her, followed with swift strides.

"It seems," Renold said with considerable annoyance, "that we are not to be allowed decent privacy. Poor Laurence. Now there's no telling who may snatch your prize."

He spoke more accurately than he knew. Michel had barely cleared the gallery steps when another man emerged from the house. His form was bent, his gait less than strong, but there was determination in every hard-won step. Angelica caught an uneven breath. It was her father.

"Renold!" Deborah cried as she came closer, "what in the name of heaven is going on? One of the house boys said Tit Jean came for dueling pistols." She stopped abruptly, her gown swaying like a bell, as she noticed Laurence, saw the pistol in his hand that turned toward her heart.

"I wonder," Laurence drawled with a sidewise glance at Renold, "how blasé you would be about my ending the life of this one."

"Not very," Renold said tightly.

"Nor I," Michel said, approaching with slow care. He gave Renold a direct look. "You might have told me about the party. I resent being left out."

"There was a reason for it," came the grim reply.

"Yes," Deborah said, "to keep me from following and maybe going into convulsions. It didn't work, did it?"

Before Renold could answer, Edmund Carew called out, "Laurence, boy, what are you doing?"

"God," Laurence said, his face twisting. "This is—"

"Ridiculous?" Renold supplied. "The element creeps in. Even in New Orleans there are those who drive by the dueling oaks like going to the theater to see a fine tragedy. Therefore, sangfroid, literally cold blood, is part of the duelist's code. He ignores the spectators. If he can."

"Shut up," Laurence growled.

"I assume," Michel said to his friend, "that you require a second?"

Renold's smile was wry. "It seems a useful precaution, though not necessary among men of honor. If Carew will stand for Eddington, we will be even in civility if in nothing else."

Angelica's father drew himself up, then ducked his head in a stiff bow. "Honored."

It was only a matter of form, of course. Any man could act for another; it implied no collusion, no allegiance, no taking of sides. Yet it seemed significant that Laurence and her father, Renold's enemies, were ranged against him.

Edmund Carew cleared his voice of a tendency to quaver. "No need to spout the tenants of the Code Duello to me, my boy: I've had my share of dawn meetings, been second more times than I can remember. My duty is to keep things fair for my principle in the fight and check his weapon. Oh, yes, and to hold myself responsible for preventing any act of—dishonor on his part."

A long look passed between the older man and Angelica's husband. Renold gave a brief nod as he turned away. "Just so," he said.

Tit Jean, breathless with haste, returned at that moment with his big hands full of knives. The meeting then took on a different, more official pace. A glaze of polite behavior attended the scene while the actors prepared for their roles. The audience contained its restlessness while it waited for the show to begin.

The weapons were spread out on Renold's coat. It was a motley collection of blades with greasy or rusty shadings and stains which it seemed better not to inspect too closely. They sported handles made of wood and bone, of cow horn and deer antlers and carved stone. Some had grips and some did not, some had hilts forged of brass or copper or blobs of lead, and some had no hilt at all. One thing they all had in common: They were sharp and they were dangerous.

Renold, due first choice of the weapons, scanned the assortment and selected one of classic shape made of quality materials and with no particular embellishments. Laurence was more careful. He picked up first one, then another, holding them to the dim yellow light streaming from the house, testing them for heft and balance. His final choice fell on a knife much heavier than Renold's, one with a bone handle, brass hilt, and a chased blade of enough extra length to give him a four-inch advantage.

Renold did not object. Michel frowned and opened his mouth, but closed it again after a quick glance at his friend.

Laurence removed his coat. The ground was cleared of debris. Some mention was made of lamps and lanterns, but Angelica's former fiancé scoffed at the prospect of extra light.

Angelica saw her father frown and glance at Michel. She wondered if he suspected, as she did, some nefarious purpose behind the refusal. However, conditions for the duel were set by the challenged party, in this case Laurence, and so there was no further discussion.

The two men were ready. They faced each other, bowie knives in hand, while their seconds stepped back out of the way. Angelica edged from where Laurence had left her, joining Deborah well back under the oak so the wide skirts of their gowns would not block the little light shining from the house.

As she glanced back along the path of the light, she felt a pang of dismay. There was a slight figure standing on the gallery, blending with the shadows at the near end. Renold's mother was there, watching. Had Renold noticed? Would it matter to him if he did?

There was no signal, no office to start. Renold, knife in hand, was adjusting the set of his shoulder bandage. Laurence scowled at him while he tested the sharpness of his blade with his thumb. Then, without warning, Laurence flung himself forward in a lunge.

Renold leaped backward, throwing his arms wide so the knife blade sliced past his shirt front with a vicious whine.

He twisted away, his laugh short as he danced out of range. Laurence, his face flushed and mulishly grim, moved after him. Lithe and incredibly agile, Renold flowed into an attack. There was a brief scuffle, then they sprang apart, circling warily.

"I thought you weren't a knife fighter," Laurence said in rough accusation.

"I never said so," Renold answered. "Duels are fought with many kinds of weapons, from sabers on horseback and island machetes to bullwhips, billy clubs, and boat paddles— anything one man can use to harm another. Preparation pays."

"For what good it will do you," Laurence said through his teeth, and tossed his knife to his left hand before slashing out with a hard, roundhouse swing.

Renold, as elusive as smoke, was not there. Laurence staggered with the force of his own attack, then whirled around with a bellow of rage as he found his quarry behind him.

"Anger," Renold said pensively, "is not good form, you know. A duelist is always calm. His indifference to his opponent's tricks is his hallmark." With a slight smile and an easy, almost negligent movement, he drifted away from Laurence's next stabbing advance.

"Stand still and fight," Laurence said between his teeth.

"Now where is the finesse in that? Or the lesson? Any pair of idiots can stand toe to toe and slash at each other in glorious bloodletting until one of them falls from sheer weakness. No. The duel is derived from ancient law, the trial by might of arms, the right of the wronged to challenge the one who gave the injury. It permitted the robbed the right to accuse the robber, the violated to have redress from the violator, the relative of the murdered to contest with the murderer. Those who were weaker had the right to choose a champion who was then, of course, invested with the same might of right. The man who lost was guilty as sin, since God favors the just."

"Idiotic," Laurence said, breathless as he retreated, scrambling, from a sudden whipping extension followed by a savage thrust.

"Possibly, but the loser was just as dead."

Renold recoiled as if the attack had been a mere object

lesson, and stood waiting until his opponent recovered. He added, "Once upon a time, any man could appoint himself as champion of another. For instance, I could fight for Angelica. There is a prayer for the occasion: *Dear Lord, gird my arm and guide my sword.* You may share it, if you like."

With that, his instructions, like his indifference, were suddenly at an end. He moved in then with a flurry of motion from which drove a hard blow homing for Laurence's heart. The other man sprang aside, but not fast enough. Renold's blade sliced across the front of Laurence's shirt and brought a streak of red at the level of his breastbone. Laurence wrenched backward frantically, scuttling for safety like a crayfish, as Renold recoiled with grace.

"First blood," Edmund Carew called. "Is honor satisfied?"

It was Laurence who spoke in savage answer. "No! Only last blood will satisfy me."

"The question," Renold corrected dryly, "is mine to answer."

"Then do it!" There was reckless fury spurred by stung vanity in the words.

Renold's gaze, there in the dark, was level, considering. When he spoke the words were even. "Last blood," he said.

They settled to it then.

The knives in their hands were like lethal, darting wraiths. The smell of crushed grass rose around them as their feet bruised the green carpet. The dim illumination shifted over them, sliding in a pale glow across their shirt backs, glinting in their eyes narrowed in fierce concentration, winking with points of fire at the end of their blades.

The two were better matched than had first appeared, being much the same in size and reach. What Laurence lacked in skill, he made up for in cunning and malevolence. Renold had patience and intelligence and the ability to think several moves ahead. The suppleness of body and lithe economy of movement Renold brought to the fight was countered by Laurence's longer blade and his lack of old and weakening injuries. Laurence used every shadow and uneven patch of ground to trip, and every artifice as a screen for further deceit.

Dangerous, the dark was so dangerous. To judge the speed

of a blow or the depth of a thrust was near impossible. The shadows hid the beginning of an assault, veiled the sudden stab. The jostling for position, the strained feinting and urgent withdrawals in the dimness were hideous reminders to Angelica of other contests she had been forced to watch. Yet this one was far more hazardous than the attack of Clem Skaggs in the alley or the grim meeting of Renold with Michel on the lamplit gallery. In those, death had been only a possibility. Now it was a certainty.

Angelica was shaking with nerves. Her chest ached with her shallow breathing and her head was pounding with the hard beating of her heart. She swayed where she stood, and her hands were clasped together with such tightness that her fingers were numb.

So intent was she on the terrible contest that she started as she felt a movement at her side. It was her father. He took her arm, holding it against him.

Was he supporting her, or she supporting him? She neither knew nor cared as she clung to him, holding tight.

The hard pace of the fight could not be sustained for long, not with death and injury being sought and evaded by inches. Both the combatants were tiring. Perspiration trickled from their hair and made their shirts cling with every lunge.

Renold made a slicing pass, stumbled on a drift of last year's acorns, then recoiled in haste from a backhanded slash. A grimace of pain flashed across his face. The white of his shirt at the right shoulder darkened to black-red in a spreading stain. He staggered, and his right arm was slow to rise to guard position. The hole made by Michel's sword had broken open.

Laurence, triumphant as a predator scenting blood, redoubled his efforts. Renold leaped and dodged, but his movements were growing clumsy, the wetness of shirt widening, shining red along his arm. Droplets of blood fell from his wrist as he slung himself aside from a reckless pass.

His recovery was sluggish. Laurence's teeth drew back in a feral grin. He gathered himself and launched a charging attack. His long knife flashed with gold fire as it struck toward

Renold's heart. The defense was delayed, without power, a mere half turn as the blade slashed toward tender flesh protected only by thin linen, toward vital organs guarded only by bands of rigid muscle.

There was the hard thud of body against body. A muffled grunt of agony. The sound of tearing cloth. The two men caught each other in a mortal clasp, swaying, their lips drawn back and teeth clenched with effort.

Then Renold wrenched free. Laurence stumbled, staggered. There was a great rent in Renold's shirt at the waist where the blade of his adversary had been allowed to pass harmlessly between body and arm. Laurence's shirt had received a new decoration, the protruding hilt of a knife embedded between the middle buttons.

Renold reached out as Laurence began to fall. He caught his shoulder, easing him down. The wounded man's head fell back and his eyes squeezed shut. With his left hand he grabbed at the protruding knife hilt while his right twitched convulsively around his own useless weapon.

Renold went to one knee beside the fallen man. He straightened the bent neck with gentle hands, turned to look for Tit Jean. The manservant stepped forward from beside Michel who was holding Deborah with her face pressed into his chest.

"Send for the doctor, then take a shutter off the hinges and bring it to get him into the house."

Practical concern, efficient action, that was Renold's way. His first impulse, Angelica saw, was to repair the damage he had done in as swift and humane a fashion as possible. It said something about the man.

She was given no time to consider it. Her attention was caught by a stealthy movement. Laurence was not as near death as it appeared. Under the cover of darkness, he was tightening his hand on the handle of his knife, straining to lift his arm for a blow at Renold's unprotected abdomen.

Angelica plunged forward, drawing breath to cry out a warning. Yet her father was before her. Clapping his hand to his waistcoat pocket, he snatched out a pocket pistol.

It was, after all, his place as second to prevent his principle from acting dishonorably. He stumbled in the direction of the two men on the ground as he steadied the pistol in his palsied fist, pointing it at Laurence.

Shaking, her father was shaking so hard with illness and strain that he could not aim. If he fired, he might hit Renold who hovered so close above Laurence. Now the knife, hidden from Michel and Tit Jean and Deborah by Renold's kneeling form, was rising, rising.

Madame Delaup, running from the gallery toward the scene of the duel as the two men went down, closed in behind Angelica and her father. She took in the scene in a single sweeping glance. She let out a scream.

"Renold, the knife!"

Renold swung with recognition and understanding dark in his eyes. Too late. He must be, would be, too late to retrieve his weapon, raise his guard.

Resolution congealed inside Angelica even as she heard Madame Delaup's cry, saw Renold turn. She did not think, had no plan; the thing was there and had to be done.

Reaching out to her father, she caught his jerking hand, steadied it. A wheezing sound of rich gratification sounded in Edmund Carew's throat. Hard on it, he curled his bony finger around the trigger of the pistol and squeezed.

The explosion blasted the night. Orange-red flame spurted with blinding light, flashing through the black smoke of gunpowder. Laurence's head snapped to one side and the pale shape of his forehead took on a dark, wet sheen. His arm dropped and the knife fell from his lax hand.

Then broad shoulders blocked the scene as Renold caught Angelica in his arms, holding her close while he turned her from the sight of death.

❧

"Aren't we civilized."

It was Madame Delaup who spoke those words some hours later. It was all over by then.

The body of Laurence Eddington had been laid out in

a wagon and carried into town for burial. The waterfront toughs he had hired had been carted away by the local sheriff. Brandy and wine had been taken as a restorative by everyone concerned, after which they had all sat down to a late supper.

Surveying them now, Renold's mother went on in the same musing tone in which she had first spoken. "Yes, indeed. Here we sit partaking of food and wine as if the late excitement has sharpened our appetites. We smile and make pleasant conversation as though the word *sensibility* should be struck from our vocabularies—or as if too far gone in shock to succumb to such a luxury. I don't mind the conversation or the smiles. What is fast becoming unendurable is the silences in between."

They were around the table in the dining room, the traditional place in a French home for a family gathering, certainly the proper one for a family council. Renold, at the head of the board, had been rebandaged and attired in fresh linen by Tit Jean, but there were lines of strain in his face and dark shadows under his eyes.

His patience had also shortened. "What do you suggest, mother?" he inquired with astringent reason. "None of us, I think, are inclined to sleep."

"I have been watching and listening these twenty-four hours past, waiting for good sense to triumph over the residue of a senseless quarrel. Nothing so enlightened seems to be imminent. I suggest, then, that some arrangements be made for a more harmonious future."

Angelica, sitting on Renold's right, sent a glance flickering in his direction. His gaze was resting on her face as he studied the distinct oval bruises left by Laurence's fingers, and also the dark circles under her eyes which matched his. Looking away, his gaze swept over Michel and Deborah, sitting close together on his left. It passed over his mother at the foot of the table, and came to rest on Edmund Carew. The eyes of the two men met.

Renold was the first to look away. Pushing back his chair with an abrupt scrape, he rose to his feet. "You prefer generosity and forgetfulness, mother?" he said, bracing his hands on the polished wood in front of him and staring at her down its length. "If so, you might have told me earlier."

"I thought," his mother said with a crooked smile, "that you had already come to it."

"Tolerance is not disagreeable to you, then. I see. The question that now arises is just how highly you value your son's life."

"It is, of course, beyond price," she said with acerbity. "If you are asking what I will give up for the sake of it, what I will endure or allow, then the answer is quite simple: Anything, everything. As you might have known if you had only considered, there is no reward for one who preserves it that I would not gladly grant."

"None?" He tilted his head as he probed for her answer.

Putting her hands to her waist, Madame Delaup unfastened the silver chatelaine draped there. She held it a moment, her gaze not quite clear, before she placed it carefully on the table, keys rattling, and pushed it toward Renold. Her smile singularly sweet, she said, "None. You may do as you will, my son, to ensure the happiness of yourself—and my future grandchildren."

Renold smiled, then, in a slow tilting of his mouth that also lighted the green of his eyes with emerald fire and wiped away much of his weariness. Pushing erect, he moved to stand behind Angelica, though he spoke, still, to his mother.

"I have been thinking," he said as he settled his hands on the back of her chair, "about the recompense due to a man who willfully throws away the final opportunity to own large property and fortune, abandoning them without qualm for the sake of honor. There is one among us who did that this evening. It has come to me that only a single reward will do." He turned his head to look at Angelica's father. "I propose that Edmund Carew make his home at Bonheur from now on, enjoying its bounty and the care of its people. And that, if it pleases him, he must consider himself its master."

"He will naturally be very welcome," said Madame Delaup while she held her son's eyes in calm approval.

What was Renold doing? That he had a purpose, Angelica did not doubt. Down the table, she thought Michel suspected

it also, for he glanced at Deborah with amazement and satisfaction springing into his face.

Angelica could feel nothing but pain. It wasn't funny. It
was, in fact, the most cruel of jests.

Her father turned slowly in his seat to look at her. There
was such grave concern in his face that she wanted to cry.
When, a moment later, he raised his eyes to the man behind
her, she swallowed hard to stop herself from interrupting,
from answering for him. She must allow him his pride.

"Your offer is kindly meant, I know," Edmund Carew said
to Renold, "and I cannot adequately express my gratitude for
it. However, I am not the only person who must be pleased
in this matter. I could not think of remaining here without
the care and support of my loving daughter, and she has
determined to go. If you wish for my presence, then you must
persuade her that the peace and happiness we all need so badly
can be found here. Together."

"Papa, it wouldn't work," she said, leaning toward him to
speak in low tones. "You know they will never forgive, will
always remember—"

"No," Renold said. "Dredging up the past is a fine way
to destroy the future, for one is built on the other. What
has gone before, then, must and will be decently buried and
planted over with the sweet flowers of atonement."

"An atonement I would make by producing a child?"

"Yes," Renold answered, his voice deep, "if that is
your pleasure. But it isn't necessary. The gesture made by
your father, in the only way he knew how, is more than
enough—his crime and atonement, if such they can be called,
balance each other. For the rest, let it go. What he did once
for your sake was an act of love. His only failure was in how
he counted the cost of it. I know now, as I did not in the
beginning, how easily such a mistake is made."

Angelica rose to her feet and brushed past him, evading
the hand he put out to stop her. She took only a few steps,
however, before stopping at the French doors that were closed
to keep out the moths and mosquitoes that might be drawn
to the candles.

Over her shoulder, she said, "So because one man died and another lived, I am supposed to forget everything that has been said and done? I am expected to calmly take my place as a loving wife—oh, yes, and doting mother."

"No." The word was calm.

"No?" She laughed, she couldn't help it. "Then in what capacity would I live here?"

"In any you choose," Renold said as he skirted the table and came to stand behind her. "Daughter, nurse, house-keeper, *maîtress*, keeper of the keys, mistress of my heart. Choose which of these things you desire, or none, if only you will stay."

"Since you never wanted a wife?"

Outrage flared in his face. She saw it reflected in the glass of the French doors with the night behind it, and waited for the storm of it to break over her head.

But just as she could see his face, he could also see hers in that makeshift mirror, see the silver streaks of the tears that she was helpless to stop as they poured over her cheekbones and down the planes of her face. He caught her arms and swung her to face him, then gathered her close against him.

"God, Angelica, I thought you knew," he said in harsh anguish. "What else could those words have been except a desperate attempt to prevent Eddington from punishing me through you, because I saw plainly that he would rather have you dead than leave me in possession of you and Bonheur. They were a lie told in sheer terror and so shaded to be believed. But not by you, my dearest love, not by you."

The rich remorse and love shading his voice was a certainty she could grasp and hold. She believed him, finally.

The great, bursting gladness of relief poured through her. She was warmed by its glory, buoyed by its power. At the same time, she knew an aching grief of her own.

"Oh, Renold, I am so sorry, so desperately sorry. I never meant to betray you out there just now."

He shook his head, pressed his chin against the softness of her hair. "You didn't, you couldn't."

"But I did. I told Laurence about your shoulder. If I had

not, he might have chosen pistols and you would never have come so close to dying."

Renold was shaken by a low laugh. "I was never close, my deluded sweetling. I could have finished Eddington twice over if I had not been so afraid of the contempt for the killing that I might see in your eyes. Everything else was a pretense to force him to show his true colors. I was pleased when you objected to the fight, saying so piteously that I might be injured, because I thought you saw what I was doing, that you were helping me."

"I didn't," she said against his throat. "I couldn't think because I was so afraid."

"If that's so, if you thought I might have been too injured to make it a fair fight, then that means—"

"It means she loves you to desperation, you prattling idiot," Michel broke in with disgust. "Will you please kiss her and take her to bed so we can all get some sleep?"

Renold's smile was beatific.

"Yes," he said simply. And complied.

About the Author

Jennifer Blake was born near Goldanna, Louisiana, in her grandparents' 120-year-old hand-built cottage. She grew up on an eighty-acre farm in the rolling hills of north Louisiana. While married and raising her children, she became a voracious reader. At last, she set out to write a book of her own. That first book was followed by sixty-four more and today they have reached more than thirty-five million copies in print, making her one of the bestselling romance authors of our time.

Jennifer and her husband live in their house near Quitman, Louisiana—styled after old Southern planters' cottages.

New York Times bestselling author

The Wildest Heart

by Rosemary Rogers

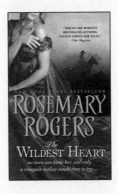

Two destinies intertwined under the blazing New Mexico sun

When passionate, headstrong Lady Rowena Dangerfield travels to the savage New Mexico frontier to lay claim to her inheritance, she finally meets a man as strong as she is: Lucas Cord, a dark, dangerously handsome, half-Apache outlaw. Fighting scandal, treachery, and murder, Luke is determined to have Rowena for his own, and as their all-consuming passion mounts, no one is going to stop him...

What readers say:

"It makes you cry, it makes you wish, and it makes you dream. It's what a romance novel is all about."

"The Wildest Heart kept me captivated well beyond the last page..."

Praise for Rosemary Rogers:

"The queen of historical romance." —New York Times Book Review

"Her novels are filled with adventure, excitement, and, always, wildly tempestuous romance." —Fort Worth Star-Telegram

For more Rosemary Rogers books, visit:

www.sourcebooks.com

My Love, My Enemy

by Jan Cox Speas

A passion for adventure...

Beautiful, naïve, and impulsive, Page Bradley inadvertently rescues English spy Lord Hazard in Baltimore during the tumultuous War of 1812. Now she must put herself at the mercy of her enemy.

An aptitude for deception...

Lord Hazard is no stranger to the atrocities of war, but he never imagined the beauty that could come of it until he meets the fiery and irresistible Page. Now he finds himself questioning every loyalty he's ever felt for King and Country.

Amidst the turmoil of war and the peril of the high seas, these two sworn enemies are destined to discover that denying love may be worse than treason.

Praise for Jan Cox Speas:

"Irresistible... This novel of high romance moves on wings from Annapolis to Bermuda to London and back to Washington..." —Library Journal

"Appealing and refreshing... a lovely romance told in a delightful swashbuckling manner." —Memphis Sunday Commercial Appeal

For more Jan Cox Speas books, visit:

www.sourcebooks.com

A Tapestry of Dreams

by Roberta Gellis

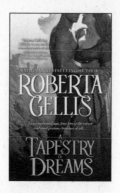

She swears she will never marry...

Though her uncle has been a kind, loving guardian to her since her parents death, running her estate fairly and efficiently, Lady Audris knows he would never be able to surrender his authority to her new husband. And so she contents herself to live her life a maid, with weaving the most beautiful tapestries in all of England.

He will not settle for another...

Hugh Licorne will push himself to his very limits for those he is loyal to. So when a corrupt steward turns over his liege's castle to the enemy, Hugh risks life and limb to escape the castle and get word to his lord that the castle has fallen. Impressed by such bravery, King Stephen recruits Hugh into his service, offering him his choice of brides to seal the deal.

From the moment Hugh sets eyes on the bold Lady Audris, he knows he has found the woman destined to be his wife. But winning her trust and defending her from her enemies will be the greatest battle he has ever faced...

For more Roberta Gellis books, visit:

www.sourcebooks.com